Warrior's Prize

WARRIOR'S PRIZE
BY

Elena Douglas

www.penmorepress.com

Warrior's Prize by Elena Douglas
Copyright © 2022 Barbara D. Brunetti

All rights reserved. No part of this book may be used or reproduced by any means without the written permission of the publisher except in the case of brief quotation embodied in critical articles and reviews.

ISBN-13: 979-8-9855298-6-9(Paperback)
ISBN:-   979-8-9855298-7-6(e-book)

BISAC Subject Headings:
FIC014000FICTION / Historical
HIS002010HISTORY / Ancient / Greece
FIC031020FICTION / Thrillers / Historical

The Book Cover Whisperer:
ProfessionalBookCoverDesign.com

Address all correspondence to:

Penmore Press LLC
920 N Javelina Pl
Tucson AZ 85748

DEDICATION

To Sonja, Joy, Sam, and Siena

You are the lights of my life

ACKNOWLEDGEMENTS

The writing of *Warrior's Prize* has been a long journey of many struggles, many iterations, and more rewrites than I can count. Often it was a solitary journey, and often I came near to giving up. Nevertheless, my family, friends, and writers' group stuck with me, believing in this book even when I was perilously close to abandoning it. To all of you I owe a tremendous debt. Thank you to my immediate family, my extended family, and all the friends who did not tire of my plaguing them with yet another rewrite of *Warrior's Prize*. Invaluable feedback and critiques were always on offer from my long-standing writers' group, past and present: Bud Gundy, Pat Elmore, Cleo Jones, Nellie Romero, Shoshana Dembitz, Susan Domingos, and the sorely-missed Charlene Weir and Avis Worthington. My fellow writers, you have taught me everything I know about the craft. A dear friend of many years, Barbara Wilkie, now deceased, was probably my most tireless supporter.

I am hugely indebted to many whom I have never met in person but only through the printed page, above all to the poet we know only as Homer. Whether he was one person or many, male or female, in composing the *Iliad* he created one of the greatest works of literature mankind has ever known. When I first read it, a whole world opened before me. When I first met Briseis in its pages, she compelled me to write her story. I am also indebted to the numerous scholars into whose works I have delved, who have offered their research, insight, and critical commentary on Homer's epics.

Lastly I am deeply thankful to Michael James and the staff of Penmore Press for giving *Warrior's Prize* the chance to see the light of print.

PART ONE:

THE BARREN SHORE

CHAPTER 1

*Reflected
glintings flashed to heaven, as the plain
in all directions shone with glare of bronze
and shook with trampling feet of men.*

Iliad, Homer, Book XIX
(Fitzgerald's translation)

I jerked awake, heart hammering in raw terror. Where was I? Then I remembered—I had dozed off in this dark cave, half-reclined against a slab of rock. I sat up, my stiff back aching. How many hours had passed since Mynes left me here? As the day waned, I'd grown hungrier and thirstier—and more afraid. Now anxiety devoured me. I groped to the cave's jagged opening and saw a dim orange sky fading to purple. Clumps of trees stood black against the twilight. The landscape seemed empty of people. There were no human sounds—no sounds at all but the whoosh of wind. Or were those faint shouts from afar that I discerned between gusts? I held my breath—heard only my own heartbeat. My ears must be playing tricks on me.

Oh, Mynes, my husband, why haven't you come back? I wondered in silent despair. *Where are you? What has happened?* Futile questions jumped around in my mind. Why had he left me for so long without news?

This morning we had set off walking up the flank of Mount Ida. He was on his way to the mountaintop to meet with the Trojan princes, who'd driven their flocks there to graze on the new spring grass. I asked to accompany him, but in his serious way he said, "Only part way, Briseis. Then you must go back. This is not for women. It's a council of war." He added, "Though it makes me uneasy when their princes venture so far away from their citadel. It's not safe."

My skin grew cold. Once, the Achaeans had been friendly traders from across the sea, who shared a common tongue with us, but nine or ten years ago they had turned to marauding. They had built a vast encampment on the Trojan shore that was, we heard, the size of a city. From there they plundered the countryside and waged war against Troy. Mount Ida and the foothills separated our city from Troy, but suddenly that distance did not seem great at all.

I said, "Mynes, I wish you would not go."

"I must. As commander I need to learn all I can from the Trojans."

Walking up the grassy slope with him, I remembered when I had romped about these hills with my brothers, a wild, carefree girl whom my father had tried to beat into submission. When he died in a drunken fall, my youngest brother, Laodokos, and I came under the care of our oldest brother and his wife, who treated us as slaves. One day I chanced to meet Prince Mynes in the marketplace when I was but sixteen and had dropped a too-heavy sack of grain. He was a childless widower in his forties, a quiet, austere man whose chief care was the governing of our city. He hefted the sack for me and carried it to our house. I never forgot his kindness.

I was away from the house one day when my sweet Laodokos dropped a full wine jug. Our oldest brother beat him without mercy. I returned to find my young brother weeping with blackened eyes and a bloody mouth. I decided we'd had enough—we would leave. When our sister-in-law tried to stop us, I was astounded by my anger. I pushed her hard enough to knock her to the floor, and felt gratified at her shock and fear. I was eighteen then, and Laodokos only thirteen. I took him with me to Mynes's home, and on our knees as suppliants, we offered the prince our servitude in exchange for our keep. He took us in and cared for us.

After we'd lived with him for some months, he said, "You shall not be my servants any longer. You shall be my wife, Briseis, and Laodokos as a son to me."

I was awed by Mynes's generosity, even as I wondered if I was too wild, stormy, and fierce for his quiet reserve. I feared he had gotten the poor end of the bargain. I esteemed him and cared for him, but although I tried to love him, I fell short.

Now, trudging up the mountain, I had a chance to redeem myself. I was almost certain I was with child. This news would bring him great joy.

I took his hand. He turned to me, and I felt surprise and pleasure sparking through his flesh. "Mynes," I said, "I am— I'm going to—" Then the words stuck in my throat. Was it too soon? Mynes's first wife had miscarried unformed babies several times, and the last one had killed her. I'd lain awake last night worrying if this was the right moment to tell him. My mother had said a woman should wait until she was completely sure, since many pregnancies resulted in early failure. I wished I could ask her more. If only she had lived past my eighth year! With a child of my own growing in me, I missed her sorely.

I couldn't bear the thought of breaking Mynes's heart. Yet the possibility of a living child was the best gift I could give him. "Mynes—" I began again.

But he stopped. Cut me off with a gesture. Stood absolutely still, straining to listen. "Hush! Do you hear that?" I held my breath and then the sound came to my ears: faraway shouts from the general direction of our town, or perhaps some distance beyond it.

I didn't want him distracted. I wanted to tell him about the baby. "Surely it's nothing, Mynes—maybe just some men having an argument."

But the shouts grew louder, still distant but more menacing, and now there were ominous metallic clangs that could only come from weapons.

His face went pale and grim. "The Achaeans! They're attacking! They're close—maybe already in Lyrnessos!" He reached helplessly for his sword, which he had not worn today.

"How can you be sure?" I protested, but I knew he was right.

"I must go back at once!"

My heart convulsed with fear. "Mynes, no!"

He only led me toward one of the caves that dotted the hillside and thrust me into its opening. "You must hide in here until I come back or send someone for you," he said.

I threw my arms around his waist. He held me a moment, and in the intensity of his grip I felt his love for me warring with his determination to defend our people.

He loosened my hold. "Briseis, we knew this day might come, and you know I must lead our men. I've trained them well. The Achaeans won't be expecting seasoned warriors. We'll soon drive them away." He bent to kiss my lips. "I want you safe. Promise me!"

"Aye, Mynes, I promise," I whispered, and he left me, running down the hill to our town. I wanted to go after him, but my knees were trembling so badly I could take no more than a few steps. Besides, I'd given him my word. As he vanished from sight, I crept numbly into the cave.

Now hours had passed; the whole day was gone. I sat near the cave mouth, parched, weak with hunger, not knowing what was happening in Lyrnessos, or if it had already happened. My helplessness nearly drove me mad.

I felt torn. I wanted, more than anything, to look for Mynes, but I'd promised to wait. A deep dread twisted my gut. I thought of all the times he sat silent at our hearth, preoccupied. He carried the weight of our people on his weary, slumped shoulders. I remembered lying in his bed at night, my body unresponsive to his caresses even as, in his every touch, I felt his desire for me. He was far past his youth, his face lined, his hair thinning. Like a silly girl, I dreamed of a godlike figure in his stead, a tall, strong man who could inflame my heart. Now I cursed my shallowness.

Oh, Mynes, come back to me!

But darkness fell, and he did not return. No one came. I feared I might be the last person left alive. I made myself close my eyes, but tears seeped out. At last, I somehow slept.

I awoke to a clamor—shouts and metallic clangs, much louder than yesterday. Chills ran over my skin. I crawled to the cave entrance to peer out into the gray morning light. *Oh, gods!* The menacing sounds came from just over the hill where Lyrnessos lay. I was desperate to know what those sounds meant. Down the slope was a knoll that overlooked our town. I could go there to see, and if there was danger, I could run back here.

I took off running toward the knoll.

After no more than a hundred paces I stopped with a cry. A man in armor sat slumped against a tree, his helmet off, spear and shield at his side. There was blood all over his leg from a long, deep wound on his thigh. "Help me!" he called out.

Fear tightened my throat. "Who are you? Where are you from?"

"I'm Akamas from Dardania." Dardania was an ally of Troy, so he wasn't an enemy. I took a step closer. He was young, not much above my age, with curly black hair and a beard. His skin was ashen, his face a grimace of pain.

"What happened?" I asked.

"Achaeans," he gasped out. "They ambushed us at the top of Mount Ida, where we'd taken the flocks." He was breathing hard. "They stole all our livestock—captured two of the Trojan princes. But my commander, Prince Aeneas, escaped. I've got to find him." He gestured urgently at his leg. "Can you bind it for me?"

"Which way did he go?"

He pointed down the hill. "That way. The Achaeans were on his heels."

Toward Lyrnessos! His commander had led the enemy to our city. *I must go—I must see—* But if I didn't staunch this man's bleeding, he would die. Forcing down panic, I knelt to examine his wound. As a child I'd learned some healing from my mother. I pressed my hand over the place where the blood was gushing. He grimaced, and I felt his pain shiver along my skin. I untied my sash and bound it tightly over the wound. "Keep pressing there," I told him. "And try to rest. You've lost a lot of blood. When the bleeding stops, you must clean it. Then keep it bound tightly."

He sat up with a grunt. "My thanks! What is your name, fair lady?"

"Briseis, wife of Prince Mynes of Lyrnessos." Distant cries, clashes of weapons came to my ears. My urgent fear returned. I stood. The need to run burned in me. Mynes, my brothers, everyone I knew was in the town. "I must see what's happening."

"Stay away from Lyrnessos! Yesterday the Achaeans raided several nearby towns. Today they're fighting to take your city." He spoke roughly and grabbed my skirts. "Listen! It's a huge raid, led by their greatest warrior Achilleus. Your Mynes is no match for him. Even Aeneas fled." He added, "Your city is already lost."

It couldn't be. I pulled free from his grasp. "I must go...to the hillock to see..."

He said more, but I was already running and didn't hear.

"I'll send you help if I can," I shouted over my shoulder as I ran.

Zeus, father of gods and men, protect our city! And Mynes and Laodokos. I froze at the thought of my youngest brother. I called his name silently. Then I reminded myself that every day he tended Mynes's sheep up the hills. Surely, so far from the town, he'd be safe.

I ran down the slope toward the knoll and saw people

swarming up the hill as they fled the town, old folk, women with children. I reached the lookout point and felt a scream of shock rise in my throat. Outside the gates of our town was a sea of crested helmets and flashing spears, warriors too numerous to count. My stomach sickened. I searched for Mynes amid the horde but couldn't find him.

Yesterday he'd kissed me and tried to keep me safe. Now he was down there. *Please gods, don't let him die!* I heard thuds, clangs, shouts, faint in the distance. The Achaeans were pressing toward the open gate, unstoppable as surging storm waves. Our men were trying to close the gate, but the invaders pushed forward relentlessly. Men vanished under their trampling feet. Cries rent the air. Even from afar, each scream pierced me.

Your city is already lost, Akamas had said. A huge weight crushed my heart. Then I saw Mynes. I recognized his stocky body and the black crest on his helmet as he broke through to the front of the battle. Fear and hope tore me apart. He would turn back the tide. *He must.*

A cheer arose as his men parted for him. His shouts rallied the faltering men, who surged forth with new courage, pushing the enemy back. Mynes advanced, driving his spear left and right, soon making a notable dent in the Achaean ranks. I was standing on my toes, screaming, "Onward, Mynes! Smite them!"

A sudden blaze of light caught my eye. The sun shone on a tall warrior approaching the city gate in bronze and silver armor with a golden horsehair crest springing from his helmet. He seemed to gather the light to himself. Never had I seen a man so tall or strong. *A god?* Goosebumps skittered up my arms. He wielded his spear with an ease and grace that belied the deadliness of his actions. I couldn't take my eyes from the clean lines of his body, the sweeping movements of his spear arm. If only he were on our side, defending us, giving us hope! But he was clearly one of the enemy, and I felt disgusted that I had admired him even for a moment.

This was the Achaean leader that Akamas had spoken of, their greatest warrior. As he cut a swath through the melee, men fell back to give him room, shouting a name that could be heard up to the heavens: *Achilleus! Achilleus!*

My heart clenched with terror. His spear flashed as he made straight for Mynes.

CHAPTER 2

> Conspicuous as the evening star that comes,
> amid the first in heaven, at fall of night,
> and stands most lovely in the west, so shone
> in sunlight the fine-pointed spear
> Akhilleus poised in his right hand, with deadly aim...
>
> *Iliad*, Homer, Book XXII
> (Fitzgerald's translation)

"*Run, Mynes!*" I cried. I lost sight of him in the press of bodies, then saw him again, standing firm, legs planted wide as he faced the tall Achaean. His arm was steady as he aimed his spear and thrust with all his strength. I watched as if in a nightmare. Light blazed from the Achaean leader's shield when he raised it and deflected Mynes's charge, throwing him off balance, knocking his spear into the dust. Swiftly the tall warrior lunged and drove his enormous spear clear through Mynes's neck.

I screamed but no sound came. Mynes staggered back. For an instant he kept to his feet. Then he fell. A voice near me shouted, "Zeus help us, that's the prince!"

My legs lost strength, and I dropped to the ground, my face pressed into rocks and dirt. "No, no, no!" I couldn't stop saying it.

Faces leaned over me. "Poor lady, she's the prince's wife," someone muttered.

A huge tumult came, a shout from a multitude of men. I scrambled to my feet to look for Mynes. But where I had last seen him there were only charging warriors.

The Achaeans, yelling, running, stormed through the gates into the town. The remaining Lyrnessos men were swept aside like chaff in the wind. Men were pinned against the walls or trampled. I pressed my hands into my eyes. When I looked again, I saw a dreadful stillness. Everything went dark and I couldn't breathe. Bodies were strewn over the open ground—these were the men of our town: Mynes's men, his comrades—and my two older brothers, who must have been in the fight. My beloved Laodokos was surely safe in the hills. But even so, I couldn't stop my gasping sobs that sounded more like screams.

When I raised my head and looked again, Mynes was still nowhere in sight. I began to hope that from this distance my eyes had deceived me and the spear hadn't really pierced his neck. He could have arisen and chased the Achaean leader into the town. *You're fooling yourself*, said an inner voice, but I clung to hope.

I took a few steps, and then hesitated. *Stay here where it's safe,* he'd said. But the Achaeans had stampeded into the town, no doubt looking for spoils, leaving the battleground empty except for the dead. That would give me time to search for Mynes. If he'd been killed, I would tend his corpse. I owed him this much and more. I owed him my very life.

My legs went wobbly. This could not be real.

As I began to run down the slope, a woman I knew from her fish stall in the marketplace reached out a hand to grab me. "Don't go there!"

I pulled away. "I must find him."

Others from the town were still climbing up the slopes, vanishing into the trees. Old Euphemos the goatherd was struggling up the hillside. As I passed him, he shouted, "Where are you going?" and he, too, tried to hold me back, but I ran by without slowing my pace. Tangled underbrush tore at my gown, scratched my skin. I took a steep, direct way down the hill, clambering over rocks and branches. I reached the bottom gasping, pain knifing through my side, and pressed on until I came to the open space where the battle had been fought.

The stench of blood filled my nostrils. Bodies were everywhere. Hardly believing that I could still stand, let alone walk, I managed a step forward and another. My skirts trailed through a pool of blood. I snatched them up, then let them fall. Flies buzzed in my ears. I knew these men. Tros the potter lay sprawled near my feet, his eyes fixed open, a hand pressed over his belly, holding a shiny, purple mass of entrails. I spun away and saw Phyleus, who hunted with my brothers. A spear was planted in his breast. And here was Mydon, who had golden hair, rare in our people. His skull was crushed, his hair matted with blood. Flies swarmed around him. And beyond him were more dead men, and more. If I looked, I would know them all.

I fell to my hands and knees and vomited in the dust. After many moments of being too weak to move, I staggered to my feet. *I must find Mynes.* I prayed he wasn't here, but my heart knew. As I searched for his familiar armor and his red-crested helmet, I stepped over tangled, bloody limbs. A few old women wandered among the dead looking for their kin, but none came near me or even seemed to notice me. I couldn't look, couldn't think. My eyes were separate from the rest of me, passing over each body as if it had no meaning. I refused to dwell on the faces of the fallen or name them. I would go mad. Yet I also looked for Laodokos, and my heart stopped every time I saw a young man's body. But surely he'd stayed safely in the hills with the sheep. I spared a thought for my older brothers. I'd search for them once I found Mynes.

Then I froze. Ten paces from me Mynes lay on his back with a great, bloody hole in his neck. His helmet was off, his head at an angle. His sparse beard was matted with blood. His eyes stared at the sky, all surprised, all unknowing. My knees gave way and smashed into the ground.

I crawled close. His skin was still warm. I searched his face. Surely his eyes would shift to me and his lips would move, speak. Why hadn't I stopped him from running down the mountain? He'd never had a chance against the Achaean leader.

I shut his poor, staring eyes. His eyelids felt soft and thin, and I was afraid of hurting him, until I remembered he was beyond pain. I envisioned his loving smile, felt his arms around me as he buried his face in my hair. *Your black, black hair*, he would say. I hugged his still body.

I remembered how I'd feared I would never wed, for my drunken father had left me no dowry. I'd prayed to Aphrodite, my special patroness, and she must have led Mynes to me that day in the marketplace. But why hadn't she put more love in my heart? With raw, aching remorse I recalled how I'd betrayed him in my imaginings. *Mynes, I belong to you, only to you forever,* I vowed. I wanted the time back, every hour and day of our marriage, so I could prove my devotion. "Mynes, I love you, I *do* love you," I heard myself saying aloud over and over, and too late, I knew it for the truth. My love wasn't passionate, but it was nonetheless real.

If only I had told him about the baby!

Heavy footfalls struck the hard ground behind me as someone approached. One of the enemy. I'd heard that they despoiled the corpses of their victims and fed them to dogs and vultures. I flung myself over Mynes. Too late, I was terrified. These men were rapists as well as killers. What folly to have come here when Mynes ordered me to stay safely in the hills! I thought of the babe inside me and backed away, folding my arms across my belly.

"Patroklos, have this body taken away with the others," said a voice.

I lifted my head to look, and froze. Just paces away stood Mynes's killer, tall and powerful, the sun reflecting a dazzle of light from his helmet and breastplate. A massive sword hung at his side. On one arm he held a huge round shield while the other hand supported a spear as tall as a young tree. Its point and haft were streaked with blood. Behind him stood another man, bareheaded, who watched me intently.

Then a strange thing happened. Instead of feeling afraid, I noticed that the warrior's armor covered his chest but left his neck and throat bare. My heart raced. Surely the gods had sent me this chance because they meant me to kill him. I owed Mynes this death. Without an instant's hesitation, I bent over his corpse and pulled the dagger from his belt. Hiding it in a fold of my gown, I stood up. I aimed the blade at the warrior's neck and hurled myself at him.

The warrior lifted his shield. I collided with it and staggered back. The shock and impact jarred my bones. The other man caught me from behind, taking the dagger and tossing it aside like a child's toy. I fought furiously, kicking my captor in the shins, but he forced my arms behind my back. Pain shot through my shoulders, rendering me helpless. My hair came loose and fell down my back and over my face. I struggled to catch my breath.

I was sure the tall warrior would draw his sword and kill me, but he only watched without moving. A sudden tension in his stillness told me something had shifted within him. Even with his eyes concealed by the helmet, I felt the intensity of his gaze. His mouth curved upward in an expression too hard to be a smile.

"Don't take him!" I cried in a shaking voice. "He's my husband, the prince."

"He fought well," the warrior answered, to my surprise. "He shall have his own funeral pyre. I'll see to it myself. Patroklos, take her to the others."

Before I could move, he hefted the spear, slung the gleaming shield over his shoulder and walked away. All my muscles went slack. When the man named Patroklos released me, I fell to my knees next to Mynes's body. I pressed my cheek against his leather corselet. I felt Patroklos's eyes on me. Looking up I saw that he was of medium height with dark eyes, brown hair. I caught his expression of pity and realized that this man, at least, meant me no harm. He would even, I sensed, protect me.

He bent to lift me away from Mynes's body.

"No!" I cried.

"He must go to the flames." His voice was oddly gentle. "So that his spirit can be set free." He made some signal, and two Achaean warriors came from nearby to lift Mynes and carry him away. I watched, too shaken to protest.

"Come with me." When I hesitated, the man called Patroklos said, "Have no fear. You will be well treated, lady." I didn't believe him, but I let him lead me away by the arm. *For the sake of Mynes's child I must go on.* He threaded his way through the bodies and led me toward a large group. He gestured. "The women of your town," he said. "They're unharmed. Our commander does not let women be despoiled on the battlefield."

Not until later, I thought.

The women stood surrounded by Achaeans with spears. I saw their faces, all known to me, all distorted with grief. A strange noise was coming from them like the howling wind but infinitely more sonorous, filled with a terrible despair that pierced my heart—a lamentation directed at the gods, at the departing spirits of the dead. Every throat pulsed with it. It came in waves, a huge sound, a hundred sounds, a hundred untold sorrows, a hundred separate laments.

Tears choked me. I felt their grief as my own, my heart crushed under the weight of all our sorrows. In front stood Amalthea, her dress spattered with blood. Oh, gods, had she seen her husband Mydon with his skull crushed in? Sharp-tongued, shrewish Speio had her face buried in her hands. I'd spotted her much-older husband among the dead. And there was my sister-in-law Pherusa, the one who had treated us as her slaves. Now her proud head was bowed, her hands tearing her hair. Did that mean my oldest brother Pylaios was dead? And what of the second oldest brother, Amphios? He would have been in the battle as well.

As Patroklos's hand on my elbow urged me forward, I stopped, hesitant. Having grown up without a mother or sisters, I was often reserved and unsure around other women. But my neighbor Nesaia put her arms around me, weeping. I noticed then that every face was marked with scratches, streaks and dots of blood. The fronts of their gowns were stained with blood where they had raked their nails across their breasts. The nearest women stared at me and fell silent, and I realized that I'd neglected to honor Mynes with this outward show of mourning. At once I brought my hands up to my face and scraped my cheeks until I felt the sting of blood. I scratched my arms, tore at my hair, and when their keening began again, I filled my lungs and lifted my voice with theirs, sending my cries to the heavens.

A long time passed before our crying diminished. I felt a touch on my elbow. Patroklos had stayed near, keeping a wary eye on our group. He pointed toward the shore "See?"

My gaze followed the direction of his arm and saw two fires blazing, one large and one smaller, the orange flames, thin in the sunlight, swirling skyward. "The funeral for your brave warriors," Patroklos said. "The smaller pyre is your husband's."

I hadn't believed Mynes's killer would keep his word. My throat closed, and I could only stare until the flames vanished in a film of tears. The others fell silent too, exhausted with grief. Then someone pointed. Nearby, the Achaeans had made heaps of gold objects, jewels, food, cloth, and cooking vessels, all our possessions and treasures.

"They're stealing our things!" Pherusa said, and we watched helplessly; some recognized their own belongings.

The Achaeans came, a few at a time, to stand about us, their numbers swelling until we were surrounded by their army. They seemed to be waiting. I heard whispers, and because I was on the edge of our group, many men's eyes stared at me. All at once the Achaeans fell silent, and their ranks parted. The tall warrior had returned. Still wearing armor and helmet but no longer carrying his shield or spear, he walked forward in that long, easy gait. From among the Achaeans came a whisper, a murmur, growing louder, like a swift-running brook. They were shouting his name over and over, pounding fists on shields and spear-hafts against the ground.

"*Achilleus! Achilleus!*"

Next to me, Patroklos relaxed. His eyes rested on his commander. When I saw those watchful brown eyes fill with warmth and pride, my stomach sickened.

Achilleus came forward until he was just paces away and stood looking over the women, his face concealed by the helmet. Then his eyes fixed on me. I stepped back and bumped into Nesaia. He came so close I could see gold hairs on his arms and streaks of dust and spatters of blood along his sun-browned skin. Not his, I knew. His gaze bored into me, forcing me to look at him. Fear rippled down my spine.

He extended his arm, holding something out: *Mynes's silver ring*. This man had torn it from my husband's corpse. The ring and the hand holding it blurred for an instant, then turned sharply clear. I understood the warrior wanted me to take it and perhaps didn't intend me harm, but I could only stare at the hand that had slain Mynes—at the blood in blackened lines under the nails and in the creases of the knuckles. Time stopped. I wanted to take the ring but could not force my arm to move. All the while his gaze never left my face.

Then abruptly he picked up my hand, put the ring in it, and closed my fingers around it. My hand burned from his touch. Before I could react, he turned his back, facing his men. "You fought well, Myrmidons!" His voice carried over the crowd. "Just look at what we've taken: food, supplies—and women. Every man shall have his share."

Their raucous cheers greeted his words. Their greedy looks devoured us. *We're their prisoners*, I realized, *their slaves*. I saw the same horror dawning on the others' faces. Never mind Patroklos's assurances, these marauders would rape us.

Achilleus lifted his hand for silence. "We'll take all back to camp so that King Agamemnon can choose his share first. We took many lovely women and much treasure from Thebe as well as Lyrnessos, and I say he is welcome to them. For myself, I shall only ask for one." Achilleus paused. Stillness. Even the group of women was listening now. *Who? Oh please gods*, I thought, *not I!* But I'd drawn his notice.

"I planned this raid—I led it," he said. "Will you support me in my choice?"

A shout arose from the men. "Aye, brave Achilleus!"

"Aye! Aye! Name your prize!"

When silence fell, he turned and lifted that bloodied hand to point at me. "This one, the prince's wife," he said, his voice deep and harsh. "She's mine."

CHAPTER 3

> "...some armed man shall drive you away, weeping,
> and take from you the day of freedom..."
>
> *Iliad*, Homer, Book VI,
> (Rouse's translation)

There was a breathless hush. My stomach twisted. I felt I was going to be sick. But Achilleus only turned and walked away through the parting crowd of warriors.

A voice called after him, "You've made your choice, Achilleus! Now let us have ours!" A buzzing, an excited stirring arose from the men who surrounded us. They stared at us with moist, glistening eyes and surged forward, their big rough bodies closing in. Blood besmeared their hands, their arms, their chests. I smelled the stink of their sweat. Their heavy breathing stole all the air. They began that dreadful pounding again. Fists against shields. Spears against the ground. Feet stomping in the dust. Voices chanted, "Give us our reward! Give us our reward!"

We women pressed close and clung to each other.

"We want them *now!*" someone bellowed.

A man wearing a bloodied corselet looked at me with eyes that seemed to pierce through my gown. He grinned, showing brown, broken teeth. Next to him, a big brute with a small unsmiling mouth nudged me aside and seized Speio behind me. As if that were a signal, all the men pushed toward us, thrusting themselves into our group, arms reaching, hands groping. Several women screamed in terror. Many were seized and held, though no man grabbed me, and I was shoved aside. Elonis, a distant cousin of mine, was pulled to the ground.

"*Halt, all of you!*" The thunderous shout stopped the men in their tracks. Hands dropped away. Silence fell.

Achilleus came forward again, shoving men roughly aside as he forced his way into the group. "Cool your blood!" he bellowed. "You know how it is! *No one* touches the women until we get back to camp and the spoils are divided." For a moment the air rippled with tension. Then a collective sigh seemed to go through the men. Some cast down their eyes and backed away. "Now there's work to do before we can go home." Achilleus began issuing orders in a voice that brooked no opposition. "Menesthios! The men of your division shall take the provisions down to the shore. Eudoros, your division is to round up all the livestock that can be found in the town. Peisandros, your men stay here and guard the women."

As the men dispersed, our miserable huddle loosened. We well knew what he had saved us from. Yet the women saw that no man had touched me. Some of them shot me resentful stares. By making his choice known, Achilleus had opened a gulf between the others and me.

Warrior's Prize

I was still holding Mynes's ring, the only thing I had of him. I was glad of it, and put it on my thumb, where I wouldn't lose it. Achilleus walked a few paces away with Patroklos. Their backs were turned. When Achilleus yanked off his helmet, his sweat-drenched hair, bright as bronze, fell partway down his back. He ran a careless hand through it and slung an arm about Patroklos's shoulder. "A successful raid, eh?"

Patroklos nodded and muttered what I thought was, "—best not set your heart on her."

Did he mean *me*? He said something else I didn't hear and cast a glance over his shoulder.

He added, "Agamemnon will likely claim her." I started in surprise. It was not the first time I'd heard that name. Agamemnon was the High King, the commander of the Achaeans.

Achilleus dropped his arm. "The Furies take him! I do all the fighting to provision the army! I don't see him risking his life. This time I intend to have what I want."

"Resign yourself, my friend," Patroklos said. "You know he gets first choice."

Achilleus only waved his words away. At that moment, before I could hide among the women, they both turned to look at me, and I saw Achilleus's face for the first time.

High brow, firm jaw, angled cheekbones—his beauty astonished me. His eyes were blue-green as the sea, but under their scrutiny I quickly turned away. I knew without looking that he'd taken a step toward me.

Patroklos, who seemed not to notice that Achilleus wasn't listening, said, "Remember, we've captured many other fair women—the ones we took from Thebe."

Thebe? Had the Achaeans sacked that town as well? Two years ago I'd gone there for the wedding of their king's daughter Andromache. My mind flashed back to that day—sunlight, music, wine, and dancing. Now that past joy was as a dream.

"Thebe." Achilleus made an abstracted gesture as if shooing a fly. He turned to face his friend. Free of those searing eyes, I breathed again. "Perhaps one of those will interest our king."

"Don't count on it."

Achilleus shrugged. "Patroklos, I've sent a runner for the ships. Go see if you can catch sight of them." As Patroklos loped off toward the shore, Achilleus approached me. I longed to flee but had nowhere to run. He drew me apart from the group of women, his hand like iron about my wrist. As his gaze traveled over me, I saw the blood spatters on my gown, which was beltless and torn at the bottom. If he noticed these things, he made no comment.

Instead he said, "You have not told me your name." When I didn't speak, he added, "You have nothing to fear from me." His voice was reassuring, even caressing. The murderer of my husband now sought my favor.

"I am called Briseis. Wife—widow—of Mynes, the prince." I tugged viciously against his grip. "Let me go."

He released my wrist at once. "No more hidden daggers?" he asked with a teasing grin. "I'm quite unarmed."

"You know I'm helpless. But if I had the strength of a man, I would kill you."

He gave a snort of laughter. "I hope to change your mind about that!" His expression sobered. "I'm sorry about your husband. But now it's your fate, decreed by the gods, to belong to someone else. There'll be a choosing at the camp, and I intend to have you for my own." When I said nothing, he gave a sudden smile and took my hands before I could pull away. He was very free with his touch. His eyes lit as his glance met mine. "I will treat you well, Briseis."

I looked down at his hands. Saw the dried blood. Snatched my hands away. I thought of the babe growing inside me without a father. I thought of the women around me who had lost husbands, fathers, brothers, sons—and their freedom. I saw their marks of grief, the blood on their cheeks stinging with the salt of tears. Rage burst within me. Before I could stop myself I lashed out with all my strength, catching him by surprise, and raked my nails down his cheek. Red streaks sprang out on his sun-browned skin.

There, I thought, *I've put the marks of mourning on his skin. Let's see how he likes it.*

Too late, I was giddy with fear. He seized my hands and forced them behind my back so hard I cried out. I saw shock, then anger on his face. *He will kill me now*, I thought.

In a rough voice he said, "Woman, you don't know whom you reckon with!"

But his ire passed as swiftly as it had come, replaced by an expression I couldn't read. As he dropped my hands, there was an ironic twist to his lips. "It does you little good to fight me. I still want you, spitfire that you are, and I *will* have you, regardless of Agamemnon."

This Agamemnon was a powerful king. The thought gave me a quiver of fear. Still, it would be better to belong to him than to Mynes's murderer. "What if you can't?" I retorted. "I shall pray that he claims me!"

He laughed shortly. "At least wait until you've seen him!"

A shout from the shore drew his attention. Patroklos stood there, arm raised to signal. "The ships are coming," Achilleus said. "I'll send Patroklos to help you aboard. And don't even think about mauling *him*, or I won't answer for my temper." Something sparked in his eyes. "I suggest you don't try the mountain lion trick on my men either. You'll find them far less merciful than I am." He gave a small, mocking bow. "I will see you on my ship." As he turned toward the shore, he repeated, "Mountain lion!" He seemed vastly amused by his choice of words, for he was chuckling as he walked away. Laughing at *me*.

I shook with outrage.

The women swarmed around me, all talking at once.

"Why did you do that?"

"He might have killed you!"

"You're trembling! Are you all right?" asked Maira, a young girl of fifteen. All at once, I was so weak I clung to her.

Sharp-tempered Speio said, "Fool! You humiliated him. You'll get us all killed."

"I don't think so," I said, thinking how he'd made fun of me.

"Still, you've made matters worse," Speio retorted. "He's the only one protecting us."

"Protecting *you*," said an indignant voice from the middle of the crowd.

I could have wept. *I didn't choose his favor!* I asked, "Is there no one else to rescue us? What of Prince Aeneas?"

Speio made a scornful noise. "We heard Aeneas escaped. Along with the Dardanians. The Achaeans took two of the Trojan princes for ransom."

"But not our men," wailed my sister-in-law Pherusa. "All our men are dead!" At her words, the women's weeping broke out anew.

All? Grasping her hand, I asked, "Pylaios is dead? What of Amphios?"

Pherusa's eyes were red and swollen. I remembered her coldness and cruelty when Laodokos and I had lived in her house, but now as she wept I could only feel pity for her. "Aye," she sobbed, "they fought side by side. Amphios fell first, and my Pylaios right after. What am I to do without him, Briseis?"

Both my older brothers. "Oh, gods!" I whispered. I had not been close to either of them. Growing up, they had scorned girls. The eldest, Pylaios, was a brutal drunkard like our father. The second, Amphios, also a roughneck, a plunderer in his own small way, had fought with the Trojans whenever they offered him sufficient reward. But they were my kin. I clung to Pherusa, my whole body clenched against the uprush of tears.

Someone gave a loud cry and pointed to the shore. We all looked. A fleet began to appear around the cape. "Their ships! They're going to put us on those ships." They would take us to their encampment up the coast. The women again began wailing with heightened agony. Nesaia, who had lived in the house closest to my home with Mynes, wept inconsolably. She had two young children. "My babies, oh my babies!"

I realized there were only young women and maidens here. "Where is everyone else—the old ones, the children?"

"The lucky ones fled into the hills. Some were left in the town," said Speio, who was childless—and dry-eyed. All the others were shrieking ever more loudly and hysterically. The marauders guarding us stood in a circle about us, and now they moved in closer, forming a barrier. One woman made a move to break away, and all at once the others charged toward the group of men surrounding us. Arms flailing at the men, they tried to push their way through. "Our children! Our children! Let us get our children!" screamed Nesaia.

The men brandished their spears. "Silence!" they shouted menacingly. "Cease this!" One lifted his javelin as if he would spear us.

"Stop!" Speio bawled. "Stop this, or they'll kill us all!"

But Nesaia pushed forward, and an Achaean struck her with the blunt end of his javelin, the blow landing across the side of her head. She cried out and stumbled to her knees. She was sobbing so hard she couldn't catch her breath. "My little ones—"

I took her in my arms. "Hush, my dear! Don't fight them —you'll only get hurt." I remembered that her parents and other kin lived nearby. "Your mother and your aunts will care for them and keep them safe. You know they will," I said, hoping it was true.

"But I'll never see them again!" Nesaia subsided against me. Her pain burned into me. I held her close and wept with her, feeling guilty that I carried my own baby in secret within me.

As I helped Nesaia to her feet, Speio said, "The old ones must take care of the children now." She added bitterly, "They'll fare much better than we will." The women fell into a silence of horror and grief. My thoughts flew to my beloved Laodokos, who was only fifteen, barely more than a child. "What of my Laodokos?" I asked. "Has anyone seen him?"

Those around me shook their heads. That boded well. If he had somehow joined the battle before the wall, someone would have seen him. Yet if he knew of the battle, would he have stayed away? He loved to drill with the warriors and had been so proud of the javelin Mynes gave him. I remembered how he had polished the point and carved his mark in the wooden handle. The young girl Maira, who had a fondness for Laodokos, touched my arm gently. "If he was tending the flocks, he surely didn't know about this until it was over. He probably fled with the Dardanians."

I nodded gratefully. "I'm sure you're right." But I sorrowed for Maira. If the Achaeans had not come, she might in time have wed him. Now instead she would become the slave of some rough marauder. I put my arm around her.

Achilleus's fleet began to fill the waterfront. The ships must have come from further up the gulf, perhaps from Thebe. I guessed there were close to fifty black-hulled vessels crowding our small harbor. At a shouted order from Achilleus, some were driven up the beach until their keels rested on sand. The men propped planks against hulls, and the loading began.

Our Achaean guards began prodding us. "Come on! Down to the shore."

But as the wailing and sobbing women began to walk, my feet rooted me to the ground. What if Laodokos came back to look for me?

An Achaean shoved me so hard I stumbled. "Move!" he snarled, hauling on my arm.

"Leave her alone!" Nesaia said. "Your commander chose her!"

The man let me go and pulled her forward brutally. "But I'll teach *you* your place!"

"No!" I hooked my arm around Nesaia's. The man gave me an angry look but let her go.

Pherusa said, "Just come quietly, Briseis! Don't make any more trouble."

Maira understood my fear. She said, "You can do nothing for Laodokos now. But don't worry. He will surely find others who survived."

She was right. If he came back now, the Achaeans would kill him. I could only hope that he was safe and would make a new life for himself. I gripped Maira's hand and walked with her, following the others, a hundred or so bedraggled women of Lyrnessos.

When we reached the shore, Achaeans bustled around us, carrying amphorae of grain, and armloads of silver, pottery, weapons, and bronze caldrons—all the treasure of Lyrnessos. I saw my loom, the cloth I'd been weaving still on it. My grandmother had given that loom to my mother before me. Two rough men lifted it toward a ship with no care, the loom twisted, my uncompleted weaving hanging off it in loose threads. As they heaved it into the hold, I bit back a cry, even as I knew this loss was trifling.

The marauders had penned up most of our sheep and goats in a makeshift corral nearby, ready to load on the ships. Listening to their pitiful bleating, I thought of old folks and children left behind. Without food and livestock, how would they survive?

As the marauders manhandled household furnishings up the gangplanks of the ships, I thought of the home I had shared with Mynes, its shady courtyard, its trellis covered with climbing grapevines. I stared up at the hills with their silver-green olive groves and piney woods. Just yesterday I'd walked there with Mynes. Tears blinded me. I remembered Akamas, the man I had tended in the hills. The help I'd promised him would never come. I wondered if he would survive.

As we were led toward the ships, I huddled close to Pherusa and Nesaia and kept my arm around Maira, hoping we could stay together. More women were led away to board ships until at last only a few of us were left, and only two ships remained on the shore. Two Achaeans came to fetch Pherusa, Nesaia, and Maira, leaving me to stand apart. "No!" I cried, clinging to Maira. "Please let me go with them." I wanted to comfort her even if I couldn't protect her.

One of the men said, "You're to wait. You're going on Achilleus's ship. And there's no room there for the others."

As Pherusa was led away, she said roughly over her shoulder, "Just let them take us and don't make them angry. We're surely all going to the same place."

Maira was torn from my grip, but I managed a quick hug and begged Nesaia to look after her. Then I stood alone on the shore, watching them go toward the smaller of the two remaining ships. These women were all that was left of my life. Most were young wives like me. We'd shared companionable hours over the washing at the spring. Mostly they talked and I listened to their tales of how to remove stains from clothes, or the best way to cook beans, or the difficulties of childbirth, or even sometimes, guardedly, how to keep a husband happy. We'd shared stories and toil, laughter and tears. Being a part of their pain would have eased my own. Their company would have lessened my fear. But Achilleus had taken even this from me.

Patroklos appeared at my side. "Come." He took my elbow and led me to the last ship, which loomed tall as a house. Achilleus stood in the prow, his profile in shadow as he stared out over the sea, head high, hair blown back in the wind. Then he turned and his gaze lanced through me with searing intensity. There was no mistaking his message.

I was his, and I'd best not forget it.

CHAPTER 4

> "In sea raids I plundered a dozen towns,
> eleven in expeditions overland
> through Trojan country, and the treasure taken
> out of them all, great heaps of handsome things,
> I carried back each time to Agamemnon."
>
> —Achilleus, *Iliad*, Homer, Book IX,
> (Fitzgerald's translation)

A plank rested against the hull. I dug my feet into the sand. I couldn't face this trip into the unknown. Yet for the sake of my baby I must.

Patroklos nudged me forward. Picking up my skirts, I splashed into water and climbed onto a steep plank that shifted with the rocking of the ship. Strips of wood served as footholds. As Patroklos steadied the plank, I pulled myself up with difficulty. My knees shook. My skirts caught and tore. I almost fell. At the top, Achilleus's shadow fell across me. He lifted me over the rail onto the stern deck and did not release me.

A gangway ran down the center of the ship, across thwarts where the rowers sat. Between the thwarts it was a sheer drop to the depths of the ship.

I tried to pull away. His hands dropped. "There are others below in the hold," he said, "the women from Thebe. But there's space for you up on deck."

I faced him squarely. "I'll travel with the other captives."

"It's much better up here. You can see where we're going, and—" I shook my head vehemently. He shrugged. "Very well. But if you change your mind—if you need anything— call me or Patroklos." I turned away without answering, and stepped too close to the inner edge of the deck. "Be careful!" Grinning, he pulled me back. "If you insist on going down there, you'd best use this!" He indicated a ladder that dropped from the deck to the bilge.

I backed onto it and descended awkwardly. Below was a world of shadows striped with sunlight from above. Thirty or so dark shapes huddled on timbers that lay across the bottom of the hull. I stood still, eyes adjusting to the dimness. A voice said, "Here," and I saw a vacant spot. Stepping from plank to plank, I made my way over. Dank-smelling water sloshed in the bottom of the ship, black as the River Styx. As I reached the place and sank down, I saw the faces of the Theban women more clearly, their rigid features and blank eyes, their cheeks bloodied with the marks of mourning.

I found no words. I didn't know anyone from Thebe. My only visit there had been two years ago when all in the surrounding villages were bidden to the wedding of their king's daughter Andromache to Hektor, the prince of Troy. Though I was only one in the crowd, I remembered how fair she looked and how the love shone in her eyes when she gazed at Hektor.

Above, Achilleus shouted an order. With a shuddering, grating sound, the ship was pushed off from the sandy bottom. I heard shouts as the remaining men scrambled aboard. Free of the bottom, the ship moved and rocked. The great oars were thrust into position, and bilge water sloshed around us as the men began to row. Looking up, I saw the undersides of oarsmen's legs, muscles straining, feet braced on the thwart in front of them. Every man sat by an oar except Achilleus and Patroklos. The rowers' rhythmic efforts were synchronized by Achilleus's shouts: "Pull! Pull—together—pull!" When the ship was underway, someone took up the rhythm by beating a drum, and Achilleus called out orders for the raising of the sail. As he and three other men hauled on the ropes, hand over hand, with furious effort, an enormous sail of white and wine-red canvas stripes unrolled against the blue sky. The sail bellied out and took the wind. The ship's progress became fast and smooth. Gradually I grew used to the rocking movement, the splash of waves against the outside of the hull.

I looked around at the other women. "Are you all from Thebe?"

A chorus of cries broke out. "Aye, our city fell!"

"The marauders killed all our men. Even our king, Eetion."

"And his sons, the princes!"

The Theban women fell silent, their gazes focused on the center of the hold. A pallet had been placed across the planks, and a pale-faced woman lay on it, motionless, eyes half open, glazed, staring at nothing. Her dark hair was streaked with gray, her thin hands half clenched. Only the slight rise and fall of her chest betrayed that she lived.

I looked around at the women. "Who is she?"

"Our queen," someone said. "King Eetion's wife."

"Andromache's mother!" I'd seen her at the wedding but hadn't recognized her in this gray, corpse-like shade. Now, in the high cheekbones, the strong, dark brows, I glimpsed a resemblance to her daughter.

"She saw her husband slain," another woman said, "and all of her sons."

"How many sons?" I asked in a hushed voice.

"Seven. The Achaean leader, Achilleus, slew them all."

"What of Andromache?" I asked.

"She is safe in Troy. But she's lost all her family. All she has left are her husband Hektor and their baby boy."

I asked, "What will become of the queen?"

"The Achaean leader will ransom her," one of the women answered. "When he saw she was stricken, he promised to send her to her father's house as soon as we reached their camp."

Another woman said, "She's been like this ever since we left Thebe."

I crept to the queen's side. Someone had seen to her comfort. There was a pillow under her head and a blanket over her. A stoppered water jar was within her reach, but the woman lay like one already dead. The left side of her face was distorted, her mouth slack. Saliva drooled from her lips and pooled under her cheek. I gasped. My mother had died like this. I felt again the unendurable pain of her loss. I took one of the queen's cold, unresponsive hands, and the pain of her sorrow assailed me as if it were my own. I whispered, "My lady, you will soon be going to your father's home. You will be cared for there."

Her eyes did not even flicker. From her mouth came a sound like dry rustling autumn leaves in the wind. "They're all gone," she whispered, and said no more. Very gently I arranged the covers about her. My pain seemed insignificant next to hers. "I'll be nearby," I said, "if you need me." I returned to my place against the hull.

One of the women said, "We've all tried. We can't reach her."

"I'm afraid she'll die," I said. *Like my mother died.*

A voice answered, "Perhaps it's better so."

"At least she has a chance," someone else said. "She'll be ransomed."

"But no one will ransom *us*," added a thin, older woman.

A silence met her words, heavy with dread for what lay before us as slaves in the marauders' camp. Then a voice spoke beside me, light and crisp, out of place in this underworld of grief. "*I* shall be ransomed."

I looked, and saw a young girl three or four years younger than I. Her smooth, pretty face bore no marks of mourning. I realized the others were as perplexed as I.

"She's unknown to us," the woman next to me whispered. "We never saw her before we boarded the ships."

Someone asked the girl, "Why you? Who are you?"

"My name is Chryseis," she replied. "I'm from Chrysa. I went on a journey to Thebe with my brother, who escaped when Thebe was taken. My father's the high priest in the temple of Apollo at Chrysa, and he'll ransom me."

That explained why there were no scratches on her cheeks. The others were looking at her with envy and bitterness.

The ship gave a sudden heave. The prow dipped and leaped. Spray rained down on us. We must have left the calm waters of the Adramyttenos Gulf and entered the rough seas beyond. With every rolling surge, I was afraid the ship would tip over. The women began to sicken, and soon my empty stomach convulsed. I leaned forward between the planks, heaving up mouthfuls of bile. The smell of sickness filled my nostrils.

Next to me, Chryseis began moaning plaintively. "I feel so ill! I'm not used to this. I'll die! I must have fresh air—" She seemed oblivious to everyone else's suffering.

I was about to answer sharply when an idea came to me. "Do you want to go on deck?"

"Oh, please!"

"Come with me." With a great effort I got up. I took her arm, feeling her softness, her fragility. Half dragging her limp form, I managed to lead her to the ladder. The constant surging of the ship threw us off balance. Grasping a rung, I called up into the wind, "Patroklos!"

But Achilleus, on the gangway, called down, "What is it?"

"This girl needs air," I shouted.

He swung himself down the ladder. Chryseis leaned on my shoulder, eyes closed. "You offered to let me travel on deck," I said. "Will you take her instead?"

He looked thoughtfully at Chryseis's fair, delicate face, slim neck, and shiny coil of dark brown hair. "She's very lovely. What a good idea!" His lips were set in a firm line, but his eyes danced with merriment. "You come too. You look a bit pale."

"I'll stay here." The words came out choked as I thought of the stricken queen. Achilleus's eyes narrowed in a look I couldn't interpret. He lifted the girl into his arms and transferred her onto his shoulder, his hand curving firmly about her thighs. As he sprang up the ladder, he seemed unable to contain himself. He gave a sudden, joyous laugh.

The sound of it outraged me, but I stumbled back to my place, thinking, *Now maybe he'll forget about me.*

The ship lurched, throwing me back against the hull. The woman next to me was heaving, and I was sick again. It was like the torments the gods devise for wicked souls in Hades. Hours passed until at last, weak and limp, I lay curled up, my head buried in my arms, and slept.

I awoke to a jolt, a grating roar, the ship being run up on sand. There were thuds on either side of the hull as the ship was braced. Through the thwarts I saw a black sky, a half-moon, and the stars of deep night. The women groped to their feet.

I crawled to the queen, who lay motionless. Her eyes were closed. There was a mess of dried sickness under her face. I removed the soiled pillow and pulled up a fold of blanket to prop her head. I touched her cheek. Her flesh was cold. I clasped her hands. I couldn't even feel if she was still alive. Then I heard her slow, shallow breaths. *I can't let her die alone*, I thought.

A light shone on us. One of the men stood on the deck above holding a pine torch. He placed it in a bracket, illuminating the hold. "Come on!" he shouted. "Up the ladder, and don't take all night about it!"

Several women looked at me questioningly. "I'll stay with her," I said. They made their way to the ladder. After they climbed out, a man came down the ladder with swift steps that rocked the ship. Without looking I knew who it was.

Achilleus knelt at the queen's other side. In the guttering light of the torch, his face showed concern but no remorse. "Leave her alone," I said. "If she wakes and sees you, it will only make her worse."

Without replying, he leaned close to check her breathing and touched one of her hands. Then he glanced at me. "The other women are on the shore. Go with them."

"But she's dying!"

"I'll have her taken to Machaon, the physician," he said.

"Let me tend her," I begged.

"No." He seemed almost regretful. "You must go to the gathering. All the women must be seen by the king." His face was grim, and I understood that, little as he liked it, he was under the compulsion of this overlord he despised. He looked down to where my hands were still linked with the queen's. Unclasping them, he lifted her with surprising gentleness.

"Go!" He jerked his head at the ladder. "With the others. I'll come after."

Having no choice, I clawed up the ladder, aware of him behind me, climbing awkwardly with his burden. As I descended the plank onto the beach, Achilleus called for Patroklos and another man to help him lower the sick woman to the shore. Someone ran up with a litter. They laid her on it. As they vanished with her into the darkness, I knew I'd never see her again.

Warrior's Prize

The ground rocked under my feet. I stood on a barren shore, the night wind whipping around me. Inland was a dark plain and long, low hills. It was a dismal place. In my damp gown I could not stop shaking. I walked toward the women, my legs so cold and rigid I could barely move. Chryseis materialized beside me. She seemed to have fully recovered from her ordeal. Her eyes were bright, her lips smiling. Someone had lent her a clean mantle, which I envied.

"I feel much better," she informed me. "Achilleus was so kind! He let me wear his mantle. Is he not handsome?"

I made some wordless, half-choked demur.

"He tells me we will be taken to the center of the camp to see the king," she continued. "And the spoils will be divided among the men."

"Spoils? That means us, Chryseis."

"Oh! But Father will ransom me soon."

I pitied her. I wondered if she had any idea that before her rescue some rough marauder, perhaps Achilleus himself, would brutalize her. As we walked up the shore, I took her by the arm, wishing I could protect her but knowing I couldn't even protect myself.

We joined a much larger group as the other ships unloaded their passengers, some from Lyrnessos and others from Thebe. As the Achaean guards herded us along the beach, I looked around for Nesaia, Pherusa, Maira, and others that I knew, but the crowd was too large, and I couldn't find them in the darkness. My despair grew. The women shuffled along like shades. Nobody spoke. To our left lay countless ships, their prows resting on the sand. Up the beach were clusters of huts. Scores of Achaeans came out of them and followed us, many light-haired and tall. Our people were mostly darker and of smaller stature than these strangers. As we walked I heard rumors of the raid, leaping like sparks from speaker to listener.

"Achilleus is back! Look at all those women!" As if we were beasts, they did not trouble to lower their voices.

"The drawing of lots will take place right now—in the center of camp."

"Agamemnon gets first choice—lucky man."

We came to an open place where a bonfire burned, the spoils of Lyrnessos and Thebe heaped around. Our Achaean guards led us to stand in a semi-circle about the fire, arranging us in several ranks, the older women in the back, the younger, more attractive ones in the front, so that we could be clearly seen, I supposed. Chryseis and I were in the first row, near the fire. I was grateful for the warmth. The crowd swelled to a vast throng. Voices clamored around us.

"...quite a raid!"

"I didn't think Achilleus would carry it off so quickly."

"...brought in enough supplies to last a long time!"

"Agamemnon will be coming..."

"...the heralds went to wake him."

"Where *is* Achilleus? He should be here, too."

There was a loud clang as a herald struck his staff on a bronze caldron.

Someone said, "The king! He's here!" A hush fell over the crowd. A voice shouted, "Make way!" As the king advanced through the cleared space, I stood on my toes to see.

A squat, broad man stepped into view. I'd expected a powerful presence, but only the gold circlet on his head and the scepter in his hand identified him as the High King.

Warrior's Prize

Rimmed in shaggy brown curls and a beard, his face was wide, bloated. His jowls sagged. Broken veins crossed his nose and cheeks. A dissipated face, a drunkard's face. Under beetling brows, his small eyes glowed with a greedy light. My heart sank. Achilleus's words echoed in my mind: *Wait until you've seen him!*

But he alone could save me from becoming the slave of Mynes's killer.

There was a stir as Achilleus, with Patroklos a pace behind, made his way through the crowd. He'd washed, changed his tunic, and donned a short dark cloak, which was slung over one shoulder. His chest rose and fell rapidly. He must have run here after completing his errand. As he made his way to the king's side, he passed quite close to Chryseis and me but did not glance our way.

"Greetings, King Agamemnon," he said in a formal tone. "I bring you the spoils of the raid so that you may choose your share."

"My thanks, Achilleus," the king replied condescendingly. "You keep our men well-provisioned. You shall have second choice of all this treasure."

"I am honored!" There was no mistaking the sarcasm in Achilleus's voice.

The king approached. His rapacious eyes passed over the group, assessing the women, dismissing all but a select few in the front, coming to rest at last on Chryseis and me. I shot her a sidelong glance. Too late I realized what he was seeing. She looked fair and fresh, while I was cold, wet, dirty, my face scratched raw, my hair tangled, undone. My torn, bloodied gown hung loose, carrying the stench of vomit. Agamemnon's lips curled with distaste. Under his gaze, I straightened and lifted my head.

His eyes went back to Chryseis, and he smiled with appreciation. "Aha!" he exclaimed. "Here's one that doesn't look like a wet rag. She's beautiful!" She bridled a bit at his words, and misgiving flickered in her face. He extended his hand. "What is your name, my dear? Speak up! You are the chosen one of the king."

I glanced at Achilleus. A savage light of triumph shone in his eyes. He'd gotten his way after all. Suddenly I knew why he'd laughed on the ship when I gave him Chryseis. He had foreseen this would happen.

A cheer arose from the crowd. I didn't hear Chryseis's reply as Agamemnon led her away. Achilleus stood before me, his eyes black in the darkness, sparking with orange lights from the fire. When he drew me forward by the wrist, I jerked back and stumbled in weakness and exhaustion. Derisive laughter erupted from the watching men. Achilleus caught me by the elbows in his firm grip and turned me to face his friend.

"Take her back to our camp, Patroklos," he said. "Look after her for me."

CHAPTER 5

"And when Achilles killed my husband and took
the city of Prince Mynes, you told me not to weep; you
promised that Achilles should take me to Phthia and make
me his wedded wife, and hold our wedding in the
Myrmidons' country."

—Briseis, *Iliad*, Book IX
(Rouse's translation)

Seeing a look of incredulity and indignation cross Patroklos's face, I understood that this was a most unusual command and he did not wish to comply. As clearly as if he'd spoken, his eyes said, *Why send* me *and not one of your underlings?* But Achilleus had already turned away.

His face sullen, Patroklos took my elbow to lead me away from the bonfire and the throng of warriors. In his touch I sensed reluctance and anger. He dropped his hand quickly. He bore no torch. Moonlight showed us the way. As the shouts and cheers of the men grew faint behind us, a small voice in my head whispered that I was better off with Achilleus than with Agamemnon. *Look after her for me,* he'd said. My thoughts were a betrayal of Mynes, but I was too tired to fight them off. Too tired to think at all. Patroklos walked ahead, along a line of ships that creaked and shifted as waves slapped their hulls. The sea was black, each ripple capped in moonlight. A wind penetrated my wet gown and pierced my bones. Sand and small rocks filled my sandals, and an aching weariness dragged at my legs. Patroklos did not speak until, after we'd passed what seemed like hundreds of ships, he halted and said, "Here is the Myrmidons' camp."

"Myrmidons?"

"Our people, Achilleus's followers. These are our ships." I saw a row of ships separated from their neighbors by a stretch of beach. Farther up the shore were low wooden huts with thatched roofs. He led me toward a hut larger than the rest, surrounded by a palisade. "This is ours, Achilleus's and mine." His lips drew into a tight line. "You'll stay there too. In the back, the women's quarters."

We stepped through a gate into a courtyard. It was eerily quiet. I asked, "Where is everyone?"

"The women are asleep. The men are at the gathering." I'd thought him kind when I first saw him, but now his answers were terse, barely civil. Clearly he wanted to be at that gathering, but, it was implicit in Achilleus's command that he keep a watch on me. He resented this duty, I was sure.

I said, "Do you always do his bidding?" He narrowed his eyes and said nothing. "Will the gathering last a long time?" I asked. *All night,* I hoped.

"Aye. After the women and the spoils are divided among the men, the priests will make offering to Zeus. They'll slaughter a score of oxen and sheep." No doubt some of those sacrificial animals had come from Lyrnessos. As Patroklos led the way across the courtyard, he added, "It will be grand

—flames rising to the sky. Afterwards they'll hold a feast with lots of wine. For some, the revelry will go on until dawn."

I was angry. "Why don't you join them? Why not celebrate your great victory? You slew our men by the hundreds. Go! Enjoy yourself. I'll be all right on my own. I have to be, don't I? You've taken everything from me."

He made no reply. Instead he said brusquely, "Wait here," and pointed to a crude timber bench by the door of the hut. "I'll bring you food and wine." He went inside, shutting the door hard, leaving me alone in the dark courtyard.

Without warning, a dam broke within me and I fell face down in the dirt, my face buried in my arms. Scream-sobs tore my throat, shaking me with their force. I couldn't stop.

After a time, hands came onto my shoulders and pulled me up. Patroklos guided me to the bench. His anger and impatience gone, he put his arms gently around me. I subsided, against his chest. My tears soaked his tunic, until at last the wrenching spasms eased into shaken sobs, and I became aware of other things. I felt how strange it was to be held by a man I didn't know, an enemy. Yet as I lay against his chest, I felt his kindness, and through it, a jumble of other feelings. I sensed that he carried a sadness of his own.

He whispered things I only half heard. "Don't weep so. It'll be all right."

It won't. Never again. Mynes, my brothers, my lost home, the grieving women, the dying woman on the ship. At last, my weeping subsided into exhaustion. I felt his firm chest beneath the wool of his tunic. I did not quite trust him, yet his presence was oddly comforting.

The baby, I thought suddenly. He mustn't know. Achilleus mustn't know. Already I had taken a tiny step back from the abyss. I loosened myself from his hold and sat up.

"I've brought you bread and some wine," he said, placing a goblet in my hands.

I forced myself to eat the bread, dry as dust, and drink the wine, which didn't warm me. I shivered. Patroklos touched the skirt of my gown. "It's wet," he said, "and you have no shawl. I can't give you another gown, but you can wear one of my tunics and a mantle. Come."

He led the way into the main room of the hut, where he had lit a lamp. As he opened a chest and searched through it, I looked around. There was a large hearth, unlit, in the center of the room, low chairs and tables around it, and two beds along opposite walls. Along a third wall were chests, storage bins, cooking pots, and a stone basin.

Patroklos handed me some folded garments. "These will do. Change in here. I'll wait outside."

When he left, I pulled off my filthy, ragged gown. Naked I fumbled into the tunic, which draped loosely about my chest and left me barelegged. I pulled the woolen mantle around me, wishing it covered more. At least it was warm and dry. My hands went to my hair, coarse and tangled as a wild horse's mane. I could only push it out of my face.

Patroklos was waiting on the bench outside. He stood. "Perhaps you should go to bed."

At the thought of a cold bed in the darkness, my stomach clenched. "Please don't send me away. Not yet." Tired as I was, I wanted whatever small comfort he could offer.

He hesitated, then sat down and motioned me to sit as well. "The first day is the hardest. You'll feel better in the morning."

"How can you say that? You don't know what it's like."

"Oh, but I do! When I was a boy of eleven years, I too was taken from my home and everyone I loved."

I was struck dumb. At last I said, "Why?"

"I killed a playmate, the son of a friend of my father's."

I had not expected this. I looked at his face in the moonlight. He gave a wry smile. "His father was visiting mine, and we were ordered to play together. He was a pompous, overbearing boy who insisted on his own way. I was humble. I yielded. Then, suddenly, I'd had enough. We were playing knucklebones, and he cheated. We quarreled. I lost my temper and pushed him hard. He fell and struck his head on a stone. I didn't mean to kill him; it was a silly child's quarrel... I—" He stopped. Clearly the memory was painful. I could picture him, a dark-haired lad standing over the suddenly lifeless body of his playmate, tears streaming down his face.

"Then what happened?"

"In our country, a death must be paid for with a blood price, and the killer must leave his home and become an exile. My father, Menoetios, took me away to the court of King Peleus of Phthia—Achilleus's father."

At the mention of that name I tensed.

He went on, "My father barely spoke as we journeyed to this strange household where he would leave me in disgrace. Then, as we stood in the courtyard with Peleus, Achilleus came flying out of the house. He was a royal prince, three years younger than I. I was to be his attendant, his servant.

But when he saw me, he knew at once how I felt. He came to me and threw his arms around me." Patroklos paused. "He welcomed me into his heart." Though he tried to disguise it, his voice quavered. "From that moment, we became as brothers."

I could envision it all: the stern, somber adults, young Patroklos shamed and heartsick, the boy Achilleus bursting on the scene like a storm, changing everything. My limbs were growing cramped from the cold. I stretched, and my bare legs came out from beneath the mantle. Patroklos's eyes darted away. Quickly I tucked in my legs. "I thank you for telling me, Patroklos. What a hard lot for you!"

"But my life took a different course—a better one. If that hadn't happened, I never would have met Achilleus. You too," he went on. "Fate has sent you to him. The gods clearly intended this. Achilleus will make up to you everything you have lost."

"He can't," I blurted.

Patroklos went on as if I hadn't spoken. "He cares for you. I saw it the first moment he looked at you. He's always attracted to a lovely woman, but this was more." Patroklos hesitated. "On the ship he said—" He stopped.

Against my will I asked, "What?"

"That there was a fire in your eyes. That you had spirit and courage as well as beauty. That you were a match for him."

I was stunned. "He doesn't even know me."

"He saw enough to know his mind. He said that when this war is over, he will take you back to Phthia, his home, where he will make you his wife."

"His wife!" I saw Mynes lying on the bloodstained ground. "I *was* a wife. He killed my husband."

"That's the way of war," Patroklos said in the brusque voice he'd used earlier. "You'd best get used to it."

"I will never wed him." *Not willingly*, I added to myself, yet Patroklos's words reminded me how many women before me must have made a similar vow in vain. I drew a shaky breath. "It would have been better if Agamemnon had claimed me."

"You're a fool to think so!" Patroklos blazed. His eyes had a hard glitter. His sudden flash of anger took me unawares. "You've no idea what Agamemnon is like. Achilleus is fair and honorable. You should thank the gods he claimed you."

"Why? He's just a brutal murderer." But I saw at once I'd gone too far.

Patroklos stood abruptly. His voice got cold, deadly quiet. "You're not to speak of him like that. *Ever.*"

I rose too and put out a hand in entreaty. "Patroklos, I only meant—"

But a chasm had opened between us. He was, after all, a stranger. He said, "You'd best go to bed now." He picked up a bundle from the bench and handed it to me. "Here's your bedding." He took up the lamp. "Come."

The night wind drove into my bones. From somewhere in the courtyard, a dog growled. Patroklos beckoned me forward with a jerk of his head. He opened the door of the hut and led me across the room to a door in the back that I hadn't noticed before. "In there," he said, pushing it open. "The women's quarters."

I stepped into a smaller, poorer room. As he held the lamp aloft, I saw a few long, uneven shapes lying in a row. Bedding stirred, heads rose, eyes stared at me.

"There are only women in there," he said.

Women taken on other raids, I realized.

"Find yourself a place. Do you need the lamp?"

I shook my head. "Good night," I said, as curt as he.

He did not answer but remained in the doorway gazing beyond me. Taking advantage of the lamplight, I found a spot between two bedrolls and spread out my rugs. Patroklos lifted his lamp toward the other end of the room. "Iphis," he said, "come."

I froze in surprise, kneeling on my bedding. There was a movement in the back of the room. A young woman arose and threaded her way between the sleeping bodies toward him. I caught a glimpse of a square-jawed face, dark eyes, straight brown hair. He drew her out, closing the door behind them. A stir passed through the others. Then silence returned.

During all the time we had talked, I had not imagined that he was waiting to be with his own slave woman, his concubine.

Then I thought of the other bed in that large, comfortable room. The revelry in the center of the camp would not last all night. At any time now, Achilleus would return to claim his prize.

CHAPTER 6

Akhilleus slept in the well-built hut's recess,
and with him lay a woman he had brought
from Lesbos, Phorbas' daughter, Diomede.

Iliad, Homer, Book IX
(Fitzgerald's translation)

Mynes, I will not lie with the man who killed you, I vowed in silence, all the while wondering how I could prevent it. Every part of me hurt. I pulled the rugs around me and closed my eyes, willing myself to drift into oblivion. Then, just before sleep took me, a sound came into my mind —the buzzing of insects, growing louder until my closed eyes saw huge swarms of flies. I was outside the gates of Lyrnessos again, looking at Mynes's dead face and all the other corpses. I saw things I hadn't seen then—my two brothers, their bodies black with flies as they decayed and were eaten by maggots. I saw Mynes calling me in helpless silence, his face eaten by worms. I pressed my hands over my ears to drown out the hideous buzzing. I squeezed my eyes shut. But the visions would not go away. I saw carrion birds digging their beaks and talons into the faces of Mynes and my brothers, tearing out their eyes.

Death was here in the darkness, its icy hand reaching to seize my heart. It would possess my body and take the life of my baby.

I pressed my hands over my belly. I tried to tell myself it was not real. Around me I could hear the soft, regular breathing of the unknown sleepers, drowned in oblivion—the noises of the living. I lay very still, alone among them, my gut clenching in terror. I could not let myself sleep, or I might never wake up. Time stretched and slowed unbearably. The night would never pass.

Much later I heard sounds of revelry from afar, growing louder as they approached. Shouts, snatches of song. The Myrmidons, Achilleus's men, were returning, some with booty, some with a new woman, all with a bellyful of wine. Achilleus would be with them. There was a harsh, brash reality to the sounds, and I almost welcomed them, for they came from the world of the living. Moments went by. My legs were so cramped and cold they ached. Voices grew louder, passed quite close, receded. Others came—an endless stream of warriors finding their way to huts and ships. The babble increased; I imagined the hut surrounded by men.

There was a creak, a slam. The hut shook. Footsteps crossed the outer room. The door to the women's quarters abruptly opened and Achilleus stood there, holding a lamp that cast light and eerie shadows upward over his features, making him look like a demon. He peered into the darkness —seeking me. I cringed and shrank beneath the covers.

"Briseis?" The call was no more than a murmur. I felt him hesitate, then take a step forward. Through the thin cover I could see the light moving as he advanced into the room.

Eliminating the others who were not hiding their heads, he soon found me. In one swift movement he crouched at my side. Holding the lamp above me, he peeled the cover back from my face. A suffocating pulse beat in my throat. He cupped his hand under my chin. His touch was beginning to feel familiar. His thumb traced the stinging scrapes of mourning down my cheeks. I wanted to back away from that touch, gentle as it was, but I couldn't move. I wanted him to withdraw his hand, but when he did, my skin missed the warmth.

He set down the lamp and was still for a long time. His face, close to mine now, looked normal now, even familiar. Twin flames, reflected from the lamp, shone in his eyes. His body emanated heat and the scent of wood smoke. My breathing eased. He pushed back the hair that stuck to my cheek and brow and smoothed the disordered cover around me as tenderly as if I had been a child. As my body yielded to the comfort, death and fear receded.

"Poor lady, you were a good wife to him, weren't you?" he said softly. Then his eyes returned to mine. "Sleep, Briseis! I'll not trouble you tonight."

In one nimble movement he sprang to his feet and stood looking beyond me into the darkness. "Diomede," he said. "Come with me."

There was an answering flurry from the depths of the room as a woman emerged—a small, softly rounded woman with a mass of curly hair. He beckoned her out and closed the door.

I lay motionless, too stunned to understand my reprieve. Then I let out a breath I didn't know I'd been holding. *Mynes, I still belong to you.*

But death hovered in the shadows, and the night was a long darkness to be faced alone.

CHAPTER 7

"...three brothers dear to me, these all my own mother's sons, these also met their doom."

—Briseis, *Iliad*, Homer, Book XIX
(Rouse's translation)

Deep in a dream, I was a little girl again, lying on my pallet in the house on the hill above Lyrnessos. My mother had gone far away and was never coming back. Sorrow filled me. I could not move, yet I must get up to fetch water and bake bread, or my brothers would go hungry and my father would beat me. I reached for Laodokos, lying beside me with his small-boy warmth, his downy hair tickling my cheek, his hands curled in sleep. But there was no Laodokos, and my eyes flew open. I was in a room with a low ceiling, walls of rough wood, and a dirt floor.

When I remembered, a cry rose to my lips, but I quickly smothered it. I was a captive in an alien world. The dimness of early morning showed me a room with several bedrolls and a few tousled heads. I heard regular breathing. Mercifully, the others here still slept. Pulling the blanket over my head, I shut my eyes and tried not to think. I managed to doze again.

A while later I awoke to rustles, whispers, mumbled greetings. I couldn't face these others. Not yet. I feigned sleep. Around me I heard the soft thud of bare feet on hard dirt.

A whisper near me said, "There she is—the new one!"

"Sssh! She's sleeping." But their low-pitched voices were clear.

"Her name's Briseis. Patroklos told me. She was taken on the raid. She's Achilleus's prize."

"Where's she from?"

"I don't know, but Patroklos said—"

She broke off. A door opened. The whispers addressed a newcomer. "Diomede!"

I ventured a look from beneath the covers. Four women were seated on their bedding. A fifth entered, carrying a tray with a goblet and a basket of bread. I recognized her as the woman who had gone with Achilleus last night.

Someone asked, "Who's the food for?"

Diomede answered, "Her—the new one."

Short, sharp hisses. "What! Why?"

Guessing they would look at me, I quickly pulled the cover back over my face. "Achilleus bade me," Diomede whispered. "She's to do no work today—only rest."

"No work! Is she a princess?"

Someone gave a low, malicious laugh. "Perhaps she's a goddess come down from Olympus!" My skin grew hot. I longed to put an end to their talk.

"We're to prepare her a bath," Diomede said.

"A bath! Carry water for a captive? *We* never had such consideration!"

"She's not to carry water at all," Diomede continued. "He commands it. And she's not to do the heavier chores. We're to treat her well. She's his favorite."

"His *favorite!*" The word was emphasized nastily. I cringed. By calling me that, Achilleus had ruined any chance I had of friendship with these women. The angry one continued, "How does he know? He hasn't even tried her yet! He slept with Diomede last night."

Someone asked, surprised, "Is this true, Diomede?"

But the spiteful voice answered in her stead. "Aye, our goddess here slept undisturbed!" She had forgotten herself and spoken too loudly.

Diomede said, "Be silent, Aglaia! You'll wake her!"

I felt them all turning toward me. I flung back the covers and sat up, trying to look as if I had heard nothing, but my face grew hot.

Diomede gave a forced smile and carried the tray over to me. "Good day, Briseis. I've brought you breakfast." She set a cup of milk and a round of barley bread before me. The women watched like a pack of wolves. I could no more have eaten that bread than if it had been a rock. I looked helplessly at Diomede.

"Let me make us known to you," she said. "I am Diomede. This is Iphis." I recognized Iphis from last night—Patroklos's woman. She regarded me neutrally and nodded. Diomede continued, "This is Kallianassa. She and Iphis serve Patroklos." Kallianassa was pretty but thin, frail, and timid-looking. "This is Helike—and Aglaia. We serve Achilleus," Diomede finished. Helike was tall and shapely, her features stolid, her manner subdued. She kept her eyes lowered and did not return my glance. Aglaia was dark and attractive. As her glittering eyes met mine, her lips sneered. So it was she who had made all those spiteful remarks.

Diomede spoke briskly to the others. "Go now—prepare her bath. It won't take long with all of you to help." I opened my mouth to protest, but with a gesture she forestalled me. Unwaveringly, she met the challenge in Aglaia's eyes as the women filed out of the room.

When Diomede turned back to me, her smile was more natural. "I'm sorry if you heard Aglaia's nastiness."

"It's nothing to me," I lied, then burst out, "But why do they hate me? Don't they remember what their first day here was like?"

"They'll come around," Diomede said. "But perhaps not Aglaia. She's always wanted to be Achilleus's favorite, only she's too harsh and demanding. At first he liked her, but now he'll have nothing to do with her."

And you? I wondered, *Do you too want to be the favorite?* I stole a look at her; her face gave nothing away. She gestured to the food. I felt nauseous. "I thank you for the food, but I'm not hungry."

"You'll feel better if you eat," she said.

Thinking of the poor little babe inside me, I drank the milk and managed to eat some of the bread. As I ate, I stole a glance at her. She had a pleasant face, her cheeks rounded, her chin small and pointed. Her dark, curly hair had a reddish cast. Her eyes were a clear golden hazel. I wondered if her solicitude sprang from kindness or was merely the result of Achilleus's commands. Those eyes made me inclined to trust her. To please her, I forced myself to eat the rest of the bread.

"Come. Your bath will be ready." She got to her feet, then gave me a curious look as I rose. She was staring at the tunic I wore.

"Oh. Patroklos lent me this. My gown was filthy and torn."

"Never mind. We'll find you another one."

She led me to a small, sunny, empty courtyard behind the hut. In the center stood a large bronze basin filled with water. "I'll fetch the clothes." Diomede left.

Discarding Patroklos's tunic, I stepped into the basin. As I washed, the cool water should have felt soothing on my skin, but I could only think how bitterly the women had resented preparing it. Their ill will seemed to swirl and ripple in the bath. When Diomede came back, holding an oblong of white cloth, I got out and dried off quickly. She helped me to drape and wrap the new gown about me, pinning it at the waist and shoulder so that it hung in folds to my ankles. She had also brought a comb. It took me painful moments to get the tangles out of my wet hair. When I finished, I left it loose to dry. Diomede handed me a sash woven with gold threads. I could not help exclaiming, "How fine this is!"

"Aye. It was taken on the raid. From Thebe, I think."

Thebe. Perhaps Andromache herself had fashioned this before she wed Hektor and went to live in Troy. Now her father, the king, was dead, her mother dying, her brothers slain. I flung the sash to the ground. "I can't wear it! Why did you give me this?"

Diomede's eyes were blank as she retrieved it. "Achilleus told me to."

"To hurt me!" *To make me a traitor to Andromache and my people.* Tears threatened.

"Nay, Briseis," she said gently. "Most likely he wanted you to have a bit of finery. You must resign yourself. This is a camp of war. Everything in it was either plundered or made by the captives."

I dropped my hands and said nothing, realizing that my refusal would only cause trouble for her. Firmly she tied the girdle about my waist, where it seemed to burn like a circle of fire. *Forgive me, Andromache,* I thought.

Diomede stood back to regard me. "There! You look lovely." But her smile was perfunctory. "You're to do no work today. I'll show you about the Myrmidon camp. You must use today to accustom yourself to this new life."

As we left the courtyard, I asked her, "Where are you from, Diomede? How long since you were brought here?"

"I'm from Lesbos. I've been here for about a year." For a moment her eyes became teary. Then she frowned and shook her head. "The past is best forgotten. Come this way."

A whole year, I thought, *when even one day seems unendurable.* Outside the courtyard, she pointed to rows of huts. "That's where most of Achilleus's men, the Myrmidons, live. Some sleep on the ships."

"Why are they called that?" I asked.

She shrugged as if it didn't matter. She pointed to some long, low buildings beyond the huts, where a man was walking a pair of horses. "Over there are the stables." I saw a few men down by the shore. Others were lounging in front of their huts. I wondered where Achilleus was but did not ask.

"The men didn't go out to fight today?" I said instead.

"Nay. There are many lulls in the fighting. Sometimes there's a big battle—more often just skirmishes. Sometimes a raiding party goes off," she lowered her eyes, "like this recent one, but often the Trojans keep within their citadel. So far it's a standoff." She lifted her eyes in triumph. "The Achaeans have failed to breach the walls of Troy."

"Why are they fighting this war?" I asked. "I've heard it's about a woman one of the Trojan princes stole from the Achaean king's brother, but—" I shook my head in disbelief.

Diomede's brows arched. "Ah, but this woman, Helen, is reputed to be the most beautiful woman in the world." She shrugged. "Still, I don't believe men would fight a war over a woman, no matter how beautiful. I think it's about greed. The Achaeans want the gold of Troy. And all men love war for its own sake."

She led the way up the shore to the place where sheep and goats were kept in pens. The animals swarmed toward us, bleating. "Oh, you poor things!" she exclaimed. "Nobody has fed you yet." She went to a huge pile of dried grass and picked up armfuls, which she dumped into the feeding trough. As the animals grazed, she reached a hand down into the pen to scratch one of the goats on the top of its head. Her face was gentle, her eyes sympathetic, as if she saw in this creature a kindred spirit.

"What is it like here for the women of the camp, Diomede?"

"We make the best of it," she said indifferently. "We work long hours, serving the men's needs, and at night sometimes we lie in their beds." A knot tightened in my stomach. "At first it's hard to endure. Then it doesn't matter. Was it any different for most of us at our homes? Achilleus is a just master. He makes sure we're provided for. Some are afraid of his temper, but I've never known him to be unfair." She added vehemently, "It's not so with all the Achaean warriors. Some women are beaten—starved. Many have died. Make no mistake about it; a captive's life is of no great value. I'm glad I belong to Achilleus."

I told myself I would never feel glad. Yet, unwillingly, I remembered his hand on my cheek. But perhaps the care he had shown me was akin to that of a man fattening up a lamb he planned to eat later.

"Sometimes women are given away as prizes—or sold." Diomede smiled wryly. "A good slave woman is worth four oxen—not nearly as much as a bronze caldron!"

I was shocked. "Why would a woman be sold?"

Diomede shrugged. "For failing to please her master, perhaps, or to pay off a wager. Of course, if a warrior dies, his women and all his possessions are given away."

If Achilleus died, I would go to another master. But it was a useless thought. As we walked toward the shore, I said, "Tell me about this camp—this place."

"I hate it!" she replied with a force that surprised me. "It's an evil place, full of flies and stinging insects from the swamps. There are no green things growing, save marsh grass and slime. It's hot and dusty in the summer—cold and damp in the winter." She made a gesture of contempt at her crumpled gown, her soiled bare feet. "It's impossible to keep clean here. The men have baths prepared by their slaves, and sometimes wash off in the sea, but the women— It's not often that we get the luxury of a bath such as you had today, Briseis."

Warrior's Prize

The words stung. I smoothed my fresh gown with a guilty hand. No wonder the other women were hostile. When we reached the shore, Diomede stopped. "I must go. I've neglected my chores. Enjoy your leisure, but don't try to leave the camp."

"Nay, wait!" There was so much more I needed to ask her. And I wanted her friendship. "Let me help you with your chores."

She shook her head. "Achilleus said not." She started to turn away but remembered something and pulled two green figs from her sash. With a furtive glance around, she put them in my hand. "He told me to give you these. I didn't want to, in front of the other women. Figs are very rare and hard to get."

"Where do they come from?" I asked suspiciously.

Diomede's eyes evaded mine. "From the fig tree just outside the Skaian Gate of Troy. Only Achilleus dares gather them." With an uneasy smile, she turned and walked away.

Feeling abandoned, I fought against welling tears. I looked at the figs. Did she really think I would eat them? I sat down and drew my legs up, resting my chin on my knees. Between two ships, I could see the horizon. The sea had a glowing stillness. The day stretched ahead of me, endless. I felt so alone. I wondered how Nesaia and Maira and the others of Lyrnessos were faring. Where in this vast camp were they? Would I ever see them again?

Footsteps crunched the sand behind me. I looked over my shoulder. Aglaia. I got to my feet, guilty to be idle, holding the precious, stolen figs. On impulse I held them out. "Here, Aglaia. Would you like them?"

She looked me over, chin lifted, eyelids drooping. "Figs from Troy." She took them and flung them to the sand, squashing them under her feet, grinding them to a thick, gritty pulp. "That's what I think of your gifts!"

I turned away quickly.

"So!" she said softly behind me. "His latest fancy! Let me look at you." Rough hands spun me around. She smiled maliciously. "You must be asking yourself why he didn't take you to his bed last night. You think it was out of kindness, don't you?" she demanded. "Well, you're wrong! He's proud, he's vain, our master." She laughed harshly. "Perhaps you failed to show the proper eagerness. I've heard him boast that no woman comes unwilling to his bed. How many other favors and gifts will you manage to get from him before you submit? You can only play that game so long, you know." She stamped her foot like a child. "You make me sick! Why don't you go away?"

"Where would you suggest I go?"

She shrugged. "We don't want you here. Diomede is only being kind because he ordered her to. You'll never be welcome—never!" Having delivered herself of her venom, she started to turn away, but her eyes fell on my sash. Her face twisted. "That's *mine!* He promised me the next fine thing he brought back." She grabbed at it and tried to yank it off. My hands went immediately to loosen the knot. Thinking I was trying to hold onto it, she struck me across the face with all her might. I was blinded, stunned. She tore at my hair, grabbed handfuls of it hard enough to tear it out by the roots if she continued. She jerked me forward, shaking me.

"Stop!" I couldn't loosen her grasp. Pain filled my head. I lost my balance. "Leave off! He'll punish you!" I said in desperation, not quite sure where the words came from, but she dropped her hands instantly, and I knew I had spoken no less than the truth.

A look of pure hatred shone in her eyes. "Go then! Run and tattle to him. But if a time ever comes when he can't protect you—" a dangerous smile appeared on her lips— "you had best look to your life!" Before I could answer, she walked away.

I stared after her. Then with no idea where I was going I started walking fast, almost running down the shore. I stopped when I heard noises, shouts. A group of men, their backs to me, were engaged in some kind of spear-throwing exercise or contest. I had no trouble recognizing Achilleus's tall form among them. There were piles of weapons strewn about. I spun away, my only thought to escape before he saw me, and collided with a stack of spears planted in the sand. I fell down, spears clattering around me. I heard a startled shout, and instantly Achilleus was leaning over me.

"What are you doing here, Briseis? Are you hurt?"

Struggling to get up, I didn't answer. Then my eyes fell on a javelin that lay nearby. I froze. An emblem had been carved, then burned, into the shaft. Now the blackened mark swam into focus. Two slanted lines meeting at an angle, one curving over the top of the other. *Laodokos!* Sitting by the fire, he had heated his knife to a red-hot point and laboriously carved his mark into the spear Mynes had given him, of which he was so proud. My body went rigid and icy. I reached out, touched the mark. There could be no mistake.

Achilleus said, "What is it?"

I sat on the ground, staring up at him. Comprehension came only slowly to my heart. I was surprised to hear my own voice, quiet, each word spoken with deadly emphasis. I held up the javelin to him. "*Where did you get this spear?*"

"Why, in Lyrnessos. Up in the hills, before we reached the town. Someone came out of the trees and threw it at me, a lad, and—" He stopped when he saw my face.

Perhaps after throwing the javelin my youngest brother had somehow run to safety. I sprang to my feet. "Then what happened?"

Achilleus lowered his eyes. "He did not have good aim or a strong arm. When I loosed my own spear, my aim was true, and he fell."

Against all reason, I hoped he was not dead but gravely wounded, and I could go to him, find him. But Achilleus said, "I had my men carry him down to the town so he could be burned on the pyre with the others who—"

"Oh, gods, Laodokos, no!" I screamed. "*NO!*" The cry was wrenched from fathomless depths. Achilleus's hands gripped my arms, but I tore free. I was sprinting, as if driven by the Furies. Scraping fresh gouges into my cheeks as I ran.

Shouts came from behind me. "Stop! Come back!" I heard him running behind me with several others. I raced with wings on my feet. I must outrun the unspeakable thing devouring me.

When at last my pursuers gave up, when there was only silence behind me, I stopped and turned toward the sea.

CHAPTER 8

"I wish the waves had swept me away..."

Iliad, Homer, Book VI
(Rouse's translation)

They were all gone. Every single person I loved. *Laodokos, my brother, my little one!* I'd promised our mother on her deathbed I would look after him.

The sea beckoned. It alone would drown my pain. I walked into it, took splashing steps until the water reached my thighs and my skirts trailed in the waves. Why do we fight so hard to live and love, when it hurts so much? The end was right here before me. Even the babe inside me would not hold me back. In taking it with me I would spare it a life of suffering.

But when the cold water smote my chest, I stopped, gasping for breath. Against my will, my body resisted.

It was very simple. I had but to keep walking and leave it all behind. I only needed resolve. I took a step forward. Another. Ahead of me lay oblivion. Behind me, a man who had murdered all those I loved.

I took two or three more steps. The wind had risen. Waves splashed my face. Far away I heard voices, shouts, but they meant nothing. The sea, only the sea, called to me.

"Aphrodite," I called to my patroness, "give me strength! Take me into the depths that gave you birth!" I pushed forward until the current tugged me. Suddenly it knocked me off my feet. My gown swirled in a heavy tangle about my legs. I couldn't touch the bottom. Waves submerged me, choking off my breath.

Sunlight pierced the sea's surface and flowed around me like honey. I floated, drifted. Salt stung my eyes and filled my mouth. My lungs craved air. I fought and thrashed toward the surface, but I couldn't reach it. Red, yellow—violent colors swirled in my head. My chest was bursting. Blood beat savagely in my ears.

I can't let go, can't die like this! The baby—

Like an animal fighting a trap, I wanted to live. Wildly, vainly my feet sought the bottom. I inhaled water. My lungs were on fire. I sank deeper. Blackness closed in.

Suddenly I was in the sky, looking down. I could see the ships, the sea spread below me, even the beach. Confused, I saw the waterlogged thing that drifted in the waves, cumbersome white robes flowing all around it. I noticed a cluster of people on the shore, shouting, pointing.

A man detached himself from the group, flinging off his tunic. He ran down the sand as swiftly as Hermes, messenger of the gods. He threw himself into the waves and swam, fast as a dolphin. When he reached the drifting body, he lifted it into his arms and bore it toward the land. Haste, urgency emanated from him. I could not understand his preoccupation with the thing he held. But he must, must bring it to the shore.

Suddenly I knew: it was *my* body—it was I! I had left it. I panicked—was I dead?

The man ran up the beach holding my body, shouting something. Another man ran to meet him, spreading a mantle on the sand. As the first man bent to lay me on it, all at once I was back in my body, a dark prison of fear and pain. A pounding shook my chest. I was rolled on my side, shaken. Deft hands turned my head to the side and rubbed my back vigorously. Salt water and the remains of my breakfast spurted from my mouth. Then something came down hard on my lips and blew breath into my lungs.

My chest expanded as air seared it. Another breath—another. After a moment I took in a painful lungful on my own. I breathed again. The gods had restored my breath, my spirit, the most sacred of all their gifts. I opened my eyes. Light flooded them.

Achilleus, breathing hard and dripping wet, clad only in a loincloth, bent over me. I lay at his knees, and my life was his.

CHAPTER 9

"...it would be better for me to go down into my grave."

Iliad, Homer, Book VI
(Rouse's translation)

Sun poured down, blinding me. For a moment my body exulted in the pure feeling of being alive. Then pain crushed me once more, and cold penetrated my bones. I shivered so hard my teeth clacked. Someone wrapped a mantle about me. I looked up into Achilleus's angry eyes, flashing like choppy seas. "*Why?*" he demanded.

I closed my eyes. When I looked again, another face was beside his. "Gently, Achilleus!" Patroklos murmured. "She's shaking. Her lips are blue. Shall I send for a physician?"

Achilleus shook his head. "No need."

"Then shall I fetch Iphis—Diomede?"

"Leave the women out of this!" Achilleus flared. "Do you think I want the whole camp to know she tried to kill herself? I'll care for her myself." He looked up at someone I could not see. "Automedon, go to my hut. Make a fire. The rest of you—leave us."

The group of men around us dispersed. I pushed up and

tried to rise. Achilleus caught me as my arms gave way. "Lie still, you foolish girl. I'll carry you." Scooping me into his arms, he got to his feet. Patroklos picked up his mantle and tunic and followed.

In the hut, Achilleus laid me on his bed of sheepskin rugs. "Patroklos, fetch a dry gown from the women's quarters. Automedon, make haste with that fire. She must be warmed."

When the two men left to obey, Achilleus removed the pins from my gown. Unwrapping the dripping garment, he pulled it from under me. I was so numb that it took me a moment to snatch a blanket and cover myself. Achilleus laughed softly as he spread the rugs over me. "Do not fear me, Briseis! You need warmth and rest." But his too-intense eyes probed mine. "Who's Laodokos?"

For a moment I wondered how he knew the name. Then I remembered. "He was my brother—my baby brother." Tears spilled. I fought to breathe. "I cared for him since my mother died, when he was three. You should have let me die!"

"The gods have ordained that you'll live. Don't reject their gifts." He added, "I did not mean to bring you sorrow." He straightened abruptly. "You need to sleep and forget."

As if I could.

"I'll fix you a potion in some warmed wine." When he got to his feet, I had a sudden view of Automedon, a dark, somber man bending over the hearth. "Haven't you got it lit yet? Out of my way. Begone!"

Automedon hastened to obey. Achilleus crouched by the hearth and soon had a fire blazing. Patroklos appeared with a folded garment, which he placed next to me. Going to Achilleus's side, he handed him a bronze vessel and a wineskin. Achilleus mixed wine, sprinkled something into it, warmed it, poured it into a cup, and brought it to me. "Here, drink this."

As he held the cup to my lips, I caught the faint, unmistakable odor of poppy. *Oblivion.* I lifted it to my lips. Then I realized I would be naked and unconscious in his bed, completely at his mercy. I mustered the strength to say, "Why do you seek to make me helpless?"

Achilleus looked astonished, then burst out laughing. "This is so you can sleep!"

Patroklos gazed down at me, disapproving. "Lady, take the drink. It's for your own good. Achilleus is learned in the art of healing."

"How can he be?" I said. "He's only a marauder." Patroklos's eyes glinted angrily, but Achilleus laughed again, and all at once I knew he spoke truth. He had not even thought of ravishing me while I slept. I downed the drink in one gulp. The wine was strong. A warm lassitude seeped through my veins.

"I do have other skills!" Achilleus was saying. "I spent part of my boyhood on Mount Pelion studying under old Cheiron, the leader of the Kentaurs. He trained many kings' sons."

The drug was already muddling my brain. "Kentaurs?" I asked.

"They are horse people and expert healers," he explained. "They train wild horses and ride them bareback with such skill it is as if man and beast were one."

My limbs were heavy and languid. As I tried to make sense of his words, I saw images in my mind of strange beings, half man, half horse, running through the hills. Then came a knife-flash of pain. *Laodokos.*

I tried to stay awake but my eyes closed. I heard Achilleus say to Patroklos, "She's almost asleep." He pulled the blankets up to my chin. "We'll leave you now, Briseis. Have no fear, you'll be quite safe."

When they left I struggled into the gown so that at least I would not be naked. It took my last strength. I crept weakly under the rugs. The bedding smelled of him. As I pulled the covers over me, I fought to keep the awful grief at bay. Mercifully the drug dulled the pain. My eyelids fell as if weighted, but in a last instant of clarity, I remembered how I had promised my dying mother that I would care for Laodokos. *I will guard his life with mine.* Those had been my last words to her. And I had failed.

Just before sleep claimed me, I thought, *I must avenge him. And Mynes as well.*

CHAPTER 10

Patroclos handed round baskets of bread,
and Achilles served the meat.

Iliad, Homer, Book IX
(Rouse's translation)

I slept, my dreams filled with shouts, challenges, clanging swords. Laodokos was in the hills and I must get to him, but I couldn't make my legs move.

Then I heard two men speaking low, quite near. "This is not a good idea. She hates you."

"Nay, she's sorrowing for her husband and her brother. Give her time."

I came fully awake, recognized Achilleus's voice, and remembered. A fist closed around my heart. I squeezed my eyes shut.

"She may try to harm you," said the first voice.

"Patroklos, we're speaking of a woman!"

"She's trouble. I feel it. Who knows? She could be the death of us both."

"What are you talking about? Have the gods stolen your wits?"

"Maybe, but I think you should give her away."

"No." The answer was sharp, quick, and angry.

"But if she—"

"Enough. She stays, and that's the end of it."

I opened my eyes. The room was in deep shadow and smelled of wood smoke. I looked toward the hearth, where the two men crouched. Achilleus was carving a shoulder of lamb into strips, which Patroklos slid onto skewers, then placed carefully over stones above the live coals. They were silent as they worked. Neither of them glanced my way. I studied Achilleus's profile, half in shadow, his brow creased in a frown of concentration.

I sat up, careful not to attract the men's attention. A sizzling sound came from the hearth as the fragrance of cooking lamb filled the room. Though I never wanted to eat again, my traitorous stomach growled loudly enough to catch Achilleus's notice. He glanced over, then stood and came toward me. I slid back against the wall. "Briseis, you're awake! Tonight you shall dine with Patroklos and me."

My mouth opened in surprise. I guessed that a female captive was not often invited to eat with the men. Where did the other women sup? And on what? Perhaps the leavings, the scraps. Nothing so fine as the feast now being prepared, I was sure. "I'm not hungry. It would be better if I went back to the women's quarters."

"Nay, stay and share our meal," he said. "Tonight I will earn your good will." When I could find no answer, he put out his hand. "Come. The place of honor is yours."

"It cannot be," I said. "You have shed the blood of my kin. We are enemies."

He smiled as if at a jest. "Spoken like a warrior on the battlefield! But what happened was ordained by the gods, who give victory to the strongest." He grasped my hand before I could pull away, and helped me to my feet. I had little choice but to obey. Later I would think of vengeance.

Around the hearth were three chairs, each with a low table at its side. Achilleus indicated the nearest chair, and I sat down. Patroklos, bringing out a basket of flat breads and placing several pieces on my table, gave me a narrow-eyed look. Did he guess what I intended? If Achilleus noticed, he said nothing. He cast a piece of meat into the fire as an offering to the gods. As it sizzled, giving off a burning odor, he mixed wine, poured it into three goblets. He placed several pieces of meat on a wooden trencher in front of me, then sat down.

While he and Patroklos feasted on their meat and bread with the appetites of strong, hungry men, I stared at my food, seeing only Laodokos. *I've lost everything and everyone.* Then I remembered the baby.

Achilleus could not have known my thoughts, but he looked up and said, "Eat, Briseis! You need to regain your strength." I took a bite and found I was famished. Patroklos got up to mix more wine. "Drink," Achilleus commanded and refilled my goblet. I drank deeply to blunt the pain and sharpen my courage. As the men talked to each other about inconsequential things, I ate and let their conversation wash over me. Outside the window night deepened. I could hear the endless advance and retreat of the waves. The lamps burned low. The men finished eating and reclined in their chairs. My own tension wound ever tighter. *Revenge.* I must do it tonight when Achilleus took me to his bed. Even if I paid with my death.

But I wanted to live to hold my baby in my arms. And I felt a terrible reluctance to take a man's life—even his. He had not known a moment's remorse in killing my brothers, my husband, all the others, but when I pictured the blood bursting from his neck, my legs weakened. He had saved my life. He had even, in his own way, treated me kindly. Perhaps, as he said, it was my fate to belong to him. Men raided and conquered. The victors killed the vanquished and took their women. It was the way of war and always had been. Perhaps it was the will of the gods.

Yet I'd made that vow to Mynes after his death: *I belong to you, only you, forever.* And the promise to my mother to guard Laodokos's life with mine. It was my duty to avenge them.

But how could I, a woman alone, do it? Even the Trojans hadn't been able to kill him.

I thought of Mynes with his mild brown eyes, his gentle smile. Would he truly expect this terrible thing of me? Would Laodokos? Would my mother? I saw another face. Andromache on her wedding day, wearing the bridal crown, her lovely dark eyes hard with determination, as they never had been on that happy day. I imagined her saying, *Kill him and save us all.* I thought of her slain father and brothers, her mother lying stricken in the ship. I saw the faces of my people, dead and living, heard their voices beseeching me. *Kill him. You alone have the chance.*

I realized it was more than my own revenge. He was the Achaeans' greatest warrior, the planner and leader of the raids that kept the camp provisioned. So many lives lost, so many towns destroyed to fill the Achaean storerooms. Killing him could change the course of the war.

Careful not to attract the men's attention, I looked around. On the wall over Achilleus's bed hung his mighty sword. It would be within easy reach if I lay with him on that bed. I had handled Mynes's sword many times, if only to polish it. I imagined the feel of the hilt, cold bronze under my fingertips. I would grip it with two hands and thrust with all my might.

I turned to study my enemy. The firelight shone on bare brown arms, muscular legs. Even in repose, his body had an aura of power. Then my eyes found the soft place in his throat, the jugular. With one well-placed thrust, a man might be killed as easily as a sheep or a swine.

Zeus and all gods send me strength, I prayed. Would some god come to my aid? *Aphrodite?* Silently I said the name of my patroness, picturing her graven face in the shrine at Lyrnessos, lips smiling, always smiling. Now I saw the mockery in that smile. I remembered my disloyal thoughts as I lay in Mynes's bed and envisioned a godlike man in his stead. Achilleus, though I hadn't known it then. Aphrodite had put his image in my mind to tempt me—*taunt me*—with what was to come.

She would not help me now.

I cast a covert glance at Achilleus. His face was lit with a smile as he listened to some tale Patroklos was recounting. Unaware of my gaze, his eyes rested on the other man's face —fond, amused—a look he seemed to reserve for Patroklos alone. Clearly he cared for him. Then I shut out the thought. He was a monster. I did not want to see him with human feelings.

"—when we were youths on the island of Skyros," Patroklos was saying. "Remember when you went looking for a wayward goat and got stuck on a high crag?"

"No, my dear Patroklos, you have it wrong. The goat got stuck, not I! I had to rescue it. Here, have some more wine. You need it to sharpen your memory!" Achilleus, laughing, leaned forward to refill his friend's goblet. Then, at the same instant, both recalled my presence. Achilleus poured me more wine and, as if reaching a decision, suddenly stood. Patroklos rose too, removed the tables, and flung the meat scraps outside to the dogs. Achilleus fetched something from a corner of the room. I heard a few notes of music and saw he was holding a beautiful, silver-bridged lyre. I gasped.

In his chair tuning the lyre, he looked up. "What is it?"

That lyre had belonged to King Eetion of Thebe. I'd seen him play it at Andromache's wedding. I didn't want to answer, but he was looking at me so probingly that I mumbled, "You stole that. On the raid."

"Stole? No, it was a prize of war. I won it." His hands rested on the lyre as he looked at me. "I would never steal. But if I am better in battle—" He smiled. "That is how I won you, my lovely one!" He reached out to caress my cheek. When I flinched, he turned back to the lyre, and a cascade of sound flowed from the instrument, each note bursting with its own color. I drew a surprised breath. He looked deep into my eyes, a *noticing* look as he continued to stroke the lyre, creating a rippling fountain of notes. The god Apollo himself could not have made greater magic. At last he raised his head. "A lament, I think," he said, and began to sing.

The words floated up, his voice rich and melodious, filling the room with the sorrowful tale of a young warrior who took on a great hero and died before his time, leaving youth and manhood behind. I suddenly couldn't breathe. The music opened a torrent within me. I tried to check my weeping but couldn't. Memories flooded me: Laodokos a baby, a toddler, then a lad, his brown eyes wide and bright, his boyish grin, a dark line of down on his upper lip, his boy's voice cracking as he said my name. I remembered a summer morning when he was eight or nine and we had gone into the green-gold foothills to search for a lost ewe. He ran bounding up the slope ahead of me. He kept hiding and wouldn't wait. Mischievous laughter bubbled out of him as he vanished behind shrubs and reappeared, his cheeks stuffed with berries, the juices running down his chin. His eyes shone with irrepressible joy. When I caught up with him at last, he had one hand behind his back.

"What have you got there, you naughty boy?"

It was a posy of wildflowers, half-crushed in his sweaty fist. "For you, Briseis. I love only you."

Sobs erupted from me. Achilleus looked up. The lyre fell silent with a clang as he set it down and got to his feet. He handed me a clean cloth, then sat again. I buried my face in it, and even as I cried, I was aware of his waiting silence.

When at last my sobs lessened, he said, "My poor Briseis, it was good for you to weep. But now, dry your tears."

Patroklos got up and went about the room quenching the lamps until only the hearth glowed. Achilleus leaned over me and scooped me up into his arms.

"Come, my beauty, it grows late," he said huskily. "It's time for bed."

CHAPTER 11

"It would be comforting to make love with a woman."

Iliad, Homer, Book XXIV
(Fitzgerald's translation)

His warm breath brushed my neck as he set me on my feet. "Come!" That taut syllable conveyed his eagerness. He pulled me toward the bed. Cold sweat broke out on my skin. I wasn't ready, but I made as if to follow. I needed to distract him, slow him down. And I needed light, to find that sword and position myself. But Patroklos had extinguished the lamps, and the only light came from the dying embers in the hearth. Not enough to see.

Midway to the bed I stopped. "What is it?" he whispered.
"I'm cold."
"I'll warm you in my bed."
"The fire," I said. "Build it up—please."
"There's no need." He tried to lead me forward.
I planted my feet. His arm muscles tightened. Then he released me. "Very well, you shall have a fire." He went to the hearth.

I groped across the floor and stopped, deep in shadow, when my bare feet made contact with the sheepskin rugs of his bed. I glanced over my shoulder. Achilleus was a darker shadow crouching over the hearth. At the other end of the hut, the door opened and closed. I heard footsteps, then faint noises from Patroklos's end of the room. I could not tell if he had summoned Iphis or was settling down to sleep alone.

A twig blazed up in Achilleus's hand, briefly sending a pale light flickering over the walls. The sword—quickly! My hands closed around it, pulled it part way from its sheath. But I dared not move it off the wall hooks. He would hear. I crouched, not breathing, watching him over my shoulder. Busy with the fire, he did not turn in my direction. I eased the sword out further. He heaped kindling over the embers, added a log, another. There was a hissing noise, a fountain of sparks. I pulled on the hilt until only a handbreadth of it remained in the sheath. Flames leapt up, crackling softly. He reached for a poker. The clang of bronze on stone gave me the chance I needed. Swiftly I pulled the sword free of the sheath and away from the wall hooks. I dropped to my knees on the bed. My hands were wet and slippery. My legs were shaking. I wished he would finish with the fire and come quickly, before I lost my nerve and my will.

The sword's weight strained against my wrists. I pulled some of the bedding over the blade to hide it. His back was to me now as he worked on the fire. Keeping both hands locked around the hilt, I gained a purchase with my knees in the soft rugs. Every muscle in my body was drawn tight. I tried to quiet my breathing as I watched and waited.

Terror filled me. *Don't think about it*, I told myself. *Just act.*

Warrior's Prize

Satisfied with the fire at last, he stood up slowly and loosened the clasp at his shoulder. His mantle dropped to the floor. He stooped, unfastened his sandals, kicked them free.

A knot constricted my throat. A tremor ran through my arms. My hands were so sweaty I could barely keep my grip on the hilt.

He turned his back to sling aside his belt and pull his tunic over his head. He stood naked in the firelight. His body glowed gold in the glow of the flames, all smooth hard planes and muscular curves.

My hands slid off the sword. I couldn't do it. Not if he was naked.

No matter! screamed a voice inside me. He had shown no mercy to my people.

I grasped the sword again. He turned, took a step toward me. He was a dark shape outlined in fire. I could not see his face, but a crescent of light curved around his cheek.

He was smiling.

"Briseis!" he whispered softly, happily, as he came closer.

My knees dissolved. *I can't!* Then came a thought that gave me strength. *Don't think of him as a man. Think of him as a dangerous beast that must be destroyed.* I focused on the shadow of his throat. The jugular. I went into a crouch, gathered my feet under me. The firelight flickered. He took a step—another.

Now! I lifted the blade and—

Without warning I lost my grip and the hilt slipped from my sweaty fingers. The sword fell clanging onto the floor.

I was trembling so badly my teeth rattled.

He stood frozen for about two heartbeats. Then faster than thought he seized me and forced me down onto the bed.

My face was muffled in the rugs, my arms twisted with wrenching pain behind my back. The length of his body lay over mine, pinning me. Long moments we lay thus in a strange intimacy, his hard breaths convulsing me, his hot closeness stifling me. My head was wedged between his shoulder and his jaw. My whole body shook.

"Briseis!" he said at last in a shaken whisper. Then his voice grew harsh. "How dare you heft my own sword against me?" I couldn't speak. He shifted me on the bed so that I was facing him. "What do you think you were doing?"

Now that I'd failed, he mustn't know I'd meant to kill him. My life depended on it. My voice came out hoarse and muffled. "I—I didn't think—"

His hands tightened around my arms. "*What were you doing with my sword?*"

"I was just—" I mumbled, "testing it. I was—curious."

"Testing it!" he said with blistering scorn.

"To see if—" I sputtered. "Your sword— So much heavier than Mynes's." I held my breath. I couldn't tell if I'd convinced him. I didn't even know if I had clumsily dropped the sword or if some part of my will had forced me to release it. I only knew that now, somehow, I must preserve my life for the baby.

"Mynes let you handle his sword?"

"To—to polish it only."

"I see." His grip tightened. "Well, Mynes is dead, and I'm your master now. You live by my mercy. Never forget it!" He broke off, breathing hard. "Don't ever, *ever* touch my sword again! Or else—" He shook me. "Or else you'll die as anyone would who went against me." I felt his eyes boring into me, and I had not a doubt he meant every word. "You couldn't have killed me, Briseis," he said. "You wouldn't have succeeded where hundreds have failed. But you took a grave risk. If I'd had to defend myself I might have done you harm. Lucky for you that you lost your nerve!"

He knew. Of course he did.

At last he let me go and lay still at my side. His breathing slowed, and he was silent for a time. I went weak, belatedly terrified, relieved I'd dropped the sword. *My baby*, I thought, *perhaps you and I will live to see another day.*

He huffed a breath. "I'll let bygones be bygones. *This time.* In your place I'd have done the same."

He got up to retrieve the sword. I thought about leaping from the bed and making a run for the women's quarters, but I could only lie there, drained of will and strength. He replaced the sword in its sheath on the wall hooks and lay down again next to me. His mood shifted. "I already know of your spirit, my fierce one!" In the darkness I sensed his smile. "I'll never forget my first sight of you—bravely defending your husband's body. You have the heart and courage of a warrior." He caressed my cheek, trailing his fingers down a long strand of my hair. "But no more! Leave the fighting to me."

He leaned over me, and I felt his warm breath on my face. Before I could turn my head, his lips met mine. I couldn't pull away—couldn't even move. I was only aware of the heat of his mouth, awakening something inside me that I hadn't known existed. His arms wrapped around me and pulled me closer. A distant voice told me to stop this from happening, but his kisses forced even that thought from my mind. I had no mind. I was a stranger to myself, observing as he loosened my gown, bundling it aside until we lay naked, flesh against flesh. His hands and lips traveled down my body. My knees went weak. When he pulled me close again and slid his legs between mine, I made no protest. I had no will. My body invited him in. A rush of feeling surged in me until my bones liquefied, and a white-hot wave carried me to an unendurable bliss that was almost pain. I wanted it to never stop. I heard myself crying out.

He was breathing hard, holding me tightly. He whispered my name as if it were the only word he knew. Then he lay against me, his breath slowing. For long moments I rested, floating, wrapped in the warmth of his flesh. I wanted never to move again.

But at last I stirred. Awareness returned. How had this happened? I was in an unaccustomed bed, in the arms of my enemy. I had failed Mynes in the only way that mattered.

I felt a shame unlike any I had ever known.

The room was in complete darkness until a log in the hearth caught, sending up a little spurt of flames, and I saw his face next to mine, the tense lines smoothed out of it. He was looking at me, sparks in the depths of his eyes.

"My beautiful Briseis!" He stroked my hair. "Patroklos wanted me to send you away. He said you were trouble—you would hurt me." He came up onto an elbow, peering down into my face. "But you're worth the trouble!" I heard the smile in his voice. I wanted to protest but I couldn't speak. He kissed the side of my neck and laid his head next to mine. His arm rested across me. His body relaxed, and his breathing grew deep and peaceful as he drifted into sleep. He seemed not to care that his sword hung just above us.

And why would he? He knew he'd won.

CHAPTER 12

"Every sane decent fellow loves his own and cares for her, as in my heart I loved Briseis, though I won her by the spear."

—Achilleus (*Iliad*, Homer, Book IX, Fitzgerald's translation)

A faint gray light seeped through the opening above the hearth when I awoke, enough for me to see the face of Achilleus asleep at my side. Self-loathing filled me. *I can't stay here in his bed.* I had to decide what to do and how to go on.

Perhaps I could even find a way out of the camp. *Escape.*

I didn't have time to think or plan. If I was careful, I could slip out of the bed without waking him. Gingerly I sat up, reached for my gown and pulled it over my head. The morning air was chilly. His blue mantle lay on the floor. I wrapped it about me.

Tiptoeing to the food chest, I grabbed some scraps of dried meat and took an empty wine skin that I could fill with water when I reached a spring.

On silent feet I made for the door and unlatched it soundlessly. A whiff of cool air blew in. Someone muttered in the room behind me. I froze. When there was no further sound, I slipped out, pulling the door closed but leaving it unlatched. I started for the gate—and saw the dogs, several huddled shapes across the courtyard. One stood looking at me through the dimness, ears pointed, tail erect. He gave a low growl. I put out my hand to reassure him. He started toward me, still growling softly. Fearful that he might bark or attack, I handed him the meat scraps, which he wolfed down. So much for having food for the journey.

The gate was barred from the inside, the bar too heavy for me to lift, but I found a place along the fence where a stack of wood and a supporting beam provided footholds. Climbing up, I pulled myself over and landed on the other side. The Myrmidon camp was quiet, the beach deserted. The water was still, the sky just beginning to brighten over the eastern hills.

I went down to the edge of the sea. In the past times of trouble, I had stood at dawn on the shore of Lyrnessos to commune with Aphrodite, my patroness. I lifted my arms to her now and prayed in silence. *O Goddess, guide me! Make your will known to me.* But if there was an answer from her, it was a deafening stillness, as if she refused to acknowledge my existence. I felt abandoned. Was she angry that I had not accepted my lot as Achilleus's prize?

I called silently to my lost Laodokos, but the pain was so fresh I turned my mind instead to my husband. *Mynes, what should I do? Shall I risk returning to our people?* I tried to see his face and hear his voice—how it sounded when he said my name. Instead, Achilleus's voice resonated in my mind. *My beautiful Briseis!*

Must I resign myself? Was this the answer I sought?

No. Not if there was any possibility of escape from the man who had murdered my husband and my beloved Laodokos. An inner voice warned, *If I get caught, things could get a lot worse.* But I had to try. What better time than now, while the men still slept? If I kept walking down the shore with the sea on my right, I would reach a place where the last ship was beached. The Achaeans, mighty as they were, could not wall off the sea. Once I got to the end, there would be a way out of the camp. And if I kept walking, following the shore, eventually I would get to Lyrnessos even if I had to walk for many days. I would find the food supply mostly gone and those few left behind struggling to survive. But never mind the hardships. I could live among my own people and bear my child there.

Mynes, is this your will? For a moment he felt present in my mind. Then his spirit gently faded. "Farewell," I whispered.

As I started walking, a vague, insistent back pain slowed my steps. The sea was beginning to shimmer with light. But its beauty only brought sadness. A lone sea gull glided by, turning on a black-tipped wing. The Achaean ships on my right seemed to stretch out without number until at last, far down the shore, I saw the end of the line. I hastened my steps. Full daylight blazed when I finally reached the last ship.

Here, the wall around the camp extended into shallow water. One hand on the wall, the other holding up my gown,

I waded into the sea, knee-deep. Then something made me look back.

A form was hurtling down the beach, swift as fate.

My heart sank. I turned quickly and waded back to the shore, hoping to conceal my purpose. *Later*, I thought. There would be another chance.

I faced Achilleus as he stood before me, his breathing barely hastened from his run. He wore a short tunic and carried a javelin. The sight of it gave me a knife-thrust of pain, even though this was not the one that had belonged to Laodokos.

"A walk at sunrise, Briseis?" Achilleus gave a harsh laugh and pointed to the wall. "You would not have gotten far. There's a sentry on the other side. But come!" He took my arm with sudden ferocity. "He will let us through."

The sentry came forward from his station. "Good day, Amphimachos," Achilleus called out. "A fair morning, is it not?"

"Prince Achilleus!" the man answered. "What brings you here?"

Achilleus grinned crookedly. "An early morning walk." He pulled me forward. The sentry returned to his post as we waded in shallow water around the end of the wall. Beyond, a brackish stream ran into the sea. Without seeking my consent, Achilleus lifted me into his arms and forded the stream. On the other side he set me down, wordlessly pulling me along, until we rounded a rocky outcropping and passed beyond the sentry's line of vision.

There he stopped, looking down at me, his eyes hard. His right hand clenched around the javelin, and I saw the knuckles whiten. "First the sword, and now this. I should punish you—lock you up." He turned, throwing the javelin with vehement force. It flew in a long, flattened arc, far down the shore, and landed point down, quivering in the sand. He ran to retrieve it, took aim and threw again, as if to fling the pent-up anger from his body.

I watched because I could not help myself. With each throw his body was a poem of fluid motion. A too-vivid memory kindled in my mind: the walls of Lyrnessos and my first sight of that lethal grace. As he ran down the beach to retrieve the javelin, I sighed sharply and sat on the sand, facing out to sea. To my left, the shore stretched toward home, tantalizingly deserted. I thought of running down that strand—but for only an instant. There was no way to escape an angry man with a spear. A man who could outrun the wind. Hopelessness weighed on my heart.

Achilleus came up to sit beside me, very close. I did not look at him but heard his hard breathing. "You cannot escape, you know. You're hemmed in by walls and sentries—and by the sea. And the sea is my friend!"

I shook my head. "How can that be?"

"My mother, Thetis, is a priestess to the sea god Nereus. The sea will never turn against me, nor those I love. Perhaps that's why I found you yesterday, just in time." He paused. "You were not indifferent to me last night, were you? Look at me, answer me, Briseis." I kept my face resolutely turned away. He already saw too much. "Sometimes when I stand on the shore," he continued, "my mother seems very near. I send her my thoughts, and I think she answers me."

Surprised, I did look at him.

"If I told her about you," he continued, "what would she say? She would tell me to be patient, that Briseis's love will be mine one day." He touched my cheek. When I drew back, his face twisted into a grimace. "I know I should listen to her, but—I can't—" He broke off, and his fist struck the sand between us. There was a stinging silence.

"What do you want?" he asked at last in a stifled voice. "I've made you welcome, shown you every kindness—"

Aye, it was true. I was not ill-treated, as were so many women who endured rape and brutality. Yet I thought, *Kindness, when you killed my loved ones!* I gave a choked, bitter laugh that became a flood of tears. As if answering my unspoken rebuke, he said, "I've done no wrong; I'm a warrior!"

He was silent as I wiped my eyes with the heels of my hands. Taking up a handful of sand, he sifted it through his fingers. "I never wanted to hurt you." But he had done that, irreparably, before he ever laid eyes on me. "Briseis," he said helplessly, "I can't change the past. But when this war is over, when we go home to Phthia—"

Not wanting to hear, I spun away, scrambled to my feet. He was up before me. For just an instant I had a glimpse of his eyes, blue-green as the sea, bleak and hungry. Then he turned his back and stood still for several moments. At last he faced me. He smiled and took my hands in his, holding them lightly, gently, while he searched my face. "Tell me how I can make amends. What can I do? Name it, Briseis."

"Leave me, Achilleus. Let me walk down that shore." I pulled my hands away and pointed. "There's nothing else I want. Just let me go. Back to my people."

He gave an exasperated sigh. "You know I can't do that."

You mean you won't. But I didn't say it. As he continued looking at me intently, I lowered my eyes, hoping he wouldn't ask anything else.

But he only flashed his radiant smile and said, "Enough talk! Let's bathe." He flung his arms toward the sky, pulling off his tunic. Naked, he plunged into the sea, jumping, arcing like a dolphin, disappearing underwater amidst a silver fountain. Mynes had never been so unabashed, so exuberantly free in his body.

His head reappeared. With a shake, he flung back the wet hair clinging to his brow. "Come join me!"

I shook my head, but he came out of the water. He tugged my gown, pulled it over my head, and flung it aside. I gasped, trying to cover my nakedness with my hands. Grinning, he took my arm and drew me irresistibly into the water.

As soon as I could, I pulled away and immersed myself, crouching on the shallow bottom. The water was cool and cleansing. Cupping his hands full, Achilleus poured a shower over my head and laughed at my cry of surprise. Beads of water glistened on his skin. I closed my eyes, feeling the sun on my wet eyelashes. I put my head back and tried to let my body float as I had seen my brothers do in Lyrnessos. But I felt myself sinking. I struggled up. His hand under my head supported me. I floated, looking up into the deep sky. A feeling of peace washed through me. Everything else emptied out—the helplessness, the rage, the pain, as if the sea had washed it all away.

But in an instant the feeling was gone, and once again I felt anguish and a wave of nausea. The pain in my back was stronger. I found my feet and began splashing toward the shore. He reached for my hand, but when I walked past him, he let it slip out of his grasp and followed me. As I bent to pick up my gown, he stopped me and held me against him. His lips found mine, but I turned my face away. He dropped to his knees and pulled me down onto the sand, where the blue mantle lay discarded.

He spread it beneath us and began to kiss me, but my mouth was dry and my stomach nauseated. I lay still, feeling all at once too unwell and depleted to resist or respond—or even care. My body ached. "Briseis?" He must have sensed something amiss, for his caresses became very gentle, and as he entered me, I had no will to oppose him.

Afterwards, I lay next to him, listless and forlorn, thankful that this time my body had not responded. As if he sensed my mood, he stroked my hair. "Briseis?" I turned aside so that I wouldn't see the question in his eyes. I knew what he was asking, but I had no answer. If the gods had brought me to this place, they had deserted me. I was alone on this shore with my baby to safeguard. I had nowhere to turn, no one to help me.

Except him.

The realization stunned me. Must I stop fighting and accept his care and protection? An answer came: *If I do, then perhaps he will accept my child as his own.* It might be the only way. But I must think it through when I wasn't so tired and weak.

"Achilleus," I whispered, "give me time. Then perhaps—" I heard his indrawn breath. When I said nothing more, he let out a sigh. His arm lay across me, and for a time neither of us spoke. Then he stirred and got to his feet, pulling on his tunic.

Warrior's Prize

"We must go back. The men will be preparing for action. I've tarried too long." Lifting me to my feet, he handed me my gown and helped me straighten it around my body. We started back up the shore. I walked a little behind, thinking of what I had just realized and almost admitted to him. But with the ache in my back raw and intense now, I couldn't focus my thoughts. When we reached the guard post, the sentry spoke to Achilleus. I heard the words "seeking you" and "mustering for battle." Achilleus thanked him and began walking swiftly. The war, the world of men, was calling him. I strove to keep up, but the ache spread to my belly and became a piercing pain, dragging at my steps. The gap between us widened. Soon I had a hard time walking at all, and I had to stop and catch my breath. I breathed against pain.

We were near the Myrmidons' camp now. I saw men arming, men leading horses from the stables. "Achilleus, please wait!" I called in desperation, but with the commotion, he didn't hear. "Help me!" I tried again, but it was only a weak croak. A spasm doubled me over. When I straightened he was far ahead where he couldn't see my distress. He slowed for an instant, turned to wave at me, and sprinted the rest of the way to his hut.

Something wet was running down the inside of my thigh. I felt a terrible fear. In the midst of all the commotion, I couldn't lift my gown to look. Stumbling, I reached the hut. Achilleus and Patroklos were arming in the courtyard, and as I staggered past them to the women's quarters, I was vaguely aware that Achilleus paused and his eyes followed me, but I was beyond being able to speak. I had to lie down. I lurched into the empty women's quarters. And saw the blood seeping down my thighs.

I don't know how long I lay on my pallet in agony as blood soaked the blanket beneath me. When Diomede came in and found me, I lay shaking, sobbing. I could no longer deny that my baby was gone.

CHAPTER 13

"So my life is trouble upon trouble without end."

—Briseis (*Iliad*, Homer, Book XIX, Rouse's translation)

Diomede, with the help of two other women, removed the bloody bedding and put clean rags between my legs. She helped me change into a fresh gown and covered me with a blanket. When she brought bread and cheese, I was too ill to eat. All I could take was a little warmed wine, which Diomede had infused with poppy juice. I wanted to thank her, but I'd fallen into so deep an abyss I could only weakly clasp her hand.

"Rest, Briseis," she said, and my exhausted body obeyed.

I awoke hours later with the afternoon sun slanting through the roof opening. At first I didn't remember where I was or what had happened. Then it struck me anew, and I couldn't move, not even the smallest muscle of my body. It was impossible that my life could go on.

I heard voices in the room outside, among them Achilleus's. My gut twisted with nausea. I wanted to turn away and bury myself in my bedding. But a silent voice deep within me, perhaps the one that impelled my survival, urged me to be still. The door was flung open, and he entered. I was so weak that when he hunkered down at my side I couldn't find the strength to turn away. He laid his hand on my brow, stroking back the sweat-dampened hair that clung there. He looked at me with concern, even tenderness. But it meant nothing to me.

"Why didn't you tell me you were carrying his child?" His words seemed to come from far away. Tears swamped my eyes. He said, "Things would've been different if you'd told me."

I wasn't sure what that meant. After a moment he said, "Once these things start, they cannot be stopped." I stared at him. My own mother had said much the same thing.

"My mother..." he began. A spasm crossed his face. "I'm told she lost several babies in this way before I was born."

I wondered why I was supposed to care. I closed my eyes. I wanted him to go away.

He took my hand and said, "When you heal—" He paused. "You and I—we can—"

My eyes flew open. He changed his mind about what he'd been about to say, and too late fell silent. But I saw it in his eyes. The unspoken words, the question, hung between us. His half-uttered thought pushed me into the pit of Hades. How *dared* he think he could replace Mynes's baby with his own? As if he could erase this child from my life as easily as he'd erased everyone else. As if nothing existed for me except him. I remembered my folly on the beach, when I thought I could accept his care and protection. But that was when my baby was alive.

He was looking at me as if he actually expected an answer. I couldn't speak, but I shook my head so hard and so insistently I made myself dizzy, my silent refusal as loud as if I had screamed it. I felt his shock. Probably no one in his life had ever denied him anything. Everything was given to him before he asked. He had only ever commanded.

He commanded me now. "Briseis, look at me. I will take care of you." He dared say it aloud. "We will have a child together."

The part of me that wanted to survive urged silence, and I tried to hold my tongue, but I couldn't. *"NO!"* I hissed, *"Not ever."* Half hoping he wouldn't hear. But he did. I knew at once I'd crossed a line and now there was no stepping back from it.

I'd heard of his temper, and I cringed, expecting him to strike me. But he only sat in absolute silence. At last he said, in a cold voice more frightening than the loudest shout, "Is that your final word, Briseis?" When I did not reply, he stood. "Then it's over. From now on you shall be my slave only, my lowliest slave, and nothing more."

He walked out, slamming the door, leaving me paralyzed. After several moments I turned over, buried my head in my arms, and wept.

Days passed. I woke up every morning feeling the loss anew like a physical pain. Though I knew I should exert myself to help the women with the chores, I couldn't summon the strength to get up, except for the barest necessities. I hardly spoke to anyone. Diomede made sure I had food and water, which I barely touched, but I sensed that even she was losing patience.

One day she said, "For your own good, you should make an effort to go on with life."

"I know," I said, to placate her. "I will. Soon." But though my body had mostly recovered, I couldn't care whether I lived or died.

Then, early one morning before it was fully light, someone crept to my bedside. I awoke from half-sleep to astonishment.

"Patroklos! What are you doing here?" I said, wary. What did he want?

"Achilleus told me what happened, and I heard you were not well." He was whispering so as not to wake the other women. "Get up," he said.

"Why?"

He was silent for a moment. "Because the gods have decreed that your life isn't over. And because you have the courage. So—stand up." Before I knew what was happening, he took my hand, helped me to my feet, and smiled. "See? That wasn't hard." There were some stirrings among the women. Shaky as I was, he drew me forward. "Let's go outside so we don't wake the others." Once we were standing in the courtyard, he said, "Come with me to the spring." He looked almost mischievous.

"What?" I thought I'd misunderstood him.

"Let's surprise the women and fetch the water before they wake up."

It was unheard of for a man to help a woman with this most onerous of chores or even to carry water at all. I looked at him suspiciously. "Where's Achilleus?"

He grinned. "He's taken his two best horses for a gallop. Far down the shore."

Warrior's Prize

A small warmth flickered in my heart at his willingness to go behind his friend's back for my sake. We went to fetch the *hydriai*, the water jars. Carrying one each, we made our way to the spring. My legs were feeble and flaccid, but the movement felt invigorating, as did the cold water swirling about my ankles as I bent to fill my jar. When I struggled to lift the full *hydria* onto my head, my arms trembled, but he was watching, so I wouldn't yield to weakness. I sensed his silent approval as he hefted his own *hydria* man-style onto his shoulder.

We made several trips and filled all the water vessels. Each trip was harder than the one before, for I had become unaccustomed to exertion, and my exhausted limbs rebelled. But the struggle made my body come alive. As we set down the last of the *hydriai* in the courtyard, Patroklos grinned and said, "Well done! But don't tell the other women I helped you."

Before I could speak, he fled to the men's hut.

"Thank you, Patroklos," I whispered after him.

When the women got up and stared at the filled water jars in astonishment, I said nothing and went to help them with the other chores.

I began to find healing in our work. When I had thought nothing remained, it alone gave me a sense of purpose and kept me from dwelling on my sorrows. I wouldn't let myself think, and somehow I kept going. I began to feel a comradeship with the other women. As we toiled through our daily drudgery, I listened to their talk but said little. They accepted me into their circle—all but Aglaia, who never lost an opportunity to make some spiteful remark. I refused to be drawn and looked upon her with pity. If she only knew how little threat I was to her!

As the days passed and my mind and strength returned, I feared for my future. I had assumed I would stay in Achilleus's camp and continue to serve as a slave. But what if I was wrong? Diomede once told me that a captive woman could be given away or sold. *For failing to please her master.* I had done worse: I'd hurt and humiliated him—wounded his enormous pride. I had rejected him when he'd shown care for me. I would never be forgiven. On some deep level I wished I could go back to that moment and reverse it. Why had I been so obdurate? What if he was waiting for the right opportunity to get rid of me—or had already made plans to do it?

I became afraid. I'd found comfort in my growing friendship with Diomede, Helike, and some of the others. I didn't want to lose the safe haven I now had. I could not bear the upheaval, the terror, of being sent to a different master— or sold to the slave merchants who came to our coast. A slave's life was worth less than nothing. There had been women in Lyrnessos, destitute women without husbands or families, who'd had to sell their services just to survive. They lived in squalid huts and made thrice-daily trips to the springs, carrying heavy jars of water. From dawn to dusk they did all the heaviest and dirtiest work at the bidding of others. Their backs were bent, their skins shriveled from the sun, their stinking bodies ailing from daily hardships, hunger, years of toil. Others had sold themselves and their children to the Achaeans across the sea, and there, we heard, they worked from dawn to dusk at the grueling job of harvesting flax, soaking it and beating it into separate fibers, and spinning it into thread, twine, and rope for their masters. Was this the fate that lay ahead for me?

Perhaps I deserved no better. The gods had decreed I would belong to Achilleus, and I had rejected their gift.

Sometimes I caught glimpses of Achilleus in the courtyard or on the shore. I heard his voice raised in command, his quick laugh at one of the men's jests, or his level, quiet tones in the next room as he conversed with Patroklos. Every evening, when the men returned from whatever skirmish or expedition had occupied them during the day, I listened through the thin wall of the women's quarters and heard them speaking over the sounds of dinner. As night deepened, tension would grow in me. For when the lamps were extinguished, footsteps would cross the hut. Our door would creak open. And the men would summon their women.

Patroklos invariably called for Iphis. I would hold my breath when I sensed Achilleus just on the other side of the door. Over and over again I heard his words: *You shall be my slave only—and nothing more.* But a slave might still be summoned to the master's bed.

I both longed for and dreaded a summons.

"Diomede!" he would call. And when she left with him, my legs would melt.

He never sought me out, never spoke to me. If our paths chanced to cross, his eyes, hard as stones, would look right through me as if I didn't exist. Each time, I went cold with fear.

CHAPTER 14

Sweat poured over head and shoulders, and the blood still ran from his cruel wound...

Iliad, Homer, Book XI,
Rouse's translation

The war grew suddenly more intense. Skirmishes became real battles. Whenever Achilleus's men returned from the fray, carrying litters with their wounded comrades, he would come to the hut to shed his armor and fetch supplies and then rush out to tend them, taking Diomede and one or two other women to help. I was never pressed into service.

One morning I was down at the shore scouring pots and thus wasn't there when Achilleus came to the women's quarters to give his orders. The men had already left for battle by the time I returned. When I reached our courtyard, the first person I saw was Aglaia. She was sitting on the ground near Helike, who was engaged in some task, but Aglaia's hands lay idle in her lap. "Where have you been?" she demanded, ignoring the load of pots I had brought back. "Who do you think you are, wandering around the camp like royalty? There's work to be done!"

Once, I'd wanted to earn her good will. I no longer cared. I said, "Just tell me what you want me to do."

"Here, you work with Helike. It's time I took a rest." She thrust a bundle of linens into my hands and stalked out of the courtyard.

Helike was sitting on the ground, busy tearing linens into strips and rolling them for bandages. "Aglaia's useless!" she said. "Will you help me in her place?"

"Of course." I sat down beside her.

She turned her attention once more to the rolls of linen. "We must have lots of these. For the men who come back wounded." As my hands worked mechanically, Helike said, "It's important to roll them just right. Achilleus gets in such a rage if one of his men is wounded, and if anything is not done perfectly—" She paused. "He used to make me help tend the wounded." I glanced up at her heavy-browed face. "I tried to help, but I hated it," she continued. "All that blood, and Achilleus shouting at us. Sometimes he strikes us if we don't do something just right." She started on a new roll of cloth. "Once, when Automedon was wounded, I had to help. When I came too near with a pot of very hot water, Achilleus shouted and frightened me, and I splattered some on Automedon's leg." Her voice shook. "Achilleus struck me hard. Now he won't let me near anyone who's wounded."

"And the others?" I asked. "Aglaia? Kallianassa? Do they help?"

She gave a wry smile. "Aglaia's hopeless. And Kallianassa's scared of blood, or at least pretends to be. The others do it when they have no choice."

Many days later, I was sitting at the loom in the women's quarters when I heard the pounding of hooves, the jangle of harnesses, the rumble of wheels driven over hard-packed dirt, the shouts that heralded the men's return from battle. There was a note of panic. Something had happened. Heart pounding, I sprang to my feet. The main door of the men's hut was flung open with a hard thud.

With an urgency I'd never heard from him, Achilleus's voice called out: "Diomede! Iphis! Come at once!"

Diomede opened our door. "Oh, gods, it's Patroklos!" she said.

I stood rooted as she and Iphis ran to obey the summons. I noticed he had not called Helike, Aglaia or Kallianassa. As Helike had said, he clearly considered them useless in an emergency. And he had not called me.

I remembered how Patroklos had saved me when I would have wasted away from the loss of my baby. Without giving myself time to think, I followed the others into the men's hut.

Inside, I nearly collided with Iphis and Diomede, who stood on the threshold. Automedon and two other men carried a burden on a litter. Two more men followed. Achilleus, his back to me, was directing the men to set the litter down by Patroklos's bed. Patroklos lay on it, a bloody cloth wrapped around his shoulder and upper arm and pressed under the edge of his corselet. Blood soaked through the cloth and pooled on the litter. His face was ashen, his eyes closed. I stopped breathing. *He's dead,* I thought. Then, as the men moved him onto his bed, I saw the faintest rise and fall of his chest.

After that I couldn't see him any more as the men crowded around the bed, all talking in frightened tones.

Achilleus shoved them aside. "Back off! Give him breathing room. You two, take this out of here!" He kicked the litter across the room. Two men took it hastily out of the hut. Two others remained, looking helpless. "What do you want us to do?" one asked.

"Get out!" Achilleus said. "I don't need you! I'll tend him with the help of Automedon and the women." They left. "Automedon, build up the fire," he added.

Automedon went to the hearth and soon had a small fire going. Then he muttered, "Need more wood," and ran outside.

Iphis and Diomede stood motionless until Achilleus turned on them. "Diomede! Bring water!" She hastened across the room to fetch a pot. "Iphis!" he barked. "The linen strips!"

Instead of going to get them, she turned away. Achilleus hadn't seen—had no attention to spare her. "The bandages are in the chest, Iphis," I told her.

Shooting a fearful look at him, she whispered, "He frightens me! I don't want to be in here if Patroklos—if he—" She didn't finish the sentence, but gripped my arm. "Please—help him in my place! He won't even notice." Before I could stop her, she ducked through the door to the women's quarters and closed it behind her. Astonished, I stared after her.

"Where's Automedon?" Achilleus shouted.

"He went out to get more firewood," Diomede said.

"Zeus the Thunderer! I need him here! Fetch him!"

Diomede went out, leaving me alone with the men. Without hesitating I went toward Patroklos's bed.

Achilleus was lifting Patroklos with one arm, attempting to undo the fastenings of the corselet with his free hand. He was fumbling, encumbered, his eyes full of rage at his helplessness. Then he saw me. "Get out," he said. But the words had no force.

"Let me help." I took a step closer and, when he did not stop me, I loosened the corselet, lifted it off. At once blood came pulsing out. I gasped. It was a huge deep gash. The bleeding must be stopped—if it wasn't already too late. I remembered my mother, learned in healing, telling me to look for the source of the bleeding and stop it there.

Achilleus stared at the wound, his face gray. I saw him drowning in fear and pain, paralyzed by his vision of loss. His hands were frozen—motionless, but there wasn't time for this. Quickly I probed the wound to where the blood was gushing out and pressed with great force. Then I drew Achilleus's hand to the wound. "Press here."

He came alive at once, his fingers pushing into the bloody flesh. He knew well what to do. He looked up at me, his eyes clear. "I have it. Now find Diomede. I need certain things. She'll tell you what."

Diomede came back in, followed by Automedon, who put more wood on the fire and went to Achilleus's side. I crossed the room to where Diomede was pouring water into a caldron over the fire. She looked shaken. "It's never been Patroklos before," she whispered. "I've never seen so much blood. I'm afraid— Fetch the linen. And his jars of herbs. Quickly!"

I went to do her bidding. When I returned to the bed, Achilleus, one hand still pressed against the wound, was cleaning away the caked blood and dirt from the edges of the gash while Diomede held the basin. Her hands shook and the water sloshed. Her face was the color of chalk.

"Hold that still." Achilleus, in command again, cast a glance at her. "Zeus!" he swore. "Zeus deliver me from a bunch of helpless women! Automedon, take the bowl. Diomede, begone! I'll not have you swooning in here. Briseis, set the bandages where I can reach them."

And just like that he accepted my help.

As he worked, I looked at Patroklos's face. His eyes were open now, bright with pain. He breathed with difficulty. His mouth was slightly agape, revealing the shiny inner side of his lower lip, where gritty pieces of dirt had caught. When Achilleus finished cleaning the wound, I took a damp cloth and wiped the grit away, murmuring something soothing, as I might have done with a child. I looked up and found Achilleus watching me, his mouth set in a bleak line that had the odd effect of making him look young and vulnerable. "Hand me the linen," he said. "Hold the sides of the wound together while I wrap it."

As I laid my hands on the wounded man, life and purpose flowed through them.

I stayed with the men until late that night. Achilleus even allowed me to sup there. There was a truce between us. Later Patroklos revived a little. He took some meat and wine, and color returned to his face. After the meal, Automedon left, and Patroklos lay propped up with pillows, Achilleus sitting by his side. I worked in the corner preparing various ointments and possets according to Achilleus's directions.

"It was quite a battle, eh?" Achilleus said, pouring his friend some wine. He was evidently making an effort to speak cheerfully, but there was a tremor in his voice, desperation and fear lurking just beneath. "When that tall warrior slashed you, I thought you were done for, and I couldn't get to you!" He paused, his face pale and strained. "I was waylaid by those two Trojans who always fight together—they cut me off from you—and you fell and disappeared."

From across the room I heard Patroklos's labored breathing. He answered almost inaudibly, "Others came to my rescue—Odysseus...Meriones, I think. The one who speared me barely got away..."

"I—I thought you were dead." For a moment Achilleus seemed unable to continue. He lifted the cup to Patroklos's lips. "Oh, my friend!" For a long time neither man spoke. Then Achilleus resumed, "I saw him clearly—I remember his armor. By Zeus, I'll look for him and I'll kill him the next time we fight!"

Patroklos said something I didn't catch. Achilleus leaned forward. "What?"

"This war," Patroklos muttered, "so senseless—why are we fighting? You don't like Agamemnon or—" His voice trailed off.

Achilleus looked away wearily and made no answer. After a moment, with forced heartiness, he began to speak of the battle they had just fought, recreating a world they shared, a world no woman could enter: a narrow world of combat on the plain, under the scorching sun—a world of comradeship and cruelty, of ground lost and gained. Listening, I could smell the sweat and dust and blood. I could hear the whinnies, the hoof beats and chariot wheels, the fierce cries, the clashing weapons, the screams of men as they died. I shivered, remembering Lyrnessos. If the gods granted me twenty life spans, I would never understand war or men.

Patroklos listened, his head sunk into the pillow, his eyes half closed. Achilleus talked until the lamps burned low. It was as if he feared to let the battle go or the day finish because Patroklos might slip away too. At last he sat silent, his arm around his friend, his face spent and defenseless. He stood up slowly, eased the pillows from under Patroklos, who appeared to be asleep, and placed a cover over him, tucking in the edges. Then he came across the room to where I crouched, cleaning the pots and vessels I had used. He watched me for a moment, his sudden nearness flustering my senses. Under his gaze I tried to hide the tremor of my hands.

"Are you finished?" he asked.

"Aye." I got to my feet, holding my breath, hoping for some word of thanks, some acknowledgment that I had helped him save Patroklos's life.

None came. He only said, brusquely, "Go to bed."

Nothing has changed, I thought.

As I started to turn away, he grasped my arm. "Tomorrow I go to battle—I have no choice. You stay with him. See to his needs. Change the dressings. Make sure he eats and rests." He looked toward the sleeping Patroklos. "I charge you with his care, Briseis." His hand fell away. His eyes burned into mine. "See that he gets well!" There was not a trace of softness in his voice. It was an order.

He had laid a heavy onus on me, and there would be no reward for success, only punishment for failure. I was, after all, just a slave.

But it didn't matter, because now I had a reason to live.

CHAPTER 15

"O Patroclos! Best beloved of my unhappy heart!"

—Briseis, *Iliad*, Homer, Book XIX,
(Rouse's translation)

A pounding on the door tore me out of sleep. "Briseis!" It took me a moment to recognize that peremptory call—to remember what he wanted me to do. Stumbling to my feet, pushing the hair out of my face, I reached the door just as Achilleus flung it open. He was dressed in battle gear but bare-headed, his helmet tucked under his arm.

"I'm going. See to him. Follow all the instructions I gave you last night." Behind me, I heard the other women stirring. He lifted the helmet onto the back of his head and held it there for an instant. "Don't fail!" He snapped the helmet down over his face, turned, and tramped through his hut, closing the outer door hard behind him.

The women were watching me when I turned to face them. Diomede said, "We'll do your chores, Briseis, and whatever else you need." I must have looked astonished, because she added, "We're grateful, because nobody else wants this task. If anything goes wrong, you'll bear the brunt of Achilleus's rage."

To my surprise I did not fear him. What I feared was Patroklos dying.

Iphis said with a smile, "We'll do anything for you! We'll bring you breakfast." That smile grated. *She doesn't care about Patroklos at all*, I thought.

I gave a small shrug. "Thank you for your help. I'll do my best. I just hope he gets well."

I straightened my hair, washed my face quickly, and went to Patroklos. When I saw the form on the bed, I stopped. He lay on his back, rigid and still, face pale, eyes closed, right hand resting limply on the bandaged wound. I took several steps forward before I saw the faint rise and fall of his chest in the dimness. I let out a sigh, realizing that I'd been holding my breath. He opened his eyes and gave the faintest of smiles. I knelt beside him.

His wound had bled during the night, soaking through the bandages. When I had cut the bloody strips away, my stomach did a queasy flip at the sight of the deep gash. I cleaned it and applied a poultice and a dressing of herbs. As I bandaged it, Patroklos tried to help by lifting the tired weight of his shoulder.

He dozed most of the day. I gave him water and barley gruel every time he awoke. Toward afternoon he seemed stronger. During one of his periods of wakefulness he looked at me and smiled. The light in his eyes told me he was glad of my presence.

A glowing warmth lit the darkness in my heart. He had helped me in my need, and now he needed me. I remembered the story of his childhood. As he lay on the bed, his face slack in sleep, I could almost see the young boy who had stood, exiled and homeless, in the strangers' courtyard. Pity stirred in me. I would care for him, and he *would* live.

I fixed him a draught of warmed wine with healing herbs and held it to his lips as he drank. Then I sat by his side as the hours passed, until the shadows in the room deepened. The light through the opening above the hearth had a coppery glow, and I heard the sounds of horses and men returning from battle.

Achilleus opened the door, entered the hut. His helmet was off, his face begrimed with dirt and sweat. He went straight to the bed and crouched by his friend. I did not wait for a glance or a dismissal from him. As I let myself through the connecting door to the women's quarters, I looked back to see him smiling down at Patroklos as he bent to examine the wound.

The next morning, after Achilleus had summoned me and gone, I found Patroklos weak but immeasurably better. He greeted me with a smile and sat up to take breakfast. After dressing the wound, I sat by his side with a spindle. The motion of my hands seemed to soothe him. As the thread flew from my fingers, there was an easy silence between us.

The fighting on the Trojan plain was hot and fierce and took Achilleus daily from the camp. But here in the hut, where I spent every day tending Patroklos, the war seemed far away. He relied on me for his most immediate physical needs. Yet care of him was in no way burdensome. He was patient and cheerful and made light of his wound, turning the smallest, most humiliating details of his recovery into an occasion for jest. One day as I helped him to the privy, he said, "Alas, the mighty warrior cannot attend to this matter without the help of a woman! Don't tell the Trojans!"

Another time, using his good hand to bring a cup of warmed wine to his lips, he fumbled and dribbled down the front of his tunic. "I'm like a little child who doesn't know how to drink properly!" He laughed, and I found myself laughing with him. I couldn't remember the last time I had laughed.

One day when he was strong enough to walk around the room on his own, he fetched a square board and a small sack of stones from a shelf. He returned to his bed and set them on a low table between us.

As I stared, puzzled, he explained, "This is a game we play, Briseis. The object is to move your stones across the board and outflank your opponent's stones."

I was baffled, but he laid out the pieces and explained the rules. After a few abysmal tries, I caught on. We spent hours at this, sometimes squabbling like children. He always won, but I managed to make it harder and harder, and when at last I beat him, I crowed aloud.

"You are vicious and merciless, Briseis! But how good it is to hear you laugh!" he said.

Often he talked, telling tales of his boyhood, his travels, some of the lighter incidents of life in the camp. As he grew stronger, there was a sparkle in his eyes. Seldom in my life had I enjoyed such companionship. Never, save with Laodokos, and at times with Mynes, had I known a bond like this.

However, there was one subject we never brought up. It was the only barrier between us. Sometimes Patroklos would start to speak his friend's name, then recollect himself and fall silent. Those silences pierced me like a thorn. And each night when Achilleus returned, constraint would fall over us. Unless he had instructions for Patroklos's care the next day, Achilleus never spoke to me, save to utter a terse dismissal.

At last the day came when the wound had knit enough for Patroklos to get out of bed for an extended time. Achilleus, before going to battle, suggested we take a short walk along the shore. After I had served Patroklos breakfast, I helped him to his feet and pulled his good arm over my shoulder so that I could ease his walking. His touch seemed as natural as that of a brother. His brown eyes were merry. As we went down to the shore, I bore his weight lightly, matching my steps to his. He seemed filled with wellbeing, glad to be outside and away from his bed. I knew that part of that gladness came from our growing friendship. I realized with wonder that I had brought him happiness as well as healing.

The ways of the Fates were strange. Achilleus didn't want me, and Iphis, Patroklos's concubine, was no companion to him. When Patroklos and I stood together on the shore, it was as if the strands of our lives had become interwoven threads that bound us: his need and my care.

Or perhaps it was my need and his care.

We walked slowly down to the water, then strolled a short way southward to a bare expanse of beach, where we sat on the sand looking out to sea.

Unexpectedly, Patroklos said, "Briseis, you've been so good to me. I owe you everything. My health—maybe even my life."

I smiled. "I'm glad you're mending."

Warrior's Prize

I thought we would subside into one of our companionable silences as we gazed at the water, but he said, "Tell me of yourself. Are you healed now?"

A darkness fell on me. His probing brought things to my mind I had tried to forget. "Healed? How could I ever be?"

He did not retreat. "Perhaps it would ease you to speak of it."

At first I made no reply. In all this time we had not mentioned Achilleus. Now his name shouted itself into the silence between us. "Achilleus—" I began, then could not go on.

Patroklos said, "He never told me. What happened?"

"When I lost everything..." I smudged away tears with the heel of my hand. "I tried to be resigned to my fate. But then..." Against my will, a gasping sob stopped my words.

"You lost the baby," Patroklos finished for me.

"My heart was hard against him after that. He wanted to console me." A knot constricted my throat. My fingers clenched around a fistful of sand. I drew a shaky breath. "I knew I should accept his comfort, his offer to give me another child. But I couldn't. When I rejected him, he was finished with me."

Patroklos gave me a look of sympathy and was silent for a moment. "I can guess you're wondering if this can ever be mended. Maybe with time, but I doubt it. Where his pride is involved, he can be hard as adamant."

Patroklos's words drove a cold shard through me. I got to my feet and walked away, fighting tears, gathering in lungsful of air. At the water's edge I picked up rocks and began heaving them at the sea. Gradually, as my breathing calmed, I felt for the flatter rocks and skimmed them along the surface, as I had done in childhood with my brothers.

Laodokos could make a stone bounce five times.

My hands fell to my sides. The tears broke through.

"Don't weep!" Patroklos came to stand next to me. He picked up my left hand and gently prized out the remaining stones. "My poor Briseis!" he said. "Your lot has been a hard one. Yet you've been such a friend to me."

When I glanced at him, his expression was full of compassion. Then for just an instant something else flickered in his eyes. I stopped breathing. But the look was gone so quickly I was left thinking it hadn't been there at all. He bent to pick up his cloak and, with quick gestures, brushed the sand from it. Carefully avoiding my eyes, he said, "I'm tired and hungry. Let's go back." When I went to support his weight, he stepped away. "I can walk on my own." He softened the words with a smile. "Thanks to your care, I'm much stronger now."

I walked by his side in silence. My heartbeat stirred up my blood so that I could hear it in my ears and feel its heat on my skin. *That look.* What did it mean? Or had I just imagined it?

That night in a dream I walked along a dark shore where dogs bayed and carrion birds wheeled over my head. In my terror I tried to run but couldn't move. The hounds and flying harpies gained ground. Suddenly Patroklos stood before me, and in those steady dark eyes was the look I had seen or imagined on the beach. He put out his arms to embrace me. But when I went toward him, it wasn't Patroklos but Mynes, his face cold and gray in death.

I awoke wondering what the dream signified. It was surely a message from the gods. Did they mean for Patroklos to take Mynes's place? How could that be when I was Achilleus's slave?

I twisted and turned and worried in my bed. Then it came to me in a blinding flash. My heart jumped. *What if Achilleus were to give me to Patroklos?*

I lay still in an effort to quiet my breathing. Surely Aphrodite had sent me the dream. Patroklos had come to mean everything to me. I had staunched his lifeblood, saved his life perhaps, and it had become as dear to me as my own. I knew his thoughts, felt his joy and pain. I felt a kinship with him. He had taught me to laugh again.

But did he care for me? I strove to see again that look in his eyes. Tenderness, compassion—and surely something more. Desire? Love? And why not? Always subservient to Achilleus, he deserved his own chance at happiness. Perhaps someday we could create a home together to replace the ones we each had lost.

Suddenly I was certain of it. But how could it come about, if neither man thought of it?

I sat up in the darkness. Patroklos must be made to see it. He must be persuaded to ask for me. Achilleus would surely deny his friend nothing, especially after Patroklos had been so near to death.

But would Patroklos's honor forbid him to ask, because I belonged to his friend?

I needed Aphrodite's help. As a young girl in Lyrnessos, thinking I would never be wed, I had given her an offering of doves, and right after that I had met Mynes in the marketplace. I flung back the covers. It was still early, and the shore would be deserted. I could go there to pray to her. A sacrifice was needed, but I had nothing of my own to give. I got up, straightened my hair and my gown, and went in search of something to offer the goddess. Outside in the courtyard stood a bin of grain. Dipping my hand in, I filled a cloth with enough barleycorns to make her a pleasing gift. Then I went down to the shore.

The sun had not yet risen. A rosy mist floated over the sea. I squatted on my heels and smoothed the sand to make a flat space, an altar. Looking out at the horizon, I tried to see Aphrodite in my mind—not the graven image in the temple in Lyrnessos but the real deity. I recalled the story of her birth: how she rose out of the sea's foam and was wafted on the west wind to the island of Kypros.

"Aphrodite!" I called softly. "Beautiful golden goddess of love, born of the sea and the wind, please hear my prayer!" I spread some barley grains over the makeshift altar. "Forgive my neglect, and accept my poor offering now. Make Patroklos love me." Sure that I felt her presence, I gazed into the mist, now tinged with gold. If Patroklos did care for me, then this prayer was already granted. But more was needed. "Make him ask Achilleus for me," I prayed.

Yet would Achilleus, with his accursed pride, relinquish me?

I sprinkled more barley across the sand. "Lovely Aphrodite, make Achilleus give me up." But the mist was fading, burned away by long beams of sunlight. I felt a sad ebbing in my mind, as if the goddess could do no more for me. A last handful of barley remained. I cast it onto my altar and looked up at the sun.

Apollo. The archer. A man's god. Patron of Troy and Prince Hektor. And no friend to Achilleus.

"Far-shooting Apollo, god of Light and Truth!" I rose onto my knees and lifted my arms to his sunbeams. "Accept this grain, and make Achilleus give me up." I closed my eyes and felt the silence and darkness within me as the sun shone on my skin, brazen, hot, assertive. "Lord Apollo," I repeated fiercely, "make Achilleus give me up. *Make him give me up!*"

After a time I opened my eyes. The barley grains lay scattered in the sand like tiny pebbles. The mist and magic were gone, and the sunlit beach looked quite ordinary. Then, just offshore, I saw a small ship sailing toward the center of the Achaean camp—a six-oared vessel propelled by brawny rowers and a breeze-filled sail.

The sight of that sail took my breath away, for it bore a large, bold, painted design: a bow with an arrow across it. *The insignia of Apollo.*

Surely it meant that my prayer would be answered.

CHAPTER 16

An angry man—there is my story: the bitter rancour of Achilles, prince of the house of Peleus...

Iliad, Homer, Book I
(Rouse's translation)

It was late. I ran back to the hut, and when I reached the courtyard I found Achilleus there, fully armed, his helmet perched on the back of his head. His face was stormy. "Where were you?"

"I'm here now," I said evasively. I felt oddly guilty and could not meet his eyes.

"Go to Patroklos. He's waiting."

He left and I entered the hut. Patroklos was sitting up on the bed, testing and flexing his wounded arm.

"Good day, Briseis! Look—it's almost completely healed." He smiled, but, as with Achilleus, my eyes fell away from his. Sudden doubt filled me. Clearly, he had not spent a tormented night as I had. Had I imagined that look yesterday? Had I constructed a lie?

I took firm steps into the room. "I'll fetch your breakfast. Then, if you like, we can walk down to the shore."

This time, at Patroklos's insistence, we walked far from the Myrmidon camp. He said he wanted to regain his strength. When we had gone a fair distance, he remarked, "I've been idle too long. I must return to battle soon."

This gave me the opening I sought. "Why do you fight, Patroklos?" I asked. "What purpose is there in this war?"

I feared the question might provoke him, but when he turned to face me, his eyes were thoughtful. "Sometimes I ask myself that very thing."

We stopped walking. Here the shore was deserted, with only a few ships drawn up on the sand. An old piece of timber lay near the water's edge. Patroklos stood for a moment pushing it with his foot. Then he sat down on it and invited me to do the same.

I said, "What answer have you found?"

He was silent for a time. "It started out as a glorious expedition. Now it's an endless, tedious war. Would that it were over!" He scooped up sand, let it run through his fingers. I studied his profile, noticing gray streaks in his dark hair, deep lines around his eyes. The war was stealing his youth. "And Achilleus—" he continued. Then he faltered and stopped.

But if we were to get to the heart of this, he must feel free to speak of his friend. "Go on."

"I think he feels the same. Sometimes he says this war is pointless and he wishes he had never come."

"Then why did he?"

"To gain honor. To be the greatest warrior. And so he fights with no concern for his own life. He says he will not survive, and it does not matter—that only deathless fame matters." Was that why Achilleus had such disregard for the deaths he inflicted on others? Patroklos added, "How can he know if he will live or die?"

I said, "No man can know his fate."

"I pray that he's wrong," Patroklos said as if I hadn't spoken. "So far nothing has touched him—only bruises and scrapes. But he frightens me. He has such morbid moods. 'Patroklos,' he says, 'when I am dead you must comfort my father and take my son home to him.'"

"His son!" I said, astonished. I had never heard mention of this.

"Aye, he has a son. Surely you knew? A near-grown youth on Skyros named Neoptolemos."

"Near-grown?"

"Aye, fifteen or sixteen—I forget."

Laodokos's age. Achilleus must have been a young father indeed, for I guessed him to be not yet thirty years. "Who is the mother?" I asked.

"Her name is Deidameia. She's a princess on Skyros, where we lived for a time. They were not wed. Achilleus had to leave the boy there when we came to fight the Trojans."

I had never imagined Achilleus as a father. With a pang of sorrow, I thought of my brother, dead by his hand. How could Achilleus have slain a lad the age of his own son?

Patroklos, lost in his reflections, didn't notice my silence. "It was a good life we left behind. I often wonder if this war is worth it. So much death and destruction..." He spread his hands ruefully. "Those are cowardly thoughts. Don't repeat what I've said."

"Whom would I tell?" I asked.

"If we don't die," he resumed, "what will our lives be when this war ends?"

My heart pounded. Now we had come to it—the future. When the men returned to their homes in Achaea, they would surely choose some of the women to accompany them as concubines, perhaps even wives. But Achilleus would never take me into his home. He had made it clear what my status was.

"As a slave, I might be given away, or sold," I said. "My life will be that of a menial. But I'm young. If only there were another fate for me!" I found that my hands were clenched. I forced them open, drew a deep breath, and plunged on. "I could be a wife and bear children. I could make some man happy."

He was silent. I ventured a glance. His eyes, full of feeling, met mine, then fell away. My heart jumped. *O Aphrodite*, I prayed, *make him say the words.*

But as the uneasy silence stretched out, I felt my hope slipping away. I turned on the log to face him. Daringly I put one hand on his knee in supplication—and felt a quiver run through him. "We get on well together, you and I. If only I belonged to you and not Achilleus! He doesn't want me." I put my other hand on his wrist. "You could ask him—" Looking into his eyes, I finished in a whisper, "Ask him for me."

He took my hand and leaned toward me. He gave a strained smile. "Briseis," he began gently. "I—I—"

At that exact moment a long shadow fell across the sand between us.

Patroklos looked up with a start—then froze. "Achilleus! You are not in battle?"

"There was no battle. The men returned." But he answered absently. He was standing there, no longer in his armor, looking down at us, deathly still.

How much had he heard? Patroklos's face had gone white. Then I couldn't shift my gaze from Achilleus. Terrible things were in his eyes. He leaned down and pulled Patroklos up by his good arm. "Go," he said in an oddly hoarse voice. "Go back—*my friend!*" His mouth twisted. "Wait for me at our camp."

As Achilleus's arm on his shoulder urged him away, Patroklos shot an agonized look at me. He muttered something to Achilleus. I thought I heard, "Don't hurt her." Then he was gone around the stern of the nearest ship.

I sprang to my feet. Murderous hands seized me, dug into my flesh—shook me. The world was blurred and jagged. I thought my neck would snap. Then he hurled me to the sand. I landed with a force that jarred my bones. Tasting blood, I came up on my knees, my arms smarting from his grip. His arm went back for a blow. I shielded my face with my hands.

The blow never fell.

"I won't strike you," he said in a strangled voice, "or I'd kill you."

He dropped his arm. For a moment, his eyes looked just the way Patroklos's eyes had on the day of his wounding. Then a lightning flash of rage lit them. He kicked the dirt violently with his sandaled foot. "I never want to look upon you again," he said. "Stay out of my sight." And he walked away.

As I got to my feet, bruised and shaken, something inside me ached far more than the pain of the fall.

CHAPTER 17

> ...Phoibos Apollo
> walked with storm in his heart from Olympos' crest,
> quiver and bow at his back, and the bundled arrows
> clanged on the sky behind as he rocked in his anger,
> descending like night itself.
>
> *Iliad*, Homer, Book I
> (Fitzgerald's translation)

I stood for a long time on the shore. Tears dammed up in my eyes, but I refused to shed them, for they would not have eased me nor washed away the wrong I had done to Achilleus. And Patroklos. Without even knowing whether he truly cared for me or even desired me, I had tried to force him to betray his friend. I'd read far too much into one look. Most likely he was expressing care and sympathy, nothing more. Now I had robbed him of the one thing that gave his life meaning. I had wrecked a life-long friendship—a life-long love.

I must seek to mend it somehow, but could it be mended? Would Achilleus even suffer me to stay in his camp?

Slowly I walked back to our quarters. When I got there, the men were nowhere in sight. Helike and Diomede were in the large courtyard. They had collected all the bedding and rugs from the huts and were airing them in the sun, beating them with sticks to rid them of dust and fleas. Many rugs hung over the palisade, and there was yet a huge pile of bedding on the ground.

As I came up to them, Diomede looked at me in surprise. "Is anything wrong, Briseis?"

"Where are the men?" I asked through stiff lips.

"Achilleus returned early. There wasn't a battle. He went to seek Patroklos. But we thought you were with Patroklos?"

I shook my head. "Patroklos doesn't need my care anymore. Let me help you with this."

Picking up a stick, I joined them at their chore, hoping for distraction. But their pleasant, inconsequential talk washed over me, and in my mind I could see Patroklos, his profile turned to me as he looked up at his friend. And Achilleus—I would never forget the look in his eyes. Though he'd tried to hide it, I knew I'd wounded him deeply.

Much later, the courtyard gate slammed open and Achilleus stood there. I froze, but he only walked into the hut without looking at us. Patroklos, his eyes downcast, followed slowly.

Diomede gave me a penetrating look. She must have guessed something had happened; yet she held her silence. Later, when we were almost finished, the gate opened a second time, and a messenger ran into the courtyard to pound on the door of the hut.

Achilleus opened it. "Antilochos!"

"You must come at once to the center of the camp," the man said.

Achilleus, already reaching behind him for a cloak, said, "Why?"

I was close enough to hear Antilochos' answer. "A priest of Apollo, from Chrysa, has come by ship to Agamemnon," he said.

I edged closer. A ship? The ship with the painted sail I'd seen early that morning and forgotten until now? And Chrysa. Where had I heard that name before? Then I remembered: Chryseis, the girl taken on the raid of Thebe. She had said, *My father is high priest in the temple of Apollo at Chrysa.*

The memory of my prayer to Apollo raised hairs on the back of my neck.

"It seems Agamemnon has this priest's daughter," Antilochos continued. "And the old priest has come to ransom her back. He comes as a suppliant to the king's knees. But Agamemnon has turned him down rudely."

"A suppliant is sacred to the gods," Achilleus said.

"Well, the king won't listen to reason. All the chieftains are gathering to try to persuade him. You'd best come."

Achilleus flung the blue mantle about him. "Patroklos?" he said over his shoulder. Both followed Antilochos out of the gate, leaving us staring after them.

"What do you suppose that was all about?" Diomede asked.

"I can guess," I said, and told them of Chryseis and her certainty that her father would come to ransom her.

Diomede shrugged. "Well, it doesn't seem as if he'll succeed, does it? Poor girl. But I don't see how that can affect us."

Just after sundown I was on the shore and saw the priest's ship return in the direction from which it had come. The painted sail hung limp in the windless twilight. The ship was too far away for me to tell who was on it, but the rowers pulled at the oars with slow, defeated movements, and I guessed that Agamemnon had not yielded, and the priest's mission had failed.

Later, Achilleus and Patroklos returned, silent and dispirited. As we women prepared bread for supper, we were aware of the stillness in the men's hut. There was no conversation, no laughter, no music from the lyre. The other women felt the mood of despondency without understanding it. Perhaps they thought the gloom had to do with the events in the center of the camp, but I knew better. I could hardly endure it.

When the darkness deepened, Diomede went into the men's quarters to retrieve the empty breadbaskets and used cookware, and returned as the women prepared for bed. I sat on my bedding, alone and apart. I did not know how, nor if, things could be mended, but I had to try.

"You look tired, Briseis." Diomede waited to extinguish the last lamp.

I shook my head, getting abruptly to my feet. There was only one thing to do. Before I lost courage, I opened the door to the men's hut and walked in uninvited—something I'd never dared do before.

The room was dark save for the dim red glow of the dying fire and one lamp. Achilleus, sitting by the hearth, twisted in surprise to look at me over his shoulder. Patroklos was in his bed, deep in shadow. I crossed the room swiftly to kneel at Achilleus's feet. "Before the gods, Achilleus, I come to you as a suppliant. Please hear what I have to say." *A suppliant is sacred to the gods.* He had said so himself. I prayed he would not turn me away.

I lifted my hands, placed them on his knees. Touching his flesh I was suddenly inflamed with such longing I couldn't speak. In that moment, I saw that all along I had deceived myself, fought against the truth. It wasn't Patroklos I wanted. It had only ever been Achilleus. *Oh, Aphrodite,* I prayed, *let it not be too late!*

If he sensed my feelings, he gave no sign. He was silent, taut, motionless—waiting.

I found my voice. "I have come to ask you—" But these were not the right words. My throat was so dry I had to stop and swallow. "I've done you wrong, Achilleus. Punish me if you must, but I beg you, do not blame Patroklos." I heard his sharp breath and ventured a look at his face, all shadows, a deep groove between his brows. "The fault is mine alone," I said.

He looked over his shoulder toward the bed in the corner. I could only guess what Patroklos had told him. To his own cost, he would have tried to shield me from Achilleus's anger.

"Achilleus, no matter what he told you, you must listen to *me,*" I said. "I only turned to Patroklos because I thought you were finished with me—that I was nothing to you. Please forgive him. He never betrayed you. And—" As I spoke, I understood the truth of this. "He never intended to."

With a quick, agitated movement, Achilleus removed my hands from his knees and got up. I felt the loss of contact keenly as he paced away from the hearth, came back. He stood for a moment looking down at me, then resumed his seat. "How do I know you're speaking the truth?"

"I swear it to you, Achilleus, by Zeus and all gods, may they strike me down if I lie."

"Ah!" He sighed and some of the tension went out of his body. "I have no need to forgive Patroklos. I know he would never take what is mine. But you—" He broke off.

I hadn't planned to say it, but I whispered, "Please forgive me, too."

He stared hard at me. "Why did you do it?" When I hesitated, he reached down, grasped my arms and shook me slightly. "You've fought me at every turn. You rejected me when I would have cared for you. You've hated me from the start, haven't you?" he demanded. "You swore to be truthful. Now tell me."

"After the baby—" For a moment I could not go on. "I was not in my right mind. But now— I no longer hate you. I haven't for a long time, despite—despite everything. Far from it." As I heard myself speak this new truth, I realized I'd laid my naked heart before him. I had never felt more vulnerable. I stumbled on. "But I thought *you* hated *me*. And Patroklos became a friend to me—that is all. Because of him, I hoped I might have a future."

His face showed nothing. Putting his hand under my chin, he brought my face into the light to study it. His thumb wiped a tear from my cheek that I hadn't known was there. At last he said slowly, "You've borne a lot. Your husband, your brother. Then the baby."

Now I couldn't stop the flow of tears. But something shifted—the past, all of it, was gone, like ground crumbling away beneath my feet, and I was left clinging precariously to the moment.

"Perhaps I was too harsh," Achilleus muttered. I caught my breath. But his tone was distant, expressing regret for something long past that could not be mended. And abruptly he was finished with the subject. He dropped his hand, turned away, and started to get up.

I couldn't let him leave it like that. Stunned at my own boldness, I took both his hands in mine and brought them to my mouth. As I kissed them, my lips traveling over his knuckles and the ridges of bone under his hard spare flesh, my whole body burned for him. My tears ran down onto our interlaced fingers. Then I laid my forehead on our joined hands and wept.

He became utterly still. When I let go and lifted my head, he drew a deep breath. He looked down at me, his eyes in shadow. I waited without breathing as he turned away with a shaken sigh, got to his feet, and extinguished the lamp. I was vaguely aware of footsteps crossing the room, the door opening, closing, Patroklos leaving the hut. The darkness was absolute.

Achilleus reached down, pulled me up, and enfolded me in his arms.

My knees went weak. Desire flowed in my veins like wine.

Without speaking, he doffed his tunic, slipped my gown over my head, tossed it aside, and took me to his bed. For a long time, we lay close and still. I listened to his breathing, the beating of his heart. I sensed his hesitation, his reluctance to trust me completely. I drew him close and kissed him fiercely, nothing held back. His arms wrapped around me. He was breathing as if he had run a race. He pulled me even closer, his kisses deeper.

"Take me," I whispered. As our bodies joined, my bones melted. My darkness filled with shooting stars.

Long after, as our breathing slowed, we lay entwined. Then he bent his head to kiss the side of my neck, a tender gesture that moved me as much as all our lovemaking.

I rested against him in a blissful languor. I sensed him drifting toward sleep. At last I slipped into a drowse. Some time later when I was more than half asleep, he stirred and slid his hand across my body, caressing me, pulling me close.

At that very moment everything inside me went dark and cold, extinguished by a malevolent shadow. Waves of ice skittered along my skin. A god had come down from the heavens and entered my mind, surrounded by blackest night.

A god with an aura of invisible flames. *Apollo*. He held a bow, with a quiver slung across his shoulder. He sank down on one knee, nocked an arrow, and let it fly. Shaft after shaft he shot. People were struck—men and women I saw every day in the camp. I heard their cries and saw them die. In a flash I knew: Apollo was bringing doom, and somehow this was connected with my prayer. I cried out, a silent scream. But the god was gone, leaving me frozen in dread.

I must have made some sound, for Achilleus roused. "What is it?" he asked sleepily.

"I—I had a terrible vision—I saw... I saw Apollo—coming in wrath—"

At the god's name, he recoiled but said, "You were just dreaming. A nightmare."

"He was angry! He was shooting arrows—killing men and women in the camp—he means you harm, perhaps because I prayed—" Then I could have bitten my tongue.

"You prayed what?" he asked.

"Nothing, it's not important, but Apollo— It felt so real. I'm frightened!"

He said, "Forget it, Briseis, not all dreams portend something." He pulled me close and took me in his arms. "Come, let me wipe it from your mind. Don't spoil our love."

I forced the vision out of my mind and accepted his comfort. I kissed his ear, whispering into it, "Love me again."

CHAPTER 18

Pyres of the dead began to burn up everywhere,
and never ceased.

Iliad, Homer, Book I
(Rouse's translation)

I awoke at first light, not remembering where I was. Then I saw his head next to mine, eyes closed. Warmth stole through me. I wanted to lie here forever. But the women would be fetching water and starting the fire to bake the bread. I sat up.

Instantly he was awake. "Where are you going, Briseis?" When I told him, he said, "Nay, stay. There is no battle today. Come." He held out his arms. "Let the other women fetch water. You can bring me breakfast later."

I returned eagerly to his embrace.

Some time after, he got up, saying he was going for a quick dip in the sea. He left, but before I could go fetch the men's breakfast, the outer door opened. It was Patroklos returning from wherever he had spent the night. When he saw me, he stood still, wary and irresolute, as if ready to bolt outside again. I felt a deep shame at what I'd tried to do, the more so since I'd spent the night in Achilleus's bed. Patroklos was an exile who had nothing save his bond with his friend. My coming between them must have rent him apart.

I had to try to make things right, and now was my chance, before Achilleus returned. I said, "Patroklos, what I did yesterday was wrong." His face looked strained. My next words were difficult to say. "I've told Achilleus it was my fault alone. He never blamed you. He has forgiven me. Can you forgive me too?"

He hesitated, then said, a little stiffly, "Aye, of course."

"Patroklos, I'll never again do anything to hurt you. Can we still be friends?"

He smiled with the old warmth. "Always, Briseis!"

With that, I went to fetch breakfast. The women were baking the bread over the fire in our courtyard. They went silent as they looked at me, their eyes full of questions. I greeted them, and then lowered my head. I did not know what to say.

Aglaia stared at me with venom in her eyes. "You shameless harlot!" she snarled. "What wiles and ruses did you use to win back his favor?"

I ignored her. "I'm to bring the men's breakfast," I said to the others.

Diomede got up to help me prepare a tray. "I hope things are well with you," she said in a tone of concern.

I nodded. "All is well."

"I'm glad," she said.

Achilleus was back when I brought the tray into the men's hut. "Sit and break your fast with us," he said. They were hungry, and as we ate without speaking, I wondered what my role would be, now that everything had changed.

At last he said, "You don't have to carry water, Briseis," he said. "Leave the harder work for the others. That was always my intention for you." He gave a teasing grin and whispered, too low for Patroklos to hear, "I want you to save your energy for me!"

"But working with the women is important to me, Achilleus. Especially fetching water from the spring. There are barely enough of us as it is." I didn't add that Aglaia always skipped out of this duty. She already hated me, more so now that I seemed to be back in Achilleus's favor and his bed. If I tattled about her shirking, she would find a way to harm me. "Besides," I added, "I am strong. I don't want to grow soft."

He looked as if he might object, but then gave an appreciative grin. "Spoken like a warrior! Very well, you shall have your way."

I felt Patroklos's eyes on me. Remembering how he had carried water with me to help me restore my life and my strength, I returned his look with a smile of gratitude.

Against all logic, now that things were well with Achilleus and Patroklos, my prayer to Apollo kept coming back to haunt me. At odd times during the day I would envision the wrathful face of the god as he lifted his bow and shot deadly arrows. Much as I tried to dispel it from my thoughts, it would return when I was alone, when my mind was not on other matters.

It was only a dream, I told myself, *as Achilleus said, a nightmare that meant nothing. And nothing has happened. All is well.* I could ignore it much of the time, I could put it out of my mind, but I could not forget it entirely. If only I could unsay my prayer!

In the late afternoon, as we women began preparing the evening meal, I went into the men's hut to look for a cooking pot and found Achilleus and Patroklos sitting before the hearth, Achilleus plucking the strings of his lyre with great concentration, trying to perfect a melody. He glanced up at me, distracted, then turned again to his instrument.

"Briseis," he muttered, "fetch me a goblet of wine. And one for Patroklos too."

I poured two goblets. Achilleus took his without even a grunt of thanks. On sudden impulse, I gave a deep, mocking bow. "My pleasure, sir! Always your compliant servant!"

Patroklos looked startled, but Achilleus burst out laughing. "Compliant servant! I would hardly describe you that way. You're more like an untamable mountain lion!"

I remembered when he had called me that in Lyrnessos. I was indignant then. Now an answering laugh bubbled up inside me. As I turned away, I sent a wordless thanks to Aphrodite for transforming my fate.

But the gods are capricious. Just when life seems good, it turns out they have other plans.

The next morning I went early down to the shore, taking last night's cooking pots to scour in damp sand. Couching at the water's edge, I was enveloped in an almost unearthly stillness, broken only by the whisper of small, limpid waves against the pebbles of the shore, and the gritty sounds I made in my scrubbing.

Without warning my vision of Apollo came back vividly, making my heart pound. A moment later a movement made me look up. A black speck appeared in the sky. A hawk that had wandered far from the hills? But when another appeared and the two came nearer, I saw their wide wingspan and ugly, naked heads. *Vultures.* An omen? Goose bumps skittered along my arms. I felt a pervasive sense of doom that I could not shake.

I told myself I was surely making too much of too little. But that night, as I lay wakeful in Achilleus's bed, my anxiety returned. Watching his restless, uneasy sleep, I guessed with a sinking heart what that meant: tomorrow the men would be going to battle.

When I heard the trumpet call from the center of the camp at daybreak, the call to arms, I went outside to watch the men muster for battle. I'd never done this before, and Diomede, Helike, and the others who often watched, gave me looks of astonishment. I realized what an upheaval had happened in me that I accepted my place in this world and was watching warriors go out to kill or be killed.

I didn't belong here. None of us did, for that matter, not even the men. Yet we were all trapped here by the Fates, who were surely madwomen.

I forced my attention back to the Myrmidon army gathering under a pearly sky. The cool air carried the odor of male sweat and horses as swarms of warriors worked efficiently, wheeling out chariots and harnessing restive steeds whose war finery was as splendid as the men's. I could feel tension building as the men prepared for battle. The air rang with sharp commands, whinnies, thudding hooves on hard-packed dirt as horses were yoked in pairs to the fifty or so chariots that would lead the charge. There were two men in each chariot, the charioteer and the one who wielded a spear. Foot soldiers, spears aloft, formed into rank behind the chariots.

Diomede pointed. In the lead was a chariot with two magnificent horses, a piebald and a bay. My eyes clung to the man standing next to it. Achilleus's helmet masked his face, its golden crest tossing in the breeze. His corselet flashed in the sun's first rays.

Then I saw his charioteer, the reins looped around his waist. "Patroklos," I whispered.

"He's returning to battle today," Diomede said. "Didn't you know?"

"It's too early. He's not strong enough."

"He will be safe," Diomede said. "Achilleus won't let him out of his sight."

Achilleus. Everyone seemed to think he was invincible. I watched him spring lightly into the chariot. As his men grew quiet, waiting, he lifted his spear and gave a shout. The charge began.

Chariots, beasts, and men crowded through the gates, their excitement rising like the wind. On the other side of the wall, they joined the swelling ranks of the entire Achaean army. Men from various camps shouted greetings to each other. The plain was a sea of glinting bronze with brightly colored waves of horsehair.

"To battle!" the chieftains shouted. "On to Troy!"

The answering roar of the men blended with the thunder of galloping hooves. The earth quivered under my feet. I stood silent and shaken until the tumult dwindled and the plain was quiet, and we heard only distant shouts like specks of sound.

"Time to be about our chores." Diomede took my arm. Helike was at her side.

"How far are the gates of Troy?" I asked.

She shrugged. "A fair distance. If you stand high enough, on one of the ships for instance, you can see the walls and towers of the citadel, but the men are as ants."

"Those ants you speak of—they'll be killing each other." I wished I had not watched.

Diomede said, "It's not always a heated battle with many casualties. Sometimes it's just a skirmish, where they shout insults and challenge each other to duels." She shrugged. "But each day there is no telling what will happen. So it does no good to dwell on it."

I could only pray that Achilleus and Patroklos would come back safely.

Helike, stolid as ever, turned away. "Let's go feed the livestock."

As we walked toward the pens, seabirds circled overhead, drawn by the return of quiet. Then I saw two black specks, the vultures again. Despite the warmth of the early sun, I shivered.

At the pens, an overpowering stench assaulted our nostrils. At first we could see nothing but milling goats and sheep. As we dumped armloads of dried marsh grass into the feeding troughs, the animals surged about us, bleating, nudging, butting. Then I spotted the trouble. Two dead goats lay on their sides, stiff legs outstretched, bellies distended, flies all over their glossy black hides. Their tails and rear legs were covered with excrement.

"Some kind of a flux from the bowels," Diomede said. "They must have died during the night. I hope none of the others catch it." We looked at each other, silenced for a moment by the thought of a sickness that could sweep through all the flocks.

"We have to get them out of here," Helike said.

The chore took the combined strength of the three of us. Diomede and I pulled the legs while tall Helike, with her superior strength, pushed each body from behind. As we dragged both beasts to the refuse pit, I held my breath often to keep from gagging. Flies buzzed as we shoveled dirt over the carcasses. It was a nasty job. With the men gone, we allowed ourselves the luxury of stripping naked and bathing in the sea.

Then we went on to other chores, thinking no more of the dead beasts. But by sundown, after the men came back from fighting, two sheep and a donkey had died in the same manner. That night a woman in one of the other Myrmidon huts sickened. By morning she was dead and several more men and women were ill. As that day and the next passed, more people fell ill, and almost without exception, died.

The Achaeans stopped going to battle.

Covertly, I watched the others in our group for signs of the pestilence. Fear was a sick taste in my mouth. Among the women there were many silences, convulsive swallows, uneven breaths, and I could tell they were thinking the same as I. Each time our paths crossed, we asked each other, "Are you well?"

As more days passed, the plague worsened. I went around with Diomede and Helike tending the other stricken women, those belonging to the lesser soldiers of the Myrmidon ranks, those who lived in poor, crowded hovels, those whom I came to know only as they died. We learned that the illness was widespread through the whole encampment, and many were far worse off than the Myrmidons.

Those who were stricken lasted only a day or two, sometimes just hours. The men who hadn't succumbed to the sickness were busy disposing of animal carcasses and building funeral pyres for their comrades and their women. An odd, heavy stillness, a pall of smoke hung over the camp. The air smelled of burning and rotting flesh. All the normal activities of the camp, save those needed for subsistence, were halted. Death ruled, and life existed timidly on its perimeters. Along with the others, I ate, drank, slept—but with a sick feeling that I had no right to do so—that darkness would come upon my eyes and death would snatch the cup from my lips. Helike, Diomede and I stayed close to each other, and I drew comfort from their presence.

As the plague worsened, I barely saw Achilleus. He did not summon me to his bed. Often he was out half the night tending men who had sickened. I saw little of Patroklos either. Sometimes I glimpsed Achilleus from a distance on the shore or heard his voice in the adjoining room. Each time I would close my eyes and think, *thank the gods he's safe. Patroklos too.*

During those first few days, busy and weary, tending the sick, with the constant fear that assailed us all, I scarcely had time to think. I actually did not make the connection. Then, on the fifth day, I heard Diomede tell one of the others, "They are saying this is the doing of Apollo. It's his arrows that are striking down the men and women and beasts. I wonder what the Achaeans have done to anger him?"

My skin froze. The god's deadly arrows—this plague! Apollo had sent me a warning, a vision, and it was coming true before our eyes. This was his answer to my prayer: *Make Achilleus give me up.* Was Achilleus going to die? Invincible in battle but brought down by a fever and a bloody flux from the bowels? And would Patroklos die too, weakened by his wound and therefore more susceptible to those swift, silent, deadly arrows from the god? And the women? All their deaths would be on my hands. What would Diomede and the others say if they knew I had prayed for this? I remembered my mother in my childhood saying, "Be careful what you ask the gods for. They just might grant it."

The next morning I went down to the shore to try to unsay my prayer. I offered grain again. On my knees I pleaded, *Lord Apollo, I didn't mean it! I want to be with Achilleus. And I don't want anyone dead. Please desist from your anger against the Achaeans—against us all.* But the god's answer was a cold inner silence.

On the eighth day of the plague, when Helike, Diomede, and I were returning from the deathbed of a woman we had tended, we chanced to meet Achilleus. He stopped us, his brows lowering, his gaze traveling swiftly over us. "Where have you been?"

My heart pounded. I couldn't speak. Helike, as usual, held her silence, and it was left to Diomede to answer. "Tending a dying woman, a captive of one of your men."

"I don't want you to tend the others." A curved furrow appeared at the inner edge of one eyebrow. "There's nothing you can do. I've tried every remedy. And I've noticed something. The arrows of the god strike those close to the ones who have died. Don't touch the belongings of anyone who has died. Stay in your quarters. So far the arrows have not reached our hut."

"Then it is Apollo?" I blurted.

"Aye." His face, drawn and weary, turned toward me. His eyes had the bleakness of winter seas. "I plan to offer sacrifice tonight, but I haven't much hope." He added, "Apollo has never been favorable to me."

Turning abruptly, he walked away. Helike and Diomede hastened back to our hut, but I stood motionless, certain that I'd heard fear in his voice.

If the god was indeed against him, here was an enemy greater than any he had faced, who could destroy him utterly.

An enemy I had summoned.

CHAPTER 19

> Nine days the god's arrows fell on the camp, and on the tenth day Achilles summoned all to a conference.
>
> *Iliad*, Homer, Book I
> (Rouse's translation)

Helike, silent and withdrawn, ate nothing at supper that night and went at once to lie on her pallet. Diomede sat at her side, one hand on Helike's brow, the other clasping her wrist. A while later, Diomede came to where I sat with the other women. Her face was rigid, pale. "Helike seems ill," she whispered.

We gathered at Helike's side. Her eyes looked up at us, filled with terror. But she said, "I'm so tired. All I need is rest."

I reached out to touch her brow. The heat of her skin filled me with a ghastly certainty. She would die through my fault, just as surely as if I had plunged a knife in her heart. And others would follow. As I withdrew my hand, letting it fall to my side, I whispered, too low for Helike to hear, "She's burning with fever."

Diomede sat motionless. No one spoke. Then Iphis asked, "Should we fetch Achilleus?"

Diomede shook her head. "He said there was nothing we could do. He would just order us to stay away from her."

"We can make her more comfortable. Bring water," I urged. "We'll sponge her down."

Iphis and Kallianassa went off into the darkness. Diomede and I tore a clean cloth into rags to use as compresses. When the others returned, we worked over her frantically, pressing dampened cloths against her face and body. Her fever burned through the wet rags. Sores broke out on her skin. She soiled herself, and we cleaned her and changed her bedding. When the cloths were used up, we tore up gowns. We fetched buckets of water from the sea. All our efforts brought her no relief. She twisted from side to side, crying out in a voice I didn't recognize. At last she fell into a torpor, beyond our reach. The other women went to sleep, but Diomede and I stayed by her side holding her hands. Her breathing was fast and shallow. At times she muttered incoherently. Then she sank into a silence, a great depth. Just after dawn, her eyes took on a glazed stillness, as if a fly could light on them and not cause her to blink. I touched her brow, but she was far away, beyond our help. *Don't leave us!* I begged her silently.

A deep, rolling rattle came from her chest. The tortured body lay still. Diomede cried out and began to sob.

I stared at Helike's face. I had barely known her, and now she was gone, taking all the stories and secrets of her life. "Who was she?"

I didn't realize I had spoken aloud, but Diomede answered in a muffled voice, "She was my dearest friend."

The poor, unseeing eyes were open. I closed them and pulled the cover over her face. I put my arms around Diomede. Her body was limp. Her head buried itself against my shoulder. I stroked her hair. "Rest now, sleep," I said. "There is nothing you can do." I led her unresisting to her own bed and tucked her in as if she were a child.

Then I went into the men's hut. Achilleus was kneeling by the hearth trying to coax a fire from last night's embers. There were harsh lines about his mouth, and his face was pale, as if he too had spent a sleepless night. He looked up, questions flickering in his eyes. "Helike's dead," I told him. As I spoke the words, all my strength and resolution ebbed, and I began to cry.

He got swiftly to his feet. His hand on my elbow propelled me blind and stumbling into the women's quarters. "Never mind your tears. Quick! We must get the corpse out of here."

I cringed at the word, but he was right—we must stop the contagion from spreading, though it tore my heart when he lifted her as unceremoniously as a piece of refuse. "Come with me." His voice was rough. "Bring her bedding, her clothes. We'll burn them too."

I nodded. Everything she touched must go. Numbly I obeyed and followed him to a pyre piled high with wood, awaiting the day's victims. Already a Myrmidon warrior lay there. Achilleus froze when he saw him. "Erymas!" he said. "That makes thirty-six of my men." In the fierce glitter of his eyes there might have been tears. He laid Helike down. As he straightened, his hands closed into fists. His face was without softness when he turned to me. "Come."

We went back to the women's hut, and from then on there was no rest, not even for poor Diomede. He flung open the door and windows, and ordered us to sweep the hut and scrub the walls and floor with seawater. "Everything belonging to Helike must go on the pyre. Also Diomede's bedding, which was next to hers. Also your own clothes. Then go bathe in the sea."

I knew we must do this to be spared contagion, but Aglaia demanded coyly, as if this were some sort of game, "*All* our clothes?"

"Don't question. Do it!"

I shot her a look that she ignored. She cocked her head saucily at him. "We won't have anything to wear, my lord."

"Zeus the Thunderer! Do you think I care?" Then he relented. "In the storage hut there's a chest with extra gowns. Wear those. There must be nothing left around that Helike touched or wore," he told her. "Then perhaps the god's arrows will not strike this hut again."

It was many hours before we were done. The day was hot, the air heavy, smoky. As we toiled, sweating, our backs aching, our eyes stinging, I had little chance to think about Helike. I only prayed we had taken actions swiftly enough to avoid becoming ill. But Diomede went about her work listlessly and hardly spoke. She did not eat all day. I was so worried about her that after the evening meal I went uninvited into the men's hut again.

Achilleus was seated before the hearth. Patroklos, cross-legged on his bed, was polishing some armor. Achilleus looked up. "What do you want?"

"It's Diomede. She's wasting with grief. I'm afraid she'll lose strength and the god will strike her down."

He nodded. "You can fix her a posset."

In the corner where the stores of food were kept, he directed me in its preparation and watched as I grated goat's cheese into barley water, adding herbs. But although his eyes rested on me I sensed he did not see me. He was brooding, distant, his brow furrowed. At last he turned away and went to his seat in front of the fire. As I brought the posset to the hearth, I passed close enough to breathe in the warm, smoky scent of his body. It distracted me for a moment, but when I held the cooking vessel over the heat, my head filled suddenly with the vision of Helike's shuddering, twitching body. Tears blurred my sight. As I brought one hand up furtively to wipe my cheeks, Achilleus's eyes focused on me.

"Why do you weep?" He spoke with impersonal gentleness, as if to a crying child or a frightened horse. "You can do nothing, Briseis, until the god has worked out his will." I flinched, hoping he would never learn that I was to blame. He got to his feet and came to where I crouched. He reached out and grazed my forehead with his knuckles, testing my skin for fever. "Are you well?" he asked. The furrow at the inner edge of his brow deepened. "Perhaps you should fix a posset for yourself—and for the others."

Then he turned his back and began to pace the hut. I was forgotten. Patroklos looked up anxiously. The silence was broken only by occasional clicks and clatters as I stirred more ingredients into the cooking vessel, and the sound of Achilleus's bare feet on the wood floor.

At last he spoke. "Why is Apollo angry? There is some treachery or blasphemy afoot, and I intend to find out what it is."

Treachery. I felt a clutch of fear. "How?" Patroklos asked.

Achilleus stopped in front of the fire, narrow-eyed. "I'll consult the seer, Kalchas. I'll get him to speak up." He resumed his pacing. "I've an idea already what the trouble may be. Agamemnon is behind this, take my word for it."

I let out a shaky breath. So he thought it was Agamemnon! But when he probed for an answer from this Kalchas, he would learn that the treachery was mine.

"Careful, my friend," Patroklos murmured. "Remember, Agamemnon has a grudge against you going back nine years. Remember his daughter—"

Achilleus paused before the hearth and stared into the flames. "Iphigenia!" he said softly. His voice caressed the name. I felt a shock of jealously. "How could I ever forget? That poor, brave girl! I did nothing for her. I could not even save her."

What was she to you? I wondered. *And what did you try to save her from?*

"Still, you tried, and Agamemnon has never forgiven you for opposing him," Patroklos insisted. "Don't speak out against him now."

Achilleus swung around. "Oh, I have no intention of accusing him myself. But Kalchas will find a way to bring it to light before all the men." Slowly he sank into his chair before the hearth and leaned forward, chin resting on his hand. The reflected flames danced across his brooding face.

What would he do when the seer revealed that I was the real culprit? All at once I knew I had to tell him. *Now, tonight.* I must spare him the humiliation of learning it before all the chieftains. Then perhaps he himself could find a way to appease the god. If I could get him to listen, many lives might be spared.

A cold, heavy lump settled around my heart. Telling him would destroy the tenuous new love between us. He would never forgive me. And who could blame him?

But I had no choice.

I lifted the vessel from the flames and set it on the hearthstone. At the same moment, Achilleus straightened in his chair, as if he too had reached a decision. His shoulders squared, and a smile touched his mouth. "I'll call all the chieftains to assembly. And I'll say—"

"No!" Patroklos interrupted sharply. "Not you. Why should you convene the assembly? Leave it to Odysseus or Nestor or one of the other chiefs." He went to Achilleus, laying a hand on his shoulder. But Achilleus shook it off impatiently.

"The other chiefs are too laggard. My men are dying! I won't wait. I'll summon them myself—tonight. If I go around to all the camps now, we can meet early in the morning."

"Don't do it!" Patroklos snapped. I had never heard him speak so to Achilleus before. *He senses danger*, I thought. But Achilleus was already at the door, one hand on the latch, a hard, reckless smile on his face. A challenging smile. Patroklos changed his tone. "Don't do this, my friend," he pleaded. "At least wait until tomorrow. If you challenge Agamemnon—"

"Agamemnon!" As if the name had filled his mouth with gall, Achilleus spat.

Now was the moment, whether I was ready for it or not. "Achilleus, wait! Please stay." My voice came out cracked and thin, out of place in this argument between them. Patroklos turned in surprise, and Achilleus went still, as if they had both forgotten I was there. "Perhaps there's no need to call an assembly. You see, perhaps I— I—" I faltered. My throat was tight and painful. "Perhaps I am to blame for this."

"*You?*" Achilleus stared in astonishment. His hand fell from the latch. He took quick steps toward me. Patroklos backed away and sat on his bed, watching. "How?" Achilleus demanded.

I tried to rise, but my legs were trembling too much. "I prayed to Apollo."

"When?" The question came like a lash.

"A while ago," I muttered, not meeting his eyes. "When I felt—differently."

I ventured a look at him. He stood before me unmoving, and I could not read his face. "What did you pray?" he demanded. "Did you make an offering?"

Under the force of his gaze I could only bring myself to answer the second question. "Just a few barley grains. And —" I fell silent. At my evasion his eyes blazed. He swung away to the hearth, picked up a stick, and stirred the glowing coals furiously, then stood staring off into space. After a moment he asked, "Then what?"

"I looked up and saw the ship with the painted sail. Apollo's ship."

A huge breath escaped him. A release of tension. "*That ship!*" He smiled, but it was a bitter smile. "What makes you think this plague has anything to do with you?"

"Some days later—that night with you—I had a vision—of Apollo shooting his arrows."

He shot me a look. "I remember!" His tone gave nothing away.

"It frightened me." I lowered my eyes. "I thought it had to do with my prayer."

He was silent for a long time. At last he shook his head. "This has nothing to do with you, Briseis. You think this plague is Apollo's answer to your prayer? That for a few words of yours, a handful of barley grains, he would kill off half the army? Nay, my foolish one, he wouldn't listen to a mere woman!" He laughed shortly. "Apollo is a man's god. This is something else. He is angry." He turned away, still holding the twig from the hearth, and resumed his pacing. "That's why I must go now to call for an assembly," he said, as if to himself. "And tomorrow Kalchas must speak up."

I sank down limply, with a relief so enormous I was faint. Surely he was right, and my prayer too small and insignificant to be worthy of the mighty god's notice. Just when I'd begun to hope Achilleus would question me no further, he leaned over me, a hard glitter in his eyes, and I felt the grip of his hand under my chin, turning my face up to his. He said with deceptive, dangerous softness, "But you never told me, Briseis. What did you pray?"

My stomach dropped sickeningly. I considered lying but knew I could not. "I—I prayed that you would be made to give me up."

He let go of my chin and went still. His eyes never left mine. His knuckles whitened, and the stick he was holding suddenly snapped in two.

I fumbled for words. "That was before—I didn't mean—"

He cut me off. "*Why?*"

"Because you had said—" I began, stumbling. "You said I'd only ever be your slave."

"I did say that," he conceded. He walked a few paces away. His back was to me when he said, "So you want to be taken from me."

"Nay, Achilleus, that was *before*—when you led me to believe I meant nothing to you. But now—" I broke off, and added in a whisper, "You *know* how I feel about you."

"Do I?" He cast me a glance over his shoulder but kept his back turned. Then he said in an oddly flat tone, "The only way you could be taken from me is if I were somehow humiliated in front of the whole army. Or dead. *That* is what you prayed for, Briseis."

I gasped, horrified. "I didn't wish you harm!" He was silent. "I tried to unsay my prayer." My voice broke. "Why won't you believe me? Achilleus, *look* at me!" I sprang up, took his arms and turned him to face me. I dropped to my knees. "Please forgive me!" My eyes were full of furious tears, and without meaning to, I said it too fiercely. *He will never take me back,* I thought. "All I want is to be with you. Can you let the past be in the past?"

"Stand up, you silly girl!" He pulled me to my feet. "Don't you see I have important matters on my mind just now? I'll deal with you later, after all this is settled."

Tears rained down my face. I said again, "Achilleus, I beg you!"

His eyes softened, and he said, "Maybe I can be merciful. Briseis, all you are is trouble to me!" But he said it teasingly. He gave a small twitch of a grin and gently mussed my hair. My scalp warmed from the touch of his fingers. I let out my breath, feeling a wild hope. Did this mean I was forgiven? *Oh, please gods!* I thought.

"Now go to bed, in your own quarters, and don't wait up for me. I'll be back quite late."

Abruptly, he straightened, all business again, and I could tell I was gone from his mind as if I had never been there. He grabbed his mantle, glanced at Patroklos, and once more was at the door, his hand on the latch.

"Achilleus, *don't go!*" The other man's voice, sharp and urgent, came from the corner.

A rectangle of black night appeared as the door swung open, sending in a whiff of sea air. Patroklos sprang out of the shadows, but the door slammed shut and Achilleus was gone.

CHAPTER 20

"You will eat your heart out,
raging with remorse for this dishonor
done by you to the bravest of the Akhaians."

—Achilleus, *Iliad*, Homer, Book I
(Fitzgerald's translation)

My first thought at daybreak was to wonder how matters stood with Achilleus. I couldn't ask him, because the assembly that would take place today absorbed his whole being. But if I took the morning bread to the men, I might know by the look in his eyes.

The assembly worried me. Why had Patroklos tried so urgently to stop him from convening it? I arose before the other women, took an empty *hydria* and headed for the spring.

When I returned, Diomede had started the fire in our courtyard and was rolling out the flat cakes of barley bread. I joined her and watched her covertly as we worked. In the cold morning light, her face was pale and etched with sharp lines, showing the old woman she would become. The slow movements of her hands betrayed her sorrow. I would have done anything to lessen her pain. I debated telling her about Achilleus's action last night and Patroklos's fears, but I sensed that the men's concerns were far from her mind. When we finished putting the bread on the hearth, I took her hands and pressed them in a silent offer of comfort.

While the bread was baking, I fretted. It was taking forever, and I had to see Achilleus before he left. When at last the cakes turned brown and the smell of cooked bread filled our nostrils, I scooped a handful into a basket, picked up the jug of fresh goat's milk, and headed for the men's hut. With a hand that shook, I opened the door.

Silence. Emptiness. They had gone.

Stopping only to set down the bread and the jug, I raced to the shore. There I saw them, already small in the distance, walking with others toward the center of the camp. Achilleus's gait was as determined as if he were setting out to meet an enemy instead of his king. His blue mantle hung from his shoulders, its ripples catching the first sunlight. For an instant that mantle was blown aside, and when I saw his sword belt under it, I felt a cold foreboding. I wanted to run after them, to reach Achilleus, to grasp his hands, to say— it didn't matter what. The urge was so strong I actually ran a few steps forward.

I stopped. He would be furious if I behaved so before all the camp. I watched them, my eyes blurred with tears, until they vanished from sight.

He'll be back before evening. But my dread did not lessen.

A hand grasped my arm. Diomede stood beside me, watching me intently. "So—you care for him." A deep pain tore through me, and I couldn't answer. When I turned to her, her face gave no clue as to her feelings, but she saw the truth in mine. She shook her head pityingly and said, in her brusque way, "Best harden your heart."

Too late for that! I wondered what her feelings were, she who had known him far longer than I. "You?" I asked in a choked voice. "Do you care for him?"

"There was a man once, in my past life. There will never be another." She paused, and I let out the breath I had been holding. "I like our master well enough. He's kind and fair, though I would sooner rest in my own bed than go to his. When he's summoned me, it's a duty, like grinding the grain, washing the clothes. More pleasant, but still a duty." She gave a small smile. "You and the other women, your friendship," she continued softly, "they matter more." Her voice faded to a whisper, and I knew she was thinking of Helike.

I put my arm around her shoulder and said, "Come, Diomede. The men are gone on some business of their own. Let's go wash the clothes and bathe in the spring. Then I'll dress your hair. How long since you've looked after your own needs?"

Her responding smile was a valiant effort. As we went to the hut to fetch the washing, I told her briefly of last night's events and the assembly that Achilleus had convened. I did not mention my prayer. After that we spoke no more of the men. At the spring, we bathed and washed our hair, trying to cleanse away the pain and fear, the death stench of the past few days. When we had washed many lengths of cloth and spread them in the sun to dry, we combed each other's hair, and as I dressed Diomede's, weaving wildflowers into it, I told her tales of my childhood exploits in the hills near

Lyrnessos with my brothers and even coaxed a few weak laughs from her.

Around mid-afternoon we had word that the men were returning. Diomede and I left our chores and went down to the shore to see if we could catch sight of them.

When I saw a group of men led by two familiar figures approaching from afar, I knew at once that something was wrong. Patroklos's movements were stiff, and he glanced often at Achilleus, who walked in long strides looking neither left nor right. I could tell that something was building inside him, a rage or grief that found no outlet. When they were still far, Achilleus turned suddenly, headed for the shore, and sat on the sand, staring out to sea. Patroklos made a move to go to him, but Achilleus, with a rude, savage gesture of his arm, signaled his need for solitude.

All my strength drained from me. Patroklos walked toward the hut, passing close but making a pretense of not seeing us. But when the corner of his eye met mine, his head jerked. His face was as white as on the day of his wound. He entered the hut and shut the door hard.

"Diomede," I said, "what do you think happened?"

"Take the clothes we washed and put them away in the hut," she suggested. "Then you can ask Patroklos."

Picking up the basket near our feet, I entered the hut. Patroklos was in his chair sipping from a goblet. He started violently. "What are you doing here?"

"We washed clothes," I said. "I've come to put them away. What happened in the assembly?"

He ran a rough hand through his hair. "Don't ask, Briseis!" he muttered. "You'll know soon enough." He drained his cup and sat staring into the hearth.

I couldn't speak. Going to the corner behind the chests and storage bins, I began folding the garments. When I was half done with my chore, I heard footsteps—someone fumbling with the latch. I peered over the lid of a chest. The door opened, and Automedon, who for some reason had not gone to the assembly, burst in. "Patroklos, what happened?" he demanded.

Patroklos rose swiftly and went to meet him. He frowned in my direction. Then he put his lips against Automedon's ear and said a few words I could not hear.

Automedon drew a sharp breath. "That's what I heard. It can't be!"

Patroklos gave a grim nod. "Take a cup of wine with me. I'll tell you how it happened."

I resumed my work, but my stomach was knotted with dread. I made a shambles of the garments I was trying to fold.

Patroklos, pouring wine, said, "I told him he should not have been the one to call the assembly. Only I never guessed it would come to this." He handed Automedon a cup and led him toward the door. "It was an outrage!" he said in a low voice. "Agamemnon humiliated him. And no one spoke up—"

I did not hear any more, for he stepped outside. Automedon followed, his profile turned toward me, a tight-skinned brown face, impassive, with a slitted eye. I flew to the door and peered out. They were standing all the way across the courtyard with their backs to me. I heard Patroklos's low voice but I could not distinguish the words.

I returned to the clean clothes and dumped them into the chest. My hands shook so that, even clumsily done, the task took longer than it should have. Then I went outside and crept along the fence, close enough to eavesdrop.

"This oath Achilleus swore," Automedon was saying. "He meant it?"

"Can you doubt it?"

"By the gods, this is no good! No good at all. But if that is how matters stand, I'd better start packing."

Packing? What had Achilleus sworn? The cold shadow would not leave my heart. Something had gone terribly wrong in that assembly, but what? I pictured Agamemnon as I had seen him my first night in camp, the un-kingly king with his greedy eyes and gloating smile. What had he said, what had he done to Achilleus? *I'll find Achilleus*, I thought. *Perhaps he'll tell me.* As I started across the courtyard my foot struck a loose rock. Patroklos and Automedon saw me and fell silent. We all stood frozen. They seemed to be waiting for me to leave.

As I made for the courtyard gate their eyes followed me. The hairs on my arms and neck lifted. I fled down to the shore. When I reached it, I searched everywhere for Achilleus, though I was afraid of what I might see in his eyes. Afraid to learn what had befallen, I had no idea what I would say to him. Though it made no sense at all, I ached to offer him comfort.

He was nowhere in sight.

I smelled fire and burning flesh. In both directions, as far as I could see, lines of smoke rose to the sky. Sacrificial fires. The Achaeans of every clan must be slaughtering bullocks and goats, burning them as offerings. To make peace with Apollo, I guessed. Every clan but the Myrmidons. Whatever had happened in the assembly had set our camp apart.

A breeze stirred, as if the angry god breathed on my neck. I looked up at the pall of smoke. "Apollo," I whispered, "lift your wrath from us, too!"

I was standing close to the spot where I had prayed before. And just as I had then, I saw a ship, closer this time. It came from the center of the camp, a black-hulled Achaean ship. In the bow stood a broad-shouldered, red-bearded man, and, at his side, a slim, dark-haired girl I suddenly recognized. *Chryseis*. Was she going home after all?

I watched until the ship faded from sight. The sun had dropped more than halfway from its zenith. A haze lay over the sea, dark with smoke. The breeze whipped up sand against my ankles. I turned away, started back.

Two Myrmidon warriors were standing near one of the ships. When they saw me, their heads drew together, whispering, watching me. As I passed them, they fell silent and stared. A cold shiver prickling down my back told me that they had been talking about me.

Impossible, I thought. Why would they be? Yet just behind them I stopped, and I was almost sure one of them said my name: "—*her*. Briseis." For a long moment I couldn't move. *What about me?* What did they know that I didn't? A frightening thought came to me. Perhaps the seer knew about my prayer to Apollo and had revealed it before all the men. For a long moment I couldn't move. At last I forced myself to walk, footsteps dragging. Just a few paces later I encountered Automedon. He gave me a narrow-eyed, penetrating look and hurried past as if he were afraid I might speak to him.

I had to reach our quarters. Surely by now Diomede would know what had happened at the assembly. Twenty paces from the hut, I encountered her carrying a large caldron with Iphis. Iphis's eyes slipped away from mine.

"Diomede!" I called out.

She looked at me, her eyes bright with tears. Then her gaze dropped. She turned away. Iphis was tugging on the caldron, and Diomede had to follow. She shook her head pityingly, it seemed, and went on her way to the waste dump.

"*Diomede!*" I cried.

My unease was full blown now, a hundred insects swarming up my skin. A hundred eyes everywhere watching me, secretive with some knowledge I didn't share.

What was it? Why would no one tell me? Quickly I went into the women's quarters, but I could not escape my growing fear.

The room was empty, thank the gods! Someone had brought a spindle and a pile of wool inside. A mindless task. Crouching on the floor, I picked up the spindle. As I spun, my fingers slippery with sweat, I could only pull out thick, lumpy strands of wool.

Suddenly I heard the outer door open, slamming into the wall. The hut shook. A voice shouted, "Patroklos!"

Achilleus had returned. His words, heavy with defeat, went through me like hammer strokes. "They are here, Patroklos. Fetch her."

The spindle fell out of my hand. I got to my feet as Patroklos's footsteps crossed the outer room. The door opened, and he stood in the entrance. "Briseis!" His stricken eyes held mine. "I wanted to tell you earlier, but I couldn't—Agamemnon was the one who offended Apollo and caused the plague, because he wouldn't give the girl Chryseis back to her father. Now he's had to yield, but he was mightily angry, and—" Then he couldn't look at me, couldn't finish. "You must come," he said at last. He took me by the hand. "Briseis—I'm sorry."

"What's happened?" He didn't answer—only led me through the hut toward the courtyard. My legs were numb as we went outside.

Achilleus was sitting on the bench. Before him stood two strangers, fidgeting uncomfortably, their eyes downcast. When he saw me, he sprang to his feet. His eyes were bright and hard. "These are Agamemnon's heralds," he said, indicating the strangers. "You're to go with them."

My mouth fell open. "Go with them? Why?"

He made a harsh sound, something that was perhaps meant to be a laugh but wasn't. "Because Agamemnon had to give up his prize, and he insists he must have another. *You.*"

My heart seemed to stop. The words had no meaning. I could only stand there stupidly, not moving.

But he spoke roughly. "Go, Briseis. You belong to Agamemnon now."

CHAPTER 21

> Back along the ships
> they took their way, and the girl went, loath to go.
>
> *Iliad*, Homer, Book I
> (Fitzgerald's translation)

I took a step toward him, and my knees gave way, hitting the ground painfully. I stretched out my arms to him and opened my mouth, but no words came.

He said, "It turns out you got what you prayed for, after all."

The gibe hurt more than I could have imagined. "No! Achilleus, I beg you! Don't let them take me!"

"It's out of my hands." He reached for me, then changed his mind and let his arm drop. "Don't fuss, Briseis. Don't make this harder. Go with them now."

The two men drew me to my feet and started to lead me away. I resisted but was so weak I feared my legs would give way again. Without my will, the heralds pulled me away from him.

As we reached the gate, I heard Achilleus give a wordless, drawn-out bellow so full of pure rage that my insides shivered. It sounded almost inhuman. I looked back. He hadn't moved; wasn't looking at me.

The two strangers took me through the gate. One of them banged it shut behind us. They led me up the shore, leaving the Myrmidon huts and ships far behind. This wasn't real. My legs felt as if they didn't belong to my body.

I kept looking back, hoping he was merely taken by surprise, and when he recovered his wits he'd jump up and stop this madness from happening.

But he didn't.

We reached Agamemnon's quarters in the center of the camp. The two men took me to a small, windowless hut. There was a bar on the outside of the door. I flung myself backward, trying to break their hold. "No! Don't lock me in!"

One of them said, "We were ordered to leave you here until the king sends for you." They pushed me in, closed the door. I threw myself against it just as I heard the thud of the bar on the outside slamming into place.

My legs gave way, and I slid to the ground. I knelt, leaning against the wall in darkness. For a long time I howled and sobbed, until, at long last, worn out from weeping, I staggered to my feet. I paced the rough hut and tried to think how this could have happened. At that terrible assembly, the chieftains must have forced Agamemnon to give Chryseis back to her father to appease Apollo. And this had ensued.

But why had Achilleus let them take me?

The answer whispered itself relentlessly in my head. *Because of that prayer. He believes you betrayed him.* The irony was that my confession had been unnecessary. I could have wept if I'd had any tears left.

Still, even if he couldn't forgive me for that prayer, I was his prize. He'd refused to give me to his dearest friend. Even if he were indifferent to me, his pride mattered above all. If Agamemnon had robbed him of a horse or an ox, a bronze caldron, or his precious silver lyre, he would have fought him to the death. So why hadn't he killed the king for taking me?

I remembered his anger last night, and what he had said about giving me up. *The only way that could happen is if I were somehow humiliated in front of the whole army. Or dead. That is what you prayed for, Briseis.*

He had been dishonored before all the men. He must hate me for it.

But he had also said, *Maybe I can be merciful.* His smile, his hand caressing my hair. Surely he knew how much I cared for him. Yet a cold voice whispered in my head. *He hasn't forgiven you.* My mind was going around in panicky circles. I would go mad.

I had to believe he would come in force to take me back. He just needed time to muster his men. Only by telling myself this could I continue to breathe.

I sat down, striving for calm, though a dreadful fear tore at my gut. Before too long, Agamemnon would send for me.

The light coming through the cracks in the door grew dim. Smells wafted in: the sea breeze, scents of sizzling meat and warm bread. It was the hour of the evening meal, and I should be outside our hut, preparing the bread with Diomede. The passing time made me frantic. I got to my feet and inhaled deeply to calm myself. It did no good. Why had Achilleus waited so long?

He's never going to come, whispered the insidious voice in my head.

I heard a noise. Shuffling footsteps. The dragging away of the beam that locked me in. Abruptly, the door opened. A small, gray-haired woman stood there with a lamp. "Come," she said. "The king wants you."

The blood stopped in my veins. Silently I asked the gods for strength. As I reached for my shawl, my hair came loose and tumbled down. I groped on the floor, looking for my clasps. Delaying as long as possible.

"What are you doing?" the woman asked.

"I've lost my clasps. I need to bind up my hair."

"Never mind that!" She grabbed my arm. "He mustn't be kept waiting."

I straightened slowly, my hair unbound like a young girl's. Dragging my feet, I followed her to a large, well-appointed hut. She pointed to the door. "He's in there." Then she scurried away like a scared rat.

I stood frozen. What if I didn't go in the door? What if I turned and ran back down the shore? But I couldn't. I'd be caught. And Achilleus had rejected me—sent me away. There was no escape. I drew a deep breath. My stomach sickened and my hand shook. I opened the door.

Inside, it was dim, yet with the glow of sunset behind me I could see quite clearly. When a hulking man lurched toward me, I recognized Agamemnon from my first night in the camp.

But the setting sun must have blinded him. He gave a hoarse, startled cry. *"Iphigenia!"*

I froze. His daughter! Only last night, Achilleus had spoken her name tenderly, and Patroklos had mentioned a grudge.

Warrior's Prize

Agamemnon pulled me into the room, shutting the door, trapping me like an animal in a snare. He lit a lamp with a burning twig from the hearth. Over its flame his bloodshot eyes stared at me. Heavy wine fumes wafted from his breath. I shrank back, from the stink of him as much as anything else, but he grabbed a strand of my hair to study it, holding it so near the lamp I feared it would catch fire.

"Your hair," he murmured, slurring his words. "Black as the sea at night. *Her* hair." Then he lifted the lamp to my face. "I thought she had come back. But you're not so like her, after all." He scowled. "You're older—not as pure. Who are you?" he asked, suddenly angry.

"Sire—" Stunned, I let out my breath, realizing I'd been holding it. "I am Briseis, whom you took from Achilleus."

"Of course. Forgot for a moment." His look turned smug. "His *prize!* He must be raging! But he can do nothing. Come, sit by the hearth."

I took a seat uneasily, while he stood. There were chairs around the hearth, spilled food, bones, and the remains of a meal. An inner door led to another room, probably his sleeping quarters. I shuddered. It hurt to breathe. Then I noticed a timid, middle-aged serving woman in the corner, wiping some goblets. Thank the gods, I wasn't alone with him—*yet*. She poured her master more wine and began to clean up the food.

Agamemnon stared at her as if he'd just become aware of her presence. "Make haste with that! Begone!"

She hurried out. He took a seat, sipped wine. My dread grew. I noted his disordered tunic. His mantle, dark red with a finely woven border, was rumpled and dirty. Gold armbands decorated his arms, and a gold chain hung around his neck. He was about to speak when there was a sudden sharp knock, and the door opened.

My heart toppled off a cliff. *He's here!* I leapt to my feet and swung around.

But it was only a man of medium height with brown hair. My disappointment was so bitter I had to lean against the wall steady myself.

"Menelaus!" Agamemnon said.

I'd heard that name. He was Agamemnon's brother, the king of Sparta, and husband of the beautiful Helen, who had been abducted by Paris of Troy, or had run off with him. This man's wife was the cause of the war—or so they said.

Menelaus was younger than Agamemnon. His hair and beard were more neatly trimmed than his brother's shaggy mane. His eyes, the same tawny brown, struck me with their lack of expression. He was ordinary looking, yet his face was hard to read. A worried frown creased his brow, though that might have been put on for Agamemnon's benefit. When he saw me, his look wavered and shifted. He cleared his throat and addressed Agamemnon. "Good evening, brother," he said. "I came to see if you needed me tonight."

I sensed he was lying. There was another reason. Whatever it was though, I was glad not to be alone with the king.

Agamemnon frowned mightily. "Why now? I've got *her* here, can't you see?" As both men's eyes came to rest on me, Agamemnon forced a note of heartiness into his voice. "You were curious, weren't you? Well, behold Achilleus's prize. Mine, now! Have a goblet of wine and tell me if you think her fair."

The men took the chairs before the hearth. Agamemnon motioned me brusquely to a stool in the corner, deep in shadow. I scurried there and sat, pressed against the wall. I felt I would go mad. *O gods, let Achilleus come soon.* I formed my words into a prayer, a litany repeated over and over. *O Aphrodite, make him come. Before Agamemnon takes me into that inner room.*

As the king filled two goblets, he avoided looking at me. I sensed he wanted to forget that moment when he had mistaken me for his daughter Iphigenia. Certainly he did not want Menelaus to know. I wondered if my resemblance to her might protect me in some way.

Menelaus stared into his cup for a moment before drinking a large swallow. Then he said, "You shouldn't have done it, brother." I listened intently. Would this man oppose the king? Could he be of help to me?

"Taken Achilleus's prize? Why should he keep his when I had to give up mine?"

Menelaus spoke mildly, almost meekly. "But it was foolhardy, don't you think?"

"Foolhardy? You heard how he insulted me! I hate that man. He thinks he's above us all. I had to put him in his place."

Menelaus swirled the wine in his cup. "So now we've lost his help in the war."

Lost his help? I gulped in air. Achilleus had withdrawn from the war?

"D'you think I need his help to take Troy?" Agamemnon growled.

"Aye, I do," Menelaus said. "But he's sworn this oath. And he'll never go back on his word." I clenched my hands around the edges of my stool, my heart pounding. Patroklos and Automedon had talked about an oath in ominous tones. What had he sworn? If only I knew. It might mean he was far from indifferent. Maybe he would fight for me after all.

"What of it?" Agamemnon demanded. "I care not what he chooses to swear!"

Menelaus shot him a baleful look and quickly dropped his eyes. My thoughts raced, trying to remember what Patroklos had told Automedon. What oath had Achilleus sworn? *This is no good*, Automedon had said, *I might as well start packing*. Did Achilleus intend to leave? To sail for home?

Without me?

But if he meant to leave, the Myrmidons had to break camp and load their belongings into the ships. Perhaps when all was ready, he would come to spirit me away.

"But without Achilleus we'll never—" Menelaus began.

"Silence!" Agamemnon roared. He gulped his wine and splashed more into his cup. "Don't plague me with your doom talk, Men'laus." He slurred the words. "It's 'cause of your whore wife that we're here at all."

Menelaus sent his brother a look of anger, quickly veiled by a worried frown, but he remained silent while Agamemnon took another swig.

When they're ready to sail, he'll come for me. He must. But how long would it take?

The king turned and motioned to me. "Bring that stool close. Lemme look at you." As I obeyed, my movements heavy with dread, he inspected me through glazed eyes. "You're fair, very fair, Briseis. Diff'rent from what I remember. When he brought you to camp, you were so dirty and ragged I didn't realize—" He shot me a sudden look of suspicion. "Why, you did it on purpose! A sly harlot's trick." His eyes narrowed with rage. "You tried to look ugly so I wouldn't notice you. Why? Because of *him*?"

I felt the blood leave my face. Drunk though he seemed, he saw too much. As I pushed my stool back into the shadows, he came part way out of his chair toward me, his fist clenched. Menelaus started to rise, but Agamemnon subsided with a muttered curse. Stealthily, Menelaus leaned across and lifted the wine skin from where it hung by a strap on the back of the king's chair. Agamemnon snatched it back, breaking the strap, spilling a gush of wine on the floor.

"I think you've had enough," Menelaus said tentatively.

"Don't you dare order me! You forget yourself, brother."

It was a snarl, and Menelaus recoiled, saying, "I was only suggesting. Remember the last time. When you drink too much, you get so—"

"Enough!" the king bellowed. "Out of my sight!"

Both men were on their feet, breathing hard. Agamemnon swayed. "Very well. Good night," Menelaus said. *Don't leave*, I thought, but he backed toward the door.

I leapt up in panic. I clung to a desperate hope. Could I enlist Menelaus's aid? Could I even trust him? Seeing that Agamemnon was busy refilling his wine goblet, I rushed to Menelaus's side. "Don't leave me alone with him!" I whispered.

"I must." For a moment, his eyes showed a weak sympathy. Then his gaze fell away from mine. "Humor him," he said. "But don't let him drink any more wine. He gets violent when he's drunk." He glanced over at his brother, who had gulped his goblet and was lurching toward us. Menelaus opened the door and leaned toward me. "Whatever you do," he warned, "don't let him talk about his dead daughter, Iphigenia, because if he—"

But before he could finish, Agamemnon slammed the door in his face and yanked my arm. "Come 'ere," he slurred. "Come with me."

CHAPTER 22

"I was blinded and Zeus took away my sense..."

—Agamemnon, *Iliad*, Homer,
Book XIX (Rouse's translation)

Agamemnon turned me around to face him, devouring my body with his eyes. "Fair, very fair!" His hands slid down my back and caressed the curves of my hips. I backed away in revulsion, but he only gestured to a board with goblets. "Fetch yourself a cup of wine 'n drink it with me. Then we'll see if you're woman enough for the king!"

I poured myself a cup. Despite his brother's warning, I also refilled his goblet. *Drink*, I urged him silently as he sat down and took it from my hand. *Drink until you fall down.* The thought gave me hope. I sat down on my stool as far from him as possible and glanced at the square of darkness showing through the hole above the hearth. A few stars shone. How long would it take Achilleus to ready his fleet?

He will come, I told myself. But a terrifying chasm opened in my heart.

"Move closer," Agamemnon ordered. "Drink your wine." I slid my stool a hand span nearer and took a sip. I choked. It was sour, full of dregs—and it hadn't been mixed with water. I set my goblet down. Unmixed wine was said to lead to madness, but Agamemnon drained his cup in one gulp and wiped his chin with the back of his hand. There were purple spots of spilled wine on the front of his tunic. His eyes had a glassy, unfocused look, and his lips smiled gloatingly. As he leaned toward me, I flinched from his fetid odor.

"I wish I could've seen Achilleus's face when they took you. The gods curse his arrogance!" He belched. "But I showed him who's stronger." He drew himself up. "Zeus himself honors me—speaks to me, sends me dreams 'n visions—lets me have what I want." He nodded sagely. "Look at you! You're much lovelier 'n Chryseis. I was meant to have you. Who'd've thought, when I sent Achilleus on that raid—"

"You *sent* him?"

Agamemnon laughed. "Oh, but he went willingly! Always the first to volunteer. Thinks it adds to his glory. I've put him to good use over the years. Look how rich I've gotten!"

He made a sweeping motion around the room. The firelight was reflected everywhere in gold: goblets, vessels, richly worked armor. Plundered wealth surrounded him. Even his chair, a tall, high-backed throne, cushioned with sheepskin and decorated with silver studs, must have belonged to some fallen king. Gold masks hung on the walls, eerie, hollow eyes staring out accusingly. I saw in their black depths the ghosts of my people. I clenched my hands and held my body taut.

"What d' you think, my dear?" he said. "Does my treasure please you?"

It was bought with blood. The words wanted to burst from me. But I bit my lips and lowered my eyes. He was looking at me, clearly waiting for a response. At last I whispered, "These things were stolen on raids."

"Aye! And Achilleus went on all those raids. He slew your husband, din' he?"

"But not for greed! He did not despoil Mynes—he gave him a funeral."

Agamemnon threw back his head and laughed. "A funeral! He's always making these grand gestures—to make me look bad! It doesn't matter. I'm more royal." He enunciated the word with care. I said nothing. His fist struck the arm of his chair. "I'm king of Mycenae, son of Atreus. No one of our line's ever been afraid of bloodshed. It's made us rich and mighty."

He poured more wine. Once again, his eyes crawled over me. "What a lovely body you have!" Extending his arm, he curved his fingers around my cheek, down my neck. His hand dipped into the front of my gown. I shot back, but my chair stuck on the gritty floor. I longed to push his arm away and leap to my feet, but dared not. Under that groping hand, that degrading touch, I sat very still and focused on the stars that shone through the opening above the hearth. They were numerous now, hard, cold jewels thrown across the night sky.

I must find a way to stop this drunken king, for if he despoiled me, Achilleus might never have me back. Yet how did he expect me to hold off Agamemnon's advances?

I remembered what he had said to me: *You have the heart and courage of a warrior.*

Then I must fight Agamemnon, I thought. *I must not fail.*

The king's filthy, loathsome hand crawled over my neck and breast. My face heated. I held myself very still and strained to hear the noises from outside—the sound of a door closing, the bark of a dog, an occasional voice. Normal night noises. He put his arm about me and drew me tight against him, holding my head immobile. His mouth came down over mine—suffocating, loose-lipped, foul with sour wine. I recoiled.

He took another swig from his goblet, tossed it aside, and groped to his feet. "Come to bed," he muttered thickly.

His arm on my neck, he pulled me into the inner chamber, where a lamp flickered in a sconce. As I passed his chair, I managed to grab the wineskin. How much more was needed to render him senseless? "Have some more, Sire," I offered, handing him the wineskin. "I'd like some myself."

He guided the purple stream into his mouth, slopping some onto his tunic, then handed it to me. I took a deep draft for courage. "Enough." He snatched it back impatiently and slung a clumsy arm over my shoulder. Half leaning on me, he took fumbling steps toward the huge bed.

I ducked under his arm—headed toward the door to the outer room. But his hand shot out and seized me roughly, knocking me onto the bed.

Slobbery lips touched my cheek as he bent over me.

I shrank back. "Sire, I—I have my courses," I lied.

"What do I care?" His movements slow and heavy, he pushed me down and slid on top of me, crushing the air from my lungs. He was very drunk, but not drunk enough. His hand fumbled between my legs. "C'mon, spread your thighs, how often 've you been mounted by a king?"

He was suffocating me, trying to pull aside my gown. I turned my face away and gasped for air. "Sire!" I cried, desperate. I remembered Menelaus's warning: Iphigenia, the forbidden subject. But what did I have to lose? "Sire, the gods will be offended if you lie with me thinking I'm your daughter!"

He stopped, lifted his head. "What—?"

"Iphigenia," I said clearly.

Rage flashed in his eyes. His body went still. His flesh seemed to shrink. Then abruptly he sat up. His lust left him, and something far more menacing took its place. "You're not fit to speak her name." His voice was deadly quiet. He sounded coldly, frighteningly sober.

"But, Sire. Your daughter— What happened to her?" I wanted only to keep him distracted, keep him talking.

He glared at me, and the hatred in his eyes made me wince. "Very well. If you would know of Iphigenia, I'll tell you."

When he wasn't looking, I moved as far away from him as I could. My eyes were on the door. *Achilleus, come now!* I prayed. *Zeus deliver me!* Agamemnon sat on the corner of the bed. The wineskin was propped against the wall. He stared straight ahead, his eyes sightless. All the lines of his face sagged, and his shoulders slumped. "Oh, my beloved daughter!" His back was turned to me now. "I summoned you. If only you hadn't come!" I started—then realized he was speaking not to me but to his long-dead daughter. He gave a gulping sob.

"Tell me, Sire—"

He turned to me savagely. "*Aulis!* Does the name mean anything to you? It was Aulis where the fleet gathered to sail for Troy. We'd sent out the call to arms to help win back Helen, Menelaus's faithless wife, from the Trojans. To regain our honor and sack that arrogant city." He reached for the wineskin. For a long moment he was silent, pouring wine down his throat before resuming. "And they've come from all over Achaea. A thousand ships, thousands of men. They've chosen me as their leader!" Ice crept down my spine. He spoke as if these events were happening now. "No man before has ever commanded such a force." He wiped his mouth with the back of his hand.

"But the wind won't blow—at least no favorable wind. How can we sail?" He mopped his brow. "It's so hot and dry. The dust clogs our mouths, our nostrils. And we've scavenged the land for miles around. There's not much left to eat. We must sail soon or the men will lose heart." His bloodshot eyes looked at me without seeing. "We've been stranded for weeks."

I sat still, afraid to move, almost afraid to breathe. "Weeks?" I whispered.

He got up slowly, began a shuffling pace around the room. "The men are restless. The army—slipping from my grasp! We'll lose this war without ever fighting it. Then Kalchas the soothsayer, that vile, false prophet, tells me—" He paused, swallowed hard. "Tells me how to right things. It seems I've offended the goddess Artemis. On the hunt I slew a stag, a beast sacred to her." He stopped before me, and his eyes looked through me. "In return for a favorable wind, she demands a sacrifice, a virgin. My first-born daughter!"

I went cold. Among my people, the gods had not exacted human sacrifices since time beyond memory. I shook my head. "Such a thing could not be."

His eyes were suddenly full of fury. "That's how it is!"

"Surely you did not obey—"

"I have other daughters at home," he answered brutally. "But I could never again command such an army. I can keep the power I hold if I slay Iphigenia. I've sent for her. But I can't say, 'Come be sacrificed.' So instead, my message is, 'I've arranged a great marriage for you—to Achilleus.'"

The name burned like a flame. I made a choked sound. Agamemnon's eyes focused on my face. Then he began to laugh. A demonic sound, growing in volume until he rocked with it, out of control. Tears ran down his face. "Of all the chieftains I could've chosen! I didn't know him then. Any other would have been loyal to me. But he—stubborn, arrogant fool! He's angry that I've used his name without asking his leave. Says he'll marry her anyway and save her from death. Thinks he can defy me, turn the army against me, take my own daughter from me—but he can't! She's mine—she loves me more!"

He drank wine. Once again he paced the room, his eyes roaming about wildly. He stumbled. Stopping before the wall where the weapons hung, he took down a long, silver-handled knife. He looked at it thoughtfully, running his finger along the flat side of the blade.

"Iphigenia!" His mood shifted again, and he addressed his dead daughter in a tender whisper that chilled my bones. "You're mine, are you not? My own flesh and blood. You'll do this for me, give me your life because I need it to appease the goddess, to control the army. To show Achilleus who's master."

And suddenly he turned. He grabbed my hair, pulled my head back, stretching and exposing my neck. "Then you begged me for your life." He was breathing in gasps. "You wept, you pleaded. I never dreamed it'd be so hard. But I'd no choice. I had to—had to— Your soft white neck, blood flowing on my hands." He gave a terrible, sobbing cry. He placed the knife over my throat. "You have to die! So the winds can blow—"

Everything froze in me. With another shift, he pulled me up hard and turned me around. He was standing over me, forcing me to kneel on the bed with my back against him. His arm around my neck was crushing my windpipe. The other hand held the knife. "Kneel, hateful woman! Beg me for your life as she did!"

His knee pressed into me, arching my back painfully. Dark spots danced before my eyes. I gagged on wine fumes, acrid sweat, the hot reek of rage and madness.

"She was pure and beautiful. You're vile—you were *his!*" His face was so close to mine that his spittle sprayed my cheek. "I hate you as I hate him! Why should you live when I had to kill my Iphigenia?"

I could get no air. I felt his muscles tightening. I clawed at his arm. Blood pounded in my ears. Everything blurred and went dark.

All at once he gave a snorting breath, as if something had occurred to him. "You think the great Achilleus 'll save you!" He gave an ugly laugh. "But your life means nothing, not even to him." His arm slackened infinitesimally, and I caught a breath—another. I hardened my mind against his words and concentrated on the feel of his arm. There was a slight tremor in it. The wine was weakening him. At any moment he might let down his guard, and I must be ready. I gripped his arm with both hands, pressing my nails into his flesh.

"He said he'd sail for home. Even now," the thick voice continued, "he's probably launching his ships, the deserter, leaving you behind." A thought struck him, and he laughed with malice. "But perhaps he'd like to have you back!" His arm jerked tighter again. "I'll send him your body—" Laughter shook him. I held myself still, breathed in slowly under the pressure of his arm. I tightened my finger-grip.

"A farewell gift." His voice rose to a mocking falsetto. "Wait, Achilleus, don't go yet! I've something for you!"

He drew the knife back, his muscles taut and quivering, the blade ready to plunge.

I made myself limp. Then with all my strength I pushed his arm away and slid out of his slackened grasp. I scrambled to the far corner of the bed.

He lunged—missed. I pulled myself onto my hands and knees. He came after me, grabbed me. Flung me onto the bed —fell on top of me. His body crushed me. I lay prone. I couldn't move. I waited for the knife to plunge.

But it didn't. He'd lost it somewhere in the bedding.

Rasping breaths came from him. I was trapped, my hands stuck under me, held immobile by his weight. My face was turned to the side. In the dim light of the lamp's flame I saw him grope slowly for the knife.

A faint red gleam shone along the blade. His fingers closed around the handle.

At that moment, he slumped against me, his body a dead weight, his breathing heavy.

He was unconscious.

Pinned under him, I could barely breathe. I was afraid to make any sound or move that might awaken him.

If Achilleus came now, he would never believe that I had not yielded.

CHAPTER 23

"...this time, for the girl, I will not
wrangle in arms, with you or anyone,
though I am robbed of what was given me..."

—Achilles, *Iliad*, Homer, Book I
(Fitzgerald's translation)

The night was far-gone when I eased myself from under Agamemnon. I was desperately uncomfortable and needed to breathe more easily. Terrified that he would awaken, I lay listening to his harsh snores. I dared not move further, but at last I slept. Deeply. Much later, when I opened my eyes, morning light seeped through the window. The door was closed. I was alone in Agamemnon's bed.

Achilleus had never come.

A voice came from just outside—a man's voice—impatient, angry. I sat upright. The door burst open, and Agamemnon staggered forward to lean against the doorjamb, his eyes focusing on me with difficulty. A mighty frown compressed his brow.

"You!" he snarled, then shouted at someone in the outer room. "Why is this woman still here? I want her gone!" A head looked over his shoulder—the serving woman who'd waited on him last night. "Phrontis, summon my heralds," he ordered her. "Then I want this room cleaned of all trace of her."

I shrank back as he approached. His eyes were bloodshot, his hands trembling. "Get out of my bed—my house! I don't want Achilleus's leavings." He gripped his head. "My men will take you away. I'm being merciful. Instead of killing you, I'm going to lock you up." The outside door stood open. Through it I saw the two men who, yesterday, a lifetime ago, had brought me here. My legs weakened. I longed so much for Achilleus that I shaped his name silently on my lips.

Agamemnon saw, and gave an angry, contemptuous laugh. He pushed the door shut so that once more I was alone with him. He shook me savagely, then released me so suddenly that I fell back. "Don't you dare even speak of him! He left you here—aye, abandoned you!" His eyes narrowed to malicious slits. "And now he's gone. Sailed away."

The words hit my chest like a rock. "I don't believe you." *He wouldn't; not without me.* He laughed harshly. "I saw his ships myself, all of them, sailing at first light, his own ship in the lead with its wine-red and white sail and Patroklos at the helm. Achilleus himself was at the prow." He gave me a malicious look. "With another woman at his side."

Was he lying? I could clearly see Achilleus's ship with its striped sail, and I remembered Automedon saying, *I might as well start packing.* And who was the woman standing at Achilleus's side—Diomede?

Agamemnon said, "Do you know what he said about you in front of all the chieftains? 'I will not fight for the girl.' If you don't believe me, ask anyone. They all heard. And now he's on the high seas. So like it or not, you're mine. Don't try anything, or I'll kill you."

My strength fled as he opened the door again and shoved me outside. I stumbled, lost my footing. Hands caught me and gripped my arms. The two men, one on each side of me, led me away from the hut.

I went. One mindless step, another. One foot before the other. We came to the familiar prison, now furnished with a straw pallet and a slop pail. They pushed me in. Dimness and stale air closed around me. The door shut. With a thud, the wooden bar locked me in.

All at once, rage burst through me. How could Achilleus abandon me? He'd killed everyone I loved and destroyed my home, so that I had no one in the world but him.

I fell on my knees, howling, choking on my tears. I curled my body, as if to keep myself from flying apart. I remembered his face as he said, *You got what you prayed for, after all.* Horrible, cruel, taunting words! Did he believe them himself? Was that why he let me go?

What if he thought I'd begged his forgiveness only to secure my position? Perhaps I'd failed to convince him how strong my feelings were. I searched my mind to remember exactly what I'd said last night. That all I wanted was to be with him. Perhaps it wasn't enough. I should have told him I loved him, but those words were perilously hard to say.

I recalled the times I lay in his bed. I thought he cared for me. It seemed I was wrong.

I will not fight for the girl.

Why? I asked the dark silence. I didn't understand. Perhaps I had never understood.

Had Agamemnon lied? His words had a ring of authenticity. *Ask anyone. They all heard.*

Now he was sailing home, Diomede at his side. My rage and grief threatened to devour me.

I remained on the floor. Hours passed. Somehow I slept. I woke up with a start when the door opened. The same stooping gray-haired woman from yesterday appeared, holding a jug and a platter. A guard urged her to make haste, and after she set down the food and water, I was locked in alone once more.

What would Agamemnon do? Kill me? Or give me away? I slept again, waking to eat and drink before slipping into sleep again. All I wanted to do was sleep, not to think or feel. When I awoke, I ate the rest of the meat scraps.

Time passed; dawns and sunsets I saw only as waxing and waning of the dim light, twice daily visits from Klymene, who never spoke more than a word or a grunt to me. Day by day I was losing strength, becoming dirtier, grittier, smellier, even growing numb to using the slop bucket. I existed like some hidden creature in a burrow—eating, drinking, falling again and again into a dark sleep. I no longer tried to count how many days had passed, but surely enough time for Achilleus to have crossed the sea and reached his home.

I began to dream of things long forgotten—green fields, wooded slopes, the blue sky and blazing sunlight of summer, the smell of sage, the cool breeze from the mountains, the ceaseless chirping of crickets as night fell. The hills of home. I saw faces from my earlier life: Mynes, Laodokos, my mother, my brothers. *Why are you penned up like a beast?* they asked.

One night a new face swam into my dreams, a face I had seen only once, though it was imprinted on my mind. She called my name, very clearly and firmly. *Briseis! We need your help.*

How does she know my name? I thought. *I was only one guest among the multitude at her wedding. And why is she calling me?* I awoke trembling and sat up in the darkness. "Andromache!" I said aloud.

I paced the tiny hut. *I can't stay here waiting to die.* I felt as weak as an old woman. Walking cleared and sharpened my mind. There was a world outside my prison, and beyond the camp a world that belonged to the Trojans and their allies, who'd fought so valiantly against the Achaeans. My people. Their faces, dead and alive, their voices, flooded my mind, filling me with a fierce resolve. *I won't stay here, alone and apart.* "I will escape," I said aloud. "I will go to them." I might even find a way to help them.

Somehow I would make my way to Troy. Or die trying.

CHAPTER 24

*...they pursued at once, like a couple of savage dogs
on the hunt chasing a fawn or hare through the woods...*

Iliad, Homer, Book X
(Rouse's translation)

The hard part was to find a way out of my prison. Once free of this hut, I could find some slave women who would hide me and perhaps even help me on my way to Troy. I had news that could be of immense value to the Trojans: the deaths from the plague, the quarrel between the chieftains— and the departure of Achilleus. All this would embolden them to fight, perhaps even enable them drive off the Achaeans and end this terrible war.

Through the flimsy walls of my prison, I inhaled smells and listened to every noise from outside. Smelling no smoke from sacrificial fires or funeral pyres, but only the evening cooking, I guessed that the plague had died out. When I heard no sounds of horses and chariots, no shouts of mustering men, I guessed the war was at a standstill. A quiet emptiness, a strange lethargy, seemed to pervade the camp. My mind ranged far down the shore to the place that had been Achilleus's encampment. I could almost hear the rhythmic splash of the surf and the whisper of wind sweeping sand across the beach, obliterating all signs that he had ever been there.

I forced my thoughts away from him. I sat passive and motionless whenever I heard the twice-daily approach of Klymene and the guard. I barely spoke to them, yet I observed their every move and listened to their every word, burning with awareness of the world beyond the tantalizingly open door. How to find a way through it? They were watchful and thorough. Then I thought of feigning illness. Even if the plague was over, there were other ailments. If my captors believed I was ill, I might be able to trick them into one unguarded moment.

That evening I was ready with my plan. When Klymene came to bring me food and water, I sat huddled in the corner. She greeted me in her usual gruff, unfriendly way. "Here's your grub." I just stared past her unblinkingly and muttered incoherent things. She hesitated, but after a moment withdrew.

The next morning I lay on my pallet with my eyes closed. "What's wrong with you?" she demanded. I only moaned. As she set the food down, I thrashed about with my arms, scattering the contents of the plate. "Lady!" she exclaimed. I sensed rather than saw her exchange a look with the guard outside. Scurrying about, she removed the spilled food.

After she left, I gobbled up the barley cakes and meat scraps she had not found and drank the water, which I'd been careful not to spill. Then I paced around, flexing my legs to strengthen them. The night would be the crucial time, when I would try to break out.

I still had no idea how I would escape the camp.

One step at a time.

When the light coming through the cracks began to dim, my nerves were wound tight. I listened at the door for Klymene's shuffling approach, and heard noises, voices that drew near and then faded off in various directions. At last came the sound of footsteps, growing louder, halting right outside the door. A shiver ran over my skin. Klymene? Or someone else? I held my breath.

A familiar scraping sound as the door was pulled open. I recognized the wheeze of her breath. Heart beating hard, I lay on my pallet, halfway off it, eyes closed, mouth open. Keeping my face muscles rigid, I made a one-sided grimace such as I had seen on the face of Andromache's mother on the ship.

I squinted my eyes open for a quick look as Klymene stepped into the hut, then held myself still, hoping she couldn't see my rapid heartbeat. I heard a thud against the dirt as she put down the water pitcher and trencher with food. Then soft steps. I felt her very close and smelled her sour breath. "Lady—?"

I stayed motionless, my breathing quick and shallow. I sensed her staring. After a moment she lifted my arm. When she released it, I let it fall slackly. Still she stooped over me, hesitating. I feared that she would turn, shuffle out, and wash her hands of me.

She stepped back. "Sir, I—" Her voice, speaking to the guard, quavered. "I fear she's ill."

The guard's voice demanded, "Are you sure?" He came into the hut. I smelled leather and sweat as he leaned over me. He shouted in my face, then grabbed my shoulder and shook me hard. It took every jot of my willpower to remain limp and still. At last he straightened, standing over me. He said, "She's in a deep swoon. It looks like some kind of seizure or fit."

"Shall we tell the king?" Klymene asked fearfully.

"Not yet. I've a comrade who's something of a healer. I'll fetch him. Stay here."

Steps retreated through the door and across the hard ground, fading. I waited to give the guard time to get far away, knowing I had to incapacitate Klymene and flee before he returned.

I opened my eyes a crack. Klymene was outlined against the open door. Golden twilight drowned my sight. My eyes fell on the water pitcher. I leapt to my feet, grabbed it, and swung it at her head. It slammed into her skull. She fell, mouth open, eyes closed. Water splashed all over. I pushed her onto the pallet, tore off my sash, and bound her hands. A dirty rag lay on the floor. I shoved it into her mouth so she couldn't cry out. Then I snatched her shawl, put it over my head, and shot through the door, shutting it quickly behind me. I slid the heavy bar into place.

Breathing hard, I looked around. There were others about, men lounging outside the huts, women going about their chores. I prayed none had heard anything. The nearest men, a pair, were strolling down the shore a hundred or so paces away. They glanced toward me. My skin prickled. I pulled the shawl over my face and hunched down like Klymene, imitating her small shuffling steps as I walked away. My legs, charged with panic, longed to run, to get far from the hut before the guard returned, but I dared not. My pace was excruciatingly slow. I ventured a glance over my shoulder. The two men on the shore had been joined by a third one. They had stopped and were looking in my direction.

Keep walking. A tight drumming filled my chest. My eyes scanned the nearby buildings. I needed to hide until after dark, when I could venture out to one of the other camps and persuade some of the women to shelter me until I planned my next move.

Suddenly—a shout. I looked back. Two men came running toward me from a different direction, yelling something. I ran. The shawl slipped down and hampered me. With no more need of a disguise, I held it around my waist and sprinted. Steps thudded behind me, gaining.

The sky had dulled to a deep rose. I veered away from the shore, gasping for breath. Ahead was a long, low, narrow building. I heard a whinny, smelled horses. The stables.

I rounded the corner of the wall. The stalls were open on the landward side. I ducked into the deeper shadows of the first stall, which held a pair of horses eating their evening fodder. Their heads reared up, their eyes suddenly ringed in white.

No place to hide here. And the men had seen me.

A diversion, then. I fumbled at ropes and tethers. One set of knots came free—another. I struck a horse across the rump and shouted. The beast whinnied and shot out of the open stall. The other followed, snorting. I dodged their hooves and went to the next stall, releasing two more. One of them reared to a terrifying height. As his front hooves crashed down, I dove out of the way. There were so many untethered horses surrounding me that their immense bodies threatened to crush me. Yet I forced my way into the next stall and the next, loosing tethers as fast as I could, until the open space in front of the stables was full of huge, rearing beasts, snorting, whinnying, running in all directions.

Shouts rang out. "Agamemnon's prize horses!"

Men came running. They dodged flying hooves and chased after trailing ropes.

"Quick, grab them!"

"There go Swiftness and Midnight—headed for the fence!"

Amid the confusion I ducked into a stall. Peering out, I saw my pursuers, but they had their hands full. I sped out of the stall and around the corner of the stable, out of their sight.

A shout came. "Where is the woman? Curse her!"

And an answer: "Search the stables! She can't have gone far."

Across an open space, I saw another building, a stall where bulky objects draped with canvas were stored. War chariots, from their shapes. I dashed across the space, lifted a corner of canvas, and crawled into a chariot. Each breath tore my lungs. My legs cramped as I crouched. I heard only muffled sounds. But if I hadn't been seen, I might be safe until nightfall.

I heard steps, voices. Coming closer.

If they found me, Agamemnon would kill me for certain.

My hand, slippery with sweat, gripped the polished rail of the chariot. Moments passed. No more sounds. I hardly dared to breathe. Someone was near—listening.

A step—another. A crunch of loose dirt. The canvas was flung back. *"Here she is!"*

My throat closed. Two men, with deadly purpose in their eyes, hauled me to my feet and led me out of the building, surely with the aim of taking me straight to the king.

The sky was deepening to purple. The sea glowed brilliantly where the sun had set. I drank in the beauty of falling night. I had not seen these sights for many days, and now I might be looking at them for the last time. My knees shook so hard I could barely walk.

The men led me to a hut I'd never seen before. One of them rapped on the door. At once it was flung open. I found myself face to face with—*Menelaus!*

"What good fortune!" he said, smiling coldly.

CHAPTER 25

*Menelaus was too anxious to get a wink
of sleep. He too feared what might happen...*

Iliad, Homer, Book X (Rouse's translation)

I stared at Menelaus, heart pounding, as he turned to my captors. "Were you seen?"

"Nay, sir," one of them answered. "Agamemnon's men are still looking for her amid the confusion she caused—she loosed the king's horses."

Menelaus's smile widened, though it didn't reach his eyes. He pulled me into the hut. "Well done!" he said to the men. "Now go stand guard outside. Not a word of this to anyone! You'll be rewarded—but only if my brother the king gets no wind of her presence here. And send the women to prepare her a bath. No need to heat the water. I want it done at once."

I went weak kneed with relief. He wasn't going to give me back to Agamemnon—at least not yet. But what did he want? He shut the door. I was in a smaller version of Agamemnon's hut. There was an inner room at the back, closed off by a heavy curtain. Several lamps were lit.

"Well!" he exclaimed. "Your little escapade has been most fortunate. Athena, my patroness, must have led you to run away in front of one of my men." He held up a lamp to examine me and made a grimace of distaste. "You look as if you've been penned up with swine. In this state you're no use to me. What sort of an offering would you make?"

Offering? What did he mean? I dared not ask. And why was he keeping me hidden from his brother?

"Your bath will be ready soon," he said. "The women will make you presentable." He gave a small one-sided smile and broke into a chuckle as if enjoying a private joke. This was a far different Menelaus from the meek, soft-spoken man I had met in Agamemnon's presence. He smiled too much while his eyes remained cold. I felt a quiver of fear.

"What do you want with me, sir?" I asked.

"My brother's made a mess of things, and I intend to fix them." His chill glance slid down my body. "The less you know the better. Just do as I say." He pointed to the door. "Go to your bath now. And don't even think of escape. My men are armed and standing guard."

In the courtyard two serving women waited beside a tub less than half filled with water. The guards hovered in the shadows, and I had to strip and climb into the tub under their watching eyes. Fortunately, by now it was almost completely dark. The water was icy, and my teeth chattered. Still I was glad of the chance to scrub my body clean of the filth and grit from my imprisonment. When I was done, one of the women helped me into a loose white robe with flowing sleeves such as a temple priestess might wear at a sacrifice.

When I returned to Menelaus, he was sitting in the chair before the hearth. He waved me to a stool and studied me with a bland smile. "Much better! Agamemnon would be furious if he knew that I have you. Still, he'll thank me in the end." He stroked his neatly trimmed beard. Then his eyes narrowed. "What did you do that night to anger him so?"

Surprised, I said, "Nothing, sir. But it seems I remind him of his daughter."

He leaned forward. "Iphigenia?" His eyes glowed yellowish, wolfish, very like those of his brother. "Didn't I warn you not to speak of her? What happened?"

I dropped my gaze. "You'd best ask him yourself."

Menelaus made an angry gesture. Then a sly look crossed his face. "I wonder," he mused, "how my brother's embraces compared with those of the great Achilleus."

I felt the blood leave my face. My hands gripped the sides of my stool. Menelaus smirked. "So! You must have done all in your power to discourage Agamemnon's attentions." The corners of his mouth deepened. I was beginning to detest that smile. "Perhaps you even played on your resemblance to his dead daughter to *cause* him to fail in bed."

I lowered my eyes. I could think of nothing to say.

"Just as I thought!" he crowed. "Things may yet turn out well for the Achaeans." Getting to his feet, he stood looking down at me in a way that roused all my misgivings. "I shall keep you hidden until the right time." He rubbed his forehead, then said suddenly, "No tricks, though! You wouldn't get far."

"Where would I go, sir? Since Achilleus has sailed—" My throat constricted.

He narrowed his eyes. "How do you know that?"

"Your brother told me, sir." When he said nothing for a moment, I asked with a surge of hope, "Was he lying?"

"No, unfortunately he wasn't. Your precious Achilleus left us all in the lurch." He gave a short laugh. "If he's had no mishaps at sea, he's likely reached his home by now. So you're stuck with us." He stared at me in such a cold, speculative way that my stomach tightened in fear.

"What are you going to do with me, sir?" I asked.

His eyes shifted. "Something that will raise the men's morale. With Achilleus gone, they'll need it. You needn't fear. It won't harm you." A lie, I was sure. He smiled again and reached out to raise me to my feet. "That stinking shed has not been good for you. We must make you healthy and fair again—and fatten you up. Why, you have lost flesh in the most important places!" His eyes grew hot, and his hands came up to touch me. At that moment we heard the slam of a gate and a loud voice outside giving an abrupt command.

Agamemnon.

Menelaus jumped as if scalded. He seized me and pushed me into the inner room, his sleeping chamber. "You stay here, and not one sound out of you if you value your life! If he discovers your presence—" He made a slashing motion across my throat. Pulling the heavy curtain across the opening, he went out.

My heart was pounding so hard I had to concentrate on breathing quietly. The room was quite dim. Only a faint light came through the opening near the ceiling. As my eyes adjusted to the near-darkness, I could see a bed, a chest, a chair. No place to hide. I crouched behind the curtain, praying that Menelaus could keep Agamemnon from coming in here.

In the outer room, Menelaus greeted his brother in loud, hearty tones.

Agamemnon was saying, "Good evening, brother! Have you supped yet?"

I let out a breath. He didn't know I was here. From the level tone of his voice, I guessed he didn't even know I was missing. His men must have been too afraid to tell him.

"My women are preparing supper now. Will you join me?" Menelaus sounded wary and reluctant. Agamemnon gave no audible answer, but presently I heard the creak of a man's weight settling into a chair, the slosh of wine being poured.

Agamemnon said, "What ails you, brother? You seem as nervous as an old woman."

"I couldn't sleep last night—I'm worried the Trojans will defeat us," Menelaus answered. "So many died in the plague. We haven't gone to battle since Achilleus left. But when we do—"

"Are you blaming me for quarreling with that man?" Agamemnon began in a threatening tone. "When at this very moment he—"

"Oh, not at all!" Menelaus interrupted. "I blame myself! If my wife hadn't left me and our child and run off with that worthless Trojan, we wouldn't be fighting this war."

So Helen had not been abducted. She had left this cold, cruel man—and her child—for her Trojan lover. I pulled back a tiny portion of the curtain to peer through. Agamemnon sat with his back to me.

Menelaus was flushed, gesticulating. "The men have lost heart," he said. "Their spirits are so low it's as if they're already defeated."

Agamemnon lurched to his feet. I shrank back. "Of course they haven't lost heart! I shall prove it the very next time we go to battle."

"How?" Menelaus sounded doubtful.

"By putting them to the test. I shall offer them the chance to sail for home—or stay and fight like men."

"I don't think that's wise," Menelaus objected. "It's likely to backfire."

"Don't you dare question me!" Agamemnon burst out.

Silence. A muffled sigh. Then Menelaus said, "I have another idea."

"I don't think much of your ideas," Agamemnon grunted. His chair creaked. "Remember when you persuaded me to send a spy to Troy, and he was caught and beheaded?"

Just then I heard the outer door open, and there was a scrape of wood across the floor as tables were moved. The serving women had brought supper, interrupting the men's talk. As clay vessels clattered onto wooden surfaces, the smell of cooked goat and fresh bread came to my nostrils. My stomach growled with hunger. For a few moments after the women withdrew, the only sounds I heard were of noisy eating. I stayed very still, my nerves as tight as warp on a loom. The disagreement between the brothers, this foolhardy plan to test the men's morale—these things would be wonderful news to the war leaders of Troy.

If I could get away.

After a lengthy pause Agamemnon spoke, his words muffled as if his mouth were full. "So the men are disheartened, eh? What do they think I should have done when Achilleus—"

Just as my ears pricked up at the name, Menelaus interjected. "I have a thought about what we could do to raise the men's spirits. Don't you think a sacrifice to the goddess Athena would—"

A sacrifice. Ice crept down my spine. I did not even hear the rest of what he said. *An offering. Fatten you up.* I remembered the unfortunate Iphigenia, slaughtered on the altar of Artemis so that the fleet could sail. Suddenly I knew.

I would be the sacrifice to restore the Achaeans' courage.

I clenched my hands tightly—tried to think. They wouldn't do it tonight. It was too late. Menelaus would keep my presence secret until he was ready to reveal his plan to the king. But he might persuade Agamemnon to do it tomorrow.

I imagined them convening the men, building an altar—

I had to escape tonight.

But where would I go? Hide among the women? With both the king and his brother after my blood, none of the women would dare shelter me. I must not only find a way out of this hut—I must get clean away from the camp and go to Troy. But how, with a high wall around the camp, and all the gates guarded?

Then suddenly, as if a god had put the answer in my mind, I saw how I could do it.

I was calm now, thinking clearly. I went over every step of my plan. Aye, it could work. I needed certain things, though, and I must find them quickly, before Agamemnon left and Menelaus came for me.

The men were still eating. They spoke of trivial things now: the weather, the quality of the wine. In the faint light I looked around Menelaus's sleeping chamber. All his personal possessions were surely here. I could make out the shape of a chest. I lifted its lid. Halfway up, the wood creaked faintly. My hand froze. The men's talk paused. I held my breath. Then Menelaus spoke again, in a natural, level tone. I eased the chest open.

It was filled with Menelaus's garments and also his treasures. Gold goblets, armbands, and jeweled brooches gleamed faintly. Fingers trembling, I examined several pieces in the dim light. I needed something of value, stamped with his identity.

Suddenly, a chair scraped against the floor. Heavy footsteps tramped across the room. Quickly I closed the lid. The footsteps retreated, followed by others. The outer door opened. Agamemnon was taking his leave.

I opened the chest again and found a clasp made from a large stone, probably a carnelian. My fingers traced the engraving on it, an embossed, helmeted head, surely the head of Athena, whom he had called his patroness. I also grabbed a gold armband.

The outer door closed. Menelaus's footsteps approached. I shut the lid and stood, stuffing the items into the side of my girdle, trying to quiet my breathing.

He flung the curtain aside. "Zeus, that was close! He mustn't find out about you until I'm ready." I gripped my trembling hands together, my arm hiding the bulge in my sash where the stolen treasures pressed into my skin. "I suppose you're hungry," he said grudgingly. "There's food left over."

He turned away and I drew a deep breath. "Thank you, sir."

In the outer room again, I sat on the same stool as before. I was ravenous, thankful for the meat scraps and fragments of bread, even if I had to gulp them down under his narrowed, calculating gaze. I would need all my strength for tonight.

To distract him, I said, between mouthfuls, "Your wife, sir—she must be very beautiful."

His brows came down like thunderclouds. He got up, paced. "When we vanquish Troy, I'll make her pay for what she did—for deceiving me. I'll kill her." He spun around suddenly to face me. "And you—I'll wager you're another like her. I know all about your trickery!"

I almost choked. The hidden objects burned against my waist. Had he guessed? I managed to stammer, "What—what do you mean?"

"You deceived my brother—and his guards," he said. I sank back in my chair, limp. "But you won't play *me* for a fool. I'll keep you tied up if I have to, until you've served my purpose."

"Oh, no, there's no need, sir," I said, my voice shaky. "I'm so glad you're hiding me from the king. As long as you let me stay here, I'm very grateful."

For a moment he was silent, and I was afraid I'd overdone it, but he said, "So you should be! Agamemnon's men are looking for you. They haven't dared tell him they let you escape. They'd do anything to lay their hands on you." He laughed shortly. "If you set foot outside this hut—"

"I won't, I promise! He means to kill me, he told me so. You'll keep me safe, sir?"

"If you do as I say." He shrugged. "You can sleep by the hearth here. No tricks, though! My men are just outside the courtyard gate."

He went into the inner room. Through the curtain opening I saw him lift the lid of the chest. I held my breath. But he only scrabbled in it for a bundle of rugs before slamming it shut. "Here!" He tossed the rugs to me. Giving me a final, menacing look, he went back into the sleeping chamber and pulled the curtain across the opening behind him.

I let out a vast sigh. He claimed he hadn't slept well last night. My plan could only succeed if he slept like the dead tonight.

CHAPTER 26

"...He told me
to go through the black night, now swiftly passing,
and to approach our enemies—"

Iliad, Homer, Book X
(Fitzgerald's translation)

    As I waited by the hearth, I tried to rest, but I could not stop thinking of the perils that lay ahead. First, I'd have to slip past Menelaus's guards. But they could not watch his entire compound, and as the night wore on, they'd be less alert. Once I left the compound, I'd have to avoid Agamemnon's men, who would be desperate to find me. But surely, if I waited long enough, they'd have given up the search until morning.

    The best time to break out was an hour or two before dawn.

    The gate sentry posed the greatest danger. The story I told him had best be convincing. To lessen the chance of being recognized, I could alter my looks. But for now I must wait. I lay down, quieted my thoughts, and dozed, coming awake now and again to check the progress of the stars. At last, when the night was deep and silent, I awoke to the rumbling snores of Menelaus coming from the inner room. *Good.* He was making enough noise in his sleep that he likely wouldn't hear me. I reached into the hearth with a twig to find a live ember and lit a lamp. I rubbed handfuls of ashes into my hair to dull it and lighten it. With a stick of charcoal I smudged shadows under my eyes, drew furrows between my brows and lines running from the sides of my nose down to my chin. I had no way to see myself, but with any luck I looked like an older woman. Wrapping myself in the gray shawl I had stolen from Klymene, I inched toward the door and opened it. The wood squeaked against the floorboards. I held my breath to listen. Menelaus was still snoring. Lifting the door to ease it open, I slipped out into the courtyard.

Just outside, I stopped. If Menelaus roused, if a guard came, I could still say I was on my way to the privy. But once I took the next fateful steps, there would be no turning back. This was the most daring thing I had ever tried. If caught, I would be put to death. A primitive fear closed my throat. In my former life I might never have found the courage, but I had nothing left to lose, and if I stayed here, the Achaeans were bound to kill me anyway.

I took a deep breath and stepped forward. A bright moon broke free of wispy clouds. Keeping to shadows, I stole toward the courtyard gate. When I was halfway there, the murmur of voices stopped me. Menelaus's guards were just on the other side.

I flattened myself against the fence to listen. A mutter. A yawn. A shifting of positions. An unintelligible curse. They were silent for a moment, the silence charged with some kind of tension. Then I heard a clicking noise and the thud of something landing in the dirt.

"Zeus!" The sharp hiss made me jump. "The luck you have! Very well. I'll wager a bronze cup on the next toss."

A low laugh. "And you, my friend, will finish the night without so much as a cooking pot or a stitch of clothing to call your own."

I let out my breath. They were gambling over knucklebones. I followed the fence to a point around the corner from the gate. Looping my shawl over one of the palisades, I pulled myself up, found a foothold, and dropped to the other side, landing in the dirt with a soft thump. I crouched motionless, holding my breath.

Silence. Suddenly, a harsh curse. Then a voice: "Your toss!"

I breathed. Got to my feet. I looked around. No one stirring. I hoped Agamemnon's men had given up for the night. Ducking around the building, I started across a large open space toward the main gate of the camp—the last obstacle. The hardest. If I found more than one guard on duty, that would make it far more dangerous.

A cold wind blew as I approached the gate. I rehearsed my story: I was Menelaus's unwilling servant, sent on a mission I dreaded, but I feared Menelaus even more.

I would not have to feign fear. My mouth was so dry I could hardly swallow. Near the gate I stopped, unable to take another step. This was madness! I was inviting death. Was it not enough that I had escaped Menelaus and Agamemnon? If I went to the farthest end of the camp, I could surely find some slave women who might shelter me.

I stood still for so long the night wind penetrated my bones. Then I took a few slow steps.

"*Who goes there?*" The shout froze my blood. A man had stepped out of the enclosure of the gate and was looking at me in the moonlight. He came across the open space toward me.

"Sir—" I was shaking, but there was no turning back. He pulled me to the gate, where a lamp burned on a ledge. He was alone, thank the gods!

"Let me see you," he growled. I held my breath, but no flicker of recognition showed in his hard face. "Who are you? Whom do you serve?"

"I belong to Menelaus," I whispered.

"Your name?"

I gave my sister-in-law's name. "Pherusa."

"What are you doing here?"

I heaved a shuddering sigh. "Menelaus wishes me to cross the plain to Troy and steal into the city in secret to get a message to his wife." Nothing showed in his face. "Helen," I added.

Heavy skepticism filled his silence. At last he said, "What message?"

"That her child is ill. That she should come back to him so they can sail home."

The guard's dark brows lowered over beady eyes. "Her child? In Sparta? Ill? How could Menelaus know that?"

I shrugged. "For all I know, it's just a ruse."

He looked at me for a long time, then asked, "How can I be sure Menelaus sent you?"

I pulled the brooch from my sash. "By this token, sir. He said you'd recognize it."

The man snatched it up, held it to the light. His breath snorted out. "This is his, all right! I've seen him wear it many times." He handed the brooch back to me but looked unconvinced. Before he could think too long, I produced the gold armband. "He also bade me give you this, sir. For your silence. He doesn't wish his brother, King Agamemnon, to know of his plan."

This would sound plausible to anyone who knew the brothers. The guard took the armband and studied it by the light of his lamp, but still hesitated

I decided to bluff. "If you doubt me, sir, you must ask him yourself." I paused, drew a deep breath. "Or better still, send me back. I don't want to go. It's too dangerous! I'll tell him you wouldn't let me through the gate."

He grunted. "Why send a captive woman?" he asked. "What assurance would he have that you'd complete your mission and return?"

I had a ready answer, and my voice shook, making the lie all the more convincing. "My lord Menelaus will kill my babe if I don't."

The guard was silent again. I dared not breathe. At last he said, "Then you must do his bidding. You're just a slave, after all." But his big body stood too still.

I realized my fear and seeming reluctance were my strongest weapons. "What if it's suicide?" I asked. "I heard that the last spy was caught and beheaded."

"If you're killed, it's nothing to me." He sounded annoyed. He turned and lifted the large timber that barred the gate. I dared not breathe. A creak, a groan of wood. He started to open the gate—then stopped. "Wait!" He stared at me narrowly. "How does Menelaus expect you to get into Troy—and out again?"

I had not thought of this. Yet from the gods, perhaps, came words of inspiration. "I've been to Troy many times, sir," I lied. "I know of a—a drainage sluice in the wall. On the far side. Big enough for a small person to crawl through in the dry season."

"And just how do you expect to find Helen?"

"The women," I breathed. "I know many of them from when I was free."

He said nothing. In the east, behind Troy, the sky was changing from black to murky gray. I looked toward it—clasped my hands together—trembled.

"Sir!" I said desperately. "It grows late! I must get into the city before dawn—or abandon the mission."

His gaze followed mine. Then he turned to me. "Go then! But if you have lied," he said, his voice colder than the night wind, "I will personally see to your death."

He shoved the gate open, and I sped through. With a thud, he lowered the beam back into place. I was on the outside. *Free!*

Elena Douglas

Warrior's Prize

PART TWO

THE DARK RIVER

Elena Douglas

CHAPTER 27

> How the night passes!
> Dawn is near: high stars have all gone down.
> Two thirds of night are gone...
>
> *Iliad,* Homer, Book X
> (Fitzgerald's translation)

The vast darkness of the Trojan plain lay ahead. When I was sure the guard could no longer see me, I sprinted like a pent-up beast set free. I wanted to get far away from the camp, to let the night wind cleanse the stench of it from my skin. But a sharp pain in my side stopped me. Weak from days in my prison, I bent over, hands on my knees, gasping for breath. When I could continue, I looked around to make sure I was alone. The camp, far behind me, was only a low, uneven line along the shore. The moon dipped toward the black expanse of the sea.

I started again on my journey. For the first time since I had left Achilleus's hut, I breathed deeply with relief. But how empty a world it was, in which I would never see him again—the pain felt as raw as when I'd first learned he was gone.

Dwelling on it only brought sorrow. I forced myself to focus on the terrain ahead, where dark hills rose behind the high ground of Troy. Along the southern horizon loomed the mass of Mount Ida, on the other side of which lay my lost home. Clouds swept across the moon, plunging me into deeper darkness. The ground became damp and uneven. I sank ankle-deep in mire, mud squelching in my sandals, until I found firmer ground. The moon reappeared, its light shimmering on water. I had reached the Scamander, the stream that ribboned across the plain.

I found a wide, shallow rocky place to cross, and on the other side walked on hard-packed dirt marked with holes and slashed by ruts. I stopped. Chariot wheels, horses' hooves, men's feet had made these marks, imprinting the soil with a tale of battle. For a moment I couldn't move or take my eyes from those moonlit scars in the ground. Had many died here by the river? A horrible vision formed in my mind: the riverbank in daylight, aswarm with hordes of men, in chariots and on foot, slashing and killing, and Achilleus in the lead, ruthless and filled with rage as he wielded his spear. I saw the waters of the river, blood red, choked with bodies, rising in an angry flood. Then the vision faded, leaving only the stillness of waning night. But its lingering horror chilled my bones.

It was a fancy, a trick of the mind. It could not be real. The night wind of this haunted place sent shivers through me. I tightened my shawl around me and walked on.

The sky had grown light behind the foothills. I came to a spring and stopped to rinse my muddy feet, wash my face, shake the ashes from my hair and bind it properly. When I started up again, I could discern the looming walls of stone, the square towers of a dark citadel.

I crept forward to stand beneath the forbidding walls. Troy, mightiest of cities, whose riches and arrogance were said to have so angered the gods that they had brought the Achaeans to these shores to besiege it. Awe-filled, I touched the huge stones of its walls, Cyclopean stones said to have been placed here by the gods many aeons ago. Tilting my head back, I looked up at the heights of a tower. Beneath it was a massive timber gate. Certain that a watch was kept there, I stood before it and called out loudly, "Let me in!"

Silence. Then a stir. A voice from above. "Who goes there?"

"I've fled from the enemy!" I shouted. "I bring you news."

A much longer silence this time. I pictured a guard coming down a staircase in the dark. Then came a creaking noise. A crack of deeper blackness appeared, widening as the gate opened slightly. Something poked at me out of the darkness, something sharp and cold that pricked my collarbone. The point of a javelin. The man who held it was a shadow that seemed not to breathe. A second shadow appeared next to him, his breastplate catching a faint glint. Both men wore armor. Some kind of wordless signal passed between them. The javelin was withdrawn and a hand seized my arm, pulling me through the opening. I heard the gate shut with a thud. The darkness was complete.

"Please," I said, "I need to see Prince Hektor."

"Hektor?" One of them gave a snort. "Hektor doesn't waste his time on spies."

"Sir, I'm an escaped captive." My voice shook. "I bring news of the enemy."

"So you say," grunted the man on my right. "But it looks like the Achaeans are using their whores as spies now. You'll come with us to the barracks."

A chill ran down my spine. As they pulled me forward, I reminded myself that at least I was safe from Menelaus and Agamemnon.

I felt them step upward, and my foot struck something hard—a stair. I thought we would climb to the top of the tower, but we only went up four or five steps, then followed a short passage, until we reached a door outlined in pale light. One of the guards flung it open, and I saw a street and houses, the sky lit with the first gray wash of dawn.

I glanced at the guards. One had a thick black beard, the other a pitted skin and a jaw covered with stubble. Both looked grim and weary. The one with the beard shouted to someone at the top of the tower. "Keep watch until we return!" He took my arm. "This way." We went up a steep, narrow street crowded with houses. Children stared at us from doorways—thin, hollow-cheeked children in rags. Sometimes a woman's face looked out, bleak and anxious. The smell of wood smoke blended with the stench of the refuse pit. Halfway up the street, a young woman ran out of a house and threw herself on her knees before my guards. She was big with child and clutched a babe of about a year.

"Please, good sirs!" She held up her free hand in supplication. "Let me come with you to the barracks for some barley meal."

"You've had your rations for the day," said the bearded guard. "What's left is needed for the fighting men."

"But my little one is ill with hunger!" Her eyes met mine as the guard shoved her aside.

"We can do nothing," the bearded guard said. Then he relented. "More supplies will be coming in from Dardania in a few days." As we moved on, my heart dropped in dismay. So this was Troy after nine years of warfare. It could not provide for its own.

We turned down an alley and came to a wide courtyard. Everywhere in the gray light I saw warriors milling about—the warriors of Troy, who so staunchly fought the Achaeans. I felt a surge of pride.

"Where shall we take her?" the bearded guard asked.

"I say we handle this ourselves," the other said. "We'll search her for weapons, then put her in the lock-up cells."

I looked from one to the other in dismay, but they did not meet my eyes. My knees were shaking. "I'm no spy," I said. "I have news for Hektor." Several warriors nearby noticed us and approached. I hoped one of them might come to my aid, but their faces remained impassive. "My husband was the Prince of Lyrnessos," I said loudly enough for the bystanders to hear. "Hektor knew him."

The guards merely looked at me in stolid silence. Then the pockmarked one said, "Hold her." He shoved me to his companion. "I'll make sure she's unarmed."

The bearded man held my arms behind me so tightly that pain shot up to my shoulders. The other guard brought his hands slowly down my body. A grin twitched his lips. My skin went hot with shame. I lifted my head and looked away, as if I were made of stone and could not feel his touch.

The pockmarked man dropped his hands, still leering. "Shall we have some sport with her before we lock her up?"

A surge of fear went through me. I tried to pull away. The bearded guard tightened his hold. I looked appealingly at the men around us—and had another shock. Lewd, arrogant faces stared back. Someone I couldn't see shouted, "Let's take turns!" and the men pushed closer.

"Aye, take her up on the walls—let the Achaeans see," another said, grabbing my arm. Big male bodies jostled me, breathing in my face.

"We have Helen, and now we have this one."

There were shouts of laughter. "Seems they can't keep their women!"

I felt sick with the same terror and helplessness I had known in Lyrnessos, surrounded by the enemy. Only this was worse, for here was betrayal where I had expected welcome. "Sirs," I said in a voice that quavered, "I too am an enemy of the Achaeans."

More jeers answered me. "One of their whores, you mean!"

I jerked hard against the bearded man's grip, but only succeeded in colliding with the men closest to me. Someone grabbed me in a rough embrace. I couldn't breathe. Then, from the corner of my eye, I saw a movement, someone pushing through the crowd. A man thrust himself into the circle with an explosive cry. *"Leave her alone!"* Faces swung around to look at the newcomer, but held fast and hemmed in as I was, I could not see him. "Free her!" he shouted, and the guard, surprised, dropped my arms. The nearest men reluctantly backed away.

He came to me and took my hands in his. "My lady! Briseis!" So startled I could not utter a sound, I found myself looking into a youthful, bearded face framed by curly black hair, with eyes as brown, as sweet, as warm as honey. I knew that face.

"Do you remember me?" he asked. "The slope of Mount Ida. You tended my wound."

His name came to me. "Akamas!" I cried. My weakened fingers clung to his hands. The welcome in his face almost made me weep.

"Don't mistreat this lady!" he told the guards. "I know her. She saved my life." His eyes came back to me, and he smiled. The sky became golden as the sun rose. His smile washed over me with the same lambent light. "I owe you a great debt," Akamas said. "I'm glad I found you."

"I'm glad too," I whispered.

The warriors backed away. But the guards stayed, flanking me with obvious mistrust.

Akamas ignored them. "How did you come here?" he asked me.

"I was captured that day in Lyrnessos," I told him. "Last night I escaped."

"That's wonderful!" He was still holding my hands. "I'll take you to my commander, Prince Aeneas."

"No, you won't," the pockmarked guard said. "Your master may be Prince of Dardania, but here he's just another fighting man."

"Then let me take her to my home—in Dardania. We'll be going back there in a day or two for supplies." For a moment Akamas's narrowed eyes challenged the two guards as if to remind them where their bread came from. Then he smiled at me. *Dardania*, I thought. The lushest valley nestled in the arms of Mount Ida, rich in clear springs and running rivers. Akamas's smile promised me refuge there. With all my heart I wanted what he offered, but, when I thought of the rutted battlefield, the hungry children, the pregnant woman begging for food, I knew I had to complete my task.

"I must speak to Hektor, Akamas. I have information. Can you help me to see him?"

Akamas nodded. "Aye, I can, and—"

"Nay!" the guard interrupted. "She may be a spy or an assassin. Just because she's a woman—" He seized my arm.

"By the gods!" Akamas cried. "Let her go!" He took my other arm protectively. But the guard yanked me away. "When Aeneas hears of this—" Akamas warned.

"What is this?" demanded a new voice, harsh with authority. We all turned. Akamas and the guard spoke as one.

"Prince Hektor!"

The sun behind him cast his long shadow over us, so that at first I was aware only of a looming darkness. But I remembered him from the day of his wedding to Andromache. He was tall and broad-shouldered, handsome in a stern, forbidding way. Straight black hair was pulled back from his forehead and hung to his shoulders. His deep-set black eyes glittered. His lips were thin and drawn, as if laughter were a stranger to them. I noted his strong, clean-shaven jaw. He held himself rigidly straight. Authority emanated from him, as visible as his shadow.

I made a deep obeisance, touching one knee to the ground. "My lord Prince, I beg you to hear what I have come to say."

"Who are you?" Hektor asked me.

"Briseis, widow of Mynes," I answered. His straight black brows were drawn together, his eyes hard. "You knew my husband—the prince of Lyrnessos. And I was at your wedding."

"Hundreds were at my wedding. I do not know *you*."

"I do," Akamas insisted. "I met her in the hills the day the Achaeans raided Lyrnessos."

Hektor frowned. "Thebe fell too, that day. My wife's family—her father, her brothers, all were killed by a single hand!" His fists were clenched so tightly that a tremor ran through his arms. "Your husband," he demanded suddenly, "did the same hand slay him?"

"Aye," I whispered.

"Achilleus!" His eyes blazed. "I will have vengeance."

"Sir," I began, "that is what I have come to tell you, that he—"

He interrupted. "How came you here? I thought all the women of Lyrnessos were taken captive. And one so fair as you—"

"I was taken captive," I said quickly, "but I escaped."

"Ah!" He shot me a sharp look. "And who was your Achaean master?"

The question punched the breath from my lungs. I had not expected it so quickly. A lump rose in my throat. "A-Agamemnon," I stammered.

"So," he asked with obvious skepticism, "you've been with Agamemnon all this time? And only just escaped?"

My heart pounded so hard I was afraid those penetrating black eyes would notice the quiver of my gown. Akamas, a pace behind me, was listening intently. One of the guards' sandals scraped the dirt. The silence stretched out until I knew I had to give Hektor the truth.

"Agamemnon took me—stole me," I said. "Before that, I belonged to— someone else."

Hektor's hands grasped my shoulders. "Who?"

"Achilleus," I whispered.

He dropped his hands and went still. When I looked up, his face was flushed. In his eyes were the banked fires of some deep emotion. "Achilleus's prize!" His voice resonated with triumph. "Apollo is good to me. Akamas, you did well to keep these oafs from harming her." I let out my breath in relief. Hektor would surely keep me safe.

Akamas took my arm again. "What are you going to do with her?"

"Leave her to me." Hektor made an impatient gesture. "You'll come with me," he said, taking my other arm. He started to walk, pulling me along.

Akamas let go reluctantly. "Tell me when I may see her again." Hektor shrugged and kept walking. Akamas, following, caught my hand. "We *will* meet again, Briseis—" But his steps faltered, and my hand slid from his grasp. He stood still, watching us go.

As I matched my steps to Hektor's, I became aware that the prince was laughing softly, coldly, triumphantly.

CHAPTER 28

"I will meet him face to face, even if his hands
are like fire and his spirit like flashing steel!"

—Hektor, *Iliad*, Homer, Book XX
(Rouse's translation)

In silence Hektor led me out of the barracks courtyard, uphill along a wide street paved with flagstones. At the top of the slope, the street leveled off and widened into a broad avenue that ran along one wing of an immense, sprawling palace. This wing was a series of connected dwellings. Here must be where the sons and daughters of King Priam lived. Hektor opened a gate leading into a large courtyard with trees and cisterns and led me to the door of his dwelling. We entered a hall where an old serving woman stood over the hearth, poking the fire and stirring a pot. She straightened to stare at us. I blinked in the dimness as Hektor shed his cloak and flung it over a chair.

"Fetch Andromache," he ordered the serving woman.

As she scurried from the room, Hektor turned to look at me. "So you were Achilleus's woman," he said softly, "or one of them. From what I hear, none but the loveliest will do for him." He had taken hold of my wrists and seemed unaware that he was squeezing them, unaware that he was holding me at all. He turned me toward the daylight that poured in from the opening above the hearth and subjected me to a piercing, impersonal scrutiny. I had the odd sense that had Achilleus's most prized gold libation cup fallen into his hands, he would have studied it in just the same manner. It was not I, but his enemy, that fascinated Hektor.

"And yet he gave you up," he mused. "Surely not without a fight? And why? Tell me *everything!*"

Discomfited, I scarcely knew how to begin. I must let him know at once that Achilleus was gone. But before I could speak, a young woman emerged from an inner chamber carrying a baby. She paused on the threshold. It took me a moment to recognize Andromache. She had changed since her wedding. Her face was still lovely and grave, but the wide dark eyes were set in hollows, filled with sadness. Hektor dropped my hands and turned to her, his tension gone, his manner gentle.

"My love, this woman has escaped the Achaean camp," he told her. "She was the war prize of Achilleus."

I expected the name to bring shock and revulsion to Andromache's face. Instead, she gave Hektor an indignant look. "Then she came at great peril. No doubt she's tired and hungry, yet you keep her standing while you question her!" Hektor looked at me, startled, as if Andromache had caused him to see me for the first time. "Here, hold Astyanax." She handed him the baby and turned to me. "Come! I shall make up for his rudeness." She smiled. Taking my hand she led me to a chair by the fire. Her small hand was thin-boned and so cold that I clasped it firmly. Over my shoulder, I glanced at

Hektor. To my surprise, the stern warrior had taken his chastisement with no more than a rueful grin. He seemed a different man in his wife's presence.

"Chloe, is that wine warm yet?" The serving woman was fussing over the fire. Andromache stirred the pot, while Hektor sat holding the baby. I noticed, in the soft blend of firelight and early daylight, how haggard the prince looked, as if the past night had not eased his weariness. There were lines under his eyes, and the skin over his high, proud cheekbones was stretched taut. But a tender smile touched his lips and lingered in his eyes as he watched Andromache. She, without looking at him, returned the smile like a caress. Theirs was no stormy love but a rare and quiet refuge. A pain struck me, making my eyes sting. Inexplicably I felt that, by stepping into that radiant circle I had brought a turmoil that would tear it apart. The feeling was so strong that I wanted to flee, though I knew I could not.

Andromache brought me a cup, and Hektor turned to me. "My wife is right to chide me," he said. "I have neglected my duties as a host. Drink and be refreshed."

I sipped, letting the warmth of the wine disperse my dark thoughts.

"Have some bread." Andromache offered me the basket.

The baby's nurse came in, took him from Hektor, and set him on a blanket by the hearth. He sat up, fluffy black hair standing on end, bright black eyes fixed on me. Then he showed two teeth in a sudden smile. The nurse handed him a piece of bread, which he shoved into his mouth, sucking it, shredding it, gurgling with delight. I reached a finger toward him and smiled as his tiny hand closed around it. Yet at the touch of his warm flesh, a darkness fell within me. *Oh, little one! I thought. What will happen to you?* I had no idea where the thought came from. I glanced up quickly to make sure Hektor and Andromache had seen nothing in my face. But they were looking at each other. Presently, the nurse came forward to take the baby into the inner room. The serving woman, too, departed and Hektor turned to face me. Andromache pulled her chair close, slipped her hand into his fingers, and regarded me with an anxious smile.

"My husband hasn't told me your name," she said.

"Briseis," I responded. "From Lyrnessos. I attended your wedding in Thebe. I have never forgotten that day."

Her smile faded, and she turned to Hektor, who frowned at me as his hand tightened around hers. Too late, I recalled how painful the thought of Thebe must be.

"Tell us," Hektor said, "what news you bring."

I began in a breathless hurry, anxious to wipe the stricken look from Andromache's face. "A plague struck the Achaean camp," I said, "and hundreds died. Then Agamemnon and Achilleus quarreled. And Achilleus has withdrawn and gone. So the Achaean forces are greatly depleted and disheartened. If you smite them now—"

"Wait!" Hektor's eyes narrowed. "You go too fast. What of this quarrel? Start at the beginning."

I told him of Chryseis and the refused ransom, the plague, and what little I knew of the terrible assembly. I spoke haltingly, omitting only what had happened between Achilleus and me. Still, as Hektor listened, I had the uncomfortable sense that he was reading far more from me than what I was telling him in words. He looked at me piercingly, mistrustfully. "And how did you manage to escape your captors?" he demanded. So I told him of my flight from

Agamemnon, then Menelaus, and the ruse by which I had left the camp. When I finished he was silent. He got up and stood with his back to me, staring into the hearth.

"Is Achilleus immortal, as I've heard tell?" he asked suddenly without turning.

"What?" I said, surprised.

"There's a story going around, because the men have never seen him wounded. They say that when he was an infant his mother dipped him into the River Styx to make him invulnerable. They say he can't be wounded except in one heel, where his mother held him. Is this true?"

A memory came to me: Achilleus in Lyrnessos, the lines of my nails on his cheek, the bright droplets of blood against his skin. "No. He is no more invulnerable than you or I," I said, more harshly than I intended.

"Indeed." I was afraid Hektor would pursue the subject, but he said, "Tell me what you know of Agamemnon. What sort of king is he, what sort of war leader?"

"A weak and vacillating one, I think, sir. Menelaus, his brother, seems to have little confidence in him."

Hektor paced the room. "Alienating his greatest chieftain is hardly the move of a wise king." He came to my chair, rested his hand on the back of it. "I thank you, Briseis! You have brought me the best of news." But still he searched my face suspiciously, his scrutiny so intense it frightened me. At last, he dropped his hand and turned away. As if thinking aloud, he said, "I wonder what Achilleus will do now."

"Do?" Astonishment brought me to the edge of my seat. Evidently he hadn't caught the import of the most momentous piece of news I'd brought. "Why, I told you, sir. He's gone. He sailed for home."

Hektor stood transfixed, looking at me, a glitter in his eyes. His eyebrows came down, compressing his brow, and he was once again the stern, aloof commander he had been at the barracks. Andromache opened her lips to speak but closed them again when Hektor shot a glance at her. "How did you learn this, Briseis, if, as you say, you were locked up?" His voice was so quiet and cold it raised the hairs on the back of my neck.

"They told me so, Agamemnon and Menelaus both," I said.

"And you're sure of it."

"Aye. Or else I would never—" I stopped, biting my lip.

Hektor nodded bleakly. "Or else you would never have come here," he finished for me. "So now we know." Under his frown, his black eyes had not a spark of light. "You want me to kill Agamemnon and avenge the wrong he did to Achilleus."

"Nay!" I protested.

Hektor waited. One side of his mouth curved upward in a bitter sickle of a smile, and his eyes demanded a fuller truth.

I drew a deep breath. "If I'd remained with Achilleus, I would have accepted my lot. Is that a crime? But he abandoned me to Agamemnon, a drunken, bloodthirsty madman who tried to kill me. Can you hold it against me that I fled? Aye, I want Agamemnon dead! But only because he's the leader of the Achaeans, the cause of all our troubles. I want this war to end." I sank back, breathless from my vehemence.

Hektor stood still, his eyes cold as polished stones. He looked at Andromache, and some message passed between them. Then he sat down opposite me, pulling his chair closer.

His smile was twisted. "With Achilleus gone, you will pledge your loyalty to Troy, is that right?"

"With all my heart." Yet my stomach knotted. He was hiding something.

"Then swear it to me!" The smile was gone, the voice like a lash.

My throat was dry. "Aye, I swear by the gods."

"Good!" He leaned back in his chair, the corners of his lips lifting slightly. "Andromache, refill our guest's goblet, if you please. And I could use a cup myself." As she bustled about, filling goblets with the still-warm brew from the hearth, Hektor got up suddenly to join her. Taking his cup, he leaned his head close to hers and whispered something. He went on at some length. Andromache looked unhappy but finally nodded. Carrying the cups between them, they returned to their chairs. My skin prickled. Hektor held up his glass with a slight smile before lifting it to his lips. What did he want from me? Something was concealed in that smile, which did not banish the coldness in his eyes.

After we all had a sip of wine, Andromache asked abruptly, "What was life like in Achilleus's camp?" I must have looked startled, for she amended, "I mean, were there many captives? How did you live? Was your lot a hard one?" These should have been natural questions from one woman to another, but her voice sounded forced.

Puzzled, I said, "No harder than the lot of most women. Many shared the work. Achilleus was fair to his captives, and —" I fell silent, thinking of all I had lost.

Hektor frowned. As if reading my thoughts, he asked, "Did he favor you?"

"I thought so. Right after I was taken captive, Patroklos said—" But it was too painful to remember the wedding once promised me in Phthia, and I couldn't go on. My head sank lower.

Abruptly Hektor's prying changed direction. "Ah! Who is this Patroklos?"

Why does he want to know this? "Achilleus's friend, his foster brother. His second in command," I answered unwillingly.

"I've seen Achilleus often in battle," Hektor said, "in his war chariot with his magnificent horses. The other man in the chariot, the one who held the reins—that would have been Patroklos?"

"Aye," I answered nervously. I had more information about the Achaeans: the number of troops, the layout of the camp, Agamemnon's foolish plan to test the men. But Hektor had not even asked me.

"I saw Patroklos fall into danger once," Hektor said. "In fact he was wounded. Achilleus fought with no regard for his own life to save his friend. This Patroklos is dear to him?"

Why is he probing? "Dearer than his own life," I admitted, then wished I hadn't spoken.

An odd light shone in his eyes. "And you, Briseis? Were you equally dear to him?"

I lowered my eyes and shook my head. "I thought—maybe—but in the end I was just his prize, his meed of honor. When Agamemnon stole me, his pride was hurt. Nothing more."

"I wonder. If that were all, I don't think he would have—" Hektor bit off what he had been about to say and changed it to, "I don't think he would have taken such a drastic step."

He got to his feet. "So it would appear that Achilleus is ruled by his heart. He can be goaded into rashness by a threat to someone dear to him."

I looked up, astonished, afraid. "What does this matter to you?"

With a burst of anger he said, "Remember, whatever happens, you have sworn your loyalty to Troy."

Andromache made a choked sound and half-rose. Hektor frowned at her. I gripped my chair, angry that he had manipulated me into speaking of Achilleus. I had been truthful, while he was withholding something. I was about to speak when Andromache burst forth suddenly, "Must you go through with this, my husband?"

I stared. *Go through with what?*

Hektor rose and touched her cheek with gentle fingers. "You know I must. But all will be well. Trust in the gods, my dear."

At that moment a woman's voice called from the courtyard. Andromache started. "It's your sister, Kassandra."

Hektor shrugged. "She's come to advise me, no doubt. Though my mind is made up. Go and make her welcome," he said, "and tell her—" His keen glance conveyed the rest of the message as clearly to me as to Andromache. *Tell her not to mention what we are concealing from Briseis.*

As she went out, Hektor came and looked down at me. "I'm sorry, Briseis, but this is war. There are some hard decisions to be made." Then he turned to spread his hands over the warmth of the fire. His shoulders slumped wearily, and I detected a slight tremor in his fingers. My anger faded as pity took its place. The war leader of Troy stood before me, suddenly only a tired, burdened man whose hands were cold.

A moment later the door went dark. A figure materialized there and stood suspended in stillness—a tall girl in a black robe. She resembled Hektor and was strikingly beautiful. Straight black hair cascaded down her back. Followed by Andromache, she entered and looked at me with dark eyes even more piercing than Hektor's. Then she turned to her brother. Her movements were tense and vehement.

"I heard about your unexpected guest," she said. When she spoke I realized that she was very young—no more than seventeen.

"News travels swiftly," he muttered.

"Andromache told me what you intend to do."

An uneasy look passed between husband and wife. "And you've come to try to dissuade me," Hektor said.

"No. I know there's no stopping you or turning you from your course. But sometimes I can see the future, and—"

"You expect me to believe that your ravings are true prophecy?" Hektor interrupted.

Kassandra lifted her chin. "It is a gift from Apollo."

"Well then, speak if you must. What is it you see for me?"

"You will prevail, up to a point." The girl's eyes had become glazed like a blind person's. Her inner sight seemed to leap across forbidden barriers and unimagined distances. Hektor and Andromache were listening, half unwilling yet frozen in stillness. "I see you standing in triumph on the battlefield," she said without joy—without hope. She lowered her face and twisted the richly embroidered sleeves of her gown. "I see you wearing the armor of Achilleus."

She's raving, I thought. *She hasn't heard that Achilleus has left*. Yet the blood left my heart. Hektor's voice, fierce, exultant, filled the room. "So Apollo will grant me victory!"

"But wait!" Kassandra said. "I see a shadow falling over you—before the Skaian Gate—Ayeee!" Her voice rose to a wail. She shut her eyes and pressed her hands to her temples. Cold ripples ran on my skin. *She's seen his death,* I thought. At last she straightened and stood still, her face wiped clean of all expression.

Andromache gave a stifled cry. Hektor closed his fists. "You're full of evil tidings! I will not listen."

But Kassandra went on, as if she could not help herself. "You will have your day of glory," she said in a muffled tone. "And you'll be remembered in the songs of men."

"Well," Hektor said lightly. "I can ask for no more."

Andromache stood rigid, her face pale. "Kassandra, I wish you wouldn't speak of these things," she whispered. "We cannot know—it is not given to us to know the future."

"I do know it." Kassandra's voice was sorrowful. "Only people choose not to believe me." She turned to go. Then her eyes fell on me. "And what of your luckless pawn?" she asked Hektor. "Will you keep her—or send her back?"

Pawn? I reared up in my chair. Send me back? His words of apology suddenly took on an ominous meaning.

"Hush, Kassandra!" Hektor said fiercely.

"It makes no difference." Her eyes lingered on me for a moment. Then she turned slowly and went out.

Stunned, I got to my feet. Andromache cast a look at me, a look of pain, I thought, but at some sound from the baby, she went into the inner room, as if glad of the excuse to leave.

I faced Hektor. "You can't send me back! They'd kill me."

"Would they? I'm not so sure."

"You don't understand!" I cried. "Agamemnon almost killed me in a fit of madness. Menelaus is sane and sober, and he plans to sacrifice me to Athena to give the troops hope again."

Hektor looked at me sharply. "How do you know that?"

"When he hid me from Agamemnon, he said he wanted me for some purpose of his own—he mentioned an offering. Then I overheard him talking to his brother, proposing a sacrifice to Athena."

Hektor gave a sudden hearty laugh. "So you concluded you were to be the goddess's victim. Oh no, I don't think so! It was not Athena he intended to give you to." Abruptly he sobered. "Have no fear, we will not send you back. The offering—the lure—must stay in Troy."

"What do you mean?"

He looked at me intently. "You are very lovely, Briseis. And all his actions prove he is not indifferent to you. Surely he wants you back." My heart gave a violent lurch. Hektor was not speaking of Menelaus—or even Agamemnon. "When he knows I have you, Achilleus will meet me face to face. And I will kill him."

The words went through me like a knife. "You can't," I whispered. "He's gone!"

Hektor shook his head. "So you were led to believe. Or else you lied." He gave a chilly smile. "But we watch their camp from our battlements. We observe them daily. And this much we know: his ships have not sailed."

CHAPTER 29

...So Andromache spoke weeping...

Iliad, Homer, Book XXIV
(Rouse's translation)

He spoke the truth. My heart knew it at once. Agamemnon had lied, and Menelaus had embellished the lie.

As the import flooded through me, I sank into my chair. *Achilleus here!* Only a short distance away. *He didn't leave me after all.* If I had stayed in the Achaean camp, I might have returned to him somehow. Yet I had allowed myself to be duped by the king and his brother, and now I'd lost all hope of ever seeing him again.

Even worse, I had made him vulnerable to his enemy. Hektor would use me against him. I mustn't let it happen. I must find a way to get out of Troy—

Watching me, Hektor laughed harshly. "It appears you didn't mean to betray him."

Betray. The word stabbed me. I thought of what I'd told Hektor. Surely not much! Only that Achilleus was not invulnerable, which Hektor must already know, and that Achilleus cared for Patroklos. The rest he had deduced for himself: *He is ruled by his heart. He can be goaded into rashness by a threat to someone dear to him.* Could I undo the harm?

"I betrayed nothing!" I retorted. "You infer too much. Achilleus *let* Agamemnon take me. He told the whole assembled army that he would not fight for me."

"Ah!" Hektor smiled grimly. "How do you know that?"

I bit my lip. "Agamemnon told me."

"Another lie?"

I was silent.

"If that's the case, why does Achilleus stay? What is he waiting for?" When I made no reply, Hektor said, "He knows his part in the war isn't over. And I'm sure he can't resist a challenge. With you as bait, I will lure him into single combat."

Mortal combat. My blood turned to ice. If he died, it would be my doing, because I had come here and allied myself with Hektor. But I couldn't give in to my terror. I must prevent this, even if I had no idea how. I sprang to my feet. "Let me go to him, Hektor! I'll persuade him to fight you if that's what you wish. It won't be hard. I'm sure he already wants to." I was babbling, willing to promise anything if only I could get back to Achilleus.

Hektor turned to face me, his eyes blazing. "You're lying," he said. "You're full of lies and deceit. I'm not such a fool as to believe you." He forced me back into my chair. "No, you'll stay right here. And don't try any treachery. All the men, all the sentries, will be warned about you. You'll no more get out of Troy than escape Hades itself."

Oh, gods! Oh, Aphrodite, help me! But there was no help, and as he swung away, I doubled over and crumpled into the darkness of my folded arms. I heard his heavy footsteps crossing the room, the door opening. Lighter, quicker steps followed. Voices from the other side of the room—the door closing. Moments of stillness. Then the light footsteps approached. A gentle hand came to rest on my shoulder. I lifted my head.

"Andromache." My voice sounded hoarse and strange to my own ears. "Where's Hektor gone? I must—speak to him." Though I had no idea what more I could say.

"He went to the barracks," she said. "Briseis, you look pale. Are you ill?" She pressed a warm goblet into my hands.

I took the cup and drank without tasting. Andromache sat in the chair next to me, watching. "You weren't lying," she said. "You really didn't know."

I barely heard her words. I set the goblet aside and covered my face with my hand. Only one thought was in my head. *I must get back to him. Somehow.*

Andromache sat so still and tense that I couldn't help being aware of her. I dropped my hand and turned to her.

"Briseis," she said, "Surely it would ease you to speak of it. Tell me—"

I drew a deep breath. Andromache might be friend or enemy. In her own way, she was more to be feared than Hektor. The grim look in her eyes showed fierce, implacable strength. Those eyes demanded a truth I could not hide. I looked up and let her read my heart.

"You love him." Her face revealed nothing. The firelight cast a gold reflection in the wet, glistening surfaces of her eyes. That revelation could imprison me more than all the walls and guarded gates of Troy. I wondered what she would do with it.

She lowered her eyes. Then, slowly, her hands came forward to grasp mine. The simple gesture lifted some of the weight from my heart. I gazed at her, feeling as fragile as an edifice of sand that might crumble in the slightest breeze.

"You don't hate me?" I asked at last.

"Nay, Briseis! We are not enemies, why should we be?" Her smile pierced me with its sadness. "We share this thing—this terrible loss for one of us."

"I've always known our fates were linked," I whispered.

"Always known? But we've only met today."

I tried to smile. "Don't forget, I watched you pledge yourself to Hektor. How I envied you that day! I envied your great love."

"And now?" she asked.

"Now I see it's only pain."

"Nay, but there's joy!" She gripped my hands. Two tears broke free and slid down her cheeks.

"I haven't had that kind of joy," I said sadly.

She made no answer, but across the bridge of our clasped hands, comfort flowed like an eddying wave so that I could not tell who offered it or who received it. We looked at each other silently until one of us made a move, and somehow we ended up clasped in each other's arms. Her embrace transported me to a territory I had not known since childhood. Mother-love, sister-love—life had until now denied me this closeness with another woman. When we released each other, she turned away, dabbing her eyes.

"I think I've always known that they must meet face to face," she said. "I'm so afraid Achilleus will kill him."

"Perhaps not." But I could not consider the alternative. I reached for her hand again. "Andromache," I said, "they must not meet. We can prevent it."

Her eyes widened with sudden hope. Then she shook her head. "You heard Hektor; there's no stopping him."

"Maybe we can stop Achilleus."

She sat very still. "How?"

"You must help me get out of Troy—tonight. Then I can go to him, and Hektor can't use me as—bait."

Doubt and mistrust creased her brow. "He warned me that you would try something like that. He—he told me to keep a watch on you."

"Because he wants to fight Achilleus above all else," I pressed. "He loves honor in battle more than his own life. They all do. And he wants to avenge *you!*" She made a small, choked sound. "But do you want that?" Her silence answered me. I leaned forward. "If I can get to Achilleus, I can surely persuade him to abandon the war and sail for home." Even as I spoke, I wondered if I could accomplish such a thing.

"Do you think so?" she asked doubtfully.

"When he withdrew, he swore some oath. He probably swore to stay out of battle." It was a guess. If only I could find out exactly what he had sworn! "He's half sick of this war already," I said, remembering what Patroklos had told me. "But I must go to him tonight, and he mustn't ever know I came to Troy."

For a moment she hesitated. Then she looked down, twisting the fringes of her shawl around tense white fingers.

"Andromache!" I insisted. "You, the commander's wife, can get me out of Troy."

She shook her head and looked up at me through tears. "He placed all his trust in me. I'm sorry, Briseis. I can't betray him."

That word again. I closed my eyes for an instant, then said relentlessly, "Not even to save his life? Think of your son —little Astyanax—"

A moan escaped her. She got to her feet, turned her back. She stood motionless for a long time, a hand pressed to her face. I could hardly breathe.

"Andromache, it's our only chance." Still she made no move. "Is it betrayal," I asked softly, "to protect your husband and son?"

Andromache sat down slowly. Her cheeks were pale as bleached bone, but she achieved a painful smile. "Hektor did not say I had to keep you prisoner in this house. If you go out the back door, you will find a gallery that connects all the royal apartments, and if you go to the left along this gallery and pass five doors, the sixth one..." She paused to draw a ragged breath. "The sixth one will take you to a woman who can help you. She knows all the sentries at all the gates, and is even, I suspect, on intimate terms with some. She is entirely without scruples." Andromache's voice vibrated with scorn. "She has no loyalty for either side in this war. If you can find a way to persuade her, she could get you out of Troy tonight."

My breath came fast. "And is she hard to persuade?"

Andromache shook her head. "I know not. Charm her, beguile her, entertain her. But hurry! You must go now, before Hektor returns." She stood up. "May the gods grant you success!"

Our hands clung for a moment, but there was no comfort now, only too much room for failure. She kissed my cheek quickly and stepped back. "I wish you well!"

I turned toward the door—then looked at her. "Who is this woman I am to see?"

"Her name is Helen."

CHAPTER 30

"No wonder Achaeans and Trojans have been fighting all these years for such a woman! ...she is like some divine creature come down from heaven."

Iliad, Homer, Book III
(Rouse's translation)

The morning sun slanted into the colonnaded gallery, dazzling my eyes with its reflection in the polished red and black paving stones. I counted the doors as I walked, and at the sixth one I knocked.

The door was opened by a dark-haired Trojan woman. I entered a large, sunny room where four or five women sat at their work. My gaze fell at once on the woman at the loom, a lovely woman wearing a rosy gown shot with gold thread. She was poised gracefully on the stool, one hand holding a length of purple wool, and she turned toward me, eyes widening. They were extraordinary eyes, the color and brilliance of sunlight shining through honey. Dark lashes fringed them, and delicate dark brows arched over them. Her hair was the deep tawny gold of polished oak. She had it drawn into thick coils and loops at the back of her neck. One solitary curl escaped to rest artlessly on the smooth naked shoulder, gleaming in the sun. Everything about Helen seemed to catch the light.

She rose and came toward me with a delighted smile dimpling her cheeks. Perhaps it was art, perhaps only an accident of facial structure and features, but that smile made me feel as if I were the very person Helen most wanted to see.

"Welcome! Welcome!" The voice was melodious and tinged with wonder. "A visitor! Sit down. Aithrê, fetch our guest a cup of wine."

A stool was brought, a goblet placed in my hand. The wine was sweet and fragrant. While I sipped, Helen sat with her hands clasped in her lap as if she could scarcely contain her eagerness to question me. At last she said, "You must be the woman who fled from the Achaeans!"

"Aye, I'm Briseis. How did you know?" I asked.

Her rosy lips came together coyly. "Word gets around," she said. "And I knew you were not Trojan. No Trojan woman would come here, except to malign me." She turned her head aside for a moment, and I saw the perfect profile with its up-tilted eye and softly molded cheek. "They all hate me, you know." She sighed. "Except for my own loyal ladies, of course!" She gestured at the others in the room. The ladies continued their work without looking up. Whatever they felt for their mistress, it was not to be read on their smooth, blank faces.

Helen smiled again. "It doesn't matter," she said. "You must tell me how you escaped the Achaean camp."

"My lady Helen." I glanced at the other women. "Gladly will I tell you, but first I have a favor to beg from you." I lowered my voice. "If we could talk alone..."

"Oh!" Swift comprehension came to her face, and her eyes took on a twinkle of mischief. "A secret! How exciting! Ladies!" She turned in her chair. "Go out for some air. Take a stroll along the walls—but tell no one about our guest."

When we were alone, Helen drew her chair up. "Now tell me." Her head tilted attentively to the side, and her face assumed a look of sweet, half-smiling gravity that set a dimple quivering in one cheek.

I mistrusted that facile sympathy. Still, I told her how I had come here and what Hektor planned to do. I left out all mention of Andromache.

"Ah!" she sighed, when I finished. "I understand very well. Men will use you for their conflicts—then they will blame you. Both sides will hate you. It is what happened to me." Her eyes took on a misty, reminiscing look. "All I did was run away with my lover. Has not many another woman done the same? Is it my fault they chose to fight a war? They are not just fighting for me! Yet everyone blames me." She lifted her hands in a graceful gesture of helplessness. "It's so unjust! Some days I wish I had never been born." But she spoke the words lightly and waved them away with delicate fingers. "Ah, well! No matter. More wine?"

She poured some for both of us. While she sipped I waited, held silent by a terrible doubt. I had nothing to offer her in exchange for the favor I came to ask. I had hoped that persuasion would be easy—a matter of asking. But Andromache had warned me. Helen would demand something in exchange. *Charm her, beguile her.* How?

Helen set her goblet down and smiled. "I so seldom get visitors, and it's such a pleasure to talk. Do you know, I have had no news at all of the Achaean camp?"

I raised my head. She was bored and isolated. Perhaps I did have something she wanted.

"You say you saw my husband." She grimaced. "Menelaus the mighty, Menelaus the anxious-hearted!" She clapped her hands together and laughed like a delighted child. "And my dearest brother-in-law, Agamemnon. How well I remember him! Has he grown any more charming with the years? I doubt it. And tell me of Achilleus. I do not know him, but I have seen him when I watched the fighting from the battlements. That one, I said to myself, would be well worth knowing. You must tell me about them all, my dear! You see how starved I am for news."

I hesitated. "About the favor, my lady—"

"Later! Later!" She waved an impatient hand. "Let's not get down to serious business just yet. Tell me about the Achaean men."

I forced a smile. I would give her what she wanted. Surely it would be a fair exchange for my favor.

I sipped wine and began to talk lightly. I spoke of Agamemnon and Menelaus, describing their faults with humorous exaggeration, as if these men had no power, no importance. And I was rewarded by Helen's tinkling laugh. She drank more wine. I tipped my goblet to my lips and drained it. Then I braced myself to tell her what she would want to hear about Achilleus. I described his beauty and his strength, though the words pained me. I watched her eyes grow wide with pleasure as the picture of him formed in her mind, and I forced myself to feel nothing when she said,

"Such a man! Had I met him in my youth, I would never have fled with Paris!"

At last I finished. I kept my lips sweetly smiling in mimicry of hers. I realized that, at all costs, Helen must smile, Helen must laugh, Helen must tell herself that she felt joy. But had I given her enough? I waited, hardly breathing while she took another sip of wine.

Then I said, "Helen, now I must beg you for your help."

She smiled charmingly. "My dear Briseis! I can guess what you've come for. It's written all over your face. You want to get out of Troy so that you cannot be used against Achilleus. You want to go to him, and cast yourself at his feet, and beg him to take you back. Is that not so?"

I nodded, dumbfounded.

"I cannot help you," she said.

I sat very still, gripping the chair. All at once there was not enough air to breathe, nothing solid beneath me.

"My dear, it would be treachery!" Helen said, as if I had protested.

And when did you ever stop at that? I wondered silently.

"I *am* sorry, Briseis! But I cannot go against Hektor. You must see that. These Trojans would kill me if I gave them the least excuse."

"Helen," I pleaded, "if you help me, the Trojans will win, and in the end they will thank you."

She smiled. Her shoulders gave the slightest, scornful lift.

I stared, astounded. "Don't you care?" Her smile never wavered, but she was silent. "What do you care about, Helen?" I demanded.

"I care for comfort—warm, perfumed water for my bath, women to wait on me, and men to admire me." She stretched her arms in the sunlight streaming through the window, holding out her white hands, the perfect nails like delicate, translucent pink shells, jewels glinting in the rings that adorned her fingers. She sighed. "I suppose I want Troy to win," she said. "But I am content to let them do it without my help. I am Prince Paris's most precious treasure, coveted by all the world. Why should I endanger that?"

Rage kindled in me. I shot to my feet. "Then you care nothing that, because you failed to help me, either Achilleus or Hektor will die?"

"That would be a great pity. Still…" Her hands gestured languidly and fell to her lap.

I wanted to strike her. "Is there nothing, no one, you love?"

A shadow crossed her face. She stood up. The bloom on her cheeks faded to a creamy pallor. She turned aside. The answer came so low I barely heard it. "I love my home—and I love my daughter."

"Daughter?" I had all but forgotten she had a child.

"My little Hermione. She was seven years old when I left Menelaus. Paris came along—a strong, tender lover. I thought I would have sons with him. What was a daughter? But still, I remember the last time I saw her. She was wearing a crown of wilted flowers she had made and holding her kitten. I kissed her goodnight as if it were any other night. Then in the morning—I was gone." Helen's voice caught in her throat, and her face disappeared behind those ringed fingers. The slender shoulders quivered.

I sat down, pulled my stool close to hers. "Helen—surely, if you chose, you could go back?"

She shook her head without looking up. "It's too late."

I said tentatively, "Perhaps if I were free in the land of the Achaeans, I could find a way to send your daughter to you, or deliver a message—"

Her head reared up. "Liar!" she lashed out. "You care nothing for me! You care only for your own lover. If you were with your precious Achilleus, you wouldn't give me another thought!"

Aghast, I said, "Helen—"

But she had sunk her head down into her hands. Her voice was thick and muffled. "Whatever happens, I am lost. If the Achaeans win, Menelaus will kill me. I must hope the Trojans win, but I will never see my home and my daughter again."

"Then help me win victory for Troy."

"No!" I realized she was weeping. She jumped up angrily. "Now you've made me cry." She went to a small side table that held pots and vials, keeping her face averted, but still I caught a glimpse of it. To my surprise, Helen did not cry prettily. She soaked a cloth in scented water and held it to her red, blotched eyes and swollen nose. "Look what you've done!" Her voice rose to a wail. "If Paris should see me like this…"

What I had done was to make her see how intolerable her life was. I felt a sick despair. She would never help me now. I stood and paced about slowly, wondering if there was a way to reverse my failure.

"You have power over men, Helen. If you chose, you could find a way to seek your daughter."

She opened the cloth and buried her entire face in it. Her shoulders drooped.

I felt a kind of angry pity for her. "You've given up. You're in love with futility. But it's not too late. If you help me, then maybe you will see that you are not helpless." I waited, holding my breath.

Helen kept her back turned. At first she was utterly still, as though she were considering my words. Then her hands began making quick, practiced movements, and in the silence I could hear the small sounds of wet cloth dabbing against skin. Each sound stabbed me with defeat. Blindly I turned toward the door.

Before I reached it, it was flung open. A tall man stood there—a man of such godlike beauty that I took a step back to look at him. Curly black hair fell to his shoulders. His eyes were large, limpid, chestnut brown, and fringed with girlishly long lashes. But a small pouting mouth and a narrow chin marred the perfection of his face. This must be Helen's lover —Hektor's brother.

I stood still, helpless. Too late to flee or hide. If he guessed why I was here and told Hektor, all was lost.

Helen glanced up, then turned her back on him. She continued to mend the ravages to her beauty. The sharp angle of her arm and shoulder betrayed her consternation. "Paris!" she mumbled. "What are you doing home so early?"

"I am not needed at the barracks," he replied. His eyes lit on me with sharpened interest. Then he appeared to notice Helen's distress. "What's the matter?" he asked her.

"Nothing! We were just talking, and I started thinking of home."

Paris took two steps toward her, frowning. "This is your home, isn't it? Or did you mean Sparta? I didn't know you wanted to go back there."

Helen turned in alarm. "I don't! Don't send me away, Paris, I beg you!"

"Then stop crying like a child. I can't stand it." He looked at me. "Who are you?"

Helen answered for me. "She's Briseis—the Achaean captive." She paused, and I held my breath, afraid. But she only said, "She's staying with your brother Hektor."

"Oh!" Paris smiled at me winsomely, displaying a flash of white teeth. "I heard about you in the barracks. Only I didn't know you were so lovely! Will you be staying long?"

At a loss, I lowered my head. I had seen the admiration in his eyes. Perhaps this could work in my favor. But Helen was watching fiercely. "Briseis was just going back to Hektor's dwelling," she said.

Paris's smile grew broader. A light danced in his eyes. "Surely there's no need for haste! It's a fair, sunny day. Let me take you on a tour of the battlements, Briseis. The view is breathtaking." He came toward me, extending his hand to take mine. "Will you come?"

He was not to be trusted. Clearly he was using me to anger Helen. Still, I felt a rush of hope. If I could get to her, make her jealous.... And a tour of the battlements might give me the faintest possibility of finding a way to escape.

Or perhaps he might be persuaded to help me.

I gave him my best smile. "That is most kind," I began, but Helen was quicker. She dropped her cloth and came toward us like a swooping crow.

"Briseis and I were just going out. I myself was going to take her there—to join my ladies. But since you're back, Paris, I'll just show her the way and return to you." Her composure was restored, the eyes only slightly red. She turned the full strength of her seductive smile on him. "Will you wait here for me?"

Paris's eyelids fluttered. "But surely—later—"

Before he could finish, she bustled me out of the door and shut it behind us. She hurried me a short way along the gallery to where none could overhear.

Then she whispered hastily, angrily, "Tonight! The Skaian Gate. You can get out that way after everyone's asleep." She took a long, shuddering breath. "I'll contrive it somehow."

CHAPTER 31

> Who is this who comes along through the dark night,
> when all others are sleeping in our camp?
>
> *Iliad*, Homer, Book X,
> (Rouse's translation)

A shaft of moonlight fell from the opening above the hearth. Deep breathing sounds came from the curtained alcove where Hektor slept with Andromache. I pictured him drowned in oblivion, black hair tousled, mouth slightly open. Weary as I was, I envied him for his slumber.

Andromache was surely awake. This mission was as much hers as mine. She'd somehow persuaded Hektor to do nothing about his plan today. Though we had not spoken when I returned from Helen, our eyes had met, and I'd nodded slightly to let her know I'd leave tonight. She'd squeezed my hands in answer, silently telling me that all her hopes rested in me. Now she would be lying rigid, breath held, ears attuned to the rustle of cloth, the soft brush of bare feet on stone.

I sat up and groped to my feet. Clutching my sandals, I crept toward the door, knowing that in her mind she followed me. When the door creaked, when the courtyard gravel grated under my feet, I felt no great alarm. If Hektor roused, she would seal his lips with hers and roll into his arms. Until I left Hektor's house, I was safe.

But as I reached the courtyard gate, my stomach tightened. I opened it, slid through. The street was a river of darkness. I sped along it downhill, bare feet soundless on the flagstones. The Skaian Gate—Helen had told me how to find it. I must look for the third turning to the left. I passed one. Here was the second, and—

I stopped. A shadow blocked my path. A tall, thin shadow made of substance and utter silence. I couldn't breathe.

A voice hissed, "I know where you're going."

A hand lifted, flinging back a hood, and I saw the pale blur of a face with wide dark eyes. "Kassandra!" I whispered.

She stood very still. Her shoulders slumped with a palpable weight of sadness. I let out my breath slowly. She knew of my errand, yet she had not alerted Hektor. "I came to warn you," she said at last. "The outcome will not be what you think."

"How can you know?" I asked.

"Do you think the future is hidden from me? Would that it were!" Her voice was a sorrowful, broken whisper. I thought she might be mad, yet she saw too much. I pitied her—and found I didn't want to hear what she had to say.

I forced myself to ask, "What do you see?"

"You think you can prevent their deaths. You can't! You think you will help Troy win the war. But even if we win, we are lost. If the Achaeans win, they too are lost." Her voice rose. "We are all lost!" It was a desolate cry that echoed from the walls of stone. I feared it would awaken the sleeping Trojans. "A great darkness is coming."

A chill ran through me. "Hush, Kassandra, I beg you—"

Abruptly she spun around and moved out of my path. "Go, Briseis, if you must!" she said softly. "You cannot go against the will of the gods, and you cannot change fate. But —" Quite suddenly, she took my hand in both of hers. She held it a moment, looking down at it. "Ah!" she whispered. "I thought so. You carry the future within you." Before I could react, she sank back into the shadows and was gone.

What did she mean? But it didn't matter. I was more determined than ever to go on. Drawing a shaky breath, I stooped to put on my sandals. I took the next street to the left and reached a narrow alley where no moonlight penetrated the gloom. I put out my hands and touched cold stone on my right. My fingers traced the outlines of huge blocks—the Cyclopean stones of the outer wall. Feeling my way, I set off in the direction I judged to be west. The wall curved inward a long way until at last I saw a faint vertical line of moonlight. When I came close to it, a cool breeze from the plain touched my cheek. I had reached the gate.

I stopped. Helen hadn't told me what to do next. As I waited, a heavy, sandaled foot clunked on the flagstones. A step. Another. A spear haft struck the ground. I shrank back, flattening myself into deepest shadow. A harsh male voice rang out. "Who goes there?"

I sensed he was only a few paces ahead of me. I held my breath. Moments passed. The unseen guard took another step. I crouched lower against the wall.

Then, from another direction came the rustle of a gown, a low, throaty laugh, a soft whisper. "Why, Chromios, it is only I! You sound so fierce. Do you not know me?"

"You!" the guard said in a husky voice. "What are you doing here?"

"Hush! You must tell no one that you have seen me." Soft steps came forward. Now I could see a graceful figure draped from head to toe in a light-colored cloak that glowed in the moonlight. I heard her sigh. "It's been so long, dear Chromios! I couldn't get away." Helen's soft voice grew petulant. "I get so tired of being cooped up. But tonight my man sleeps like the dead. And the moon is lovely! Can we not walk outside the walls and look at it?"

The guard let out a long breath. Then the gate creaked wide open and moonlight flooded the alley. Two figures, arm in arm, slipped through the opening. I sped to the gate and took a cautious look. Their backs were to me. Their steps took them eastward, around the wall—away from the path to the Scamander River and the Achaean camp.

Unchallenged, I slipped out through the gate, walking quickly in the moonlit darkness until I was far from Troy.

During the long walk I thought about how everything had changed. I'd sought a haven and a way to help the Trojans win the war—never dreaming of seeing Achilleus again. Now I hoped only to keep him alive and be with him again. And Hektor's life as well hinged on this. I carried the burden of the promise I'd made to Andromache. I prayed to the gods I could keep it. Pausing for a rest, I looked back at the citadel of Troy, looming pale and almost ghostly in the moonlight. I thought of Kassandra's words. *We are all lost!* A shiver ran over my skin.

One more hurdle remained. I must find Achilleus's camp and gain entry.

When I reached the wall of the encampment, I followed it to my left, seeking the gate nearest to Achilleus's quarters, which would be guarded by his own men. But how would I recognize it? At last I came to a wide gate, surely the right one, as it was nearest the end of the encampment. I hesitated for several moments, then smote upon the rough wood.

The gate opened a crack. A head peered out. "Who's there?"

"Are you Achilleus's man?" I asked.

"Aye." The voice was suspicious. "Who wants to know?"

"I—I'm Briseis. I've escaped." I paused, not sure my name would mean anything to him. He shone a torch in my face, its bright flame blinding me.

"From Agamemnon? What are you doing outside the wall?" He knew who I was. He withdrew the torch and I saw his face. To my relief, a name surfaced in my mind.

"Trechos! I—how glad I am to see you!" I gulped in a breath. "I got away from the king, hid among the chariots, got outside the gate—" My words stumbled over each other as I concocted an explanation that I hoped sounded plausible.

He looked at me for a long time in silence. At last he said, "Achilleus can sort it all out, I suppose. You'd best come in."

"For your master's sake, please say nothing, sir, not to anyone," I said.

He only grunted.

Inside the camp I breathed deeply, savoring the breeze, the smell and sound of the sea, even the dirt and grit in my sandals. This was home. For now I had no other.

But I'd best be careful. Menelaus would have his men searching for me on the quiet. Agamemnon's men, too, would be looking. At least, I thought, no one would have any reason to suspect I had been to Troy.

I reached Achilleus's hut and stopped. Now that the moment had come I couldn't face him. I remembered how strangely distant he'd been when he let me go. I had no idea how he'd receive me. For that matter I had no idea if he was even alone in his bed.

I could go to the women's quarters and face him in the morning. But I'd have to explain everything to the women. All at once weariness overcame me. I had not slept much the previous night, and this one was half gone. Too exhausted to think or plan, I decided to go to Achilleus's ship, where I could sleep until daylight.

The night wind had turned cold. Drawing my shawl about me, I walked toward the shore. As I passed the stables, I saw a movement against the shadowed wall. I hesitated. There was no sound, no further movement. I waited. Nothing. Surely it was only one of the men obeying a call of nature. I went on.

At the shore I paused to look at the long line of ships, their prows resting on the sand like strange, quiescent beasts. Only the soft lapping of water against their black hulls broke the stillness. It seemed as if the whole world slept and I alone was abroad, under this gibbous moon that lit the sky and silvered the sea. The breeze stirred and sent tiny ripples racing, racing, going nowhere.

I recognized Achilleus's ship by the carved serpent's head adorning its prow. A plank leaned against the side of the hull. Icy waves splashed against my ankles. Shivering, I hitched up my skirts and found a purchase on the plank. My strength was almost gone as I climbed, scratching my way upward until at last my fingers found the rail. I started to pull myself over it—and froze.

He was here—Achilleus, asleep on the moonlit deck, enveloped in a mantle that looked black as the midnight sea. My hands locked on the rail. I stared at the dark-lashed crescents of his closed eyes, the furrow between his brows. He slept, but not at peace.

I was unprepared to face him and terrified that he'd awaken to find me here. As I tried to back down, my desperate feet fumbled for the gangplank—and knocked it over with a splash. I clung to the rail, hands slipping from their grip.

In an instant he was awake. He sprang up, clutching a javelin. Then he saw me, and the javelin clattered to the planks. "*Briseis!* By the gods, what are you doing here?"

He grabbed me and pulled me up onto the small triangular deck.

CHAPTER 32

"If I go home to my native land, there will be no great fame for me, but I shall live long and not die an early death."

—Achilleus, *Iliad*, Homer, Book IX
(Rouse's translation)

He stared at me for a breathless instant. The grip of his hands sent shivers along my skin. "How did you come here? Does Agamemnon know?" He released me abruptly and scanned the shore, his right hand reaching for the sword that wasn't there. "Who saw you? Who knows you're here?" He shot the rough questions like stones.

"Only the gate guard—Trechos." I sputtered.

He let out an explosive breath. "You *escaped*." I heard amazement in his voice. "How did you do it?"

I tried to remember what I'd told Trechos. "I managed to get away from—where I was confined. I hid among the chariots until near dark." I hesitated, hoping he wouldn't notice the holes in my story. "When I—when some men took the horses out onto the plain, I—I slipped out unseen. It seemed safer to stay outside the camp until everyone slept, and—"

"And no one saw you? Besides Trechos?"

I shook my head. "I don't think so."

He was quiet for a time. Then he said, "You can't stay here—you know that, don't you?"

I gasped. "*Why not*?"

"I have been dishonored, Briseis. If I take you back now, I will be further dishonored."

"I don't understand."

He hesitated and seemed not to know what to say. "We have to talk." I waited. He settled himself back against the rail and moved me to his side. "If I keep you here, I'd be a thief. I'd lose all chance of ever regaining my honor."

"Honor!" Rage surged in my heart. "What about *me*?"

Again he was silent. Then he said, "This isn't about you."

"Then will you please tell me what it *is* about?" I was beginning to realize that in this struggle between the two men, I was nothing but a hostage. *Luckless pawn*, Kassandra had called me. "Achilleus," I cried, "you can't send me back to him!"

"Hush!" He looked quickly around as if he feared someone might hear. "Listen. I want you to understand." He put his arm around my shoulders. His touch was soothing, but his words were not. "When Agamemnon took you, I was disgraced before all the army. I wanted to kill him, but that would have been a great evil. So I mastered my rage. I expected the other chieftains to support me, but even though they knew the king was in the wrong, they did *nothing*." He paused, breathing hard. He withdrew his arm. "Which made them as guilty as he. So I swore an oath before them all."

The oath. I raised my eyes fearfully to his face. "What did you swear?"

"I was holding the speaker's staff," he picked up the javelin, "like this. I told them I was leaving the war. And I swore that when they were so hard pressed they begged for my help, I would no more fight for them than the dry wood of the staff would turn back into a living tree." Vehemently he flung the javelin away.

I was stunned. "Then you will never return to battle?" That meant he wouldn't fight Hektor now, and my plan to get him away from the war might be easy after all. I had but to find a way to make him take me back, and—

"But—" he said, and my heart sank, "if I don't fight, I will never regain my honor." He paused, breathing harshly. "So I prayed to Zeus."

"What did you pray?" I asked, wondering if I really wanted to know.

"That the Achaeans would be utterly defeated," he said bleakly. "Then my honor would be restored."

I sensed no good would come of this, even if it benefitted the Trojans. "So you're going to wait here to see if it happens?"

His eyes fell away from mine. "I must."

I stared at him. A chasm separated him from me. And from everyone else, it seemed. I wondered what Patroklos thought. "Is honor so important?" I whispered.

"It's the only thing that gives my life meaning."

"None of this makes any sense." The wind gusted, penetrating my bones and my heart. "I don't understand you at all."

He gave a sudden, short laugh. "No one else does either! My parents want different things for me. My father wants me to win honor, to be the greatest warrior. But my mother wants me to live. She tried to keep me from this war by sending me to the island of Skyros when I was a youth. She would be happy if I never returned to the fighting."

"Your mother sounds like the only sensible one. And what do *you* want?"

He said, "There's a prophecy about me: If I fight in this war, I'll die young but win everlasting fame. If I go home, I'll live a long life without glory. So when I came to fight at Troy, I made the choice."

"An early death." The words caught in my throat.

"Undying glory. It was my birthright. A promise from Zeus. But now Agamemnon has turned me into an outcast. My life's purpose is gone. And the only way I can get it back is if the Achaeans beg me to return to battle."

Each word filled me with fury. Honor—undying glory. He would choose it over life itself. "And will they?"

"I don't know. All my hope is in that prayer, for if I'm dishonored, I can't face my father. I can't go home."

"What is honor?" I said. "A word, no more. It won't fill your belly or ease your pain. It can't make you happy."

He gave me a look of sorrow. "I was taught that happiness doesn't matter. Only one's name and one's deeds."

"There's nothing left for you here, Achilleus. Why do you stay?"

"Enough!" he snapped. "I've told you—the Achaeans must restore my honor."

His honor or his life. This was beginning to seem like a repeating nightmare. But nothing I could say would change his mind. And how would I ever keep my word to Andromache?

I turned away furiously—then turned back. "And where does that leave me?"

His glance dropped from mine, and he was silent.

A cloud fell over me. He had become a stranger. How could I have thought his camp was home? I had no home, and if it came to it, nor did he. We were both adrift. I groped for the rail. Without any idea of where I would go, I swung one leg over the side. The plank was gone, and I would drop to the hard-packed sand, but it didn't matter. I lifted the other leg. Before I could jump, he grabbed me and pulled me back.

"What are you doing? You can't just leave. I must think what to do with you." I shivered as the night wind gusted. "You're cold." He draped his mantle around me. His nearness, his sudden concern brought tears to my eyes. But he looked away. "Briseis, you don't know what this has been like for me. If only I could—"

His voice faltered, and he did not go on. At that moment I understood this was tearing him apart. I stepped toward him and lifted my arms to embrace him.

He drew a sharp breath. Backed away. "I—we can't, Briseis. You're his now."

"By the gods! He stole me!"

He said in a whisper so low I barely heard, "And he *had* you."

"*No!* I fought him—I never lay with him, Achilleus. I held him off until drunkenness overcame him, even though he nearly killed me. After that he kept me locked up in a filthy hut." When he made no reply, I sagged in defeat. "You don't believe me. But I too have my honor."

"I do believe you, Briseis," he said. "You're very brave. Many men don't have half your courage." He made a move toward me, quickly checked. "I *wish* I could take you back. None of this is your fault. The fault is mine. My accursed fate —the vow I made—"

Acting on pure instinct, I drew him into an embrace. His breath caught. I rested my head on his chest and heard the pounding of his heart. My arms tightened around him. An insatiable hunger swamped me. For a time neither of us moved. Then his mouth fused with mine. The taste of him left me weak with longing.

After we broke apart, I said breathlessly, "Love me, Achilleus. Whatever the gods have decreed, we have this moment—maybe only this moment." Our lips joined and parted again, and I whispered, "This means more than honor," but he was breathing too hard to hear.

At last, with a shaken sigh, he drew back and bent to spread his mantle on the deck. He lowered me onto it, pulling me hard against him. There was only him, only us, in all the world, and as our bodies became one, joy flooded through me, deeper than any I had ever known.

Afterwards we lay entwined. He freed a hand to caress my hair. He raised himself up on an elbow and kissed my cheek, my lips, my neck.

"My Briseis! I don't want to give you up," he said. I opened my eyes. His words brought me back to the unresolved question. "But if I keep you," he added, "I can't stay here."

I seized those words like a lifeline. "Then surely you need *not* stay! Oh, Achilleus, your mother is right—your life matters more than anything!" When he was silent, I went on rapidly, "If Zeus answers your prayer and the Achaeans can't win without you, your honor will surely be restored, even if you leave, for they'll understand the wrong they did to you." The wind whipped up, sending shivers deep into my bones. He pulled me closer but made no reply. "There's nothing for you here anymore," I whispered, burying my face in his shoulder. "Take me home with you."

He sighed sharply. At last he said, "What you're saying, I've already thought to myself a thousand times. Something tells me you're right. I should set out at once—tomorrow, or even tonight—or I will never see my homeland again." I heard yearning in that desolate whisper. His voice came, soft and broken. "I do—want—happiness."

Hope filled me like wind rushing into a sail. "Then why don't you—"

"Perhaps. Now hush!" His fingers stole across my lips. "I must think." He wrapped the mantle more tightly around us. I was muffled in warm wool that carried the scent of his body. Yet, he had withdrawn from me, and for a long time said nothing. At last he lifted a hand to stroke my hair again, trailing a loosened strand through his fingers. "In my home, not many women have hair like this. What will they make of you, I wonder? They will call you Raven, or Midnight, or perhaps Melanippe—little black mare." I heard the smile in his voice. Then he paused and gave a start, as if at some new thought. "If we sail tonight, while they yet think you are locked up, they won't know I stole you back—"

My heart jumped. "Oh, Achilleus!" I tightened my arms around him. I listened to the sound of his breathing as if it could tell me his inner thoughts. "Take me to your home. I want to see it. I want to know it."

He let out a shaky breath. "Home!" That whisper was so fraught with longing it pierced me through. *Home.* A safe refuge. I shut my eyes and nestled my head against his chest, so close I could hear his heart. I imagined the green fields and hills of Phthia. Half asleep, I could see black mares galloping, their hooves drumming, drumming, like his heartbeat.

All at once he thrust away from me and sat up, listening. Cold air surged between us. I heard a wild rhythmic pounding. The hooves of galloping horses. A long, frightened whinny tore the air. Fear stopped my breath. He sprang to his feet, pulling on his tunic, and went to the rail.

"Balios and Xanthos! My horses! How did they get loose? The horse boy must have not secured them properly." I pulled myself up and saw two dark equine shapes galloping down the strand. I slipped on my gown and started toward him as he swung one leg over the side. "Stay here," he said. "It won't take me long to bring them back." He caught me in his arms and kissed me fiercely. "Wait for me here, my love," he whispered, and sprang overboard.

He ran swiftly down the beach after his horses. They paid no heed when he whistled. He kept running until the gray edges of night swallowed him.

Then I heard a cry. By the nearest hut, not far up the shore, a form lay crumpled in the sand, enveloped in trailing robes. A woman.

What was she doing out here? Perhaps going to or from the privy. Had the horses hurt her? My instinct was to jump off the ship and run to her aid, but caution held me back.

The cry became a sobbing whimper, as if from pain. She needed help. I recalled my distress when I'd been about to miscarry my child. Perhaps her need was equally dire.

I stayed glued to the railing. I should at least go see. I hesitated—on the ship I was safe. But I couldn't bring myself to turn away from her. At last, after looking far up and down the shore and seeing no one else, I lowered myself off the ship and dropped to the sand. I could run back if it wasn't safe. I took a few cautious steps toward the woman. I couldn't see her face, and I dared not call out. But as I approached, she got up and staggered toward the nearest hut, shouting, "Help! Here! Quickly!"

I stopped. Her voice sounded familiar, and she did not appear hurt. "What do you want?" She glanced at me over her shoulder. I saw her face—the hard glare of her eyes. "*Aglaia!*" I remembered her hatefulness from the very first day, and the words she spoke. *If a time ever comes when he can't protect you, you had best look to your life!*

Achilleus, the horses. *Treachery.* All at once I smelled male sweat, leather. I turned and ran back toward the ship.

Heavy footsteps crunched the sand behind me. Something hard smashed against my head. The moonlight splintered into fragments, and I fell in darkness.

CHAPTER 33

> ...with loud clamour they rushed toward their ships,
> the dust rose under their feet and hung over them in clouds,
> they shouted to one another to get hold of the ships
> and draw them into the sea...
>
> *Iliad*, Homer, Book II
> (Rouse's translation)

Crashes and thumping noises jolted me awake. When I opened my eyes, light stabbed through my skull. I was in a dim, cavernous place with curving walls and no roof, only beams that crisscrossed the blue sky. Like ribs. Something familiar nagged at me. The beams were thwarts. A ship—I was in the hold of a ship.

How did I get here? I must have fallen off the deck—hurt my head—after Achilleus left. I had the faintest memory of him running down the beach in the darkness. But now it was day.

The shouts, thumps, and crashes from outside grew into a deafening din. The ship was shaken violently. Someone shouted. "Home! We're going home!"

Joy filled me as I remembered—we'd talked of going to his home. He must have gone to summon his men, and now they were launching the ships. If I listened carefully, I would hear his voice giving the orders. But when I lifted my head, the thwarts blurred and the sky disappeared.

I awoke to silence. There were no rowers sitting on the thwarts above me, no one around at all. What had happened? I moved my head and dizziness overwhelmed me. When I pulled myself up onto my elbows, I was sick. Afterwards I lay back, too weak to move.

Much later I heard footsteps. A man came to my side, a small, balding man of middle years, whom I had never seen before. He busied himself cleaning up the mess of sickness. When I tried to speak, I managed only a weak croak.

He turned at once. "So you're alive! The physician thought you might live."

Physician? Was I beyond Achilleus's help? As the stranger crouched, I heard water splashing. He held a cup to my lips. I drank, fighting dizziness, then laid my head down and kept it motionless. "Who are you?" I managed to ask.

"My name is Odios." The name meant nothing to me. Why had Achilleus sent a stranger? "That's a nasty bump on your head," Odios said.

I touched a large, tender swelling on my temple. I closed my eyes. I wanted Achilleus very badly. "When will he come?" I asked.

Odios frowned, his small features compressed between bushy brows and shaggy brown beard. "I expect he'll send for you when you feel better. I'll bring you food. Then you must rest."

Send for me? Why didn't he come? Tears stung my eyes. "Why aren't we moving?" I asked Odios. "How long will it take?"

"What?"

"To reach his home."

He shook his head. "This ship is beached. We're not going anywhere."

"But—I felt the men launch the ship."

He sighed. "They *tried* to launch the ships. They thought they were going home. But he was only testing them."

I stared, completely at a loss. "Why test them?"

Odios shook his head. "It was an ill-judged scheme. He thought it would rouse their fighting spirit, so he told them we would give up the war and sail for home. He expected them to protest. But instead they ran to launch the ships. That's what you heard. It took all the leaders to stop their flight."

His words made no sense. I pulled myself up. The ship seemed to spin about me. "That's absurd. Achilleus has never lied to his men. And I don't believe he lied to me."

Odios stared at me as if I had lost my mind. "Achilleus? What are you talking about? I was speaking of Agamemnon."

Agamemnon? He'd planned to test the men in this way. Pieces of memory came back: A blow on the head. Treachery. *I was on Agamemnon's ship.*

I gave a great cry and struggled to sit up. My head pounded. I fell back hard. The taste of blood filled my mouth. "My lady—Briseis!" Odios's voice was faint, far away. Silence and blackness swallowed me.

I sank below pain into deepest dark. Mists swirled. I was floating in some dank rocky place. When I tried to move, it was like wading through a swampy thickness. Cold fear filled me, but I had no voice to cry out. I heard the murmur and splashing of water. Before me was an open place where a river glided, black and smooth, between banks of gray sand. I stopped. There was a boat on the shore. A hooded figure rose from it and came toward me, a stooped old man. His strange-looking, milky eyes gazed from an ancient wrinkled face, translucent as wax. His hand stretched out. The seamed palm was open. He wanted something. A fee—to ferry me across.

I looked at the far bank of the river. A man stood there—a man with thinning brown hair and a beard. Smiling, he held his arms open in welcome. A boy crept up behind him, insubstantial in the mist. *I knew them.* Mynes and Laodokos! Waiting for me.

But I had no gold to give the old ferryman. His hand dropped. He turned away. *Take me!* I cried, but my throat made no sound. Then I remembered the gold-threaded girdle I wore. I reached for the knot. The ferryman was leaving. My nails scratched and tore at the fabric in desperate haste. At last it came loose.

No! cried a soundless voice. *Don't go with him!*

I stood still. The girdle dropped to my feet. The boy and the man vanished into the mist. The old boatman too disappeared. I stood alone in a dark dream.

I drifted through shadows. Nothingness. Then, out of nothingness I heard voices. I tried to shut out the sounds, to go back to the dark river, but the voices pulled, distracted me.

"—insensible as you see her now."

"How long has she been like this?" This voice was harsh, ugly, familiar.

"Days, my lord."

There was silence. My skin prickled. Men, very near, were watching me.

"*Days,* you say?" The harsh voice rang out. "Why wasn't I told? Why wasn't the physician brought back to see her?"

I opened my eyes. The dim gray light made me blink. Two figures stood by my side, one broad and large, one small and cringing. Neither looked at me. "If she dies," said the large man, "you shall pay the price."

"Look, my lord Agamemnon, she wakes!"

The larger man bent, and his face loomed right over me, a wide face rimmed in bushy hair and beard, with small yellow-brown eyes. A face I'd hoped never to see again.

"You had better find a way to heal her," he said to the other man. "Send for Machaon, the physician. And get one of the women to tend her. See that she mends. See that she puts on flesh and her looks are restored." His voice became a snarl. "As she is now, she's no use to me."

CHAPTER 34

"These are the gifts I shall arrange if he desists from anger. Let him be subdued!"

—Agamemnon, *Iliad*, Homer, Book IX
(Fitzgerald's translation)

Agamemnon's heavy steps thumped up the ladder, followed by the lighter steps of Odios. Silence returned. The rock crushing my heart wouldn't let me breathe. For a long time I lay inert with despair. How I hated the king! How I hated Aglaia, who had betrayed me to his men! But most of all, I loathed myself for letting it happen.

I had to move. I had to think. I started to sit up but my stomach sickened, and dizziness overwhelmed me. I lay back against the side of the hull. What did Achilleus do when he found me gone? He would have questioned his men—perhaps learned of Aglaia's betrayal.

I had to get back to him. Somehow. I had escaped before and could escape again.

A terrible thought struck me. What if he had decided, after all, to sail for home?

Oh, gods, surely not! I prayed. But I couldn't think anymore. I was so weary and sick that I fell into a torpor from which I could not rouse myself.

As I lay only half aware, a dark-haired man of middle years came to kneel at my side. I shrank in panic. He said, "I'm Machaon. The physician. The king bade me examine you again to see how you fare." I let him feel my pulse and inspect my wound. At last he got to his feet. "There's nothing I can do. You will heal—or not. The next few days will tell."

Much later a woman came, carrying a bowl. "My name is Ianeira. I'm here to help Odios care for you." She was large and strong looking, with brown hair. "Try to eat. You must regain your strength." The bowl contained some kind of gruel, which she proceeded to spoon into my mouth. I swallowed each spoonful although it was a huge effort. Before the bowl was empty, I retched without warning and was sick until nothing remained in my stomach.

She sighed. "It was too much too soon. We need to give you smaller amounts until your head heals." She put a gentle hand on my brow. "Rest now."

Reassured by her kindness, I slept.

When she returned, she fed me small sips of broth. Again my stomach rebelled. Her brow creased with worry. When my retching stopped, I asked the question that burned in me.

"Achilleus?" I whispered. "Has he—have he and his men sailed to their home?"

"Nay, he has not stepped foot out of his camp since the day of the assembly when Agamemnon took you."

I let out a breath and asked, "Does he—Achilleus—know where I am?"

"How should he not? Agamemnon never let it be known that you escaped his camp."

I wondered if she knew I'd been in Achilleus's camp when Agamemnon's men caught me. I wondered if I could trust her and persuade her to help me. Too weary to ponder these things, I closed my eyes. I would rest until I was healed. Then I would think of escape.

"I don't understand. The wound on your head is much better, and you say you're no longer dizzy," said Ianeira several days later, when I was still unable to keep anything in my stomach. "The physician says you should be well. Why are you still sick?"

I will be sick no longer, I vowed. *I will regain my strength.* Once a day I made myself climb the ladder to pace the gangway. But the fresh sea air did not lift my nausea, and my energy soon drained like water from a leaky pot, forcing me back to my pallet.

Whenever I was on the deck, I observed what I could see of the camp. Several armed men stood on the shore, spread evenly along the sides of the ship. "What are they doing here?" I asked Ianeira.

"Agamemnon fears you'll try to flee again. He ordered them to keep watch day and night. He wanted to put you in chains, but Odios and I promised we'd guard you, and you wouldn't try anything. You won't, will you, Briseis?"

"Of course not," I answered promptly, secretly determined to find a way. But it seemed impossible. A black cloud fell over me. It would have been better if I had died before ever going to Troy—if I'd never met Hektor and

Andromache, never returned to Achilleus. All I'd accomplished was to betray Andromache and make everything worse for Achilleus.

One day as I was dozing, loud shouts and clangs jolted me awake. *Men fighting.* I pulled myself up in a panic, still confused with sleep. I was again on the hillside above Lyrnessos watching the slaughter. But when I managed to get to my feet, I only saw my familiar prison. I struggled over to the ladder. "Ianeira!" I called. "What's happening?"

She climbed down into the hold. "They're fighting today for the first time since the plague, and the Trojans have pushed the Achaeans back almost to the wall of the camp. We can see the battle from the deck. Come with me and you'll see." Brooking no refusal, she pulled me to the ladder and helped me up it.

I stared, dazzled by the blinding sun. Masses of warriors were fighting just on the other side of the wall. Shouts, challenges, and clashing weapons burst upon my ears. Was Hektor attacking because of what he had learned from me?

I hoped Achilleus was still safely out of the fighting. Looking over the railing far down the shore toward his camp, I saw only the long line of beached ships that separated me from him.

I asked Ianeira fearfully, "Is Achilleus—has he returned to battle?"

She shook her head. "I would certainly have heard if he had." She added, "I've never seen the battle come this close before." She smiled grimly. "This is good for the Trojans!" These were her people, but I did not miss the quick, anxious glance she shot toward Odios, who stood on the shore near our ship. Clearly her emotions were mixed. "I'm glad

Agamemnon ordered Odios to stay out of battle and guard you," she said.

I looked again toward the fighting. The wall of the encampment was five hundred paces from the ship. The men were on the other side of it, too far away for us to see their faces clearly, and I couldn't always tell Trojan from Achaean. At first it seemed to be just an unbridled display of ferocity and shouting. Then I heard the screams of the wounded and saw growing splotches of blood all around. I saw a man fall dead. My stomach heaved. Whether friend or foe, I had no stomach for watching men die.

"Ianeira, I'm going below." I crawled down the ladder. Alone in the hold, I vomited.

Much later she came down to tell me that the Trojans had been pushed back and all was quiet again. "Come and get some air on the deck."

I went. When Odios saw us there, he clambered up to join us. "It's good to see you up and about, Briseis," he said. "Are you well?"

"I'm better, thanks to your care and Ianeira's," I told him, touched by his concern. I didn't tell him how little I could eat, or how often I was sick.

He gazed back at the plain and pointed. "We've pushed them back." I saw a swarm of men, small as insects. For a moment we three watched the conflict in silence—with very different feelings, I imagined.

Odios said, "It went very badly. Many died here by the wall. Many were wounded." On the open ground on the other side of the wall, men were moving around, many stumbling from their own wounds, as they lifted the corpses of the fallen. "Those will come home for burial. The Trojans tried to carry off the bodies for trophies, but we fought them off." He seemed shaken, and Ianeira looked at him keenly and laid a gentle hand on his arm.

Odios continued, "It was a near thing. They almost breached the wall of the camp. Agamemnon is worried." He shot a glance at me. "I heard he wants Achilleus back."

My heart jumped. Would the king give me back to Achilleus in exchange for his return to battle? I felt torn in two. If Achilleus rejoined the war, I wouldn't be able to keep my promise to Andromache. But if Agamemnon didn't make this bargain with him, I'd never see him again.

I had to be ready for whatever happened. I went up on deck every day and relentlessly paced the ship, fore to aft, to regain my strength. Ianeira and I watched what we could see of the battle, though mostly the fighting was far away. The next few days were hot, the air still. Insects swarmed and stung. Each day the Trojans pushed the Achaeans hard. Each day we watched them bring back the wounded and dead in great numbers. With difficulty they managed to keep the Trojans far from the camp. But Odios said the men were losing strength and courage. He did not again bring up the subject of Achilleus.

Then came a day when clouds covered the sun and weighted the air with heat and moisture. "There'll be a storm," Ianeira said as we watched the army march out. The heat grew more oppressive with the passing of hours. Late in the day, when we were on deck trying to find a cool breeze, we heard shouts, a growing clamor.

"The Achaeans are in retreat," Odios called from the shore. Chariots, horses, men were approaching with furious desperation. The noise grew to thunder. Men were bellowing, "The gates! Open the gates!"

Odios ran to the aid of his comrades.

"The Trojans are slaughtering them. This might mean victory for our people!" Ianeira cried. Her eyes met mine with a fierce look of triumph. Then her gaze fell, and I knew she was adding a silent prayer—*May Odios be spared*.

The gates were flung open. Men hurtled through, while the battle raged on the other side of the wall. At last every Achaean left alive was in the camp, and the gates were shut. Twilight had fallen when Odios returned.

The Trojans did not retreat. A watch fire blazed in the purple darkness of the plain—then another and another, until hundreds of fires glowed like stars. The Trojans had encamped just on the other side of the wall, a relentless presence the Achaeans could not ignore. An eerie stillness settled on the camp. The wind arose, bringing a sharp bite of cold as darkness deepened.

A begrimed, weary warrior emerged from the dark to speak to Odios, who listened tensely. When the man left, Odios climbed up to the deck.

"The leaders are in council," he told us. "They want to make peace with Achilleus this very night. The king wants to give you back, along with many gifts and treasures, in exchange for his return to the war."

I sprang to my feet. Thunder shook the air, and goose bumps skittered along my skin. *Zeus, the thunder god!* I remembered Achilleus's prayer to him: *that the Achaeans will be utterly defeated without me.* I added a prayer of my own. *Zeus, let me go back to him.*

But if he took me back, he would return to war and either he or Hektor would die.

Nothing is sure until it happens, I told myself. If only I could be with him again!

Odios said, "They've summoned me. They're sending me with the emissaries as one of the heralds."

Emissaries? Why did Agamemnon not go himself to make atonement? Had the arrogant, high-handed king doomed his mission from the start?

As Odios vanished into darkness, I went to the seaward deck and stared at the stormy waters. I paced the gangway, breathing deeply and watching the play of lightning as it faded in the distance. The clouds parted and pale stars appeared. Restlessness seized me like insects crawling over my skin. As night deepened, I looked at the Trojan watch fires. Somewhere on that plain, Hektor sat by a fire, his eyes like a wolf's, hungry for blood, and Andromache waited for her man in a lonely bed.

"Try to sleep, Briseis." Ianeira's voice came out of the dark. "It'll be a long time. You want to be rested when they send for you." After a while she went below, and I returned to the seaward deck. The rain had never come. Night was waning when I lay down, wrapped in my shawl, and somehow slept.

A voice woke me. Ianeira—urgent, excited. "What word, Odios?"

In the east was a faint wash of light. I rose and raced along the gangway as Odios heaved himself up, his shoulders sagging from weariness.

I opened my mouth to echo her question, but I remembered Achilleus's oath.

Warrior's Prize

I swore I would no more fight for them than the dry wood of the staff would turn back into a living tree.

My knees went weak, even before Odios said, "We failed. Achilleus refused."

CHAPTER 35

Then Hector leapt within, his face like sudden night, his eyes blazing; light flashed from his armor, two spears were in his hands. No man alive could have checked that rush.

Iliad, Homer, Book XII
(Rouse's translation)

I had hoped I was wrong. Now, with my last hope gone, my legs dissolved so suddenly that I slumped against the rail and buried my head in my arms. Ianeira was at once beside me, her arm around my shoulders.

She rebuked Odios. "Why did you break the news so roughly?"

His anxious voice asked, "What ails her? I thought by now she was well."

"This was too much of a shock," Ianeira answered, "and she's with child." I lifted my head, stared at her. "Didn't you know?" she asked me.

"No," I whispered, but unconsciously I had known—and denied it. *It can't be!* I'd thought. *I only lay with him a few times since I lost the baby.* I'd paid scant heed to the changes in my body. Diomede had said that a captive woman's courses often stopped. And lately, when I was weak and sick all the time, I thought it was from the blow on my head.

I remembered Kassandra grasping my hand. *You carry the future within you.*

Oh, gods, she had known!

"You've that look about you," Ianeira said. "I can always tell." She turned to Odios. "The king must know nothing of this, do you hear? Swear it!" Odios nodded. "Do you want to go below?" she asked me.

I shook my head, and went to sit on the seaward deck. She fetched me a blanket, then left me, evidently sensing my need to be alone. My hand slid down over my belly. *Achilleus's child!* For a moment I allowed myself to savor a joy almost too great to bear. Then it was swallowed in fear. If I never went back to him, he'd never learn I was carrying his child.

But if he'd known, would it have made a difference? No, not with his fierce pride. Not when Agamemnon's offer was nothing more than an attempt to bribe him and dominate him. The king had not even gone in person to ask pardon for the wrong he had done.

At least for now, Achilleus would stay out of battle. He was safe from Hektor, and Hektor from him.

Small consolation, when I needed him so.

I pulled Ianeira's blanket around me. Gone were all thoughts of escape. I was adrift, with a new life to fend for in an unknown future. Weary beyond measure, I lay down and slept.

When I awoke it was day. Ianeira was holding a cup to my lips. "Briseis, you must take nourishment." I sipped the goat's milk, willing myself to keep it down. But immediately I was sick. She sighed and wiped my face. "I've seen women like you who can hold nothing in their stomachs. I'll make you an herb draught."

She was getting to her feet when she froze at the sounds of battle, suddenly audible, growing louder. Shouts, crashes, cries. The fighting was once more drawing near. Without a word, she ran to the foredeck.

I lay without moving, my thoughts very far from the battle. Much later I realized there was silence again, broken only by the soft slap of waves against the hull. The Achaeans must have driven the Trojans back across the plain. Feet thumped along the gangway—Ianeira returning with her potion. "Drink this, Briseis. I have known it to work wonders." I drank and lay down again, wanting to be left in peace, to drift—not to think. But once again the battle turned, and its clamor assaulted our ears.

Odios shouted from the shore. Ianeira hurried to him and came running back. "The Achaeans are in full retreat. Agamemnon is wounded!" she told me, triumph in her voice. "Also Odysseus and Diomedes, two of their chieftains. And many others."

"Is the king's wound serious?" I asked hopefully.

"Alas, it's only a flesh wound. But the Trojans have backed the Achaeans almost up to the wall. Come see!" She pulled me to my feet and led me to the landward deck.

On the deck we were high enough to have a clear view of the battle just outside the wall. The potion had strengthened me, but the blinding reflections of the sun on a thousand helmets and shields, the moving, seething masses of men, made my head hurt. I turned away from the play of spears, the slashing blades.

Ianeira cried, "The Achaeans are fighting for their lives!" Then her glance slid to Odios, who was watching from the shore. I understood that look: out of all the loyalty for our own people, a spark of love for one of the enemy. That spark could become a conflagration. But it would turn to ashes. My heart went out to her. I clasped her hand.

"See that chariot, those black horses. Isn't that Hektor?" Her grip tightened in mine. She leaned over the rail. "He's leading the charge! The Achaeans are yielding!"

I looked. The Trojans, a tidal wave of men, were driving the Achaeans back toward the wall. With their chariots leading the retreat, the Achaeans began to push through the gates in a disorderly, panicked throng. Wild and fierce, the Trojans pursued them.

"Just like yesterday," I said. *A lifetime ago.*

"No, it's different today!" Ianeira cried. "Look! Hektor is leading the men straight to the gate!" I saw him at the front of his men, a tall figure with a black horsehair crest on his helmet.

Amid the deafening tumult, we could hear the Achaeans' desperate shouts.

"Leonteus! Hold those gates open!"

"Polypoites, help! To me, to me!"

"Close the breach—fast! They're coming! Ayeee!"

The Trojans' shouts were harsh with triumph.

"Onward, onward!"

"Come on, men! We have them now!"

Below us, Odios gave a shout of dismay. "*By the gods! They're going to breach the wall!*" He gestured wildly at us to go below deck, then turned away, groping for his sword.

Ianeira paid no attention to Odios's unspoken command. "They're doing it this time!" she cried. "We'll be slaves no more. We'll be free."

But I knew the Trojans cared nothing about us. To them we were whores and traitors.

The Trojans ferociously battered the gates, which the Achaeans held open only wide enough to allow those left outside to enter in twos and threes with the occasional chariot, the horses screaming in fright. When they closed the gate at last, many Achaeans were stranded and slashed down savagely. I saw one receive a spear in his face. Blood spurted over his nose and mouth. Sickness rose in my throat. I turned away, but Ianeira gripped my arm. "Look!" she screamed. "Look at Hektor!"

He was advancing toward the gates just as the Achaeans closed them, massing themselves on the inside to keep the Trojans out. The gates appeared oddly fragile, their wooden slats cracked and dried. Hektor picked up an enormous rock that most men couldn't have lifted. As he trudged toward the closed gates, a space cleared around him, and a hush fell. The Achaeans crouched in terror. Then a Trojan shouted, "Hektor!" A thousand throats took up the cry: "Hek-TOR! Hek-TOR! Hek-TOR!" The pulse beat in my blood. The Trojans were still but for that chant—all massed ferocity, a flood held momentarily in abeyance, waiting to surge forth in a torrent of destruction.

Hektor lifted the boulder above his head. The black horsehair crest of his helmet quivered with the fury of his effort. He came so close to the palisade that he vanished from my sight. Then his forearms rose above the gate, holding the boulder aloft. His muscles bunched as he hurled it with all his strength. Wood splintered and shattered with a crack like thunder. The broken slats bulged inward. A thousand Trojans roared with victory as they flung themselves forward and burst through the gates.

CHAPTER 36

> His own death
> came upon him as he spoke, and soul from body,
> bemoaning severance from youth and manhood,
> slipped to be wafted to the underworld.
>
> *Iliad*, Homer, Book XVI
> (Fitzgerald's translation)

The Achaeans howled and scattered like pariah dogs driven off by lions. As the Trojans stormed into the encampment, I saw Hektor very close, his face under the helmet dark as nightfall. He was everywhere at once, shouting, exhorting the Trojans, his presence so powerful it was as if he spoke to every man personally.

"Trojans, Dardanians, Lykians! Onward! Press forward! We have them now! We will destroy them!"

The beach swarmed with men. The battle surged around the ships so close that we could have reached down and touched them. Ianeira and I clung together, terrified.

"Let's go below!" she shouted.

I shuddered. "It would be worse—not knowing what's happening."

So we stayed, cowering below the rail. Our ship shook with the force of the fighting. The men were intent, unremitting, slashing, stabbing with swords, thrusting spears. Blood spurted everywhere. Numbness overcame me. I could no longer see the Achaeans as enemies or find any comfort in the Trojans' victory. An arm's length below me, men were dying like butchered animals.

Suddenly someone threw a plank against the side of our ship, and five or six Achaean men leapt up shouting onto the deck and began thrusting spears downward into the melee. They paid us no heed. We dodged as they leapt, nimble-footed, as if performing some strange dance before the altar of a god.

A volley of arrows flew toward us. The man nearest me howled and pitched off the deck with an arrow in his chest. "Let's go below!" I screamed to Ianeira, grabbing her hand, but the men blocked our way to the ladder. We crouched beneath the rail like animals in a lair. We heard shouts, grunts, screams, and hollow thuds as bodies hit the hull, shaking the ship. There was blood on the rail, the deck, the ropes—and on our gowns.

"Odios!" Ianeira sobbed. We lifted our heads to look for him. He was backed up against our ship, helpless. He had lost sword and spear, and two Trojans were bearing down on him. "He'll be killed!" She started to climb over the rail, but I pulled her back. Her lips moved, praying wordlessly. Suddenly a spear sailed over my head, almost striking one of the men, who dodged as it clattered onto the thwarts. I grabbed it and crawled to the edge of the deck. Seeing my intent, Ianeira shouted, "Odios!" He looked up, and we managed to lower the long, unwieldy spear into his hands.

More arrows flew at us. "Down!" I screamed. We smelled smoke, and I dared a quick glance. Black clouds billowed up from leaping flames, consuming a nearby ship.

Ianeira pointed. "They've set fire to that ship! And the one beyond it!"

The Achaeans surged toward the fires, screaming, shouting, desperate to staunch the flames. With shields and bare hands, they flung water from the sea. The Trojans pressed forward, forcing the Achaeans to let the ships burn. The fires raced and devoured the pitch-soaked wood. Flames and smoke engulfed both ships.

In a sudden stillness, Achaeans and Trojans alike lifted their eyes to the sky to watch the black cloud swirling up. I saw tears of futility on many Achaean faces. "By the gods," Ianeira whispered. "This could mean the end for them."

They'll be driven into the sea and slaughtered, I thought. Was this the answer to Achilleus's prayer?

I gripped Ianeira's arm. "What will happen to us women?"

Another ship farther down the shore went up in flames. The smell of smoke burned my lungs. A blood-red sun hung suspended in the sky. With a roar, the Trojans sprang forward again.

Then, from far down the beach came shouts—vigorous, triumphant roars. Fresh horses raced to battle, pulling warriors in chariots. The distant Trojans fell back. A surge of alarm stilled the rest of their army. The Achaeans soon noticed, and all the men turned.

Sunlight burst through billows of smoke. A dazzling blaze of light shone from the center of the advancing warriors. Sun rays, striking off silver armor. A fearsome warrior in a chariot led an army charging with vigor. Hope lit the faces of the beleaguered Achaeans.

Ianeira grabbed my arm. "Who are they?"

My insides twisted. I knew that armor, those splendid horses. *He's going to fight them off, perhaps even rescue me.* But I felt a terrible fear. *Oh gods, what if he's killed?*

At my feet, a Trojan warrior dropped his sword and cried in dismay. "*Achilleus!*"

A hundred voices took up the cry, but I barely heard. Everything blurred and went still. I saw only that silver-armored figure advancing in the sun. My legs would crumble if I moved. All my being went forth in my eyes as I followed the figure cutting a swath through the Trojans, pushing all before him. Pushing, pushing, his advance heralded by fierce shouts and challenges, until the Trojans, depleted of bluster and victory, gave way. Space opened up in the crowded field, and the battered, bruised Achaeans, Odios among them, emerged from where they had been backed up against the ships.

Achilleus bellowed menacingly and thrust his spear about him. As his chariot wheeled by, I stared at that spear. It was not the great long ash spear that he usually wielded. Nevertheless, he used it with chilling efficiency, and the Trojans fled.

The retreat was slow but inexorable. The figure in the silver armor did not yield, and his soldiers, so filled with drive and momentum they were like a river in spate, pushed forward bit by bit until the ground cleared, leaving open patches of bloodied dirt. The Trojans surged toward the fence like liquid forced through a funnel. After a last, desperate stand, they scrambled through the broken gate they had so recently demolished and ran in full retreat toward the plain.

The silver-clad warrior shouted to his charioteer, who drove the horses toward the gate and through it. The horses picked up speed, began to gallop after the fleeing Trojans. The fresh soldiers followed their commander onto the plain, the entire Achaean army, with suddenly rediscovered courage, in pursuit. The battle had turned.

"It's Achilleus!" Odios shouted up from the shore. "He's going after them—all the way to the walls of Troy!"

I pulled myself to the highest point of the deck, grasping the curved timber of the prow as I strained to see. Something was wrong.

The name. The spear.

It wasn't Achilleus.

I continued to watch the imposter in silver armor until my eyes stung and I could see his chariot no more. Soon all I saw was a dazzling point of light where the sun shone on his armor. Then that too vanished. I blinked, and then I saw him again, even more clearly than before, and very near. It was as if I were just above him, looking down. I saw the way he leaned into the chariot rail, his shoulders slightly hunched as if a shadow or a pain followed him and would not let him be. I saw the curl of dark brown hair below the rim of his helmet.

A shock went through me. *Patroklos.*

I could see him as plainly as if he was very close. I thought I was imagining it, but the vision did not go away. Instead it came clearer, as when, once before, I had left my body and drifted above the sea, seeing everything. Now, just as then, I was floating—above the man in the chariot. I was deeply shaken. Perhaps I was near death again. Yet it was real. Somehow my fate was linked with his. I was with him on that hot and dusty plain, in the jolting, speeding chariot with Automedon at the reins. I breathed with him, I followed him, feeling every rut on the sunbaked ground, my heart and mind attuned to his. I tasted his exhilaration and his fear. And I alone knew his secret.

He was wearing Achilleus's armor, leading Achilleus's men. What had possessed Achilleus to send out his dearest friend in his stead? Even though he had prayed for the Achaeans' defeat, even though he wavered between his two fates, he must have been unable to watch the slaughter. Bound by his oath, he could not go forth to save them. Patroklos must have entreated him: *Send me in your stead! Lend me your armor—let me lead the men! I can save our ships and drive the Trojans out of our camp.* And Achilleus had yielded.

Trapped in my vision, I was with Patroklos as he reached the walls of Troy. He leapt from the chariot into the thick of the fighting. With that driving will, he felled Trojans left and right and set his foot on the base of the wall, as if he would scale it. He was forced back, but with a great shout he sprang up once more. Again and again, he lunged with his spear, its length streaked with blood, and the Trojans fell back before him.

I remembered the gentle companion who had been like a loving brother, shared pain with me, and laughter and closeness. I could find no trace of him in this relentless warrior. It was as if he had taken into himself the fierce heart of Achilleus.

Then I felt a jolt of fear. It came from him, not me. Hektor's chariot pushed its way through. Patroklos picked up a huge rock and flung it with all his force. With a thud it hit the charioteer, who fell headlong in the dust. Hektor's mouth opened in a howl of rage. At once, the men of both sides closed in, fighting for possession of the body of the fallen man—the Trojans to defend it, the Achaeans to gain it as a trophy, to desecrate it. With a snarl of triumph, the Achaeans dragged off the corpse.

A space opened in the turmoil, and Hektor advanced on Patroklos. The fear was all mine now. It crushed the breath from my body.

Patroklos! I didn't know if I cried aloud but my throat felt torn. *You can't fight him!*

I knew with terrible certainty that Achilleus had said the same thing. *Don't fight Hektor.* But Patroklos, drunk on victory, advanced across the open space toward Hektor, and I knew that, from the walls of Troy, Andromache watched, her heart in her throat.

Zeus and all gods, I prayed, *Let them stop now! Let them both live.*

I could feel Hektor's ferocious intensity. The black-haired prince advanced, and Patroklos, in his disguise, faced him boldly at the base of the walls of Troy.

The two men began to circle each other warily. Time seemed to stop. "Let them live—let them live!" I prayed aloud over and over.

Then something changed. The sunlight dimmed, as if a malevolent shadow had cut off its warmth. Deep cold struck my heart. I knew that shadow. A god had come: the only being in the universe whom Achilleus feared.

Go back, Patroklos! I cried desperately. *You cannot win against Apollo!*

Patroklos flinched slightly. Surely he felt the god's cold breath on his neck. *Run!* I thought. *Run for your life!* But he stood his ground. At once the shadow seemed to engulf him, and Trojans closed in on him, cutting him off from his men. A spear was flung from behind him with such force and accuracy the god himself must have guided it. It caught him at the back of the neck just above the corselet, and he staggered. Dark blood streamed out. His arm fell, dropping the shield. He was helpless, his strength draining. It took the lifeblood from my own heart and limbs. My fingers gripping the prow slipped, and I felt I had lost my hold on his life.

"Beloved friend!" I whispered, sobbing.

Another blow struck him, and as he stumbled, Achilleus's helmet came off Patroklos's head and rolled on the ground, the golden horsehair crest trailing in the dirt.

Hektor must have realized then that he had been cheated of the vengeance he desired above all else. Yet, if he felt disappointment it was short lived. As he advanced under the sheltering shadow of Apollo, he crowed in triumph. I sensed his exultance that through this killing he could inflict so much suffering upon his enemy.

Patroklos had lost shield, spear and helmet. His corselet was torn and loosened. Blood flowed from the base of his neck. For a time Hektor jabbed at him and taunted him cruelly. Then he rushed in for the kill. I felt the bronze point tear through my own flesh as Hektor's spear plunged into Patroklos's belly. Patroklos fell at last and lay too long dying, his blood gushing out to stain the dirt beneath the feet of the victorious prince.

I had to watch as Hektor deliberately stripped away the silver armor and left Patroklos's poor, torn body naked in the dust.

CHAPTER 37

"I never laid a hand on your Briseis!"

—Agamemnon (*Iliad*, Homer,
Book XVIII, Fitzgerald's translation

Everything went dark. I fell and lay on the deck of the ship. Sobs tore me. My body curled itself around the pain. *Oh, Patroklos—it can't be!*

He was the dear friend who had saved my life, made it bearable, comforted me when I would have died of grief.

I heard footsteps, then Ianeira's voice. "Briseis—" she said breathlessly, "a messenger came. Patroklos has been killed! It was he who went forth in—" She stopped. "You were calling out his name. You knew." I nodded, unable to speak. "Now they're fighting over his body," she said, "just outside the wall of the camp."

I struggled up. In my befuddled state, her words made no sense. "His body?"

"Hektor has threatened to cut off his head and feed the corpse to his dogs," Ianeira said.

"Oh gods!" I pressed my hands over my eyes. Hektor was as savage as any marauder.

"The Achaeans got it back, brought it almost all the way here, but now they're losing it again. Someone's gone to break the news to Achilleus."

Achilleus. The grief would slam him into the ground, break his heart into pieces.

At that moment a great howl of anguish arose from our side of the wall. I knew that voice. And I knew that the world had changed irrevocably.

Odios called up to us, "A messenger brought Achilleus the news. He's shouting to scare off the Trojans because without armor he can't go rescue the body."

As Achilleus shouted twice more, the Achaeans surged forward with renewed courage.

"It's working!" Odios cried. Moments later a messenger ran up to him. "They've recovered the body," he shouted to us. "Patroklos will come home for his funeral rites."

I was gripping the rail so hard that my knuckles were locked around it. I forced my fingers loose.

Evening was falling as a great group of bloodied Achaeans trudged down the shore behind somber men bearing a litter. Their burden seemed intolerably heavy. A mantle covered the body, but I saw a limp arm dangling, streaked with blood. The right arm of Patroklos, who had set out so fiercely and proudly earlier today.

Darkness came. I lay on the deck, wrapped in a blanket. Though my heart was unbearably heavy, I slept. At first light I awoke to a voice coming closer, calling out repeatedly in urgent tones. "Awake, Achaeans! Come to assembly! I have something to say!"

Achilleus. I struggled up to the rail, but he was gone, his voice fading in the distance as he ran up the shore.

Men emerged from huts and ships. The cry was taken up. "Achilleus is back! He wishes to speak in assembly!" They started to make their way to the gathering place.

A man came to Odios with a message. Odios climbed up to the deck. "Briseis, make ready. You're being given back to Achilleus."

I couldn't speak. I longed and dreaded to see him.

Ianeira scrambled off the ship and came back a short while later with a clean gown, a comb and a bronze basin filled with water, which Odios carried up the gangplank. I clambered down to the hold to wash and change, my hands fumbling in haste. When we climbed down the plank to the shore, my knees wavered and I stumbled.

"Steady." On the shore Odios put a hand under my elbow. "Come."

My legs refused to move. I clung to Ianeira. She embraced me. "You must be strong. I can't go with you. I haven't been summoned. Only you and—" She cast her eyes down. "—the other women."

"Other women?"

Odios gave her a stern look. "You don't know if that agreement still stands." He turned to me. "She means the seven other women Agamemnon promised Achilleus when he sent us to him the day before yesterday. He offered him many treasures, a dozen horses, seven captive women from Lesbos—and you, my lady."

I remembered Ianeira telling me of it, but I had forgotten—had barely noted it. Those other women meant nothing to me. My heartbeat was saying his name, the very sound of it piercing my insides. I embraced Ianeira and bade her farewell.

Odios took me to an open place with an altar, where the Achaean chieftains and many of their men were gathering in a vast half-circle. Those in front seated themselves on the ground. "This is the place of assembly," Odios said. Nearby was a small hut. "You will wait in here." The door was open, and several women were sitting inside. The women of Lesbos. As I stood in the doorway, they stared at me. I took a step forward, then stopped. I didn't want to have to speak to them.

"I'd rather not go in there," I whispered.

"Very well." Odios pointed to a spot just outside the hut. "You can watch from here."

More men assembled until I couldn't see the edges of the crowd. Achilleus was nowhere in sight. When at last he appeared, I almost didn't recognize him. His tunic, always spotless before, was rumpled and streaked with dirt, his hair dulled. His face, translucently pale, distorted by grief, had a kind of terrible, alien beauty. As he stood still before the crowd, the entire assembly of men fell silent. My heart hurt. I felt Odios's hand on my arm, restraining me. Without realizing, I had taken several steps forward. I was in plain sight, no more than fifty paces from where Achilleus stood, seemingly unaware of my presence.

"My lord Agamemnon, son of Atreus!" He turned, evidently facing the king, whom I could not see. His voice rang out. "I wish the woman Briseis had died in Lyrnessos, before I ever laid eyes on her! What good was it that we fought over her? Look what harm it has done."

My knees buckled. I must have cried out, for Odios hissed, "Be silent, Briseis, or you'll have to wait in the hut with the others."

"But he said—"

"Never mind, he's possessed by grief—I'm sure he didn't mean it." Odios's hand on my arm was steadying. "Hush now, and listen."

"We can't carry on our resentment forever," Achilleus went on in a harsh voice. "Here is the end of our quarrel. Tell the army to get ready for battle. I will fight now, I will meet Hektor face to face. I will make him pay—"

A roar drowned out the last of his words. Cheering and shouting men leapt to their feet, brandishing spears, pounding on their shields. Long moments passed before they quieted. Then a raspy voice strove to rise above the clamor.

"Brave Achaeans, hear what I have to say! Be silent and listen—none of what happened was my fault!" It was Agamemnon, seated among the chieftains. He addressed the crowd without rising. The men were restive, stirring and muttering, interrupting as he told some long tale about how the gods were to blame for what he had done. Then he pointed at Achilleus. "Go, then, lead out your men to fight. Or stay back if you choose—I don't care! But all the gifts I promised you will be delivered to your quarters, that all may see how richly I reward you."

Achilleus made a brusque gesture. "My lord King Agamemnon, the gifts are yours to give or to keep. I don't care. We've wasted enough time. To battle!"

The men cheered again. Then a man with reddish hair announced that the men needed to eat before fighting. "But first," he said, "let the king give the treasures to Achilleus and swear before all, that he has never gone into the woman Briseis's bed, nor had anything to do with her."

There was a buzzing from the men. Many were looking at me. I stood rigid. My face burned. The king rose and came forward. He issued some orders. A group of men hurried off and returned laden with the promised gifts: tripods, cauldrons, ingots of gold. The Lesbos women were summoned forth from the hut and stood behind me. The audience made appreciative sounds. Two men kindled a fire, and someone brought a young boar and laid it across the altar at the front of the crowd.

Agamemnon lifted the ceremonial knife. "Let Zeus be my witness, before the sun and earth! I never touched Briseis—never brought her to my bed nor took her for any other pleasure. If any word of this is false, may the gods punish me for perjury." And he slit the boar's throat.

Never touched me! Even though he had not completed the act, rage filled me as I remembered that terrible night in his bed. Still I should be glad of the oath he had sworn, for he would be believed.

Achilleus's glance slid over me. "It was all folly. Now it's over. Go to your meal, men, and then we will fight!"

As the men dispersed, Achilleus turned and came in our direction. My heart jolted. But he walked right past us without looking my way. His profile was ravaged, gaunt, his mouth bracketed in new lines. There were streaks of dirt on his face and in his hair.

Odios said, "Come. I'm to escort you to his camp."

We took the long trip down the shore, followed by the men bearing the treasure, and the seven women from Lesbos. When we reached the courtyard gate, Odios went to look for Achilleus so that he might formally present us, but he came back saying Achilleus was busy with armor and horses and was not to be found.

"Well, my lady, he knows you're here—you and the others." Odios took my hand and pressed it between his. "I wish you well."

As he left, a voice called my name. Diomede came rushing up and caught me in an embrace. "Briseis! They said you were coming back. Are you well?"

I shrugged. "And you?" I barely waited for her answer. "Where's Achilleus?"

"He's getting ready for battle."

"Diomede, I must see him."

"Perhaps you shouldn't seek him out just now. But if you're determined, I'll go with you. He's either in the stables, or—" She led the way into the courtyard.

I froze. A bier stood near the door of the hut, and on it lay Patroklos.

The cold finality of his death swamped me. And a horrifying fear as well. *Oh, gods! Did he die because of what Hektor learned from me?* All at once I understood Achilleus's dreadful words. If he had never laid eyes on me, Patroklos would still be alive. My worthless life had brought nothing but trouble and grief.

"Diomede—" Tears choked me before I could finish.

She put her arms around me, and I sobbed on her shoulder. "Leave me with Patroklos, please," I whispered.

"As you wish."

His body had been washed, his hair combed. There were deep gashes and scrapes on his face. He was draped in his familiar brown mantle. How alone he was, beyond my reach, beyond the reach of anyone, cut off from any human comfort. I sank to my knees before the bier and touched his cheek, finding not flesh but some hard, alien substance.

"Oh, Patroklos!" I spoke aloud, hoping my cry could reach his spirit. "When I first came here, you comforted me. You were my only friend. And all I brought you was pain and trouble. I brought you death." I raked my cheeks until they were bloody. Then, burying my face in a corner of his mantle, I wept.

A sound made me look up.

Achilleus entered the courtyard, dressed for battle in shining new armor. He held his helmet under his arm. I stood, aching to comfort him. Then I saw his face, hard as adamant, the blazing blue-green eyes rimmed in red. Death was in those eyes. He paid me no more heed than if I'd been a rock in his path. He went straight to the bier and looked long into the face of his dead friend.

"Why did you do it, Patroklos?" he cried out softly. "I told you not to challenge him—only to drive the Trojans away from the ships—" He straightened, squared his shoulders, lifted his helmet to his head. "You will be avenged, I swear by the gods." His breath was ragged, his voice broken. "Before the sun sets, I will bring Hektor's body back to you!"

CHAPTER 38

> ...Akhilleus like the implacable god of war
> came on with blowing crest, hefting the dreaded
> beam of Pelian ash on his right shoulder.
> Bronze light played around him, like the glare
> of a great fire or the great sun rising,
> and Hektor, as he watched, began to tremble.
>
> *Iliad*, Homer, Book XXII
> (Fitzgerald's translation)

As Achilleus snapped the helmet over his face, the bright sheen of his armor transformed him into an angry god, remote and terrible. He turned his back and walked across the courtyard, the dark red plumes in the crest of his new helmet dancing in the sunlight, and I remembered Andromache's small cold hands in mine as I promised to prevent the very thing that was about to happen.

"Achilleus, don't do this!" It was a weak, futile cry that he didn't even hear. I ran forward calling out again, but he opened the gate, and a thousand battle-ready men massed outside the courtyard shouted and cheered in unison. Automedon and another man stood by Achilleus's war chariot. Automedon climbed in and took the reins. Achilleus sprang up beside him. The other attendant handed Achilleus the huge ashwood spear.

"To battle!" Achilleus shouted. "Death to the enemy!"

The men roared. The charioteers cracked their whips over the backs of horses and wheeled about. Foot soldiers brandished spears. With a deafening clamor, Achilleus's Myrmidons surged to the main gate.

The sounds of the departing army dwindled. I slipped to the ground and for a long time sat motionless, too gripped with dread to move. *Vengeance.* It mattered more to Achilleus than his own life. I remembered that I, too, had sought it once. But now I saw its emptiness and futility. It wouldn't bring Patroklos back. My mind kept seeing the rage in Achilleus's eyes. The death of his friend had turned him into a terrifying stranger.

I wanted to know what happened yesterday when he had learned that Patroklos was slain.

I got up and went to find Diomede. She was sitting in the women's courtyard, forming a circle with Iphis, Kallianassa, Aglaia, and a group of others—strangers—grinding grain. I stopped. These were the women given to Achilleus by Agamemnon. Diomede was speaking, her face animated, welcoming. *Of course.* She too was from Lesbos, and she knew most of them.

She looked up, smiling, pushing back her red-brown curls. "Briseis, it's good to have you back." Her smile faded when she saw my face. "You're very pale. Are you ill?"

"It's nothing," I said distractedly. "Diomede, please tell me—"

She glanced apologetically at the women. "Of course. Join us. Let me make these others known to you. This is Theano, and Halia, and..." She gestured at each one, but their names did not stick in my mind.

I sat down and put an insistent hand on her arm. "Diomede, I must know how it was yesterday—when Patroklos was killed."

A flash of impatience was replaced by a look of sympathy. "We were talking of home, but there'll be other times for that." She shook her head gravely. "When Achilleus was brought the news, he gave a great cry and flung himself onto the ground. He poured handfuls of dust and ashes on his head and tore his hair."

Iphis, looking pale and strained, said, "He reached for the knife at his belt and might have killed himself but that the Achaean who brought the news—Antilochos was his name—threw his weight on him and grabbed his hands."

I understood, all too well, his wish for oblivion. "Then what happened?"

Diomede's glance fell. "He said some words, but perhaps I heard wrong. I was on the other side of the fence."

"Tell me."

"He said, 'Let death come. For me. For everyone. So long as Hektor dies.' He would have rushed into the battle right then, but he had no armor. So last night he had new armor made, the smiths working all night, melting down gold and bronze vessels, and—"

But I was no longer listening. *Let death come. For everyone.* All his grief had turned to rage, and death had overtaken his soul.

Iphis asked suddenly, "What if Hektor wins?"

I froze in the middle of a breath. Hektor's cold voice came back to me: *I will meet him face to face. And I will kill him.*

Diomede said somberly, "Then we'll all go to new masters."

One of the Lesbos women laughed. "For us that would mean having three masters in two days!" Her laughter scraped like sharp rocks.

"Hush, Theano!" another said. "It's not funny. We'd probably be sent back to Agamemnon."

That silenced them. Then one of them asked, "Tell us—what is it like here?" and the women of our camp all began talking at once.

Their voices pounded in my head. I stood up. "I'm going to the shore."

Diomede started to rise, but I laid a hand on her shoulder. "Nay, stay and help these newcomers feel at home."

I envied her, sitting in the circle of her friends, exchanging news and stories, almost untouched by the events of these past days. My thoughts turned to Andromache. At this moment she would be standing on the wall of the citadel holding her little boy in her arms and watching from afar as her Hektor went forth to face his enemy. She had not even slept in his arms last night, for the army of Troy had again encamped on the battlefield. Perhaps even now Hektor and Achilleus were advancing toward each other on the windy Trojan plain. I imagined Hektor's impassioned face, his glittering black eyes. I also remembered him at his hearth that day in Troy, his face weary, his shoulders slumped with the weight of his people's destiny.

How foolish and vain had been my promise to Andromache. Hektor's killing of Patroklos had made this meeting with Achilleus inescapable. Failure lay on my heart with the weight of a mountain. *Father Zeus*, I prayed, *let Hektor and Achilleus both live.*

But as I remembered the look in Achilleus's eyes, I knew my prayer was wasted. I imagined his face contorted with rage as he hurled his spear with all his mighty strength.

In the late afternoon I was near the shore when a great clamor signaled the Achaeans' return from battle. Fighting the leaden weight of my legs, I stood up and started toward the place where we always watched the men's return. Diomede appeared at my side. Half a league away the men poured into the encampment. I began to tremble. A swarm of men and chariots charged in our direction, dust billowing up in clouds. Soon we could pick out the leading chariot. Thundering hooves brought it closer until we could see the man next to the driver. A tall man in flashing armor, shield and spear held aloft. Four red plumes nodded from the crest of his helmet.

Diomede cried, "He's back! He's safe!"

A cold, terrible certainty pierced me. I turned away. "Briseis, what's wrong?" Diomede asked. Before I could answer, she gripped my arm hard. The other hand was pressed over her mouth. "Look!"

Achilleus's chariot swept by, dragging something. It was the torn, naked body of Hektor, attached by the feet to the back of the chariot. His neck and chest were dark crimson with blood. His eyes stared sightless at the sky, and his hair was spread behind him trailing in the dirt, no longer black but an unrecognizable gray brown, streaked with blood. His head bumped over the ruts in the ground, and his arms flopped about like broken sticks. Dust swirled around him.

I crumpled to my knees, covering my face with my hands. Thudding hooves went past me, grew faint, then increased again, passed again. Achilleus gave a fierce shout. He was leading the Myrmidons in a victory procession around their camp. I looked up just as they passed once more, and saw the body, the head to the side now, the mouth slack and open, those sightless eyes looking right at me. My stomach heaved, and I was sick.

One of the Lesbos women bent over me. "You're with child, aren't you? Ianeira told me." I nodded weakly. "Perhaps you should let Diomede take you inside to lie down."

"Briseis! Is this true?" Diomede asked. "We should tell Achilleus—"

I gripped her hands. "No! Don't tell him!"

Diomede drew a deep breath. "Very well. But come lie down."

She led me to my bed and put a cool cloth over my brow. "Rest. At least he's alive, and we won't be given to another master." I shut my eyes, knowing this security had come at the cost of Andromache's happiness. Silent tears ran down my temples. I wept not only for Patroklos and Hektor and poor bereft Andromache, but also for the part of Achilleus that had died when his friend was killed.

Diomede, watching me, said, "Briseis, don't let this affect you. You'll make yourself ill unto death."

If I died, I thought, Achilleus wouldn't care or even notice.

After she left, I could not close my eyes for fear of the images that would come to my mind. After some time passed, I got cautiously to my feet and crept to the door of

Achilleus's hut. I cracked it open, peered inside. No one was there. I stole across the room toward the courtyard door, barely breathing, fearing that he would be there by the body of his friend.

But the courtyard was empty of any living man. Where had he gone? From afar I heard shouts and smelled fires, smoke, cooking meat. It was the hour of the evening meal, though the normal routine was disrupted. I guessed the men were preparing some kind of feast on the shore. The women must have been pressed into doing extra chores, baking many rounds of bread and waiting on the men. The sky glowed with the dull rose of twilight. I looked out and saw something on the ground by Patroklos's bier. At first I took it for a shadow. But it had a cold, dark substance. Chills ran over my skin. Gathering courage, I stepped outside—and stopped.

Hektor's body was thrown face down in the dust at Patroklos's feet.

I stood motionless, not breathing. Then I nerved myself to walk outside to the two dead men. I went to Patroklos first and looked down at his face. *Forgive me,* I whispered, *but even though he killed you, he should not be so dishonored.*

I knelt at Hektor's side. With great effort I rolled him over. *Andromache, this is where you belong. But I will tend him for you.* I reached out to close his eyes.

As I looked over his body, with the gaping wound at his throat, I took a deep, steadying breath. I went into the hut and returned with water, cloths, and an old blanket. Just as I knelt down, I heard a shout close by. I froze, my heart pounding. When there was no further sound I began my work. I cleaned the soiled flesh, straightened the dead man's hair, and covered him decently with a blanket. Lighting a lamp, I set it by his head. I hesitated. I should stay with him, holding a vigil, but I feared Achilleus finding me here.

Just as I was leaving, the courtyard gate slammed open. Night had fallen, but the lamp's light showed Achilleus clearly. The sight of him sent a shock through me. His tunic was torn and dirty, his hair tangled, his face smeared with ashes. His limbs were streaked with blood and dust. In great furious steps he came toward me. I shrank as he towered over me, eyes blazing.

"Why are you here? I traded away Patroklos's life—for you!" He looked down at Hektor and saw what I had done. "This one is to be left for the dogs and vultures!" He bent and stripped the blanket off the corpse.

"Achilleus, stop!" I cried. "You gave my husband Mynes a funeral pyre."

His breaths were short, ragged. "Mynes was an honorable enemy. Hektor slew my friend." He choked on the word. "And he would have desecrated Patroklos."

He bent swiftly and rolled the corpse onto its face, pushing it into the dirt. Then his foot came down between the shoulder blades as if to grind the body into the ground. I gasped, one hand pressed over my mouth, too afraid to try to stop him. But he only straightened wearily, a dark shape against the night sky. He drew a deep breath and leaned over Patroklos's bier to look into the star-washed face of his dead friend.

"Tomorrow the Achaeans will build your pyre, Patroklos, and give you a funeral with all honor. Then we will hold your funeral games." He rested his hand gently on the dead man's chest. "I did what I promised," he said hoarsely. "I've brought you Hektor. And I've captured twelve Trojans alive, whom I will sacrifice at your funeral pyre."

I went cold. "Achilleus—*no!*" I cried. "You can't mean to —!"

He stared down at me. "No one shall stop me." He seized my jaw, forcing me to look up at him. "Stay out of this, or I'll kill you!" I held still. "Now begone!" He dropped his hand and turned away.

"Come, Patroklos," he said in a broken voice, "they are waiting down at the shore to mourn you and hold your funeral feast."

He picked up his friend's corpse as tenderly as a mother cradles a newborn baby and carried it from the courtyard.

Twelve Trojans to be slaughtered! The gods would surely strike him dead for such a monstrous outrage.

CHAPTER 39

The twelve noble young Trojans he slew without mercy.

Iliad, Homer, Book XXIII
(Rouse's translation)

After a long time I got to my feet slowly, like an old woman. When I reached our quarters, it was very dark, very quiet. Alone, I sat on my bed, shivering from a deep inner cold as I thought of Achilleus slaughtering those twelve men.

I tried to tell myself that it would be no different than if he had slain them in battle. I told myself it was not my business and I could do nothing. But it did no good. I lay down, too troubled to sleep. Something else occurred to me. What if one of the twelve was Akamas, the man whose wound I had tended and who had come to my aid in Troy? The thought of such a warm and kind soul waiting for death was unbearable.

I slept haunted by nightmares. Just before dawn I awoke and bolted up with a new horror. If the gods were angry with Achilleus, they might also kill his progeny: his living son far across the sea—and his unborn child. I put a hand on my belly. I could do nothing to shelter the tiny life within me from the wrath of the gods.

I must stop Achilleus.

I could not do it alone. The other women had returned, and my only friend Diomede slept in the next bed. I awakened her and told her about the terrible deed Achilleus planned. "He means to kill those men in cold blood at the pyre of Patroklos, Diomede. We can't let him do it."

She sat up. "Are you mad? There's no one who can stop him. None of the Achaeans will even try."

"But we can't just stand by!"

"Don't be a fool," she said. "He'll kill us if we try to interfere. Those twelve Trojans went to battle knowing they were risking death. Do you think they wouldn't have killed Achilleus if they'd had the chance? Why waste your pity on the men? It's we women who suffer the most."

"The gods will strike him down for such an act," I said.

Diomede lay down again. "I doubt the gods care."

Only Patroklos might have had the influence to stop him. Then I remembered Automedon, who'd replaced Patroklos as second-in-command. I doubted he would concern himself with my worries, but I had to try. At first light after I helped the women with the most basic chores, I went to search for him.

Outside the courtyard men scurried to and fro, driving mule carts laden with wood. Down the shore, a huge pyre was rising. I set out for it and nearly bumped into a man carrying an armload of logs. "Out of my way!" he bellowed.

Another shouted, "Go back to your chores, woman! You've no business here."

I hid behind one of the ships, watching for Automedon until at last I saw him. He was sitting on a timber for a moment's rest. I rushed over and crouched on one knee before him. "Automedon, I beg you!" My mouth was so dry that my voice sounded strange to my own ears. "Can you stop Achilleus from killing the twelve Trojans tonight? It's a terrible deed—"

He looked at me as if I had taken leave of my senses. "The lives of those Trojans are nothing—to him or anyone." He spat on the ground.

"But surely it will offend the gods, particularly Apollo, the patron of Troy. Achilleus will be punished—accursed."

He shook his head roughly. "Revenge is his duty—his right. The gods will not interfere. Stay out of this, woman. You understand nothing." Getting abruptly to his feet, Automedon left me kneeling in the sand.

Why did no one but me see the obvious? The gods were capricious and needed far less reason to curse a man. They might send the Furies to pursue Achilleus, torment and punish him, and kill his offspring. Even if I was wrong, it was no comfort. Twelve helpless men would die. I looked up at the sky, deep blue with white clouds that scattered and reformed into feathery shapes, lofty and distant. *Zeus*, I thought. Zeus had brought things to this pass. I lifted my arms. "Father of all the gods," I prayed, "spare the life of Achilleus, but don't let him do this evil. And don't let Akamas be among the victims." I listened deep within me for an answer but heard only the faraway shouts of the men as they prepared the funeral pyre and the indifferent wind, whipping across the sand. I dropped my arms in defeat.

Warrior's Prize

At twilight hundreds of men from all over the encampment gathered around the huge pyre far down the shore. Achilleus appeared suddenly in our camp. His face was dirty, unshaven, his eyes sunk in hollows. His beautiful mane of bronze hair was gone. I was with Diomede and others near the gate. I shrank in fear, but he did not even see us.

"Diomede, he's cut his hair!"

"It's an Achaean custom to cut one's hair in mourning."

Achilleus shouted orders. A group of Myrmidons hitched their horses to their chariots. The body of Patroklos was lifted onto a chariot, and the men processed solemnly toward the funeral pyre. Silent and grim, Achilleus stood watching. Then Automedon brought his own chariot to him. Achilleus climbed in, and they followed the chariot bearing Patroklos.

I watched until they were out of sight. The moment had come. I couldn't put my body between Achilleus's victims and his sword blade, but I prayed I would somehow find a way to stop him. I prayed for courage. When Diomede and the others went to the hut to eat their meal, I set out along the shore.

Darkness had almost completely fallen. The sea glowed with an eerie, tenebrous light. Ahead of me, the dark mass of hundreds of men was grouped around the pyre. Etched against the sky, several men were carrying Patroklos on his bier to the top of the pyre.

It felt as if his death had taken all kindness and reason from the world. "Farewell, my friend!" I whispered.

At the bottom of the pyre stood a tall figure, withdrawn, solitary, the darkness around him somehow colder and deeper.

I steeled myself and crept closer. My gray shawl helped conceal me in the deepening twilight. Crouching behind a small shed, I searched for the Trojan captives in the dim light. My straining eyes landed on a group of bound men, indistinguishable shadows until someone planted a lit torch, and I saw clearly.

Frantic, I studied their outlines. One man was too stocky, one too short, one was balding, another had thin straight hair down his back. Only one had thick curly hair like Akamas. My heart dropped. Then I saw that he was far too tall. It was scant comfort, for here were sons, brothers, husbands, fathers. They ate and drank and laughed. They made love and held children on their knees. And now they waited to die.

An ominous mutter emerged from the silent crowd as Achilleus turned to the captives. No one moved.

Achilleus, don't! It won't lessen your pain. I felt as though I had shouted, but my throat was so dry I could not even whisper.

He pulled the first Trojan from the line of captives and lifted his sword. I leapt into a run but before I had gone five paces, he slit the man's throat as if slaughtering a sheep. I froze. Blood spurted, black as the night. Achilleus heaved him onto the pyre.

A roar from the men drowned out my cry. My knees gave way and I fell to the ground, but somehow found the strength to rise and stagger forward again.

Someone small and hard grabbed me from behind, taking us both to the sand. "You fool!" Diomede hissed, holding me down. "What are you doing? He'll kill you too!"

"Let him!" I cried. "Since he—"

"Hush! Listen!"

That roar again—the Achaeans cheering, shouting as Achilleus murdered the next captive and flung him onto the pyre. I pressed my hands over my ears as more men died and more roars came. Diomede seized my wrists. "Do you hear?" she demanded. "They're all as hungry for blood as he. Come away!"

I shook and sobbed, feeling as soiled as if I had assisted in the slaughter.

"Get up!" She had a tight grip on my arm. "Quickly, before anybody sees us."

She led me along the shore, pulling me so hard I was forced to run. When at last we stopped to catch our breath, she looked over her shoulder.

"No one will come after us," I told her. "They only care about the bloodletting."

Nearby, dogs barked, a hound bayed. The sky began to glow with lurid, pulsating streaks of red.

They had lit the pyre.

CHAPTER 40

> The first dawn, brightening
> sea and shore, became familiar to him,
> as at that hour, he yoked his team, with Hektor
> tied behind, to drag him out, three times
> around Patroklos's tomb.
>
> *Iliad*, Homer, Book XXIV
> (Fitzgerald's translation)

    The men stayed with the burning pyre until dawn. Achilleus did not return to the hut. When morning came, the women awoke and went to fetch water and milk the goats and bake the bread. As if nothing had happened. As if there was a reason for life to continue.

Having no other choice, I went with them.

Later, as Diomede and I worked in the courtyard airing out the bedding, some of Achilleus's men appeared. Two went to the stables and came out leading three horses. Others headed for a storage shed and came out bearing several bronze caldrons. Automedon and another man went into Achilleus's hut and carried out cooking vessels, gold drinking cups, and other treasures. They took all these things and headed toward the center of the camp.

As we watched from the courtyard, Diomede asked, "What's happening?"

"He said something about funeral games for Patroklos today," I said. We had all begun to refer to Achilleus only as *he*, and always in a hushed voice.

"That probably means he sent for all those things to offer as prizes," Diomede guessed.

One of his attendants, a man named Alkimos, approached us and asked, "Where is the woman Aglaia?"

Diomede pointed to our room in the back of the hut, where Aglaia often sat alone, sulking and shirking. "In there." She shot a puzzled look at me as he went in and summoned Aglaia, who came out preening now, simpering. With a disdainful glance at us, she set off with Alkimos, who had also summoned several other women from nearby huts.

Diomede, watching them walk up the shore, gave a wicked grin. "I'll wager our dear Aglaia is about to become a prize in one of the funeral games!"

"What makes you think so?" I asked.

"*He* knows she betrayed you to Agamemnon's men that night. I overheard him say so to Patroklos. He said he was looking for an honorable way to get rid of her."

I was silent. If Aglaia had not acted as she had, none of this might have happened. *Might have!* How many such broken threads are woven into the strands of our lives? How the Fates must laugh at their work!

All the men went to the games. Throughout the day we heard occasional shouts and cheers from the center of the camp, carried on the wind. It was late afternoon when the men returned, spent as if from a battle. Achilleus disappeared into his hut and closed the door hard. Shortly afterward, we went to his courtyard to hang up some clothes we had washed. I opened the gate and froze. A sickly carrion stench wafted out. I gagged, pressing my hand over my nose and mouth. Diomede, a step behind me, looked over my shoulder. "What is it?"

We stared. The body of Hektor lay naked and prone in the dust. Flies buzzed around him.

"Come away!" Diomede tried to pull me out through the open gate.

But I held back. "I thought—last night—he would have been put on the pyre with the others. So his soul could pass into the realm of Elysium in Hades."

The door of the hut burst open. Achilleus charged out. Diomede pulled me behind the gate. I peered back in. He stood staring down at the body with haunted eyes. Then in a swift movement he bent over the corpse and turned it onto its back. He grasped some leather thongs that had been bloodily threaded through Hektor's ankles. Achilleus dragged the corpse on its back by the thongs, toward the gate. Diomede and I dived out of sight around the corner of the palisade. He pulled the corpse to where his chariot stood hitched and ready, and attached the body to the back. He jumped up and drove down the shore, Hektor trailing behind.

I stood for long moments with my shawl pressed into my mouth.

Much later he returned, still dragging the body, which he left again on the bare ground. It looked like some large broken animal half devoured by wolves.

Warrior's Prize

After that we stayed away from the courtyard, carrying out our tasks elsewhere. But it did no good. With my eyes closed I could still see Hektor's body dragged along for its dreadful ride down the shore and around Patroklos's tomb— just as I could see the first captive Trojan falling with his throat slit.

At dawn the next day, I heard sounds outside: the opening of the gate, the creak of wheels, the thump of hooves. Achilleus was once again wreaking his senseless, terrible vengeance.

"Don't think about it," Diomede said when she saw my face. "That's how I've survived. Hektor is naught but a piece of earth now. The dead feel nothing."

But what of his soul, which without proper burial must wander forever homeless? And what of Andromache and the fatherless little boy Astyanax? I'd wanted Achilleus to live. I'd asked the gods for his life. And the gods, laughing, had granted my prayer.

Death hung over the camp. The sickly stench from the corpse pervaded everything and would not let me forget, even for a moment. Achilleus made his vengeance a daily pattern. Each morning I, the only one awake, listened to those dreadful sounds. Death was in my heart too, as if I had taken part in all his bloodletting. I felt a terrible fear for the babe growing in my womb. Who would care for him and protect him? What would he become? His father was a monster, and I— a child should not be born to a mother such as I. I could never give love to anyone or anything ever again.

On the third morning I arose with my mind made up. Achilleus's child would not be born.

With the flat calm of despair, I waited until after the morning chores were done and the women left to wash clothes at the spring. Diomede, when she saw that I had no wish to join them, did not press me. Though she kept a watch over me, she enjoyed spending time with the women from Lesbos—her friends. They managed to separate themselves from the dreadful events. At the spring, far away from the stench of death, there would be much talk, even laughter.

After returning from his terrible chariot ride, Achilleus went down to the shore, where he spent hours staring at the sea. I watched him leave. I entered his hut. He had many herbs stored there—though even he did not know all their uses. The one I sought was secret women's lore, passed down by women to their daughters and granddaughters from time out of mind. It was an herb I knew he possessed, for it could also be used to staunch the flow of blood from wounds.

I searched through jars and bundles of herbs, sniffing them, examining the leaves until I found the one I needed. I prepared a strong potion and heated it over the hearth. Then I carried the steaming goblet out to the women's courtyard.

As I sat on the ground, breathing against the pain of my leaden heart, trying to keep my resolve while I waited for the potion to cool, the gate swung open. I lurched and almost spilled the cup. Diomede stood there. When she saw my face, she came up quickly and sniffed the brew. Without a word she tried to yank it from my hands.

I struggled fiercely, but standing over me she had the advantage. She twisted my wrist and dashed the cup to the ground. We both watched the contents soak into the dust.

Then she sat next to me, leaning against the wall, breathing hard.

She picked up the cup and used a finger to scrape out the residue of herbs, which she flicked onto the ground. "I'll help you stay out of his way," she said. "You need never see him or speak to him. But this—" She stared at the cup, then flung it across the courtyard. "This hurts only you. And the little one. There's been enough killing. Don't be like *him!*"

She got up, reaching down to help me to my feet. I took her hand but couldn't move. I pressed my other hand over my face and wept.

CHAPTER 41

"Akhilleus,
be reverent toward the great gods! And take
pity on me, remember your own father."

—Priam, *Iliad*, Homer, Book XXIV
(Fitzgerald's translation)

The Achaeans did not return to battle. A dreadful quiet pervaded the Myrmidon camp, for the unburied corpse haunted us all. Every time my chores took me near the courtyard, I held a cloth over my nose and mouth, but I could never be free of the stench. I tried not to think, for there were too many places where I could not allow my mind to go: Achilleus, Patroklos, the babe growing within me, the lost soul of Hektor, and most of all, Andromache.

At night sleep often eluded me. One night, when the sleeping quarters were hot and close, I gave up on rest and decided to walk along the shore. Careful not to wake the others, I groped for my sandals. Crept to the door. Let myself out into the night.

A half-moon sailed above feathered clouds. All was still. The sea sent black ripples against silver-gray sand. Near the water's edge I heard a muffled groan, and stopped. A man lay face down on the shore—Achilleus, seemingly insensible to the world. I stood staring at him, feeling hatred swell within me. He had turned the world into a place of utter evil.

He must have sensed my presence, for without warning he sat up and turned to me. I wanted to flee, but before I could move, his fathomless eyes, black in the darkness, looked into mine—and revealed his heart.

I saw that, in his abuse of Hektor's corpse he sought to blunt a pain that gave him no respite—the knowledge that he brought about the death of his friend. He was a prisoner of his rage and grief, as much as he had made the rest of us. And he would never, ever forgive himself. To my surprise, I felt a deep, unwilling pity for him.

I said, "Achilleus, let go of your revenge! Do you think Patroklos wants you to suffer like this?"

Something sparked in those eyes and was gone. He buried his face on his bent knees. He was silent for so long I turned away.

At last he said in a muffled voice, "I have little time left."

A chill ran along my skin. "What do you mean?"

"Left to live."

"You can't know that," I said.

He looked at me. "I do know it." I took a step toward him, but he lifted his hand to ward me off. "Leave me."

I hesitated, then turned away, my hopelessness deeper than before. He was broken beyond mending, and he had made a pact with death.

The next morning he once again took Hektor's corpse on that terrible chariot ride. When he came back, he closed himself in his hut and stayed there for hours. Much later in the afternoon, as I was returning from the spring with water for the evening meal, I saw a strange sight: a wicker cart loaded with goods and pulled by a team of mules, driven by an old man. Another gray-bearded man in a plain, soiled brown cloak followed in a horse-drawn cart. He bowed down as if under a great weight. The ancient travelers were heading along the shore. Where had they come from, and what were they doing here?

As they drove past me, the driver of the horse cart glanced my way. He looked like Hektor's father Priam, King of Troy, whom I remembered from Andromache's wedding. But it couldn't be. Many graybeards, sunken in age, looked alike. These two were surely peddlers who had come from some nearby town to trade goods for food.

Even so, I hurried after the carts. At Achilleus's gate I set the water jar against the fence and watched the old men continue up the shore. They paused when they met a man near a hut. They seemed to be asking for directions. The Achaean turned and pointed—right to where I stood. The men reversed the carts in a wide turn. I watched with horror as they approached.

They must not come here!

They halted near the gate. The one who had driven the horse cart tossed the reins to his companion, climbed down, and walked toward me.

My blood turned to ice. It *was* Priam.

He spoke in a quavering voice. "Good woman, is this the hut of Prince Achilleus?"

The dreadful carrion stench wafted up behind me. I held up my hands. "Sire, this is a place of death," I said. "Go back!"

He squared his thin shoulders. "Take me to Achilleus."

"Sire, he will kill you!"

"I've come to ransom the body of my son. I won't leave without him."

I backed against the gate, shaking my head, spreading my arms.

He said, "Stand aside. Let me pass."

It was a command. But I didn't move. In the courtyard he'd see the body. Unless I could find a way to conceal it. "Wait!" I drew a deep breath. "Please wait, Sire." Though I was sure Achilleus was in the hut, I said, "I—I'll go see if Achilleus is within."

I sped through the gate to where Hektor lay. Holding my breath, I covered him with my gray shawl, scattering swarms of flies. Now, in the deepening twilight, he was hidden from sight.

Just as I turned away, the king and his servant came through the gate.

I bowed before him. "Achilleus is inside with his companions, Sire. But you shouldn't—"

Priam went silently past me to the door of the hut and opened it, followed by his attendant.

Achilleus would kill him. I had to stop it—or at least try. I sped around to the rear door that connected Achilleus's room to the women's quarters. Diomede, kneading bread there, looked up in surprise. "Maybe you shouldn't go—" she began.

I pulled the door open a crack and peered in.

And stopped dead. Achilleus sat in his chair by the hearth, looking down in astonishment. I saw him in profile, but could only see Priam's hunched back as he crouched trembling at Achilleus's feet. *Oh gods, had Achilleus already harmed him?*

But then Priam lifted his head. Taking his enemy's hands, he brought them to his lips and kissed them. I silenced a gasp.

Achilleus's face went still. His eyes filled. The firelight caught the silvery line of a tear running down his cheek. Neither man saw me. Nor did Achilleus's two companions, who sat back in the shadows watching. After a moment Achilleus reached for Priam's hand.

I knew then that the old king was safe.

I pushed the door a bit more ajar and crouched, looking through the crack, listening, hardly breathing.

"What—?" Diomede whispered, but I waved her to silence.

"Achilleus, think of your own father, old and alone, and take pity on me!" Priam said. "No man has ever done what I've had to do—kiss the hands of the man who slew my son."

Achilleus grasped the old man's hand and moved him gently away from his knees. He covered his face with his other hand. He wept.

Priam too was weeping. Tears stung my eyes.

Long moments passed. At last Achilleus straightened. "How could you have the courage to come here to me? Your heart must be made of iron." Achilleus got up, took the old man by the hand, and raised him from his knees. He said, "Zeus brings all men evil things as well as blessings. My father too. Though you have many sons, he has only one ill-fated son—me. I've left him alone in his old age, while I am far away, bringing *you* trouble and—grief." His voice broke on the word. "Your sorrows are great. But you must not mourn endlessly. It will not bring your Hektor back. Let your heart find comfort. Now, come, sir," he invited, "sit and—"

But Priam interrupted harshly. "Do not invite me to sit when my son's body lies untended. Release him to me, Achilleus!" *Oh, Priam,* I thought, *you will reawaken his rage.* "I've brought gifts—ransom. Take them, enjoy them. I wish you a safe return to your home, since you spared my life."

A spasm crossed Achilleus's face. He turned away from Priam and sprang to his feet, his eyes blazing. "Do not provoke me, sir! I intended to give back Hektor's body. But I have sorrows of my own. If you stir up my wrath, I may lose my temper and forget that you are a suppliant."

He stood still for a moment, his hand pressed to his brow. Then, leaving Priam standing there, he came abruptly toward our quarters and the door that hid me. "Briseis! Diomede!"

I scrambled away, collided with Diomede and the breadboard, and plunged my hands into the floury dough. My back was to Achilleus, my heart thudding as he entered our hut.

"Come," he said. We stood quickly. "Get the other women. I need you to wash the body of Hektor and make it presentable for his father."

"Aye, my lord," Diomede said. As he turned away, she stared at me. "Briseis! You're white as a shroud! Achilleus," she called after him. "Briseis can't help, she's ill with—"

"Hush!" My hand flew to her lips. "*I can!*" Achilleus hadn't heard. He walked out of our door to the courtyard. "Quickly!" I said. "He needs us. Call the others."

She went to summon the women, and we followed Achilleus. In the main courtyard he called to Automedon and Alkimos and gave them orders to unhitch the wagon, tend the mules, and take the old King's attendant to another hut to eat and rest. Then, going to the wagon that contained the ransom, Achilleus lifted out a fine-spun tunic and two mantles and carried them to where the corpse of Hektor lay.

"Dress the body in these," he told us. Glancing at the open door of the hut, he added, "I don't want you working out here. The old man mustn't see him as he is now." When he noticed the shawl over Hektor, he cast a puzzled look at us, his eyes coming to rest on me. But he said nothing. He only bent and lifted the body in his arms. He carried it around the building to the women's courtyard where he called for a clean blanket on which to lay it.

As I followed him, the odor of death swept over me, and I was afraid my stomach would betray me. Yet my spirit stayed strong, because at last we could do this for Hektor and for the living. When Achilleus removed the shawl, the body was mangled, dirty, the wounds caked and blackened. But my stomach remained steady. I knelt down next to the corpse.

Achilleus crouched next to me. When he glanced at me, a heightened resolve sparked in his eyes. I expected him to leave us to this work and go back to Priam, but to my surprise he stayed to help, lifting the corpse as we washed it and rubbed it with scented oil, holding the head when I poured water to wash the hair. I could feel the intensity of his purpose. It mattered greatly to him that this was well done.

Warrior's Prize

When we were finished, he lifted the body with care and reverence and placed it on a bier. Then he called to Automedon and Alkimos to take it to the horse cart. As they left, he stood looking down at us. He said, "Bread. Get it ready and bring it in. I will be preparing the evening meal for the King."

He left. I stared after him, recalling how afraid I had been for Priam a short time ago. But, strange as it seemed, compassion had bloomed between these two desperately grieving enemies. I realized that Achilleus could offer the old king more comfort and healing than anyone else.

But I wanted more. I wanted healing for Achilleus as well.

Later, after we had cleansed the death stench from our hands, changed our gowns and prepared the bread, we inhaled the aroma of grilling lamb. It had been so long since I had smelled this that it seemed to come from another life. When the flattened barley cakes had been browned over our fire, Diomede placed them in a basket. "I'll take this in."

I reached for the bread. "Let me."

As I walked in, Automedon took it from my hands. Achilleus was busy over the fire, turning the grilling spits, sprinkling salt. Alkimos mixed wine, poured it into goblets. When the food was served, Automedon and Alkimos retired to the far end of the hut, leaving Achilleus in privacy with his royal guest.

But I lingered. To stay near him, I thought of another duty. I brought a cloth and a basin so that they might wash their hands before eating. First I offered these to the king, who barely noticed me. Then I went to Achilleus, who gave me an unfathomable look and nodded thanks.

"If you need anything else—" I whispered.

"Aye. Not now." Although it was a dismissal, I sensed only his urgent need to offer hospitality to the king. He gestured in the direction of the door to the women's quarters, or perhaps the corner. I chose to interpret that he meant the corner and I could stay. I backed into the shadows there.

As the men ate, sometimes one or the other would speak, or silence would fall between them, a companionable silence. When at last they finished, they looked at each other with a kind of wonder. The firelight burnished Achilleus's skin and the smooth lines of his brow and cheek and jaw, and highlighted the ravaged nobility of Priam's features.

At last Priam said, "I have tasted pain and grief a thousand times since Hektor died. This is the first time I've tasted bread and meat. Another cup of wine, please! Then make a bed ready for me that I may sleep. I've not slept a full night since then, either."

"Nor I!" Achilleus responded. He beckoned toward my corner. "More wine, Briseis, and take these away." As I refilled the goblets my trembling fingers brushed against his. But his eyes remained focused on Priam. I removed the platters, taking them to the corner to wash them.

Achilleus said, "My friend, you should sleep outside in the courtyard under the stars. We'll make your bed there. I've spoken to my men. At first light they'll guide you out of the encampment so that Agamemnon and the other chieftains do not learn of your presence." He stood, raised Priam by the right hand and said, "One more thing. How many days do you need for the funeral of Hektor?"

Priam replied, "Eleven days. Nine days to mourn him and to bring in wood from the far hills for his funeral pyre. On the tenth day we will have his funeral feast, and on the eleventh day we will make his tomb."

"Then for eleven days," Achilleus said, "I will hold the Achaeans back from fighting."

I should have been surprised, but somehow it was part of this strange evening, this transformation of the world—and Achilleus's return to life. Warmth filled my heart. He had done what was needed for the living. I spared a thought for Andromache. She would embrace her Hektor one last time.

Achilleus looked at me, his eyes deep as the sea. "Briseis, fetch the women. Tell them to bring bedding for King Priam and his servant."

He stood holding a lamp for us as we prepared the beds. When we had finished and Priam was lying down, Achilleus extinguished the lamp. "Good night, sir!" he said softly and turned toward the doorway of his hut.

Our work was done. The other women went hastily ahead of him through his hut to our own quarters. I followed slowly, my pulse racing.

He came in, closed the outer door, and approached the hearth. As I was about to leave, I heard a sigh so soft I might have imagined it. The only light in the room came from the dying fire. I turned. He was a black outline, motionless.

He said, "Stay with me, Briseis."

I flew across the room to him. I would have crossed the dark river itself to hold him in my arms.

CHAPTER 42

*Achilles himself lay to rest in a corner of the hut,
with lovely Briseis by his side.*

Iliad, Homer, Book XXIV,
(Rouse's translation)

We lay in his bed and loved and loved again, our passion all the deeper for our shared sorrow. He fell asleep before I did, and as I lay drifting off, the sound of his breathing filled me with a sense of peace. When morning came, I saw the soft, unguarded look in his eyes as he awoke. He kissed me, gave his radiant smile, and pulled me once more into his arms.

A long time later, he sat up, and his mood changed abruptly. I watched his thoughts take him far away. He bent to plant another kiss on my lips before springing to his feet. I felt a rush of cold air from his side of the bed. As he pulled on tunic, sandals, and the blue mantle, there was tenseness and urgency in his movements.

"Where are you going?" I asked, afraid.

"To Agamemnon's quarters."

"Now? Why?"

"I must make sure of my promise to Priam. Agamemnon must tell the Achaeans they won't fight for eleven days."

"What if he won't agree?"

He gave a grim smile. "The army will do as I say. I have regained my honor. Although it doesn't seem to matter so much now." He bent to kiss me again. "Wait for me here. Have the morning meal ready." And he was gone.

I lit the fire and fetched bread and a jug of milk, which I set on the lip of the hearth. He returned in less time than I had thought possible. "All is well. We have eleven days," he said, flinging off his mantle. "Now, where's that meal?"

He ate in silence. I guessed from the sudden bleakness in his eyes that the eleven days loomed as a vast emptiness in which to miss his friend. He would spend the time doing things the men did when there was no battle: drills and hunting, exercising the horses, mending weapons, armor, harnesses, sometimes engaging in races and contests. But for me the truce was a god-sent gift. I would fill his emptiness, tell him of the child, and make his return to battle unthinkable.

I said, "Achilleus, today will you take me beyond the camp where we went once before?"

"Aye, if you want, but why?"

"I'd like to bathe in the sea. And I have something to tell you."

He gave a teasing grin. "How do I know you aren't going to try to run away again?"

I was dismayed. "I would never—"

But he burst out laughing. "Do you remember how ferocious you were when you first came here? You tried to kill me, not just once but twice!"

Abashed, I lowered my gaze. "Don't remind me!"

He laughed again, and then grew serious. "My Briseis, I love your fierceness—your fiery spirit." He tilted my chin up to his face and kissed me.

After a moment he said, "Get some food ready to bring, and let's go."

We set out in the shimmering stillness, walking to where there were no more huts or ships. When we reached the last sentry post, Achilleus greeted the guard and told me, "This is one of my men." He introduced me to the man, saying, "If Briseis ever comes here without me, let her through. She has my trust. Tell your fellows."

After we crossed the shallow stream onto the empty beach, he said, "There, my sweet! You can come to bathe here any time you want. And if my company grows too tedious, you can take a long walk and leave me far behind, as you tried to do the last time we came here."

He was laughing as he said it, and I wanted to answer with a jest, but could think of nothing. What I said at last was the simple truth. "I was afraid that day. Afraid of my heart."

He took me in his arms and I felt raw emotion surge through him. "My Briseis! I wish we'd had a better start. We would have had so much more time."

Would have had. The import of this sank into my heart like a stone. This was the crux of it, the thing he believed but wouldn't say, the shadow hanging over us, its sadness pervading even the joy of our reunion: his belief that in recommitting to the war, he had chosen death.

I wanted to shake him, scream at him, tear my hair out. But I forced myself to say lightly, "We have lots of time. Our whole lives."

His answering silence was weighted with meaning.

How do I get us past this? How do I get him out of this war?

In silence we walked far down the shore to where the beach widened and the sand was soft, and we sat side-by-side looking at the sea, smooth and silvery under the blazing sun. Gulls dipped and soared on black-tipped wings, their cries the only sounds we heard.

It had been several months since I'd come to his camp in early spring, and now, though the weather was still mostly warm, the days were growing shorter.

At last he said, "What did you wish to tell me?"

Now that the moment had come, I struggled for words. I reached for his hand and brought it to rest on my belly. "Achilleus, your child is growing here inside me."

A sudden intake of breath. "Mine?"

"Who else could it be? After Mynes there was no one but you." For a long time he said nothing. When I ventured a look at his face, he was staring at the horizon, the familiar curved furrow between his brows. "Are you glad?" I asked.

"Aye!" He turned to me smiling. "That's wonderful news. A son!"

"It might be a daughter."

"Then she would be like you." But a shadow fell on him. *The* shadow. He lowered his head. "It doesn't—it can't change things," he muttered.

"What do you mean?"

He pulled me close. "Look after my child, Briseis."

"Of course." But now was not the time to delve into this. *We will speak more of it later.* "Achilleus," I said, "you've never told me about your parents—your home."

He picked up a handful of pebbles and flung them into the shallow water. "My father, the King of Phthia, lives mostly alone. My mother spends much of her time with her people, on the coast. Our home is in the hills near Mount Pelion. There are rivers and springs and woodlands and rich pastures for the horses and cattle." He spoke as if it were far removed from him. As he described a great house filled with servants and attendants, he smiled sadly. "I was the only child," he said. "How lonely it was—until Patroklos came to our household." His face brightened. "When he arrived, we were both young boys. He was older, but shy and afraid."

I saw that he needed to talk about his dead friend. "Patroklos told me of his exile and how you helped him."

"I cared nothing for his past. He was the brother, the friend I'd always longed for."

"Tell me about your home after Patroklos came," I said.

But it turned out that too little of his childhood had been spent there. There had been no softness or nurturing. "We were sent away to Mount Pelion to be tutored by Cheiron of the Kentaurs. He was a wise man who taught me not only riding and hunting and spear-play but healing and music as well. Then, as young men, we were sent to King Lykomedes on the island of Skyros because my mother wished to hide me from the coming war." His face sobered. I felt it—the shadow.

"What was your life like on Skyros?" I asked quickly.

"The king and his servants paid us little attention, but Patroklos and I had each other and needed no one else. We wandered all over the island and had many adventures."

I began to understand the full measure of his love for the only companion of his solitary youth. I was a latecomer in his life. No wonder he had thought me a poor trade for his friend. I remembered something else. "You fathered a child on Skyros."

His eyebrows lifted. "So you know about my son!"

"Patroklos told me."

"The king had a daughter a year older than me. Deidamiea. She was wild and wayward, a difficult, bossy girl. Often she wanted to join in our adventures. We tolerated her at times. Her nursemaid did not watch her well, and I, as lads will—" He broke off.

"Did you love her?" I asked.

A spasm crossed his face. "Not enough. We were too young..." He paused. "Too young to understand love. But now there is Neoptolemos, my son, a fine young man of fifteen summers." He reached down, took another handful of sand and pebbles, let it sift slowly through his fingers. "I've had many women since then. I've led the life of a warrior, a wanderer." He brought out his next words slowly. "If the gods will let me live long enough to take a wife—" his voice caught on those words, "it will be you, Briseis, or no one."

The world was suddenly full of light. A sea bird burst aloft with a shrill cry, and my spirit soared with it. I wanted to speak but no words came. The bird cried out again, but this time it was a sound of such plangent sadness that my heart stilled. Achilleus, silent, gazed out to sea. He gave a sharp sigh.

He looked at me then and smiled. "Where is the food you brought? I'm very hungry, and you should eat for the sake of that baby."

After our meal he jumped up and flung off his tunic. "Race you to the water!" I'd always been swift on my feet, but

I had no chance against Achilleus the Runner. He plunged in waist-deep just as I reached the water's edge. But after he swam a bit and surfaced for air, I caught him unawares, jumped on him, and dunked him underwater. He came up sputtering and laughing. "You demon!" Picking me up, he threw me bodily into the sea.

When we got out, shivering and laughing, he pulled me up the shore to the soft sand and spread his mantle so we could lie down. For a long moment he lay next to me, propped up on an elbow, looking at me, grinning wickedly.

"What?" I asked.

"We should do this more often—lie together in daylight. I love looking at your body!"

Our lovemaking was long and slow. Afterwards, as we lay sated, with our wet, sandy bodies touching, I closed my eyes. I had only dreamed of what it might be to know a day like this, the sky cloudless above us, the sun on my skin, and my beloved at my side. I wondered if the gods only allotted one such moment in a lifetime, and at that thought a gray sadness tinged the edges of my joy. The shadows were lengthening, the sun dropping toward the sea. The chilly wind picked up, and the sea became restless, each deep blue wave crested with gold. Achilleus rose and pulled his tunic over his head.

"It's time to go back." There was a heaviness in his voice.

Ten more days of the truce, I thought as we walked toward the encampment. Ten short days in which to persuade him to sail home to Phthia. *But how?*

CHAPTER 43

"My fate I will accept, whenever it is the will of
Zeus and All Gods to fulfill it."

—Achilleus, *Iliad*, Homer, Book XXII
(Rouse's translation)

The next day I mustered the courage to ask him outright, "Why don't you abandon this futile war and sail home?"

He lashed out with more anguish than anger. "Briseis, why can't you leave me alone?"

After that he became withdrawn and distant.

It was clear I was not allowed to speak of the future or his leaving the war. It was a solid wall between us. I had to find another way. On the third day, as we sat together over the remains of the evening meal, I thought of a new tactic. I spoke to him of my own home in the days of peace: of harvest festivals in Lyrnessos; of gathering grapes in the vineyards, and how as a child I had stolen grapes and gorged on their sweetness until I was sick. I spoke of going with my brothers when they led the sheep to the high pastures to graze on the new spring grass, and what it was like to breathe

the clean air of Mount Ida and drink icy water from streams on its slopes. Achilleus listened, smiled, but said nothing.

The next evening I came upon him playing the lyre, drawing from the strings a tune of almost unendurable longing. *What is devouring your soul?* I asked him in silence. *What do you pine for? Your home? Your lost friend? Life itself?*

I thought, *if I can't breach this wall I must find a way around it.*

Two more days passed swiftly. Each day, when he was with his men, all their activities and speech revolved around the war. I must counter that. I recalled the board game I'd played with Patroklos. That evening I said, "Achilleus, I played a game with Patroklos when he was wounded. A game on a board. Do you—can you—?"

His face lit up. He went to fetch it.

For a time we played happily, a hotly contested game, and I thought I would best him, but at the last moment he made a move that defeated me. "Not fair!" I said as he laughed. "I will have revenge!" I quickly set up the board for the next game. But halfway through it, his eyes lost focus, and his face went sad.

He stood up. "It's no good, Briseis. Let's just go to bed."

After our love, I lay awake wondering what else I could try. Another walk down the shore? A chariot ride? Get him to teach me a song on the lyre? But when I suggested each of these things, he turned me down.

Two days slipped by in which he went off with his men, returning late in the afternoon. We shared meals and walks on the shore and lay in his bed at night, but nothing changed.

I felt a growing desperation.

Warrior's Prize

That night I dreamed of his homeland, Phthia. I was outside a house with a beautiful garden where birds sang and fruit trees grew. A house he had built for us. He asked me, *Isn't this much better than the cold stone palace?* I awoke with a happy memory of that place. I could see it clearly and hear birds in the trees. On this godforsaken shore, how I missed trees!

An idea formed in my mind. I would make him believe in my dream.

That night in bed I told him of the dream, embroidering it with vivid details. "Achilleus, it was lovely! You built us a house where we could raise our child."

"That's wonderful," he said, his voice slurred as he slipped into sleep.

With four days left I shared my dream with him again. "When we live in Phthia, your son can make his home with us. He could be a mentor to his new brother—or sister—"

Achilleus said nothing.

"I'd love to meet your father, Achilleus. Your mother too."

"Enough. Let us talk of something else."

With three days left, I was in despair. I watched Achilleus jump into his chariot and take his magnificent horses for their daily gallop down the beach. He stood straight and tall, his shortened hair whipping out behind him, and I remembered the times I had watched him leave for battle. My nostrils imagined a carrion stench, as if I had actually inhaled it. The memory of butchered bodies, the corpses of Patroklos and Hektor, the burning pyres, filled me with horror. *Oh, gods, no!* I couldn't stand the thought of the war resuming.

With just two days left, the somnolent mood that had pervaded the camp was over. I saw heightened activity, men flinging spears at targets and sparring with swords. Achilleus's tension increased. On the last night, after I cleared away the remains of the evening meal, I found him sitting by the hearth, honing his sword and testing the fittings of his armor.

"Achilleus, no!" I cried involuntarily.

His hands went still. He looked up at me for a long moment. Then his gaze fell, and he began again with his work. "My father will take care of you," he said, "you and the child."

The world went dark. I clung to the back of a chair. "What do you mean?"

He met my gaze squarely. "You know it is my fate to die in this war."

I'd expected these words, but they still jolted me. "You—you can't be certain!"

He got up, unclasped my fingers from the chair back, and guided me into the seat. "Briseis, we've spoken of this. You must accept it, as I've known and accepted it from the start."

"But that night on your ship, you said—" Remembering how Agamemnon's men had ambushed me and stolen me back that night, I could not go on.

His face twisted momentarily. He said, "I told you then about my fate."

"You called it a prophecy. But prophecies don't always come true, and you said you wanted to return home."

"Everything has changed, Briseis. That's no longer possible."

"*Why not?*" I almost shrieked. "You've regained your honor!"

"How can I make you understand?" He got to his feet. "When I withdrew from the war, I hoped that I'd somehow cheated my destiny, but it was a vain, stupid hope, and it cost Patroklos his life. *He* was not meant to die. When in my folly I sent him out to help the Achaeans, he died the death that was meant for me."

I was shaking uncontrollably.

"It was my duty to avenge him," Achilleus continued, "even if it meant taking back my fate. I owe Patroklos my death."

I reached out blindly toward him. "Nay! He would want you to live, Achilleus."

"But I promised his spirit that I would not leave him alone on an alien shore. That my bones would lie with his in the same funeral urn."

"Let him go, Achilleus." A jagged rock lodged in my chest. "Bring his funeral urn home. Build a tomb for him in your homeland."

He shook his head. "I did not mean *this* shore. I meant the shore on the other side of the river of death. I abandoned him once. I will not do so again."

It was as if I had plunged into water so icy I couldn't breathe. "Surely you still have a choice. You could leave this war now and—"

"Enough!" He came to me and drew me into his arms. My skin felt so cold I wondered he didn't notice. "Briseis, you mean everything to me. Come, let's enjoy the time we have." He pulled me toward his bed. I could not understand the heat of his flesh after the words he had just spoken. As I lay beside him, joy was far from my heart.

All too soon morning came. He arose, ate a quick breakfast in silence, and began to don his armor. His face was pale with a sheen of sweat. I had a terrible fear that he would go to battle heedless of his safety and submit willingly to death.

He fastened his corselet, reached for his greaves. "Help me with these."

"No! I won't help you get yourself killed."

His eyes grew hard. "I can manage on my own. But it's bad luck to send me off like this."

Instantly I was wild with remorse. As I bent to fasten the straps, my tears blinded me, and all I could do was fling my arms about his legs and kneel with my face pressed against his thigh. But he needed my strength, not my tears. I said, "If you are strong, if you guard your life well, perhaps the gods will let you live. Promise me you'll have a care, Achilleus."

He smiled and reached down to touch my cheek. "I give you my word."

With trembling hands I fastened the straps about his calves and ankles, praying, *Zeus and all gods, keep him safe.* I reached up the sides of his legs to his hips, his waist, his chest, as if my touch could cover him with an invisible shield. *Aphrodite, don't let him be taken from me!* I got to my feet slowly. *Hera, mother of the gods, my little one needs his father.* As I continued to run my hands over his body, as if my prayers could wrap him in protection, the door opened. Automedon and Alkimos stood there.

Wait! I wanted to cry. *I'm not finished!*

He gently detached himself, kissed me, picked up his helmet and shield, and was gone.

CHAPTER 44

The beautiful greaves, fitted with silver anklets
first he put upon his legs, and next
the cuirass on his ribs; then over his shoulder
he slung the sword of bronze with silver scabbard;
finally he took up the massive shield...

Iliad, Homer, Book XIX
(Fitzgerald's translation)

Though he came back whole that night, he continued to go to battle day after day, whenever there was a sortie or a skirmish. If I made the slightest protest, either by look or gesture, his eyes, hard and bright, would ward me off, and he would turn away abruptly. So I learned to hold my tongue and guard my face.

When I shared my fear with Diomede, she shrugged and said, "No one can foretell the future. He can know no more of his fate than any man." I had once thought the same, but now I was not sure. Someone who believed in a certain fate could inadvertently make it happen.

Each time he left for battle, I pleaded, "Have a care, my love. Guard your life." I spoke softly, wary of angering him. "The gods are capricious. Perhaps it's their will that you live."

Each time he smiled and said, "I will take great care to come home to you."

He never again spoke of his fated death, yet it lay on my heart like a stone.

The baby was pushing out a little mound in my belly. At night, when I lay against the warmth of Achilleus, I savored a fleeting happiness. As weeks passed I even began to have hope, for there was a lull in the war. Without Hektor the Trojans seemed to have lost heart. They often stayed within their walls, coming out only now and again for skirmishes. Perhaps they were sick of the war. If only they would agree to hand over Helen and a large amount of treasure, the Achaeans would go home satisfied.

Then one day it all changed. After the Achaeans went forth to meet a Trojan onslaught, we heard shouts and clashes, unusually loud, even from afar. Diomede, the others, and I climbed onto Achilleus's ship. Straining our eyes we saw a huge multitude fighting on the plain. "Those can't all be Trojans," Diomede said. "Some other tribe or nation must have come to their aid."

I climbed down and sat crumpled in the sand. *Zeus and all gods, let him come back safely!* Hours passed before the men returned, Achilleus's chariot in the lead, galloping, urgent. In a chariot behind him, a man was doubled over, bleeding from the shoulder. As Automedon brought the horses to a halt, sending up a shower of rocks and sand, Achilleus sprang to the ground and shouted to his men, "Quick! Take Menesthios to his hut. I'll follow."

Throwing off his armor, he ran into our hut and came out with jars of herbs, ointments, and bandages, some of which he thrust into my hands. "Help me with these, Briseis. Menesthios was shot with a poisoned arrow, and—" As I followed him, he said, "Today the Amazons came to the aid of the Trojans."

Amazons? I'd heard they were a tribe of warrior women from the eastern plains. I wanted to ask Achilleus more, but at Menesthios's hut he took the medicines from my hands and rushed in alone. Much later he returned to wash and change into a clean tunic. "We drove the Amazons away, and Menesthios will live, but many others died. We are holding their funerals tonight. There's not even time to mourn. We must be ready for the next enemy."

Next enemy? Was there another? I felt cold inside as I watched him go up the shore. Soon the sky was aglow with light from the pyres. Very late he returned to the hut and fell into bed, exhausted. "Women," he said. "We killed women today. What has this war come to?"

I crept under the covers with him. "Were they huge, these Amazon women? Did they have magical powers?"

"No, but they fought like men! I did not believe such a thing could be. They used wiles and tricks as well as strength, and poison in their arrows and spear tips."

"What did they look like?"

"Like other women, though they wore armor. Their queen—" He fell silent.

"Tell me," I whispered.

"I—I slew her myself, after she killed many of our men. Her helmet came off as she fell, and she was—beautiful." His voice caught. "Now we hear that another, even stronger nation is coming from afar to the aid of Troy." He was silent for a moment. "And now the Trojans are using the Amazons' poison in their own arrows."

A stronger nation. Poisoned arrows. Achilleus slept, but I lay awake, alone in my fear.

A few days later, when the men had left for battle, word flew through the camp that a great army was marching from the south. The other women and I ran to the main gate where a crowd had gathered. An Achaean sentry, mounted on top of the wall, shouted down to us. "There are hundreds of them, with many chariots and horses. And the men—they're huge and—they're dark skinned!" A gasp of surprise went through the crowd. "They're a head taller than ordinary men, and—"

But I heard nothing more. There was a rippling movement deep inside me, like a little fish swimming. I stood very still and, for the first time, felt the baby moving, kicking, strongly alive, as the other one had never been. My thoughts sped to Achilleus. I wanted him to feel it too.

Then noises penetrated my mind. Tramping feet and hooves, creaking chariot wheels, jangling harnesses, shouts of men on the move, not far beyond the wall of our camp. My fear returned with such force I was sick with it. I slipped away before the others took notice. At the water's edge I sat looking at the waves, imagining those fearsome dark warriors driving at Achilleus with spears and swords. *Oh, gods!* Would I lose him just as our child was quickening?

When the sun was low and copper colored, the sentries' shouts heralded the army's return. Chariots and men poured through the gate. The women of our camp ran to watch, some calling out in relief, some in alarm when they did not see their men. My feet dragged as I followed, afraid to look.

Clouds of dust arose as chariots came to a halt and men jumped down, milling about, yet I couldn't see any sign of him. Then I saw his chariot, Automedon at the reins, but he wasn't in it. My knees buckled. "Where is he?" I screamed at Automedon.

He gestured stolidly behind him, where Achilleus followed on foot, helping a wounded man to his hut. I went weak with relief. As I ran to meet him, he said, "I'm here only to take off my armor and wash. There's an assembly to decide how to deal with this new enemy."

He returned late at night and sank into his chair by the hearth. "Warm some wine, Briseis. Take a cup with me."

I served us, and knelt next to him, my hands clasping the arm of his chair. "Our baby is kicking inside me," I told him. "He moved for the first time today!"

He stared at me as if he hadn't heard. "Briseis, these Trojan allies who arrived today, these Ethiopians—"

He said more, but I could barely keep my attention on his words. I was desperate to draw his mind away from the war. I had a wild hope that if only I could make the baby real to him, he might reconsider his determination to fight. I waited until he paused to sip wine; then I pulled his hand to my belly. "Feel our baby. He's moving!" He was restless, his hand tense, as if he willed himself not to pull it away again. When there was a ripple, he started and jerked back. Even though I couldn't be sure it was a boy, I said, "This is your *son*, Achilleus! What will happen to him if tomorrow—if—"

He interrupted harshly, "What are you saying?"

"Only that he needs a home," I said, barely above a whisper. "He needs a *father*."

"He already has a home—in Phthia. You're not to worry, Briseis. There's nothing we can do to change fate." *You could leave the war.* But I dared not say it. "I told you—I've given orders to my men to take you home to my father when the war is over. No matter what happens to me, my name will protect my son—and you—even if I die tomorrow."

"But our child—"

He said wearily, "Briseis, I can do nothing better for him than to be what I am."

"You can care for him—teach him. Oh, Achilleus!" A howl of agony. *"Don't go!"*

He stared at me, his eyes hard. He stood, paced restlessly, turned to me again. "The Achaeans need me more than ever. A huge army has come—swarthy men, a race of giants. I've never seen their like. Their leader Memnon is taller than I. He's my match or more."

I was stunned. Was this the enemy the gods had sent to kill him?

"I would be a coward without honor if I stayed away now."

Honor! I wanted to scream the word, but I knew better than to venture down that path again. "No one could ever accuse you of being a coward. But why is it you who must fight this fearsome warrior? Why not someone else for a change? There is Ajax, who is as tall and strong as you. You could back away and let him earn the honor and glory."

Achilleus's eyes blazed. "I have never backed away!"

And that was the crux of it. He was so bent on being a hero he wouldn't even spare a thought for our child. I was suddenly so angry I wanted to hurt him.

I was on my feet, the words coming in a raging torrent. "You don't care about your sons—the one you already have, and this one not yet born." His eyes narrowed dangerously, but I couldn't stop. "If you had any concern or love for them, we could have a life in your homeland. The house I dreamed of—you could build it for us. We could raise our children there. We could have an orchard where they could climb trees together and gather sweet fruit, and—"

"Enough!" He shook his head incredulously. "I'm about to face the battle of my life and you speak to me of *fruit trees*? You understand *nothing*, woman!" His voice went deadly quiet, "If you keep seeking to unman me, I shall not come near you again."

Turning away abruptly, he threw his mantle over his shoulder and strode toward the door.

"Achilleus, wait!" But he stormed out of the hut.

I raced after him and watched the darkness swallow him. My anger ebbed, leaving me weak and shaky. I was right, of course, and I'd meant every word, but he'd never change. To rage against him would only drive him away.

All at once I understood what he had been saying all along. The truth hit me hard in the gut. However difficult, however painful, *I had to let Achilleus be Achilleus.*

I could only take each day as it came, and pray for the strength to endure it.

My hopes faded. I felt immensely sad. I had lost husband, home, and baby before. I could not survive it a second time. Yet I couldn't force him to be what I wanted for the sake of our child. And he had laid the onus on me. *Look after my child, Briseis.*

Warrior's Prize

I spent an anxious, restless night waiting in vain for his return. At daybreak I stepped out of our courtyard and saw him coming up the shore. He did not even glance my way, but went straight to the hut of Automedon and Alkimos, where he took his morning meal. He returned to fetch his gear but would not look at me. As he gathered the pieces and fittings of his armor, I said what I knew I must to settle things between us. "Achilleus, I'm sorry. Please forgive me."

But he walked by me as if I didn't exist. He armed himself outside in the courtyard, fastening greaves and corselet under the gray sky. Around him the men, many wearing bandages, mustered in grim silence. Automedon brought his chariot, the horses snorting and pawing restively.

As Achilleus mounted, he stumbled and had to grab the rail. Never before had I seen him stumble! I cried out and ran toward him, but he only lifted his helmet onto his head. Automedon snapped the reins, and the horses surged forward, the chariot disappearing in a cloud of dust.

Oh, gods, I prayed, *if you let Achilleus live, I'll ask for nothing more.*

CHAPTER 45

"For to me life is worth more than all the wealth
of that noble city Ilios in peace time..."

—Achilleus, *Iliad*, Homer, Book IX
(Rouse's translation)

    The day was endless, as if the sun was suspended at midheaven. Only through force of will could I perform the daily round of chores. When finally the shadows deepened and daylight faded, I heard sounds of men and horses and raced out of the courtyard, ahead of the others. At first I saw no sign of him. My legs started to give way, but Diomede grabbed my arm. "Look!" she cried, and I saw his chariot. He was in it, slumped, dirty, his left arm bloody—but living and breathing. My heart overflowed with relief. I forgave him everything just for coming back alive.
    I ran forward as Automedon reined in the horses. I reached up to touch Achilleus's arm. "You're back! You're safe!"
    He lifted the helmet from his head. As he stepped down, Automedon said, "Shall I attend you tonight, my lord?"

I held my breath. Achilleus looked at me long and hard, and I held his gaze, pleading with him silently, telling him with my eyes that I would not revisit our quarrel. At last he gave a nod, letting me know that all was right again.

"No," he said to Automedon, "Briseis will be with me."

He leaned a heavy arm over my shoulders. "I'm very tired. Can you fix me a bath?"

I hurried to the women's quarters. The women were already heating water. Diomede helped me carry the bronze basin into his hut, and we filled it. When the women left, he took off armor and tunic. I saw the gash on his arm. "You're wounded!"

"It's nothing. That man Memnon had the strength of a giant. Never have I fought for my life like that!" I saw bruises on his body as he lowered himself slowly, painfully, into the water. "I slew him, and his men have fled."

I felt nothing but relief at this stranger's death. "Oh, Achilleus, I'm so glad!" *Now you can leave the war.* But I did not say it.

For a time he was silent, eyes closed, leaning back against the rim of the bath. Then he lifted his head. "Before I could fight him, he killed Antilochos, my friend."

I remembered a smiling young man who came often to visit. Diomede had told me that he was the one who had brought Achilleus the news of Patroklos's death. "I'm sorry," I whispered.

"Antilochos died defending his aged father Nestor." A tear slipped down his cheek. "It should have been the other way around."

I took his hand. "You would have done the same as Antilochos."

"He was a dear friend, Briseis, and yet—" He broke off, and continued with sudden intensity. "The shadow of death hung over me today. Then it lifted, as if the gods took Antilochos instead of me. And though I grieve for him, I want to live. For my son. For you. For myself." He looked at me and smiled. The warm wine of joy ran in my blood. "I went after Memnon to avenge Antilochos," he continued, "and the closer I came to losing my life, the harder I fought. I stayed alive because my will to live was so strong. Maybe—" I held my breath, but he fell silent and stared unseeing at the rafters.

"What, Achilleus?" I whispered.

"It could be that I'm meant to live after all."

My heart soared. Perhaps all my prayers, all the times I had begged him to fight for his life, all the dreams of home I had shared with him had not been in vain after all.

Oh, Aphrodite, I thought, *I will offer you a hundred doves when I am able.* I wanted him to say that he would stay out of battle, and that we would sail for home tomorrow, but I held my tongue. He must come to this decision on his own. And I had promised the gods to ask for nothing more than his life. I bent and kissed his brow in silence, lingering over the feel of his warm flesh against my lips. Then I wet a cloth and began to rub his back, his shoulders and arms, trying to soothe away his weariness and pain.

"Achilleus," I said, "let me fetch dressings for your arm."

He forced a laugh. "This is barely a scratch." But he got out of the bath and let me bind it.

He was quiet and somber as we ate the evening meal. I knew he was thinking of his friend Antilochos. When we lay together in bed, he took me swiftly, almost roughly, as if to exult in being alive. But in the waning hours of the night he awoke and made love to me again, gently this time, every touch infinitely precious, his lips caressing, his hand curved around my cheek so tenderly that if I close my eyes, I can feel it still. As he lay drowsing at my side, I nestled close and whispered, "I love you," marveling at those words bursting golden on my tongue like ripe grapes gathered at the harvest.

I had thought him asleep, but he answered, "And I you," and tightened his arms.

The next day dawned so fair it seemed the whole world was washed clean. Leaving Achilleus asleep, I went down to the shore. Sea and sky blended in a glowing lavender mist. I lifted my arms to the sky and thanked the gods for the gift of life.

When I returned to our quarters to bring Achilleus the morning meal, he was up, stretching, smiling at me. I hoped that with the Ethiopians gone there would be no fighting today. But after he ate, he fetched his armor. My heart plunged. Seeing my face, he said, "Only one last time, Briseis. I must make sure of our victory yesterday." He put down his corselet and took me in his arms. "Then I will have done the whole of my duty to the Achaeans."

A wild thought came to me. Distract him somehow, then go into his store of herbs and fix him a draught to render him so sick and helpless he couldn't fight. But I knew better. I could not betray his trust. And surely there was very little danger. He had removed the last great threat.

Silently I prayed to the gods for one day more.

As he armed, I helped him with his greaves and whispered the words that were my talisman. "Come home safely." The men gathered as usual, Automedon waiting with the chariot. As Achilleus stepped up into it, some impulse made me run to him. My hands gripped the wooden railing. I smiled up at him. One of the horses sidestepped, whinnied.

"Go back, Briseis! You'll get hurt." But he bent to touch my cheek, and gave me his luminous smile, then put on his helmet. As I backed away, the horses leapt forward.

In the late afternoon, when we went to watch the men's return, I recognized his horses from afar. I saw his chariot, Automedon at the reins.

But Achilleus's side was empty.

Aphrodite, where is he?

Now the men were much closer. I could see them clearly in the swirling dust. A large group trailed on foot behind Automedon. Their shoulders slumped, they were carrying a litter.

I went icy cold. But surely it wasn't my beloved. I rushed to meet the men, trying to get close enough to see who was on that litter, in what condition. They plodded on, a forest of moving men.

And then I saw. Achilleus, covered in a rough gray cloak, lay very still.

Oh, gods! My heart was smashed between rocks.

His bright hair was disordered, dusty, his eyes half-closed, rolled back, slits of white showing through the lashes. His mouth was open, caked with dirt, dried blood. Though I saw no other hurt, I knew he was gravely wounded.

Hurry! I tried to shout. *Send for the physician! Get him to his hut. I can find the herbs, the potions.* But I couldn't make a sound. The men went on walking too slowly, their faces rigid, eyes staring straight ahead. I ran toward him. I wanted to wipe his mouth, brush the hair out of his face. I must touch him, hold him. I pushed forward. Rough hands thrust me out of the way.

"Let me go to him!" I cried. "I can heal him!"

They kept moving, and I was flung aside. I landed on my knees. A harsh, agonized voice said, "Can't you see he's dead!"

CHAPTER 46

> "...take him out of the play of spears,
> a long way off, and wash him in the river,
> anoint him with ambrosia, put ambrosial
> clothing on him."
>
> *Iliad*, Homer, Book XVI
> (Fitzgerald's translation)

Something was crushing my heart and my bones. I was running down the shore. I had never run so fast. I heard screams. They were coming from me. I reached the water. I fell.

Then Diomede was kneeling by me. I lay face down in damp sand. My feet and the hem of my gown were in the water. Something was wrong with my lungs. It hurt to breathe.

"Come," she said. "They've brought his body to us. Do you want—?"

"They're lying!" I gasped. "He's alive!"

But from afar I could hear the high, keening lamentations of the women.

She started to help me up. "It'll do you no good to lie here. At the hut you can rest while we wash him, prepare his body for—"

"*No!*" The cry was torn from me. I pulled away from her grasp and leapt to my feet. "*I must do it.*" I started running up the shore.

In the courtyard the women stood about a bier, keening, making the ritual motions of mourning, dragging their nails down their arms, pounding their fists against their breasts. His men, the Myrmidons, stood behind them. When they saw me they all fell silent and made a space for me. As I approached, I thought, *it can't be him on that bier.* Then I looked down at him and couldn't breathe.

He lay as if made of stone, his skin so drained of color it looked gray. Someone had closed his eyes and smoothed the lines of anguish from his face.

Yet this was not Achilleus. He had gone far away and left me behind.

I raked my nails down my cheeks until the blood ran. Then I looked around at the men. "How—?" I asked.

Automedon spoke bitterly. "An arrow in the back. Another in his heel. We learned too late that the arrows were poisoned. He died—he died in—"

In agony, I thought, though Automedon didn't say it. His face wore the same stunned look that I saw on the others'. "The best and bravest of us all, shot down from afar by the coward Paris."

Helen's lover. I remembered his weak-chinned, petulant face.

"But Paris could not have done it alone. Apollo himself guided the arrows." The hairs rose on my arms. Had Achilleus felt the god's malignant breath as he died?

"Now the Trojans are boasting," Automedon said, "threatening us, because our invincible warrior is dead."

I felt myself falling. The darkness threatened to swamp me, but I couldn't let it. Not yet. When Diomede and another woman grasped my arms to lead me away, I struggled free. "I will tend him—wash him." Though each word tore at me, I said, "The men must bear him to the spring, the spring of Simoeis."

For a moment no one moved. Then Automedon said, "The guards at the gate will warn us if the Trojans try to attack. Do as she bids."

Only then did the men come forward to lift the bier. Blackness fell over my eyes, but somehow I followed them to the spring.

"Lay him in the water," I said. They lowered him into the spring, then left him to the women. The clear, pure waters ran over him, slowly clouding with a watery red as his wounds washed clean. I fell on my knees in the icy spring, and the water bore his weight so that I could hold him in my arms. Though it didn't matter, I lifted his face above the surface. His hair flowed and rippled in the spring like water reeds.

Diomede knelt at my side, the other women behind her. But this duty was mine alone.

"Take the others," I said to her. "Fetch herbs from his hut. Lavender, rosemary, hyssop." Herbs like these must surely grow in the hills of his beloved Phthia, and their essence might comfort whatever part of his spirit lingered. "Bring oils to anoint him. The best, only the best." He must be wrapped in fragrance and beauty. "Bring his finest tunic, his blue mantle. Wait, it's soiled. Wash it, then bring it here." Diomede hesitated. "Go!" I commanded.

They left, and I was alone at his side. It was better thus. No one who bore him a lesser love should be here. All those others who loved him were far away. I called out to them in my mind: his mother Thetis, priestess of the sea god; his aged father Peleus; his son Neoptolemos; even the mother of his son, Deidamia. Faces I couldn't even imagine. How alone he had been in his life! But for Patroklos. But for me.

Patroklos, I prayed, *be there to greet his spirit on the other side. Don't leave him alone.*

I bent and lifted his ice-cold body in my arms, running my hands over his strong shoulders, his torso, cleansing the bruises, the cuts. My heart turned over as I touched the cut on his arm, which I had tended only yesterday. I found the wound in his back, the deep puncture in his heel. *Shot from behind.* My fingers probed to wipe away the last of the dirt and poison. After I had finished, I held him against me and pressed my face to his still, cold chest.

The women returned, and we pulled him from the spring. I dried him with my loosened hair and with the clean linen Diomede had brought, then rubbed fragrant oils over his limbs. When the men came to fetch him, I stood, dripping wet, trembling. All my strength deserted me now that I had done this last duty.

I followed the men as they carried his body back to our camp. In the courtyard I stood by his bier one final time, memorizing each feature of his face so that I could hold it forever in my heart. I bent to kiss his lips, cold and hard, tasting of spring water and herbs.

Then I straightened quickly. I had one last gift for Achilleus. I looked at Automedon, who had a knife at his belt. I pointed. "Give it to me."

He took it from its sheath, yet hesitated. I reached for it, and as my hand closed around the hilt, I thought how easy it would be to plunge the point into my throat. But there was the baby. *Look after my child,* Achilleus had said. I brought the blade to my hair, cutting all of its length in great hanks. Gathering them up, I placed them in his cold, still hands.

Now he belonged to the men. Automedon, Alkimos and others came to stand on either end of the bier. They would take him up the shore to the place where they had mourned over Patroklos. I flung myself across his chest and held on hard one last time until someone pulled me away, and the men took up the bier. Then he was gone forever from my sight.

I let my knees drop me to the ground.

CHAPTER 47

*...the Myrmidons were stirred again to weep.
Then Dawn with rose-red fingers in the east
began to glow upon them as they mourned
around the pitiful body.*

Iliad, Homer, Book XXIII
(Fitzgerald's translation)

Diomede and Iphis leaned over me. "Come, Briseis, to our quarters," Diomede said. "We'll be together there."

In the women's hut, I found myself sitting on my old bed, where I had not slept for a long time. Darkness had fallen, and someone had lit a lamp. The women formed a circle around me. They were speaking, but I couldn't make sense of their words. I leaned against the wall and closed my eyes. Diomede reached for my hand. I forced myself to listen to the women.

One of the Lesbos women, Theano, said, "The men are saying that he was their greatest warrior ever, that his fame will never die."

You knew, I thought. *All along you knew that you could not escape your destiny.*

His own words came back to me. *True honor can come only from the gods... I prayed to Zeus.* And Zeus had granted his prayer. Glory or long life—it had never been a choice. Honor had kept him in chains. Honor had killed him.

Even now I didn't understand honor.

"You're lucky, Briseis," Theano continued. "You're carrying his child. You will be in a very good position when we are chosen by new masters."

It took me a moment to grasp her words. Then I shook my head. "I won't have a new master. I'm going to his father, to his home in Phthia. He promised me his men would take me there."

Theano looked at me pityingly. "Automedon is the leader of the Myrmidons now, and he has no standing among the Achaean chieftains. He won't be able to protect you when they fight for Achilleus's possessions. But never fear; you'll be chosen by someone of high rank, for it would be deemed an honor to raise the son of so great a hero."

"And if it's a girl?" someone asked.

"Then many would want to wed her to link their name and their bloodline with his," Theano answered.

You foresaw this, Achilleus, I thought. *You knew that the honor of your name was your legacy to your child.*

But that meant the strongest chieftain would claim possession of the child and me. We might even be given to Agamemnon.

At that moment I felt a sharp movement inside me, as if the little one protested against this fate. All at once I knew—my child must never become the prize of any Achaean chieftain.

I must run away from the camp this very night.

I looked around at the kind, concerned faces of the women. If they guessed what I intended, they would try to stop me. They could be punished, even killed, if they helped me. I would have to manage on my own, and soon, before the men returned.

I would find my way to Lyrnessos, where those who had escaped the raid were surely eking out a living on whatever had been left behind. *Forgive me, Achilleus, for rejecting what you tried to give our child. But this is the better way.*

I asked, "Is—is the funeral pyre tonight?"

"Nay," Diomede said gently. "Tonight, and many nights more, they will mourn him in the center of the camp. The Trojans mourned Hektor for nine days. The Achaeans will not give Achilleus a lesser mourning."

The men would likely be gone most of the night. The mourning ceremony for Patroklos had lasted until dawn. I got to my feet. My legs were shaky. I leaned for a moment against the wall. The women were all looking up at me questioningly.

"I want to be in his hut for a while," I said. "Then I'm going down to the shore."

"I'll go with you." Diomede got to her feet. As I sought a way to put her off, I saw the love and compassion in her eyes. From the beginning she had been my dearest friend, had helped me and comforted me more times than I could count, and now, when I had the greatest need of her, I would never see her again. I put my arms around her, and my tears spilled over. "Thank you for your care, Diomede," I whispered. "Thank you for saving my baby. I can never repay you."

"Hush!" she said. "It's nothing. Now why don't you let me fix you a potion so you can rest and—"

I put a hand on her shoulder. "I'm sorry. I need to be alone. Just for a while."

"Very well. You won't do anything stupid?" she asked in her blunt way.

"You mean try to kill myself?" I forced my lips to smile. "Of course not. I have this little one to think of." I squeezed her in a last embrace, saying a silent farewell.

"Come fetch me if you need me," she said. I shut my eyes against bitter tears.

As I moved out of the circle, wrapping my shawl around me, several hands reached up to touch me, to comfort me.

"Come back soon. Get some sleep."

"You'll be all right. It will pass. I, too, lost my master." This was Iphis, but she and Patroklos had never been close.

In his hut I lit a lamp from the hearth. My glance fell to his bed, still tumbled from our sleep last night. I kneeled, buried my face in his pillow—inhaled his scent. Sobs washed over me, great gulping cries from the depths of my body. I lay on his bed, curled in on myself, feeling that my weeping would never end, but at last the spasms slowed. I pulled myself to my feet. I did not have the luxury of endless weeping. I must be on my way before anyone could stop me.

I opened chests and took his knife, a warm mantle, a cooking vessel, some bread and hard cheese, and a pair of water skins. I rolled everything into a carrying pack, slung it over my shoulder, and let myself soundlessly out of his hut.

As I walked away from the Myrmidon huts along the dark shore, the sky was lit with a glow but the camp was dark, quiet, and empty. At the post at the end of the encampment, a lone guard stood, holding a wineskin. When he lifted his lamp, I recognized the sentry who had been here when I came with Achilleus. "Who goes there?" he called out.

I stopped. "You remember me? Achilleus said to let me through."

"Achilleus is dead."

"All the more reason to honor his word," I said firmly.

"Very well, go. But don't be long." He returned to his wine.

I waded across the shallow ford and walked swiftly down the shore. As I looked back toward the camp from far away, the sky was lurid with the flames of bonfires. I saw in my mind the cold stiff body on the bier.

Perhaps he had intended this escape for me all along. Perhaps those words he had spoken to the sentry to allow it had been his last gift to me. *My Briseis, I love your fierceness—your fiery spirit!* That same day he had also said, *look after my child.*

I will, I promised him silently. *Your child will grow up free.*

I would not say farewell. I would take him with me always.

Elena Douglas

PART THREE

THE BOUNDLESS SEA

Elena Douglas

CHAPTER 48

> "...look out and see
> my ships on Hellê's waters in the offing,
> oarsmen in line making the sea-foam scud!"
>
> *Iliad,* Book IX
> (Fitzgerald's translation)

When Achilleus sacked Lyrnessos and made me his captive all those months ago, it took one afternoon and most of a night for his ships to sail up the coast to the Achaean camp. The return journey on foot though the hills would be rugged and difficult. And so it was. Five days later, footsore and weary unto death, I came to what was left of my home. Only a few people remained, old folks and children, who lived off stores of grain the Achaeans had missed and livestock that had escaped the raid. There was wild game in the mountains and fish in the sea. A young boy and his grandmother, who lived in the hills above the town, took me in to live with them. The boy, Dymas, hunted and foraged for food while I did household chores and cared for his ailing grandmother. Eventually we buried her, but I continued to share a home with Dymas.

One day Dymas and I saw a great migration of people—all ages of men and women, as well as children. Some moved into the empty houses of Lyrnessos. Some built a camp on the shore. The men began dragging timbers from the forests and set to work with hammers and axes.

"What could they be building?" I asked.

"Ships," Dymas guessed.

We learned they were Dardanians, led by Prince Aeneas, who had escaped from Troy. The war had been lost. The Achaeans had gone home. The gods had told Aeneas to construct a fleet and sail away, to found a new empire across the sea. Dymas decided that, when they sailed, he would go with them.

Dymas was with me in the house when my birth pains started. He ran to fetch an old woman who lived on the edge of the town. She sat by my side while pain battered me. Hours passed, and then a day, and the baby did not come. Putting her hands on my belly, she said. "Your body is not opening." She shook her head. "Only the goddess Hera can save you and the baby. I will go to her temple to offer sacrifice." And she left.

I lay alone, sinking into a sea of pain. I could endure no more. I saw the dark river, the old ferryman reaching his hand to me, and I welcomed him. *Achilleus, I will soon be with you.*

Then I heard his voice again. *Look after my child.*

Dymas came into the room. "I'm going to the Dardanians," he said. "They may have a midwife who can help." He left, returning much later with a woman who touched my brow, looked into my eyes and knelt at the foot of the bed. She reached a hand inside me. I bucked with agony. "Now!" she urged. "Push it out!" Pain tore me apart. Then I heard a loud, lusty cry. The woman said, "A little girl!"

A tiny, perfectly formed body, taut with indignation, squirmed against the hands that held her. My eyes flooded with tears.

Later, when I was resting, holding my daughter in my arms, a man came into the hut. His face, tender and concerned, leaned over mine. He had warm brown eyes, curly black hair and a beard. "Do you know me, Briseis?"

"Akamas," I said in wonder.

I had forgotten that he was a Dardanian, one of Aeneas's men. He told me he'd been wounded in the shoulder and left for dead on the battlefield the day of Patroklos's death, but he had recovered. When Dymas came seeking help, Akamas heard my name and followed him here.

I called my baby girl Thalassa—the sea.

It took the Dardanians many months, but bit by bit a fleet emerged. Akamas brought Dymas and me to live in the encampment on the shore. At the hearth, at night, he told us of the tragic last days of the war. The Achaeans had left a huge wooden horse outside the city, supposedly a gift, but secretly filled with warriors. The fleet pretended to sail away. The Trojans brought the structure into the city and celebrated. In the dead of night, the warriors climbed out of the horse and opened the gates for the invading army. The people of Troy were slaughtered as they slept. Hektor's father was killed, and even his baby son Astyanax was not spared. Andromache, Kassandra, and Hektor's mother were all taken captive. I wept for them. Achilleus, I thought, would have opposed such a dishonorable victory.

All the things I had done—all the machinations to save Hektor, to save Achilleus, had been in vain. The gods had decreed their fate and willed their deaths. Kassandra, that sad Trojan princess, had foreseen it all. I heard her voice in my mind. *You cannot go against the will of the gods, and you cannot change fate.*

When the fleet was almost ready, Akamas said to me, "Come with us to seek a new homeland." Softly he added, "I owe you my life, and more. You are very brave, very fair. I want you for my wife, Briseis."

I agreed to go with him. Lyrnessos was a dying city. I needed a real home for Thalassa—for myself. But I was not ready to wed. There was still turmoil in my heart. Akamas had fought with the Trojans, who had killed my beloved. "One day, maybe," I told him, "when I have had time to heal. If such a thing is possible."

Akamas told me he would wait as long as it took.

The day came when the ships were finished, loaded and provisioned. With my daughter in my arms, I climbed the steep plank of Akamas's ship. As the fleet sailed out of the Adramyttenos Gulf, I stared at the retreating shore until my eyes ached. All my life, my past, was fading in the mist. Then I looked down at Thalassa and found her gazing over my shoulder with her father's eyes at the far horizons of the sea, and I felt that his spirit was with us.

There followed a long journey into the unknown. Eventually we came to a fair land far to the west, a land of fertile plains, woodlands, and rolling green hills. Aeneas and his men fought a series of bloody battles against the inhabitants to establish a kingdom there. But Akamas and I, along with Dymas and some others, sick of war, broke off from them and became wanderers, seeking neighbors with whom we could live in peace.

Though I was content with Akamas and our growing family, Achilleus remained in my heart. Sometimes I fancied I could hear his quick laugh, feel his hand on my cheek. I saw him in his daughter's smile, the small furrow that creased her brow in serious moments. And even, at times, in her tempestuous temper, which always passed as quickly as a summer squall.

Now, many years have gone by. Thalassa stands before me, adorned in bridal finery. The sight of her fills me with pride. She is tall—taller even than her stepfather Akamas, who watches us, our sons at his side. I glance at him and smile at the love in his eyes.

Thalassa is marrying the son of the King of Etruria, a wedding that will unite our people with those who dwell here and make this land truly our home. When the king persecuted us and threatened to cast us out, Thalassa, bold and fearless, went to his court to offer herself in marriage to his son, pointing out that our people united would form a stronger nation. When the king learned that she was the daughter of the legendary hero Achilleus, he accepted the alliance eagerly.

It will be a marriage of love, for when Thalassa had met the young prince she'd known at once that he was the one. And from the way he looked at her, I could tell he felt the same.

As I lift a crown of flowers onto her head and caress the golden brown hair that cascades down her back, she smiles at me. Her eyes are blue-green, startling against the pale gold of her skin. In those eyes, in the high cheekbones, the straight dark brows, the proud lift of her chin, I see how like him she is.

She knows the story of all his deeds. Once, when she was young and angry, she asked me, "With all that happened to you in the beginning, how were you able to forgive him?"

Even after the passage of time, my eyes had filled with tears as I remembered all the sorrows and joys that had finally brought me to a place of peace in his arms. I said, "When there is love, we can learn to forgive, no matter what bitterness has gone before. That is how I came to be healed."

Now as the tambourines and flutes begin their melodic clamor, she leads the wedding procession in her lithe, long-legged walk, not girlish at all but graceful as a panther. My heart overflows. *Oh, Achilleus, if only you could see her!*

THE END

AFTERWORD:

THE BACKGROUND AND LANGUAGE OF *WARRIOR'S PRIZE*

While there are many varied and sometimes conflicting myths about the gods and heroes of Ancient Greece, the *Iliad* tells one magnificent tale, whole, coherent, and complete in itself. It moved me to write the story of Briseis, a minor character in the *Iliad*, a mere woman, who is nevertheless pivotal to the plot. I have used the *Iliad* as my primary source for *Warrior's Prize*.

As often as possible, the story line of *Warrior's Prize* closely follows that of the *Iliad*. In chapters 20 through 41, Achilleus' public actions, as well as those of Agamemnon and Patroklos, reflect as accurately as possible events that occurred in the *Iliad*. The relationship between Achilleus and Briseis I have developed on my own, and also Briseis's relationship with Patroklos. Homer does not tell us what happened privately between them, but this much is clear from the *Iliad*: Achilleus loved Briseis, and she seems to have reciprocated. She enjoyed a close friendship with Patroklos and grieved deeply over his death. I invented her secret trip to Troy as well as the wounding of Patroklos (although there is a vase painting that portrays Achilleus binding the injured arm of his friend). For the events after chapter 41, I have relied on various sources from Homer's time and later. A lost epic called the *Aetheopis* tells of the battles with the Amazons and with Memnon, as well as the death of Achilleus. In describing his death, in which he was famously shot with an arrow in the heel, I have added a second arrow to his back and poison to both arrows since it stretches credulity to believe that a single arrow to his heel could kill a strong man in his prime. A much later work of literature (Propertius: *The Elegies*, Book II) has Briseis tending Achilleus' dead body, anointing it, and drying it with her own hair. Of what became of her after his death nothing is known, so I have chosen to give her a future with the fleeing Dardanians and Trojans led by Aeneas, who built their fleet in Lyrnessos and sailed from there to the country now known as Italy. Akamas was one of Aeneas's men in the *Iliad*, so he could have met Briseis in the raid on Lyrnessos. He was left for dead on the battlefield the day Patroklos died, though his demise was not certain. I have chosen to believe he survived.

Without intent to plagiarize Homer, when characters speak words they actually spoke in the *Iliad*, I have paraphrased their speeches from various translations of the *Iliad*. This is particularly true of Chapter 41, where the dialogue between Achilleus and Priam comes from the beautiful and moving scene in Book XXIV of the *Iliad*.

For information about the raid that begins our story, I have relied upon *Troy: A Study in Homeric Geography*, by Walter Leaf (MacMillan and Company, London 1912) for his informative and scholarly reconstruction of what he calls "The Great Foray," which he posits might have been the subject for its own separate epic that has not survived the passage of time. In the interest of the plot, I have taken some liberties with the details.

On the spelling of names: in order to more closely approximate the ancient Greek, I have used "k" instead of "c" ("Hektor" for "Hector", "Kassandra" for "Cassandra") since "k" is closer to the Greek kappa. Rather than spelling Achilleus' name in the traditional way ("Achilles," which is Anglicized from the Latin), I have followed Latimer's translation in rendering it as "Achilleus", since this is the closest transliteration of the ancient Greek. His name has four syllables, not three. In the *Iliad*, written in dactylic hexameter, "Achilleus" is metrically identical to "Odysseus." Furthermore, "-eus" is a Mycenaean ending. It fascinates me that the two heroes, Achilleus and Odysseus, as well as others in the epics, have names that come down to us from Bronze Age Mycenaean times. Since some scholars believe there was an actual Trojan War (or wars) in the Mycenaean era, it leads me to wonder whether there could have been a real Achilleus, now lost to us in the mists of time, from whom the legend is derived.

NOTE: In the quotes at the beginnings of each chapter I have spelled the names according to my two sources, W.H.D. Rouse and Robert Fitzgerald. Rouse calls him "Achilles", and Fitzgerald, "Akhilleus."

For further reading, I recommend the following: *Why Homer Matters*, by Adam Nicolson, Henry Holt and Company, New York. 2014, which will make you want to delve into Homer; and *The War that Killed Achilles,* by Caroline Alexander, Viking. New York, 2009, in which the author examines the epic's characters and motivations, as well the *Iliad*'s theme that the war was "a pointless catastrophe that blighted all it touched."

About the Author

BARBARA BRUNETTI

Barbara Brunetti, who writes as Elena Douglas, was born in Paris, where she lived until the age of seven, when her parents divorced and her mother remarried. After immigrating to the United States, Barbara and her newly blended family lived in New England. During a summer spent in an isolated cabin in the White Mountains when she was eight, her mother read her the *Iliad* and the *Odyssey*. Thus began a lifelong fascination with the legends of ancient Greece.

When she was a teen, the family moved to Berkeley, California. She attended U.C. Berkeley and enjoyed a long career teaching middle school and junior high English. She left teaching to pursue her writing career. *Warrior's Prize* is her second published novel. The first one, *Shadow of Athena*, is also available through Penmore Press. She and her husband live in Berkeley, California. They have two grown children and four grandchildren. For more, see her website: http://elenadouglas.com

IF YOU ENJOYED THIS BOOK

VISIT

PENMORE PRESS

www.penmorepress.com

All Penmore Press books are available directly through our website.

SHADOW OF ATHENA
BY
ELENA DOUGLAS

In a cruel, centuries-old tradition, lovely sixteen-year-old Marpessa of Lokris is chosen by lot to serve as a slave for one year in distant Troy, across the Aegean Sea. She can return, but only if she survives. Marpessa leaves behind her devoted mother, and also a ruthless oligarch, Klonios, who vows to have her as his wife upon her return. The young slave Arion is sent to escort the maiden on her treacherous journey. After delivering her safely, he escapes slavery to eke out a living on the Trojan shore, until barbarians raid Troy. Captivated by the girl from the sea journey, Arion rushes to save her. The two find themselves marooned in a rough, unforgiving land teeming with dangers. Struggling to survive, they yield to a forbidden love. Marpessa longs to remain with her beloved, but Arion knows he must give her up. When they lose everything in a deadly flash flood, he must return her safely home, despite the price on his head as a runaway slave and the evil Klonios who lurks in wait. By the time they reach Lokris, Marpessa is with child. Enraged, Klonios orders their deaths, but Arion will stop at nothing to save Marpessa's life. Even at the cost of his own.

PENMORE PRESS
www.penmorepress.com

Carrie Welton

by

Charles Monagan

Eighteen-year-old Carrie Welton is restless, unhappy, and ill-suited to the conventions of nineteenth-century New England. Using her charm and a cunning scheme, she escapes the shadow of a cruel father and wanders into a thrilling series of high-wire adventures. Her travels take her all over the country, putting her in the path of Bohemian painters, poets, singers, social crusaders, opium eaters, violent gang members, and a group of female mountain climbers.

But Carrie's demons return to haunt her, bringing her to the edge of sanity and leading to a fateful expedition onto Longs Peak in Colorado. That's not the end, though. Carrie, being Carrie, sends an astonishing letter back from the grave and thus engineers her final escape—forever into your heart.

PENMORE PRESS
www.penmorepress.com

Mistress Suffragette
by
Diana Forbes

A young woman without prospects at a ball in Gilded Age Newport, Rhode Island is a target for a certain kind of "suitor." At the Memorial Day Ball during the Panic of 1893, impoverished but feisty Penelope Stanton draws the unwanted advances of a villainous millionaire banker who preys on distressed women—the incorrigible Edgar Daggers. Over a series of encounters, he promises Penelope the financial security she craves, but at what cost? Skilled in the art of flirtation, Edgar is not without his charms, and Penelope is attracted to him against her better judgment. Initially, as Penelope grows into her own in the burgeoning early Women's Suffrage Movement, Edgar exerts pressure, promising to use his power and access to help her advance. But can he be trusted, or are his words part of an elaborate mind game played between him and his wife? During a glittering age where a woman's reputation is her most valuable possession, Penelope must decide whether to compromise her principles for love, lust, and the allure of an easier life.

PENMORE PRESS
www.penmorepress.com

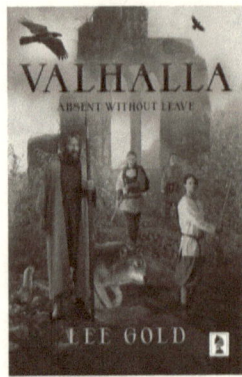

VALHALLA

Absent Without Leave
By
Lee Gold

The Age of Heroes is not done...

"An axe age, a sword age," Bookwyrm chanted. *"A wind age, a wolf age."*
"Brothers shall fight and slay each other," sang Knut. *"Garm howls in Hel, and the wolf runs free."*

    Robin Johnson died a hero's death, rescuing people from a hospital during a California earthquake. So how is a hero rewarded? Robin finds herself not in Christian Heaven but in Valhalla of Norse myths, welcomed by heroes and the guardians of Asgard. But Robin had been something of an oddity in life and continues to be so in the afterlife. She's not content to spend the better part of eternity feasting and fighting and... drinking to Odin's honor. Accompanied by two fellow-heroes, a wolf, a telepathic sword and a chatty red squirrel, the renamed Robin Grima sets out to prevent Ragnarok, the doom in which nearly all the Asgardians die.

    Their first quest: slay the dragon Nidhog, who gnaws away at the root of Yggdrasil, The World Tree. If they succeed in that, they can confront sea giants, hill giants, mist elves, Fenris Wolf, the Midgard Serpent, and Hel, corpsequeen of the dead. But the only way to really stop Ragnarok is to deal, once and for all, with the mastermind of plots and Odin's foster-brother — Loki himself.

PENMORE PRESS
www.penmorepress.com

Assassins of Alamut
By
James Boschert

An Epic Novel of Persia and Palestine in the Time of the Crusades

The *Assassins of Alamut* is a riveting tale, painted on the vast canvas of life in Palestine and Persia during the 12th century.

On one hand, it's a tale of the crusades—as told from the Islamic side—where Shi'a and Sunni are as intent on killing Ismaili Muslims as crusaders. In self-defense, the Ismailis develop an elite band of highly trained killers called Hashshashin, whose missions are launched from their mountain fortress of Alamut.

But it's also the story of a French boy, Talon, captured and forced into the alien world of the assassins. Forbidden love for a princess is intertwined with sinister plots and self-sacrifice, as the hero and his two companions discover treachery and then attempt to evade the ruthless assassins of Alamut who are sent to hunt them down.

It's a sweeping saga that takes you over vast snow-covered mountains, through the frozen wastes of the winter plateau, and into the fabulous cites of Hamadan, Isfahan, and the Kingdom of Jerusalem.

"A brilliant first novel, worthy of Bernard Cornwell at his best."—Tom Grundner

PENMORE PRESS
www.penmorepress.com

Penmore Press
Challenging, Intriguing, Adventurous, Historical and Imaginative

www.penmorepress.com

www.ingramcontent.com/pod-product-compliance
Lightning Source LLC
LaVergne TN
LVHW091615070526
838199LV00044B/811